SUFFERING THE SCOT

BROTHERHOOD
OF THE
BLACK
TARTAN
BOOK I

NICHOLE VAN

Fiorenza Publishing

Suffering the Scot © 2019 by Nichole Van Valkenburgh
Cover design © Nichole Van Valkenburgh
Interior design © Nichole Van Valkenburgh

Published by Fiorenza Publishing
Print Edition v1.0

ISBN: 978-1-949863-03-1

Suffering the Scot is a work of fiction. Names, characters, places and incidents are the products of the author's imagination or are used fictitiously. Any resemblance to actual events, locales or persons, living or dead, is entirely coincidental.

To Kian—
My little Mr. Positive.
Always keep shining.

To Dave—
So, about this kilt swish thing . . .

HADLEY & MONTACUTE FAMILY TREE

(Characters in bold appear in the story.)

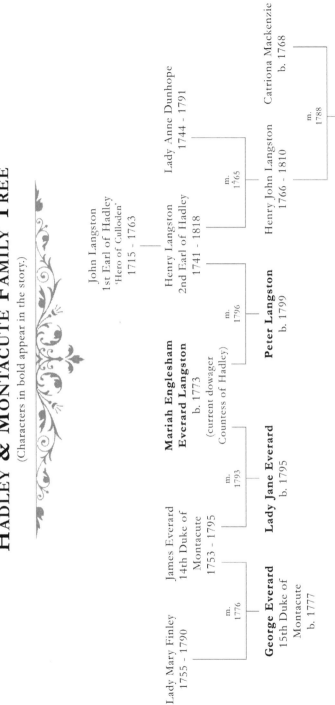

John Langston
1st Earl of Hadley
'Hero of Culloden'
1715 - 1763

Lady Anne Dunhope
1744 - 1791

Henry Langston
2nd Earl of Hadley
1741 - 1818

m. 1765

Catriona Mackenzie
b. 1768

Henry John Langston
1766 - 1810

m. 1788

Andrew Henry Mackenzie Langston
3rd Earl of Hadley
b. 1789

Lady Mary Finley
1755 - 1790

James Everard
14th Duke of
Montacute
1753 - 1795

m. 1776

**Mariah Englesham
Everard Langston**
b. 1773
(current dowager
Countess of Hadley)

m. 1793

m. 1796

Peter Langston
b. 1799

George Everard
15th Duke of
Montacute
b. 1777

Lady Jane Everard
b. 1795

But to see her was to love her,
Love but her, and love forever.
—ROBERT BURNS

PROLOGUE

The notice appeared in *The Edinburgh Advertiser* on a blustery Tuesday in March.

> *The Brotherhood of the Tartan will hold their second annual meeting at the Black Bull Inn on Falkirk Road on Friday, March 19, 1819. Let nothing be forgotten.*

The notice was not on the front page with the other announcements. Instead, it was placed on page seven, nestled between the deaths and the corn share report, clearly having been added in haste after the front page had gone to print.

The Rake was the first to see the notice as he sat eating toast soldiers and eggs in his father's townhouse. The butler laid the newspaper—freshly ironed to set the ink—beside his breakfast plate.

The Physician saw it next when he stopped to purchase a newspaper on George Street after a night spent at the bedside of a dying, elderly patient.

The Artist spotted the announcement that afternoon as he took a break between client portrait sittings in his studio in Old Town.

The Sailor didn't see the notice until the evening when he finally retired to his rooms. He had spent the day assessing damage to his ship docked in Leith harbor.

The Merchant saw it last as he flipped through the newspaper the next day, curious about the price of corn shares. But then he had no need to look for the notice, as he had been the one to post it in the first place.

The nineteenth of March marked the third anniversary of Jamie's death.

And on that night, the Brotherhood of the Tartan would gather to honor Jamie's life—to drink a dram and unburden their collective grief and guilt. Most importantly, they would plot ways to bring Jamie's murderers to justice.

Nothing would be forgotten.

Everyone knew it was an unmitigated disaster.

Some even deployed the adjectives "biblical" and "calamitous."

For her part, Lady Jane Everard simply hoped to survive the afternoon without anyone drawing blood.

She took a sip of her tea, politely listening to the women buzzing around the drawing room. Her younger half-brother, the Honorable Mr. Peter Langston, sat beside her. The black mourning band around his upper arm spoke tellingly of their situation.

After six months of full-mourning for her stepfather, the late Earl of Hadley, Jane's family had resumed afternoon at-home hours. Their neighbors had called upon them, ostensibly to lend support during their current hardship. Such concern only thinly veiled their delight in watching the Langstons of Hadley Park descend the social ladder.

Jane's mother, the widowed Lady Hadley, sat across the room, holding court over the tea tray. Lady Hadley had overcome the death of two aristocratic husbands—a duke and an earl. A few venom-tongued busy-bodies would not defeat her.

Though Lady Hadley declared herself a devout Anglican, Jane believed her mother's true religion was a fervent belief in her exalted station in life. The lady defended her social position with the ruthless tenacity of a medieval Crusader, carefully calibrated silences and chilly reserve being her weapons of choice.

"Gracious, what a disaster," Lady Whitcomb declared, leaning to take a teacup from Lady Hadley. "You are scarcely out of full-mourning, and the new Lord Hadley is at your door."

"Is it true what they say? That Lord Hadley is barely civilized?" Mrs. Smith asked, darting a glance up from her own cup.

"But, of course." Lady Whitcomb tilted her head, her graying curls swaying with the motion. "He is an impoverished, coarse *Scot*, after all."

Jane considered Lady Whitcomb's opinion to be slightly redundant, as all Polite Society knew the word *Scot* already encompassed *impoverished* and *coarse*.

"You have the right of it." Mrs. Burton tsked, accepting a teacup with a mournful shake of her head. "Rumor says Lord Hadley was raised in a crofter's hut deep in the wilds of Scotland."

The way Mrs. Burton pronounced *Scotland* imbued the word with a thousand years of history—the medieval battles between Robert the Bruce and King Edward, the horror of England suffering a succession of wastrel Scottish kings after Elizabeth's glorious reign, the more recent Battle of Culloden and the current Highland Clearances, all threaded through with Scotland's uncivilized behavior and loose understanding of decorum.

Lady Hadley did not react, proving again her ruthless control over her emotions. Jane followed suit, keeping her own expression polite, resting her cup and saucer on the table beside her before folding her hands in her lap with exacting precision.

Lady Hadley and her daughter were well-known for their exquisite manners. It was what made the current situation all the more horrific and, to be honest, horrifically delightful to those observing from the outside.

Peter, predictably, snorted.

Jane forgave him. What else could she do? Growing up, she and Peter had only had each other and that fact had not changed over the years. No matter what he did, she loved Peter more than anyone else in the world.

That said . . . snorting was decidedly ill-mannered.

Jane surreptitiously nudged Peter with her foot, a silent reproof.

"Indeed," Mrs. Burton replied. "Given the Earldom of Hadley's history with Scotland, the situation is decidedly . . ."

"Ironic?" Lady Whitcomb supplied, mouth pursing into a simpering moue before sipping her tea. "That the hunter has become the hunted?"

Lady Hadley replied with a taut smile.

The facts *were* decidedly ironic, Jane supposed.

The first Earl of Hadley had been raised to the peerage for, *Invaluable services to the Crown in assisting His Majesty's troops to defeat the unruly Scottish rebellion at Culloden.* In short, the first Earl had been a celebrated English war hero noted for his savagery in dealing with wild Scottish rebels.

However, his grandson, Henry—born to be the third Earl of Hadley—did not view Scots in quite the same fashion. So much so that, while on a hunting trip in the Highlands, Henry had abruptly married an impoverished local lass. (*Lass* was the kindest way Jane could describe the woman. Others used more colorful words, the politest of which were *trollop* and *light-skirt*.)

Horrified at finding himself with a low-born, Scottish daughter-in-law, the old earl had cut Henry off without a farthing and never spoke to his son again. If it had been within his power, the old earl would have even barred Henry from eventually succeeding to the title. Fortunately, Fate listened, and Henry had died before his father.

So it was now Henry's son, Andrew Langston—the Scottish lass's offspring and therefore uneducated, crude, and completely unfit—who had become the third Earl of Hadley. The very sort of Scot the first Earl of Hadley had valiantly tried to exterminate.

Irony, indeed.

"They say Lord Hadley is a veritable savage." Lady Whitcomb practically quivered in delicious excitement, her pinched face narrowing further. "He certainly doesn't mix in polite company. There has never been a whisper of him at any *ton* event." She arched her eyebrows before biting into a buttery biscuit. "My cousin, Lord Wanleigh, stated as much in his most recent letter."

Lady Whitcomb's cousin was the aging Marquess of Wanleigh—a fact no one was allowed to forget. Jane had never met the man, but she often wondered if he was as pompous in person as he sounded on paper.

"And why *should* the new Lord Hadley have mingled with Polite Society? Savages don't attend balls." Mrs. Burton pronounced her words with zealous conviction. Jane was quite sure fealty had been sworn with less fervor.

Peter angled himself fractionally closer to Jane, snorting again. "Of course savages attend balls," he muttered under his breath.

Jane concentrated on not smiling.

Do not react.

She pressed her fingernail into her palm, pressing hard enough to feel a bite of pain but never breaking the skin.

Peter leaned into her ear, clearly undeterred. "One must be nearly feral to survive the London Season. Cannibalism is the *ton*'s *modus operandi*. We thrive on devouring our own—"

Jane barely swallowed back the laughter climbing her throat. She shot Peter a quelling side-glance.

"Hush." She managed to say the word without moving her lips, for all the good it did.

Peter was determined to win this round.

It was a game they played. Peter said outrageous things, and Jane bravely refrained from reacting beyond a discreet pinch or *sotto voce* reprimand. Abruptly smiling, frowning, smirking, eye rolling, or heaven forbid, *giggling* would earn Jane a dressing down from their mother after guests departed.

After all, she had an image to maintain.

Ladies never indulge in broad emotions, Jane, Lady Hadley would say. *Emotion, if it must be shown, should be conveyed through a raised eyebrow or slight tonal inflection. Nothing more.*

Peter, of course, had no such constraints. He could make faces all he wished, and their mother would never say a word. Facts he well knew.

Thankfully, Peter obeyed Jane's quiet reprimand and sat back, crossing his arms, his black armband straining from the movement. But the smile lurking on his lips promised more harassing torment.

Her brother knew her polite, elegant manners were studiously learned; a facade she carefully donned. Unladylike behavior and rowdy thoughts lurked just beneath her polished veneer, defaults she constantly strove to quash.

In true younger brother fashion, he delighted in reminding her of these facts. Over and over again. Endlessly.

Jane forced herself to focus by pressing another fingernail into her palm, leaving a clear half-moon shape. It was a habit born years ago. She had found that the small pain channeled her emotions, keeping them off her expression. After a particularly trying afternoon, her palm would look like fish scales, the markings taking an hour or more to fade.

"However will you manage, Lady Hadley?" Mrs. Burton tsked, reaching for a biscuit. "A coarse, bawdy Highlander as the Earl of Hadley—"

"Oh, a Highlander." Mrs. Smith's gaze went wide and a little dreamy-eyed. "Like one of the heroes of a Walter Scott novel?"

"No, Martha. The man is not to be fictionalized," Lady Whitcomb admonished, much as one might reprimand an overly-eager poodle for jumping up on the furniture. "I shan't permit you to romanticize the severity of this situation."

"Hear, hear. The new Lord Hadley certainly does not belong to the Church of England." Mrs. Burton nibbled her biscuit daintily, obviously enjoying the conversation immensely. "More likely he is a pagan heathen."

Peter huffed, quiet and low.

"Or, worse," he whispered, "a Presbyterian."

He nudged his foot against Jane's.

I know you want to laugh, his movements said.

Jane pinched her lips, keeping her head determinedly faced toward their mother. *You shall not defeat me.*

She supposed most sisters would feel aggravation over such teasing. But Peter's actions showed louder than anything that he understood, that he *knew* her.

And Jane adored being known. Being known meant she was loved, accepted just as she was.

Was it any wonder she loved Peter so thoroughly in return?

The ladies continued their gossip.

"Indeed," Lady Whitcomb agreed. "A pagan Scotsman might do for a novel but place such a man in an English drawing room . . ." She drifted off, giving a violent shudder.

In that moment, Jane nearly pitied Lord Hadley. The man would be walking into a hornet's nest of expectations and rigid etiquette rules he clearly did not understand, crofter's hut or not. He was in for a brutal time of things.

Lady Hadley offered a restrained smile, expression politely arctic. "It has been a dreadful shock. Thankfully, we have the care of kind friends to buoy us up."

Her mother delivered the words with dripping sweetness. Lady Whitcomb did not miss their venom, her lips pinching in response.

Jane longed to roll her eyes and lounge back in her chair, posture slumping.

She took another sip of tea instead.

The Langston family had already survived four Scottish kings, three German ones, and pink powdered wigs. It would surely outlast this catastrophe.

Jane herself was no stranger to disaster. Her father, the Duke of Montacute, had died when Jane was still a babe. When Jane was a toddler, her mother had remarried, this time to the widowed Earl of Hadley. Lord Hadley had not been a cruel stepfather to Jane. He had simply never acknowledged her existence beyond the occasional polite nod or word.

Jane might have taken offense at this, but the old earl treated everyone that way—his wife, relatives, his deceased son, Henry . . . even Peter, his only child with Jane's mother. No one mourned when, after years of poor health, the earl had finally passed on six months ago. Only his lordship's creditors and immediate family considered his death a calamity.

No, the true horror came in the aftermath of his lordship's funeral.

Jane vividly remembered the palpable gasp in the room as the family solicitor politely informed them that the old earl had made a series of unwise investments, leaving the earldom heavily in debt and on the verge of bankruptcy. Lady Hadley would receive her dower portion, as was legally required, but no other allowances had been made.

Peter, his lordship's *English* second son—the spare, not the heir—had received nothing.

Instead, what little remained had been left to his lordship's Scottish grandson, the new Lord Hadley.

Laws of primogeniture being what they were, the title *had* to pass to the eldest son of the eldest son—the Scot, Andrew Langston.

But . . . the ailing estates, lands, and investments were not currently entailed. Some portion of them—or all, quite frankly—could have been left to Peter. Yet, for some unfathomable reason, the old earl had utterly cut his second son from his will. The question was why?

The old earl had been ill for years before his death. Had he simply neglected to update his will in a timely fashion? Or, had he truly been so uncaring of Peter? Regardless of the old earl's finances, to deny his son any inheritance whatsoever seemed excessively callous.

Peter had borne it all with a stoic, white-lipped silence—the same wretched, suppressed fury with which he greeted all information about the new Lord Hadley. Having spent her whole life concerned for her brother's welfare, Jane found it physically painful to witness.

The disorderly heart of her—the inner wild self she kept contained and thoroughly battened down—raged at the injustice. *That* Jane wanted to raise the old earl from dead, just so she could send him to his Maker again. This time in a more painfully lingering fashion.

Of course, such thoughts merely underscored *why* she kept her inner self thoroughly contained. No one wanted a lady who behaved in such a manner. Her past had proved this most cruelly.

"When do you anticipate his lordship's arrival?" Mrs. Smith asked Lady Hadley, interrupting Jane's thoughts.

Though Lord Hadley had immediately petitioned Parliament for a Writ of Summons, he had waited six months before making an appearance in Sussex.

The previous week after Sunday service, Mrs. Smith had the audacity to muse that it was to his lordship's credit that he had waited until the family was out of full mourning before visiting them. She was immediately silenced.

"His man-of-affairs said to expect him in three weeks' time," Lady Hadley replied.

"The earl did not write you himself?" Lady Whitcomb was all astonishment.

"No."

Silence greeted Lady Hadley's curt response. Unspoken assumptions hung in the air—if Lord Hadley hadn't written the letter himself, was his lordship even literate? However, he *did* employ a man-of-affairs, so perhaps opinion was divided on that score?

Smiling stiffly, Lady Hadley motioned toward the tea tray. "Would anyone care for another biscuit?"

Eventually the ladies rattled through their gossip about the new Lord Hadley and took their leave.

"Well, I cannot say I missed afternoon calls when we were in full mourning," Peter said as the door closed on the last of them. He stood, walking over to the fireplace. "I'm quite sure my ears are bleeding from their lacerating witticisms."

"You acquitted yourself well, Peter, as usual," Lady Hadley smoothed her lavender skirts, before turning to Jane. "You were far too quiet, however, Jane. You need to speak more."

"Of course, Mother." Jane gave her reply automatically. If she had said more to their visitors, her mother would reprimand her for speaking too often.

Jane pressed her fingernail into her palm. *Half-moons*, she thought. *Concentrate on making half-moons.*

"Why are you harping on about Jane's manners, Mother?" Peter rolled his eyes and snorted, sarcasm dripping. "The new Lord Hadley will not notice one way or another."

He pronounced *Lord Hadley* with a hostile wince, as if saying the man's very name hurt his mouth.

Jane shot Peter a grateful look. She could see them both reflected in the mirror above the mantel, their heads nearly touching, Peter's tousled blond overlapping her brassier auburn. Symbolically always beside her.

"Hadley . . . perhaps not." Lady Hadley glanced her way. "But I've had another letter from Montacute, Jane, and your brother is hinting, again, at you joining him and his duchess in London for the Season. If that happens, we must focus on perfecting your behavior."

Jane narrowly avoided a wince herself. Only the biting pain of her nail into her palm stopped her reaction.

Her other half-brother, the current Duke of Montacute, had exacting expectations of her. Words from his latest letter rattled through her skull:

> *You must ever be mindful, sister, of the honor your name does you. You are the daughter and sister of Montacute. Your every breath should reflect the exalted circumstances of your birth.*

Nearly twenty years her senior, Montacute had always been a menacing figure, more stern father than brother, truth be told. Jane revolted at the thought of living with him and his duchess in London, forced to interact daily with their caustic selves. Worse, it would separate her from Peter.

Her mother continued, motioning toward Jane with a languid hand, "Montacute has increased your pin money since the old earl's death, Jane, but with the earldom on the brink of bankruptcy, I do not know how much longer you will have a home here. It all depends on what the new earl decides when he arrives. Unmarried, you are simply a drain upon both Hadley and Montacute."

As was proper, Montacute had assumed financial responsibility for Jane since her stepfather's death and provided her with a monthly allowance. But her mother's words were true—unmarried, Jane was nothing more than dross.

Peter moved to sit, sprawling in the chair opposite, shooting her an understanding look. While neither of them was enthusiastic about having to tolerate the new Scottish earl himself, they genuinely dreaded the consequences of his choices.

"Well, we are *all* drains on Hadley now, Mother," Peter said, again distracting Lady Hadley's attention. "He holds our purse strings, such as they are. We are all reliant on his good-will for our every need. I consider it prudent to politely avoid the man as much as possible."

Given that Peter could scarcely say the man's name without grimacing in distaste, her brother was far more troubled than he let on. He was justifiably angry that Hadley—uncouth, unrefined, and currently unknown—now held Peter's future in his hands. The hurt of being abandoned so thoroughly by his sire ran deep. Peter had been cut adrift, floating away from her, and Jane felt powerless to bring him back to shore.

Jane sat straighter in her chair.

"I agree with Peter," she said. "We shall simply endure Hadley's coming the way all English have faced Scots over the centuries—with impeccable manners, reserved politeness, and sardonic verve."

Peter grimaced and saluted her with a raised eyebrow. His expression mirroring her own sense of impending doom.

2

His friends were arguing again.

Andrew Mackenzie would never tire of it.

The sound of their bickering was home and camaraderie all mixed into a male-acceptable tonic—endless, pitiless teasing.

"Ye cannae eat haggis without a dram or two of good whisky, that's alls I'm sayin'." Master Kieran MacTavish angled his tumbler toward Dr. Alexander Whitaker sitting across the table.

"Too much strong drink is bad for the body," Alex countered, tilting his own water glass in response.

"Aye." Andrew nodded, joining in. "Whisky is the enemy, Kieran." He winked and then took a healthy swig of his own dark ale.

"Och, away wi' ye both. The Good Book says I'm tae love my enemies, aye?" Kieran lifted his glass and sipped before placing his free hand over his heart. "An' I've always been a devout follower of the Good Book—"

The door cracked open, bringing a rush of voices from the taproom and a blast of smells: alcohol, leather, horse. Two more men followed swiftly behind—Lord Rafe Gilbert and Ewan Campbell.

The men stood, exchanging greetings and hearty back-slaps before settling around the central table, all five of them.

The group of friends were gathered in the private dining room of the Black Bull Inn, midway along the road between Edinburgh and Falkirk.

A fire crackled in the hearth, casting shadows along the wood paneling on the walls. The ceiling timbers creaked from footsteps above. The noise of the taproom beyond the closed door was a distant murmur broken occasionally by a boistrous laugh.

This evening, the nineteenth of March, marked the second anniversary of their gathering, the third year since the fateful events which changed all of their lives.

Andrew nursed his ale, watching his friends laugh and continue their good-natured ribbing of Kieran. The men were much the same as they had always been.

Lord Rafe was quick to deflect a personal question and even quicker to flirt with a beautiful lass.

Alex was their moral compass, a physician who could be relied on to keep a steady head, regardless of the situation.

Ewan was quiet and watchful, thoughts and words carefully considered, as if he were determined to commit them all to one of his canvases.

Kieran's pale eyes still hung with dark shadows. His easy laughter hid the grief and guilt Andrew knew ate at his friend's soul.

Andrew, as ever, felt the weight of their lives on his shoulders.

The innkeeper bustled into the room with more ale and a bottle of whisky for the table, promising to return shortly with haggis and neeps 'n' tatties.

Silence descended as the door clicked behind the man.

"I'm right glad tae see ye all tonight," Andrew said. As the one who had brought them together in the first place, he continued to act as their leader.

Facts which made his task tonight even more difficult.

He had to tell them. It was far past time. He should have told them years ago. Tonight, he would correct that.

But first, there was a weightier matter to address.

Andrew cleared his throat. "We journeyed tae the far corners of the world together and returned changed men. We were strangers tae one another before we left, but now we are brothers in every way that matters except blood."

"Aye," Alex murmured, "though we have shed enough of our blood together tae be counted as blood brothers in truth."

Rafe smiled, the motion pulling at the white scar which ran from his right temple to his cheekbone.

Silently, Andrew took the bottle of whisky and poured a single finger in each glass.

Raising his own cup, he said, "A toast to Jamie and all those who did not return home with us. We drink tae their memory, tae the secrets we keep, and tae the justice we seek."

"To Jamie," the others chorused, clinking their glasses.

Five years ago, Andrew had decided to fulfill a lifelong dream—to embark on a voyage of scientific discovery. The four men in the room had responded to his entreaties to join him.

Andrew had met Lord Rafe while studying at St. Andrews. Both of them shared a passion for the natural sciences, though Andrew preferred mineralogy to Rafe's botany.

Alex and Ewan had replied to Andrew's advertisement for a physician and artist, respectively.

Kieran had been master to their ship, *The Minerva.*

Their voyage had been pleasant enough for the first six months, but then—

"I cannae believe it's been three years since that day," Ewan said. "My memories are still so vivid."

"Aye . . . Jamie's death haunts us all," Andrew said.

None of them looked at Kieran.

As master of *The Minerva,* Kieran had been given charge of the ship's navigation, as well as ensuring she was outfitted and in ship-shape condition at all times. Though not the captain—that honor belonged to Captain Martin Cuthie—Kieran had been the ship's second. If Captain Cuthie was the ship's father, Master Kieran MacTavish was her mother.

Jamie Fyffe had come aboard as the carpenter's mate. Jamie's father, Mr. Charles Fyffe, had been Kieran's mentor and friend.

Jamie had been new to life at sea, but charismatic and clever, drawing all their attention. The five of them—Andrew, Rafe, Ewan, Alex, and Kieran—had each taken an interest in Jamie's well-being. It was as if their affection for Jamie was the initial bond that had brought them together as friends. Jamie, of course, had returned their friendship ten-fold.

When events had turned deadly on that night three years ago, Jamie had defied Captain Cuthie and saved their lives. But the youth had paid the ultimate price as a result.

Unbidden, memory washed over Andrew.

Blinding pain smashed into the side of his face. He struggled to stay upright, but an agonizing slash cut across his legs. He collapsed in agony.

Kieran bellowed into the night, an inferno of flames rising behind him, fist shaking at the moonlit sails on the ocean. "Ye'll not get away with this. I'll hunt ye tae the ends of the earth!"

To say they mourned Jamie's death would be an understatement. The heavy guilt and nauseating grief felt endless at times. The youth had relied on them for protection, and they had failed.

But then . . . some things were not to be overcome, simply borne and woven into the fabric of the soul.

Along with that—

"I have something for you tae see." Andrew slid back his chair and snagged a paper parcel he had set with his hat on a small desk in the corner.

Untying the string, he opened the package. A length of dark wool tartan tumbled onto the table, a cross-hatch pattern of red, green, yellow, and white on a black ground—the colors all the more vivid for the dark background.

"What's the point of this?" Kieran reached out a hand, gently rubbing the wool between his fingers.

Obviously, the length of tartan seemed to be a *non sequitur*.

But . . .

"I had the manager of my woolen factory outside Perth weave this for me," Andrew replied. "It's merely a sample, mind ye."

"I don't recognize the pattern." Rafe took the fabric from Kieran's hands. "It's quite dark for a clan tartan."

"Aye," Andrew said. "You wouldn't recognize it because I created the pattern myself. I call it 'Jamie's Tartan.'"

Silence descended.

Andrew cleared his throat. "I ken that we named ourselves the Brotherhood of the Tartan tae honor our joint Scottish heritage and the trials we faced together. But I liked the thought of having an actual tartan as a symbol."

Andrew reached down and spread a hand across the wool, flattening a section on the tabletop. He tapped the dark ground.

"Black for grief and anger." He traced a wide, cherry-red band. "Red for our guilt over innocent blood spilt. A little gold for hope, a wee bit of green for growth." He drew a nail along the last color. "White for the purity of our hearts and goals."

He cleared his throat, tone abruptly gruff. "I wanted something more tangible tae remember Jamie. I thought I'd see if ye would be interested in each having a length of plaid for a sash or great kilt. Or both." A pause. "If ye like the thought, I'll instruct my manager tae make multiple lengths of the tartan."

Alex slid the cloth toward him, staring at it. "That is a beautiful idea, Andrew."

"Aye," Ewan all but whispered. "Jamie needs tae be honored and remembered."

Kieran bolted another shot of whisky before nodding his head.

"Nothing about that dark night should be forgotten," Rafe added, the scar on his cheek flashing in the firelight. "Shall we rename ourselves the Brotherhood of the *Black* Tartan then?"

A moment of silence greeted Rafe's question.

"Aye," Andrew's voice had gone hoarse. Given the similar 'ayes' from his friends, he was not alone. "We'll be the Brotherhood of the Black Tartan."

"We *will* have justice for Jamie," Ewan whispered.

Silence hung for a moment, as they each wrenched emotions into submission.

"Any luck trackin' down the bastard responsible?" Kieran asked. His words were casual, but Andrew didn't miss the venom laced through them.

Revenge and justice had been Kieran's lodestar for nearly three years. They were the only emotions strong enough to keep him from succumbing to the morass of his grief and guilt.

"Nothing solid yet, but we're making progress," Andrew replied. "Last month, I employed the most celebrated Runner from Bow Street to find him. I'm hoping this Runner can succeed where others have failed."

They knew the man responsible for the events that led to Jamie's death—Andrew's one-time business partner, Thomas Madsen. The man who had betrayed them and left them for dead, marooned in the South Pacific.

The problem? They couldn't *locate* Madsen. They had returned to Edinburgh to find the man had cleaned his accounts of money and utterly disappeared. Andrew had employed men to find Madsen over the past year, but only recently had he hired the-best-of-the-best from Bow Street. Hopefully, the Runner would produce results.

"Madsen may be dead," Rafe said.

"I hope he isnae," Kieran replied. "I want ma pound of flesh."

"Blood thirsty." Rafe shook his head, clicking his tongue.

"I'm Scottish," was Kieran's shrugging reply.

A polite rap on the door stopped the conversation. Two barmaids entered, each balancing a laden tray. They set down plates and cutlery before placing a trencher of browned haggis in the center of the table. The haggis rolled slightly, steam escaping from a slit in the sheep's stomach that encased the ground meat. The smell of black pepper and sausage filled the room. Bowls of mashed neeps 'n' tatties followed.

Ewan was the first to heap food on his plate. Alex continued to study Jamie's tartan and ask questions about Andrew's weaving processes. Rafe flirted with both the lasses until they were giggling and blushing. Kieran rolled his eyes. Andrew lifted a finger to request more bread and whisky.

Basically, everyone precisely as they should be.

Their conversation wandered as they ate, Kieran describing a recent galley fire aboard his ship, and Alex recounting a horse race in Leith. Andrew dug into his haggis while listening to his friends bandy insults back and forth, trying to decide when to tell them his *other* news.

Somewhere in their years together, particularly after being marooned and nearly dying on a small island in the South Pacific, Andrew *should* have told them.

And yet . . . he hadn't.

Mostly because he never thought about it. His father's past had never defined Andrew's own future. But, as often happened, the past had caught up with him just the same.

They had all pushed back from the table, Ewan still picking at the leftovers, when the topic moved on to Rafe's recent trip to London, dancing attendance on his father.

As the younger son of an English duke, Lord Rafe was the least Scottish of them all. But his mother hailed from Ayrshire, south of Glasgow—she even professed to have met the celebrated poet, Robert Burns—and Rafe attended the university in St. Andrews in eastern Fife, so he identified strongly with his maternal Scottish heritage.

"I'm surprised your father allows ye tae spend time with us at all," Alex snorted.

"Aye, well, most English think of Scots as unruly louts," Rafe chuckled. "Scotland has been bandied about London drawing rooms even more the past couple months. Do you all recall the Earldom of Hadley?"

"The title created for that English bastard who vowed tae exterminate every last Scot at Culloden in '46?" Alex asked.

"The very same." Rafe nodded. "Though I think the situation is rapidly proving that God has a sense of humor. The old earl passed away a few months ago, and his grandson, the new Earl of Hadley, is a Scot."

Kieran and Alex let loose loud guffaws.

"A Scot?" Ewan raised his eyebrows.

Andrew pursed his lips. *Now* would likely be a good time to say something.

He cleared his throat.

"Aye," Rafe talked over the noise. "The old earl's heir married a lowly-born Scottish woman—"

"That old earl received his just desserts in the end, aye," Kieran grinned.

"Perhaps," Rafe said, "but, of course, now Parliament is stalling over granting the new earl his Writ of Summons. There are *concerns*, as my father put it. Was the heir tricked into marrying a woman of questionable morality? Were the new earl's parents properly married in a church? Is a lowly Scot even fit to lead an English earldom?"

Kieran growled. Andrew joined him.

A woman of questionable morality? Truly?

He cleared his throat louder.

Four heads turned his way.

Right.

"Och, she wasn't a woman of questionable morality and the marriage was absolutely proper." Andrew drummed his fingers on the table-top. "Bunch of bloody English gossips."

His friends stared, one-by-one their eyes widening with realization. He met their gazes, wincing slightly.

Guilty conscience and all that.

Andrew let the silence proclaim his truth.

Rafe was the first to speak. "This is where you tell me what we're thinking is madness. You are Andrew Mackenzie, aye? Not the new earl, Andrew Langston?" Scotland drifted into his consonants, as it was wont to do when he became agitated or deep in his cups. "Or has one of ma best friends been keepin' a secret of this magnitude all these years?"

Andrew sighed, sitting back in his chair. His gaze drifted to the fire crackling in the hearth. He dragged a weary hand over his face.

"I didnae mean to keep it from yous," he said, accent slipping further from crisp aristocratic to the brogue of his Scottish grandfather. "In all honestly, I never think about ma father's English family. But, aye, I was christened Andrew Henry Mackenzie Langston."

His friends' stunned silence stuffed the room, tightening Andrew's breathing further.

"I should have told yous years ago," he muttered. "I just dinnae like thinking about that part of my life, tae be honest. Though it makes me right crabbit to hear that my ma's good name being slandered so. She is a gently-bred lady."

"Her father was a wealthy man of business, aye?" Alex said. "Owned cotton mills and iron works and the like?"

"Aye." Everyone knew Andrew had been born and raised a wealthy gentleman. "My dey—sorry, my grandad—was lowly born, but he built a financial empire. My mother was his only child. My father didn't speak much about his English upbringing. Only that he came tae Scotland on a hunting trip and never left. Said he saw my ma and that was it for him. He loved her tae distraction until the day he died.

"I knew growing up that my pa was the heir tae an earldom, but he didn't ken tae his family. They washed their hands of him, said they never wanted tae see him again. After that, my pa preferred to be called Henry Mackenzie, adopting my dey's surname as his own. I followed suit, dropping the Langston name . . ." His voice drifted off.

More silence.

Andrew felt the weight of their judgment, that keen sense of betrayal.

Kieran let out an explosive blast of air. "I cannae believe ye didnae tell us," he muttered.

"Aye," Ewan agreed.

Alex nodded his head.

Rafe grimaced.

Kieran waved a hand. "It's as if ye hate us."

"Kieran," Andrew began, "it's not like that—"

"Nae, it is." Kieran jabbed a finger at Andrew's chest. "Years! Ye have deprived us of *years* of teasing ye over this." He threw up a hand in disgust.

"Aye!" Rafe smacked a flat palm on the table.

Kieran wasn't done. "I could've been calling ye your lordship—"

"Bowing and sich," Ewan mourned.

"Tugging a forelock."

"Always insisting on giving ye precedence," Ewan continued.

"You have never done that with me." Lord Rafe looked at Ewan.

"Och." Kieran waved a hand at Rafe. "Your lofty lordship isnae fun to tease."

"Aye," Alex agreed, "you're no' serious enough. But Andrew—"

"Andrew would've been a dream." Kieran looked off into the mid-distance, eyes wistful. He jabbed a finger at Andrew again. "I dinnae think I can ever forgive ye . . . yer lordship." He gave a mocking bow.

His friends all laughed.

Andrew frowned.

Not *quite* the reaction he had expected.

"How are ye getting on with it?" Ewan leaned forward, snagging Andrew's gaze. "Given your family's acrimonious history, are ye content to assume the earldom?"

Trust Ewan to ask a kind-hearted question. His artist's soul always thought of people first.

"He cannot refuse the title," Rafe said. "English laws of inheritance will not allow it."

"Rafe has the right of it." Andrew chewed on his cheek. "More to the point, I am not one to shirk my responsibilities. So even though I don't necessarily *like* that I am an English earl, I will do my duty there. My father wished it and, tae his credit, he ensured I knew how tae run an estate and manage the demands of an earldom." He shook his head. "Though, I can't imagine living as an English gentleman is supposed tae—endless parties and empty entertainments. I've labored in business my entire adult life—"

"Ye're a cit, as the English would say," Ewan said.

"Aye, but I wear being a cit as a badge of worth—"

"Nae, that's just yer bourgeois upbringing speaking," Kieran snorted.

"Regardless," Rafe said, "Father was talking about you all last week. Your Writ of Summons is taking some time—"

"Aye, the process has been fraught. The Committee on Privilege keeps demanding more proof, particularly regarding my parent's marriage, as ye said," Andrew replied. "Clearly there is a faction in Lords that wishes tae humiliate me before I even arrive."

Even though he was the rightful heir to the earldom, Andrew still had to petition the Crown and Parliament to be recognized as the next Lord Hadley. Usually receiving a Writ of Summons—a legal document summoning Andrew to take his seat in the House of Lords—was a mere formality. But someone in Lords had decided to make the entire process fractious.

"You *are* the rightful heir." Rafe frowned. "They can make noise, but they cannot legally remove you without writing a new law. Chancery *has* to issue the Writ of Summons at some point."

"Precisely. I'm waiting tae receive an update from my solicitor."

Alex nodded. "I imagine a new earl, particularly one that does not come from the peerage's exalted ranks, will always cause a stir."

"Aye, the *ton* is fascinated by you." Rafe rolled a hand. "And by *fascinated*, I mean abhorred."

Andrew snorted. "I certainly didn't anticipate the antipathy I would cause. Why should these unknown English dislike me so, sight unseen?" he asked. "Regardless, there is still much tae resolve with my late grandfather's estate—"

Rafe nodded. "I had heard that the earldom was on the verge of bankruptcy."

"It is," Andrew said bluntly. "My grandfather, the old earl, made some catastrophic investments."

"The Caribbean Affair of '14?" Rafe asked, referring to an investment scandal that had rocked London nearly five years ago.

"The verra same."

The Caribbean Affair involved shares in a once-profitable bank based in Nassau. Heavily invested in the sugarcane trade, the bank collapsed due to mismanagement and a series of disastrous hurricanes. Many members of the *ton* had lost fortunes, Rafe's father included.

"I leave in two days tae visit Hadley Park in Sussex tae sort it all out," Andrew said. "The earldom desperately needs an influx of cash—"

"It's fortunate, then, that ye're known as the Scottish Vulcan," Ewan said, naming Andrew's current nickname in the newspapers. Mackenzie was rich as a god, they said, forging everything he touched into money.

Luckily, no one yet had connected the wealthy Scottish Vulcan, Andrew Mackenzie with Andrew Langston, the new Earl of Hadley.

"Aye," Andrew grimaced. "I've already extended a hefty sum to settle the earldom's creditors. I have faith—with enough time and effort—that I can resuscitate the earldom's finances. It's the relatives I've inherited that worry me more: a step-grandmother in Lady Hadley, and her son— Mr. Peter Langston, my heir."

Rafe chuckled. "Aye, I believe Lady Jane is still at Hadley Park, too."

"Who?"

"Lady Jane Everard, Lady Hadley's daughter. Before marrying your grandfather, Lady Hadley was married to the Duke of Montacute. Lady Jane is the daughter from her first marriage."

"No one has mentioned a Lady Jane. Are you sure she's there too?" Andrew frowned.

"Last I heard, she was, but it's possible she is living with her brother, the current Duke of Montacute." Rafe shrugged. "I have a passing acquaintance with Lady Jane, as she is a cousin of sorts. She and her mother are decidedly . . . English."

Andrew grimaced. "That I believe. The brief letters I've received from Lady Hadley have dripped with condescension and disdain. She obviously dreads having to accept me into the family."

"Once a Scot, always a Scot," Rafe nodded.

"You will never be anything *but* that to them—a bawdy, clownish oaf," Alex added.

Just what Andrew feared. It explained why he had waited so long to visit Hadley Park. Its citizens were already predisposed to dislike him. Polite Society considered him to be a barely-literate barbarian. Why foist himself on them a second before necessary?

"What tae do then?" Andrew asked.

"Dinnae be anything other than yerself," Ewan suggested and then clarified. "Yer true Scottish self."

"And I'll be there to support you," Rafe said. "I have business to attend to, as my father's demands never cease. But I should be passing near Hadley Park in about four weeks' time. I'll pay you an extended visit."

"I would welcome your company. I fear I shall need the help."

"That's why I'll be coming with ye directly," Kieran added.

"You'll be coming?" Andrew asked.

"Aye. My ship won't be repaired for at least another month. I'm in the carpenter's way at this point. Besides, ye'll need assistance that only I can give."

"Only you?"

"From the sound of things, yer English relations have definite opinions about ye. As Ewan said, you need tae be yer *true* Scottish self." Kieran wiggled his eyebrows.

"Why do I have a feeling you mean more than me as I am at this moment?"

"Och, the English have already assumed the worst about ye. Just listen tae what they're saying about yer parents. They consider Scots tae be loud-mouthed, vulgar, glaikit eejits. Nothing any of us do or say will convince them otherwise. Chancery wants to humiliate ye, and yer English relations are going out of their way tae make ye uncomfortable." Kieran's grin was slow and wicked. "I ken ye need to mount a proper defense against that."

"You're not helping me tae feel any better about this—"

"I say ye revel in yer Scottishness, ensure they're just as uncomfortable as you." Kieran pressed a hand to his chest. "Honestly, it's practically yer civic duty tae live up tae their lowest expectations."

Andrew paused, thinking of the curt letters he had received from the Chancery and Lady Hadley, the cruel rumors about his mother, the abrupt assumptions made simply on the basis of his nationality.

The problem was easily summed up: England would always look at Scotland as the troublesome scoundrel that needed to be suppressed, the scapegrace who offered endless teasing and ribald jokes.

Nothing Andrew said or did would change their preconceived notions.

So . . . why *should* he try to behave in any other way? Why *not* derive some enjoyment from watching his English relatives snub their noses at him? Counter the cold disdain of their English manners with his own flamboyant Scottishness?

He grinned at Kieran.

Scotland.

Living up to England's lowest expectations since 1296.

All of a sudden, Andrew couldn't wait to leave.

Thank ye for comin', my lady." Mrs. Brady curtsied to Jane.

"I wished to greet your latest addition." Jane handed off the basket she carried to an older child and then folded her hands primly in front of her. She gave a slow nod of her head, eyes drifting to the tiny babe in Mrs. Brady's arms. "She is beautiful." The baby scrunched her face, sighing in her sleep.

Jane had escaped Hadley Park and her mother's critical eye today. Visiting Mrs. Brady—one of the estate's tenant farmers who had just welcomed her eleventh child—had simply been a convenient excuse.

Mr. Brady worked hard with his older boys, but as he was missing the lower half of his right leg courtesy of Napoleon and a French mortar, his farm did not produce the yields required to support a family of thirteen. Jane tried to augment their meager rations with supplies from Hadley Park's larders when she could.

"We are always grateful for your ladyship's kindness." Mrs. Brady nodded to the basket of jams and butter. Jane had even included a portion of ham, as she knew meat to be a rare luxury.

"Think nothing of it," Jane replied, glancing again at the tiny baby. She longed to hold the infant, to drop a kiss atop her small head and breathe in her warm scent.

But the daughter of a duke would never condescend to cuddle a farmer's babe. It was simply not done. And Jane had long ago given up wishing for things that could not be.

A few moments later, Jane was back in her pony phaeton, reins loose in her gloved hands. She clucked Thunder to walk on, guiding him down the lane toward the other reason she liked visiting Mrs. Brady.

The Brady's cottage was close by Rosehearth.

And Jane adored Rosehearth.

The spring weather had turned sunny and warm, hinting at summer. Newly-green trees rustled and sheep baaed in the distance.

Jane wheeled through a clearing. Rosehearth came into view with its red brick facade, mullioned windows, and forest of chimneys. Medieval in structure, the house even had a small moat with a drawbridge extending out. *Charming* seemed too tame a word to describe it.

Rosehearth was said to be the original great-house of the Hadley family, dating from the late Middle Ages. Once the family fortunes expanded during the reign of Elizabeth I, they had abandoned Rosehearth and built (and built and built) Hadley Park. Rosehearth had become the place to deposit superfluous relatives—typically dowagers, spinster aunts, or unruly children—keeping them out of sight and mind.

Jane and Peter had lived there until she was twelve years old. During those years, Lady Hadley was too busy with her social life in London and house parties in the country to worry about her children. The old earl, for his part, had enjoyed showing off his young, beautiful, vivacious wife. Children were not to be seen or heard. This was more easily accomplished if the children were housed elsewhere.

Rosehearth always reminded Jane of her carefree, younger self. Of her and Peter running wild through the garden, laughing in the kitchen with Cook, sneaking past Nanny Smith to visit the home farm, cuddling together in the timber-lined library while winter winds raged outside.

During those years, Jane watched over Peter, bestowing on him all the love they lacked from others. She had helped him ride his first pony, walking beside him, scarcely taller than the pony herself. She had kissed his skinned knees and laughed at his silly jokes. Peter and Rosehearth had been her entire world.

Jane nearly sighed. How simple life had been then? And she, in her naivety, had assumed that such a life would continue unaltered.

But then came a disastrous visit from Montacute and everything had changed. Her ducal brother arrived unannounced and found her swimming in a nearby river with Peter and other children from the estate.

As her legal guardian, His Grace had *not* been amused to discover his only sister in such a state. Twelve-years-old and swimming? With lower class *boys*, no less?

Jane still vividly recalled the vein near to bursting in his neck, the violent bulging of his eyes. His Grace, in a word, had been incensed.

The duke had instantly whisked her away with him to Montacute House, vowing that if Lady Hadley could not raise Jane to be a lady, then he and his duchess would take over her rearing as was their right. After all, Jane had been left in Lady Hadley's care only at Montacute's sufferance.

Jane had sobbed the entire journey to Montacute House, three days of hiccupping and tears.

She missed Rosehearth.

She desperately missed Peter.

Montacute House was an inhospitable place—the building and its inhabitants both echoing and cold. The Duchess had raked Jane from head-to-toe, lips pursed, before making a scathing comment about Jane's wild red hair, already gangling height, and freckled skin.

Her sister-in-law dripped aristocratic hauteur—hard eyes, clipped tones, and not a hair out of place. Jane could not imagine the duchess had ever *smiled*, much less splashed with abandon in a river.

Montacute and his duchess had been pitiless. Since Jane's unfortunate hair and height would never win her admirers, her only hope of ever marrying lay in cultivating elegant comportment and manners.

And so they fumed over Jane's behavior. Her table etiquette was atrocious, her posture abysmal. She could scarcely execute a proper curtsy when called upon, much less competently preside over a tea service.

Jane could not stomach it, quite literally. She refused to eat for nearly a week in protest.

Finally, Lady Hadley was summoned. Peter, she reported, was distraught without Jane. Separating the children was proving difficult for both families.

A truce was reached.

Montacute relented to placing Jane back into Lady Hadley's care, with the caveat that Jane be molded into a perfect lady, as benefited the daughter of a powerful duke. Montacute would inspect Jane's progress on an annual basis.

Lady Hadley, embarrassed and wishing to stay in Montacute's good graces, readily agreed. For her part, Jane would have consented to anything in order to be reunited with Peter.

As Lady Hadley led Jane from Montacute House, the Duchess had her parting shot:

"You must stamp out your tendency toward base behavior and speech, Jane. No gentleman will ever align himself with a hoyden," the Duchess said, peering down her nose. "Become a lady, in every sense of the word. Remember—no one will want you otherwise."

Jane heeded that warning. The threat of being permanently separated from Peter loomed large.

She rooted out that wild girl running amok in the woods around Rosehearth, diligently excising the base parts of her psyche.

Every year, the duke would summon Jane to Montacute House where she would be subjected to a week of meticulous examination, her every breath scrutinized for less-than-perfect behavior.

The first couple years had been abysmal, but by her eighteenth birthday, Jane had even earned the duchess' distant nod of approval. Since then, Jane had not been required to present herself for inspection. It did not escape her notice that the visits had ceased only when Jane herself had become a woman like the Duchess of Montacute—cold, haughty, and colorless.

Become a lady . . . no one will want you otherwise.

Even her *hair* had finally acquiesced to the demands to be more contained, darkening from fire-red to a more sedate auburn, though her fair skin—more fickle—still freckled at the slightest ray of sunshine. It was as if her very hair and skin had conspired to be emblems of her outward and inward nature.

Jane clucked at Thunder, keeping the pony on the road. He was small, even for a pony, but generally well-behaved and liked to please. Though on occasion, he displayed a distressing tendency toward independent thought. He needed to have his wayward impulses checked, as well.

For her part, Jane did not know how to be warm and vibrant in moderation. She had silenced the girl she was at Rosehearth so thoroughly, sometimes it felt as if she had no personality left to offer. She worried that any glimpse of that wild, hoydenish Jane would cause her entire facade to crumble.

And so she remained Lady Jane—distant and chilly . . . as a lady should be.

She considered herself none of those things.

For example, Jane was passionate about the importance of caring for the poor on the estates that she inhabited. She always longed to run through a summer rain storm and had a decided taste for strong drink (though only Peter knew that vice). She secretly wanted to dig in the dirt and wade in streams to find minerals and other interesting stones.

As if proving her point, the phaeton rolled into a large clearing, skirting the edge of an abandoned, medieval quarry. The quarry cut into the hillside, creating a distinct horseshoe shape and exposing layers of stone. She studied the rocks as she passed.

It was her one indulgence. Jane supposed it was no surprise that she found stones so fascinating—minerals were simply another manifestation of imposing order on something seemingly chaotic. They were endowed with everything she enjoyed. Unmoving and unchangeable. Pretty to look at. Sometimes valuable. And offering endless ways to be organized: color, hardness, material, gemstone inclusion, and so forth.

She had drawers of her finds in the library at Hadley Park, all tucked into specially-designed cabinets. Periodically, she would rearrange them according to her whim.

Peter said she did it most when she was feeling alone and "sedimental."

He was excessively proud of the pun.

So she scoured the layers of stone as her phaeton slowly crept past, but she didn't see anything worth stopping for.

Or it could simply be that her heart wasn't in it.

Chaos awaited her at Hadley Park.

Lord Hadley arrived tomorrow.

The staff were aflutter with nerves and worry. What changes would the new Lord Hadley make? How could an uneducated Scot understand the complexities and tradition of running a large English estate?

All this worry naturally communicated itself to Jane's mother. Lady Hadley had become more waspish and authoritarian with each passing day until even Peter had closeted himself in the billiards room, only emerging for meals.

This left Jane to fend for herself against her mother. After a few days, her palms had been nearly reduced to half-moon ripples.

Her life, as she knew it, was about to change.

And likely not for the better.

"MA TREWS ITCH." Kieran shifted in his saddle.

"No true Scotsman would say such a thing." Andrew shook his head.

"I'm going tae pretend I didnae hear yous just now." Kieran gasped, mock hurt. "I'm merely stating a fact." He squirmed again. "They itch."

Mmmm.

Andrew rocked in his saddle. Kieran wasn't wrong; the trews did itch something fierce. Not that Andrew would give Kieran the satisfaction of admitting as much. His friend was whining only to annoy him.

"Quit your whinging," Andrew said, sliding into the deep Scottish brogue he would be using for the rest of the day. "Ye're the one who wanted tae wear them, no' me. 'We need tae be exceptionally Scottish today,' ye said. As I asked earlier, what demented ancient Highlander decided that leather-and-tartan pantaloons were a wise fashion choice?" Andrew stared down at his red-and-blue tartan trousers.

Kieran snorted, tugging on the length of green-and-yellow tartan he had slung over his left shoulder. The sash wrapped around his chest, matching the tartan of his trews. "Scotland isnae supposed to be comfortable, I suppose."

"Aye," Andrew agreed. "It's our national pastime. It's how we keep the English from overrunning the place . . . convincing the Sassenach that they dinnae want it. I only wear trews when I'm hunting deer or grouse in the Cairngorms. Then it's too wet and damp to wear anything *but* trews—"

"I'm no' finding fault with yer argument, Andrew—"

"I'm just saying trews are unnecessary in Sussex." Andrew waved a hand, indicating the lush green forest and dappled sunlight surrounding them. "I'm still puzzled why ye wanted tae wear them today."

"Spoken like a true English lordling." Kieran's grin was absolutely unrepentant.

Andrew ignored the jab. "I suggested kilts. Why didnae we wear kilts today? Kilts itch less."

"Trews are better on horseback."

"We could have taken ma carriage."

"No. That wouldnae do. Yer relatives expect a proper Highlander. We're no' about to disappoint them." His friend shook his head. "Highlanders wear trews."

"But we're no' proper Highlanders." Andrew had to say it. "I'm a Fifer."

"Speak for yourself."

"What? You hail from Dumbarton. Dumbarton isnae the Highlands either."

"Ma maither was from Inverness and my faither from Wester Ross—"

"Fine, then—"

"—but, regardless, the English dinnae understand the subtleties of Scottish origins. A Scot is a Scot to them. So . . . we wear trews."

"Now, Kieran—"

"Enough! I think yer a bit nervous, yer lofty lordship, and it's making ye tetchy."

Andrew held his tongue.

Kieran was likely right.

The latest round of letters with the Committee on Privilege had been arduous. The members of the committee—all peers in the House of Lords—were requesting more documentation of Andrew's birth from the parish records, further proof of his parent's kirk marriage, and the most galling of all, affidavits attesting to his *character*. An English-born heir could drink, carouse, and gamble away his inheritance and still be welcomed into Lords with smiles and hearty back-slaps. Whereas Andrew—who never caroused and rarely gambled, though he admitted to being fond of a wee dram, at times—found himself not only temporarily barred from taking up his seat in Parliament, but *literally* black-balled.

He had requested a membership at White's—the exclusive gentleman's club in London—thinking that acceptance there might help push his suit with the Committee on Privilege. But when the lid was lifted on the voting box, there had been three black balls nestled in the midst of the white ones, officially barring him from entry.

Before ascending to the earldom, Andrew had been generally ambivalent toward the English aristocracy. He hadn't had much interaction with its members, and so the entirety of the English government existed as a distant hum beyond his everyday life.

But after six months of dealing with English prejudices and cruel assumptions . . .

Who were these faceless English lords to unilaterally decide he was unwelcome in their ranks? And, worse, attack his good mother and his own character in the process? It was clear there was a faction within Lords who wished to teach him a lesson, make sure he understood his lowly place before taking his seat and discourage him attempting to help govern.

After all, Andrew *would* win the battle and be issued a Writ of Summons from Chancery. He had law and precedent on his side. It was only a matter of time.

Bloody English.

Andrew and Kieran rode in silence for moment. A gentle breeze rustled through the trees. It was only early April, but already England was in full bloom. Scotland wouldn't leaf out for another month, at the soonest. In a cold year, trees could remain bare until June.

Spring always came late in the far north.

Traveling south from Edinburgh had been like watching Spring arrive in a rush. Every mile closer to the south had been a smidge greener. Flowers had moved from snowdrops to crocuses through to daffodils before finally arriving at a few overly-eager bluebells already making an appearance in Sussex.

Andrew had never been to Sussex. He had rarely stepped foot in London, for that matter. He and his late grandfather had a delicate, unspoken truce. His grandfather allowed Andrew to live in peace and, in return, Andrew could inhabit every corner of the world save London and Sussex.

The planet was large enough for the two of them to coexist in their own spheres without overlapping. But now . . . being here . . .

Sussex was as gentle a place as Andrew had ever been.

He would know; he had been most everywhere.

He had sailed the world. Climbed a mountain in Rio de Janeiro simply to see the view from the top. Dined in Sydney, Australia with Governor Macquarie. Explored the dense forests of the Kingdom of Hawaii.

Sussex certainly wasn't the greenest or most dramatic or most awe-inspiring place he had been.

But it *was* the gentlest. The sun shone with just the right amount of warmth. The wind lacked the biting edge always present in Scotland. The Sussex Downs were hilly enough to be beautiful, but not so hilly as to render riding through them a chore.

Sussex, Andrew decided, was the pastoral equivalent of a wool blanket—comforting at the outset, but guaranteed to make one itch for a change after too much time spent wrapped in it.

Or maybe he simply had itching on the brain.

Kieran wasn't wrong; he *was* tetchy.

They were nearly to Hadley Park. Today he would meet his father's relations for the first time. Given the letters he had already received from Lady Hadley, he anticipated his relatives icing him with glacial English condescension. Were they also part of the plot to ostracize him in Lords?

Asserting his Scottishness seemed the only defense. A way of thumbing his nose at their haughty presumption. Though why, when someone expected him to behave poorly, did Andrew insist on meeting their poor expectations?

It was a character flaw he chose not to examine too closely.

As per Kieran's plan, the two of them would arrive in full Highland kit, Andrew employing his strongest brogue, both playing unruly Scots to the hilt for an afternoon.

Once they had a bit of fun and Andrew had called his haughty relatives on their preposterous assumptions—Scots were always civilized and mannerly; they simply didn't take themselves as seriously as the English—Andrew would send for his retinue who were happily biding their time in an inn a few towns over. Not only had Andrew brought his valet, coach, coachman, and two grooms, but also three secretaries, his man-of-affairs, and an experienced land steward. The needs of his financial and landed empire never ceased.

After his staff arrived, he would trade his itchy trews for more civilized trousers and a starched cravat. Then he would get down to business, assessing what needed to be done with the estate.

The road wound through the forest. Fortunately, after taking a wrong turn at the crossroads, a kindly farmer had pointed out a narrow country lane that would lead them through to Hadley Park. The lane was strait and rutted in places but in otherwise decent repair.

They passed by a defunct quarry with some interesting rock striations. Sussex was well-known for its mineral wealth, particularly the fossil-rich layers in its chalk beds. His scientific brain perked up at the thought of doing a wee bit of mineralogy hunting while in the area.

Ahead, Andrew could hear the gurgle of water. A stream, most likely.

His thighs pricked where the wool clung to his legs.

He shifted again in his saddle, adjusting his tartan sash. All the heavy wool swaddling his body made the day feel a touch too warm.

Kieran chuckled at his unease. The fiend.

"Devil take ye," Andrew muttered.

"I cannae think why—"

A crash rent the air, coming from the road ahead.

A terrified feminine shriek and loud splash followed.

Both men had kicked their horses into a gallop before the sounds faded.

J ane staggered upright in the stream, gasping for breath, water sluicing off her body.

Her pony danced forward, pulling the wheel of the phaeton back onto the bridge.

"Don't you dare continue on, Thunder!" she ordered. Thunder darted her a sheepish look at the sound of his name and thankfully stopped in place.

Wretched animal, acting on independent thought!

Ugh!

Shaking her head, Jane looked down at her dripping spencer and sodden, clinging skirts. She shook the water draining off her fingers.

Now what was she to do?

Her drive home had been uneventful. But while crossing a bridge over the river, Jane had pulled Thunder to a stop, as she always did, to study the quartz vein in the riverbed. She had spotted what looked like topaz glimmering in a newly-turned rock and bent over the side of her phaeton for a closer look.

That had been her undoing.

Thunder had decided he did not wish to linger on the bridge, so he had suddenly lurched forward. This, in turn, had sent a wheel partially over the edge—as there was no railing to stop it—tilting the carriage slightly, and pitching Jane headfirst into the water.

She was lucky to have not broken her neck.

But now she was *wet*.

And . . . *muddy*.

And . . . *disheveled*.

Jane wasn't sure which of those three adjectives horrified her more. She stringently avoided being any *one* of the three and to be them all at once—

Bloody hell! What if someone saw her like this?!

She simply stood and breathed for a second, the motion loud in her ears.

It did not escape her notice that she was only yards away from the same spot where Montacute had caught her swimming all those years ago.

Was this her doom then? To be soaked and dripping in this dratted river?

Would her base inner-self *never* be fully tamed?

More to the point, how was she to sneak back to Hadley Park without her mother or Peter catching wind of it?

Her mother would blister her ears with a scathing lecture on decorum—threatening to tell Montacute and pack her off to London—all of which would end with the same refrain that Jane was twenty-four years old, still unmarried, and could she please stop behaving as a recalcitrant child?

If Peter were to learn of this, she would have *years* of his teasing comments to deflect. She loved Peter. She did. But sometimes he failed to see the stinging barbs embedded in his words.

Brothers.

Thank goodness Lord Hadley didn't arrive until tomorrow.

She pulled her sodden bonnet off her head, tossing it up onto the carriage floor of the phaeton. Her hair dripped into her eyes, determined to underscore the horror of her current state.

Argh!

That wild little girl fumed and seethed inside her, battering her cage, rattling the bars, seeking to burst forth—

No!

Jane swallowed, taking in gulping breaths.

All was not lost. Surely if she found a sunny field, she could dry out her skirts. Anything to hide the worst of the damage.

She pulled her skirts forward, trying to see if there was mud on the back of her dress.

There was. A prodigious amount.

Too much to hide.

Grrrrrrr.

Everything piled on at once.

The ceaseless pressure from Montacute. *Become a lady . . . no one will want you otherwise.*

The fear of not knowing what the new Lord Hadley would do.

The frustration of being unable to completely mold herself into what others expected—

ENOUGH!

"Bloody, bloody hell!" Jane screamed, the tether on her messy inner-self abruptly snapping.

She tossed her arms in the air, raging at the sky, allowing that long-lost, emotionally-honest girl to soar free.

The loud sound startled several ravens in a nearby tree, nearly scaring her half-to-death and causing her to stumble sideways. They cawed their displeasure, fluttering away.

Argh! Could her day get any worse?

It was at that point that she realized . . .

. . . why, *yes*, her day could in fact become much, much worse.

"Och, lass, it's no' bad as that." A very Scottish, very male voice said behind her. "I'm sure the mud will launder out. No harm done."

Oh, no.

Please no.

"Aye." A second voice joined the first. "We can set ye to rights in no time." This voice was also Scottish, also male, gratingly cheerful.

Oh no. NO!

Bloody, bloody hell!

Her heart sank through to join the rocks underneath her feet. She prayed for a tidal wave to sweep down the river and wash her away. Or, at the very least, another dunking to cool the fiery blush currently scouring her body.

This was her fate, was it not? The last time she had been wet and muddy in this river, an unwanted man had found her.

Foolish her to think this instance would go any differently.

Would this be the final nail in the coffin then? The thing that saw her packed off to Montacute in humiliated shame? Was there any way to prevent her mother from learning of it?

Her extensive etiquette training had never covered this particular scenario:

When a young lady of excellent breeding finds herself tumbled into a muddy stream and cursing like a sailor before a group of Scotsmen . . .

The men behind her must be part of Lord Hadley's retinue. The coincidence was too great. But as the earl wasn't set to arrive until tomorrow, why were they here? Were they the advance scout party? The earl wanted to take the lay of the land, as it were?

And, most importantly, *whatwasshetodo!*

If she turned around, they would clearly see her and, more to the point, recognize her if they encountered one another again. Any hope she had of this not making its way to Hadley's ears, at the very least, was rapidly evaporating.

Her best hope was to send them on their way without turning around herself.

A rustle sounded behind her. "Here, let's lend ye a hand—"

"I'm quite all right," Jane snapped, head turning slightly. "Leave me be. Go on your way."

The noises stopped, the men hesitating.

And then . . . "Are ye quite sure?"

"Aye," the first voice joined in. "I ken that maybe ye need—"

"As I said, I am quite fine," Jane interrupted, tone as frosty as possible. "I do not need help from the likes of *you*. Carry on your way."

She flipped a dismissive hand over her shoulder, waiting for the men to take themselves off. She couldn't very well hike her skirts up to her hips and clamber up onto the bridge with Scots behind her.

Unfortunately, she did not hear sounds of the men leaving.

"Do ye think she means it?" the second Scot asked, voice low.

"I ken she might," the first replied. "I dinnae know why she would refuse our kindly offered help. She cannae get out of the burn alone. The banks appear too steep and the bridge too high."

Of all the idiotic . . . !

Her rational mind knew it wasn't their fault. They had simply heard a noise and come to offer help.

But that didn't stop a fiery flash of anger. Their presence here practically ensured endless humiliation and complications for her. If they were gentlemen at all, they would be sensitive to this fact.

But of course they were *not* gentlemen.

They were Scots.

"Aye, and her swearing and screaming sounded a wee bit distressed. I didnae ken ladies knew how tae swear like that, tae be honest."

"Maybe they learn it in finishing-school nowadays? They hold swearing class right after embroidery lessons but before bonnet trimming?"

"If so, they're doing a bang-up job of it. It was bloody brilliant."

Jane gritted her teeth, that same blush flaring back to life, righteous indignation bristling. The men's blatant disregard for decorum only underscored the chasm between English and Scottish behavior.

A slew of angry words choked her, desperate to escape her mouth. She swallowed them back. Yelling at the men like a fishwife would not help the situation. That messy little girl might still be inside her, but Jane did not have to *be* that little girl.

Never again.

There was no helping it. The men clearly were going to require a firmer hand. They would see her face. Perhaps she could request they not report this incident to Hadley.

Poise and grace. Deep breaths

Sucking in a fortifying breath, Jane slowly pivoted around.

She had to blink several times.

Two men sat on horseback on the riverbank, frankly observing her. *That* she had expected.

Their clothing, however, was an affront to the senses. A cacophony of pattern and color.

Her eyes instantly locked on the man to her right, his horse prancing sideways before he easily pulled the animal to a standstill. He sported red-and-blue plaid trousers and more red tartan wrapped around his chest in a broad sash. A jaunty bonnet sat on his head, cheerful feathers matching the dark blonde of his hair. Everything about him shouted a loud declaration of Highland patriotism; a Sir Walter Scott novel come to life.

But it was his amused, smiling eyes that held her attention—a blue gaze that reflected the color of the summer sky and danced just as merrily.

Here was a man who did not take himself or life too seriously. Some-one who clearly reveled in his inner wild-child, never bothering to tame his baser impulses.

Jane felt her lips tense into a straight line.

Granted, his companion was not much better. Swathed in green-and-yellow tartan, his pale blue eyes smirked at her.

Oof! This whole situation was simply unsupportable.

"We cannae leave you like this, lass," the first Scot said, those laugh-ing eyes never leaving hers. She mentally categorized him as Red Scot based on the colors of his tartan. He motioned toward her sodden state, standing knee-deep in the stream. "Wet clothing might be all the rage in London this Season, but we cannae, in good conscience, hurry off without—"

"As I keep saying, I do not require your assistance." She nodded her head with regal precision. "I *order* you to carry on your way."

"*Order* us? Ye cannae be serious?" the second man asked, shifting his green tartan. Jane dubbed him Green Scot.

"Aye," said Red Scot, "how will ye clamber out of the wee burn there—"

"With my fully-functional limbs, I am sure. Off with you both." She made a flapping motion with her hand and clucked her tongue, much as one would shoo away an overeager dog.

Red Scot merely blinked at her actions and tone. Did *nothing* get through to the man?

He loomed on his horse, broad-shouldered and strong-jawed, those blue eyes drilling into her. The weight of his gaze squeezed her lungs and hiccupped her breathing. If the man had to be Scottish, must he be so *large* about it, as well?

"I fear she's serious," Green Scot said conversationally to his friend. "She has to be chilled, wet to the bone."

"Maybe it's the latest fashion?" Red Scot removed his eyes from her—*thank goodness!*—turning in his saddle. He appeared to be the leader between the two. "I've heard tell some ladies dampen their petticoats."

"Aye, it was only a matter of time before they moved on tae wetting down the whole skirt."

"Perhaps we should mention it in Edinburgh? See if we cannae start the trend up there?"

"It wouldnae work." Green Scot pursed his lips. "The lasses are far too smart to wear wet clothing on a dreich Scottish day. Catch their deaths."

"Aye," Red Scot said mournfully. "'Tis such a pity." He shot her an appraising glance.

Heat washed through Jane, as scalding as it was unwelcome.

Even without the peacock-like display of his Highland origins, Red Scot would have stood apart from English gentlemen. Something unbroken and untamed lurked in his eyes. Perhaps the same Scottish spirit that a thousand years of English influence had never managed to quash.

Jane literally *felt* the wildness of him. A lone wolf howling at the full moon, beckoning others of its kind to respond.

Her wild self perked up, peering out at him.

Oh! Hello, you . . .

His gaze tangled something in her stomach and rendered her very skin so achingly alive. Acute physical awareness washed in behind—

No!

Jane viciously squelched that skitter of attraction, mentally pressing it under her foot as she would a spider. Her base self would *not* have the upper hand with this. That part of her had already caused enough trouble today.

A true lady would never harbor such feelings toward one of the lower classes. And a *Scot*, no less.

This encounter proved worse and worse.

"We cannae leave her like this," Red Scot said to his companion, still not speaking to her directly.

"Aye. We must provide assistance."

Jane barely stopped an outraged gasp. The last thing she wanted was either of these ruffians touching her. Just the thought of Red Scot wrapping his strong hand around hers sent heat chasing her spine again; gooseflesh pebbled her arms.

"As I keep saying, I do not need assistance, particularly from a . . . a *person*, such as yourself." Jane used her ducal tone, the one that helped others understand their place in relation to her. She might also have imbued the word 'person' with a scathing bite of contempt.

She was a duke's daughter, for heaven's sake. When those of the lower classes spoke to her, it was usually accompanied by bowing and fawning.

Society functioned as it did because Englishmen followed the rules. Even the lowest chimney sweep knew to show deference in the presence of a lady. There was a harmony and structure to things.

She might have an inner wild self, but Jane deeply cherished the English sense of order. She had a distinct fondness for a crisply laundered chemise, glowing white and neatly ironed. She insisted on her dresses being sorted according to color, descending through the clothes press like a rainbow. Such structure, like organizing minerals in a cabinet, offered comfort and stability in a chaotic world—a soothing pattern supporting the lattice-work of society.

Without it, they were all little more than savages.

Scotland had never been adept at obeying England's rules.

Obviously.

Jane felt as if this entire conversation distilled a thousand years of English/Scottish relations into a solitary exchange.

England: *Behave! Stop being uncivilized animals!*

Scotland: *Och! We cannae be bothered tae change.*

England: *We mean it! We will not tolerate such outrageous behavior.*

Scotland, laughing: *Haud yer wheesht. Could someone pass me a wee dram o' whisky?*

What was she to do? As the current roof over Jane's head existed courtesy of Lord Hadley, was she expected to treat his impertinent servants—attendants? henchmen? minions?—with respect?

Even when they showed her none?

And based on their behavior, how would the earl himself be?

ANDREW STUDIED THE drenched lass staring daggers at him, her auburn hair hanging loose, gray eyes snapping.

She was, in a word, *stunning*.

Lithe and long-limbed—he refused to allow his eyes to dip lower to the skirts clinging to her legs—she vibrated with an energy as fiery as her hair. For sure, her tone was chilly and moderate, but the air around her nearly crackled with suppressed emotion.

Her haughty tones and the expensive cut of her spencer (despite being dripping wet), clearly proclaimed her to be a lady of means. Was she the daughter or sister of a local lord? Would he meet with her again? And if her haughty behavior was indicative of all his neighbors, Andrew was going to find his time at Hadley Park even more trying than he had first supposed.

That said, he couldn't, in good conscience, leave a gentlewoman standing knee-deep in a stream, no matter how condescending and rude her attitude.

Slowly, Andrew dismounted. Kieran followed, gathering both sets of reins and looping them over a low-hanging branch.

Andrew took a step in her direction.

The woman's eyes widened, her nostrils flaring wide.

He stopped.

If she had seemed afraid, Andrew might have reacted differently. But nothing about this woman spoke of fear. Instead, she bristled with hostile outrage.

How to diffuse the situation?

"Perhaps before we help ye out of the burn, we should make some introductions," he said.

Kieran brightened. "A right proper introduction would be appreciated—"

"No, I will not be introducing myself," she quickly replied, those same arctic tones in her cultured voice. "Your behavior is already far too brazen. I have not sought, nor do I wish to have, your acquaintance."

"Och, that's no' verra nice." Kieran frowned.

"Aye, perhaps ye meant to say kinder words—"

"I assure you my vocabulary is exact in its precision," she said. "Moreover, it is far clearer than that butchery you lot pass off as the English language."

Andrew's eyebrows flew upward. She was insulting their speech now?

Well, if she expected her acerbic answer to quell them, she was instantly mistaken.

Andrew and Kieran both roared with laughter, heads back, teeth flashing.

"Och, we cannae help it," Andrew spoke first. "Yous English taught us yer Sassenach language in the Middle Ages and then up and changed the bloody thing without informing us.""Aye. You've only yerself to blame." Kieran grinned.

"Yous English are terrible teachers."

The woman sniffed and lifted her chin, her fists clenched. "You poor victims," she deadpanned. "It's no wonder we ceased our aid, if this is what passes for gentlemanly behavior in Scotland."

Andrew blinked at her stinging remark but refused to allow his smile to slip. They were *trying* to help her. It wasn't their fault she had more spines than a hedgehog.

He took a few steps onto the bridge, approaching her slowly, like one might stalk a Highland deer. He wanted her to clearly understand they only meant to help.

The pony, who had been standing patiently on the bridge, decided he did not like the sight of a burly Scot advancing toward him. The animal whinnied and took two steps forward.

"Thunder, no!" The lady whipped her head in the pony's direction. "Stay."

The pony's ears pricked at hearing his name, obediently stopping.

Andrew couldn't help it. He laughed. "Thunder, eh? That's an ambitious name for such a wee fella."

"Do ye suppose he has a companion named Lightning?" Kieran came past Andrew and caught Thunder's harness, making soothing noises.

Andrew reached the lady, surveying her in the water.

She frowned in return. "I am *quite* through with this conversation. My feet have gone numb—"

That was all she got out. Andrew reached both hands down, wrapped them around her upper arms, and—unceremoniously, without warning—hoisted her straight out of the water, depositing her on the bridge like so much baggage.

She barely had time to eke out a high-pitched squeak. She wobbled as her feet hit the bridge but managed to keep upright.

Unhelpfully, his brain pointed out that this unknown lady had a darling wee nose and very fine eyes—gray irises surrounded by thick brown lashes. Those lashes caught the color of the freckles dusting her porcelain skin. She likely detested her freckles, but Andrew found them amusing. They were rebellious wee interlopers dotting her cheeks.

She blinked up at him, as if unsure whether to offer thanks or reprimand him for so casually touching her person.

He took both options away from her.

"Yer welcome." He grinned, saluting her with two fingers. "Would ye like us to accompany ye tae your destination?"

"Gracious, no." She sniffed, that wee nose of hers rising in the air. "I have had my fill of your company."

Andrew might have been insulted by it, but as she was muddy, disheveled, and wet—decidedly resembling a half-drowned kitten, spitting in outrage—it was difficult to take offense.

"If you will excuse me." She stepped past Andrew and primly lifted herself the short distance into her low phaeton. Her skirts slopped onto the seat with a sodden *thwump*. She took the reins Kieran handed to her and, clucking poor Thunder into a walk, rolled away.

She did not look back.

Andrew and Kieran watched her drive off with matching bemused expressions, waiting until the carriage disappeared, turning down a side lane.

"Well, now, that was enlightening." Kieran clapped his hands together.

"Aye. She was verra high-handed. We simply wanted tae help."

"I ken that." Kieran chuckled. "If those are the manners of a lofty lady needing help, imagine how entertaining it will be tae tease yer relatives. Come along yer fancy lordship—" He motioned Andrew forward. "—we have more English to horrify afore the day is over."

Andrew hadn't given much thought as to what Hadley Park would look like. If he had pondered it at all, he would have imagined a building somewhat similar to his own Muirford House in Scotland—a majestic property built in the last fifty years.

But as he and Kieran crested a hill and looked over the green valley to the great house nestled in the trees, Andrew realized his error.

Hadley Park was less harmonious lines and more the awkward love child of the Tudors and the Stuarts. Not that Andrew intended to make the house itself an emblem of problematic English-Scottish relations, but there was no other way to describe it. One half of the building featured the red brick and expansive mullioned windows of earlier English Tudor kings, while the other half displayed the honey stone, pedimented windows, and harmonious architecture of later Scottish Stuart monarchs.

Ironically, it was the Stuart half that was structured and elegant. Andrew was quite sure his English relatives would *not* see the humor in that observation.

"Are ye sure they're expecting us?" Kieran motioned toward the lawn laid before the house. "The place is fair humming with activity."

A line of gardeners swung scythes in a synchronized motion, methodically cutting and tidying the grass. Other workers busily trimmed hedges along one side of the house, while a team of maids snipped spent flowers.

Mmmmm.

The scene was decidedly industrious. A prepping, planning sort of industriousness.

"I had my man-of-affairs write ahead," Andrew said. "Though tae be honest, I cannae rightly remember which day I was tae arrive, today or tomorrow."

Travel and weather being what it was in Scotland, arrival dates were always loose estimates at best.

"I dinnae think they're expecting us today, yer lordship," Kieran grinned. "It's like ma day just keeps getting better and better."

"At least one of us is enjoying this."

Kieran, the eejit, laughed merrily at Andrew's sardonic tone.

They followed the worn carriage lane, winding their way toward the main house, pausing at every vista and picturesque bend in the road. Heads turned as they passed, workers stopping to stare, some even raising a hand in greeting. Eventually the lane passed through an impressively-decorative gatehouse before ending in front of what had to be the main entrance—an enormous oak door topped by an imposing archway.

On the Tudor side of the house, naturally.

Andrew didn't dwell too long on the symbolism.

A groom *did* come forward to take the reins of their horses as they dismounted. But that was the extent of it.

No one else greeted them or seemed to notice their arrival. When Andrew traveled to Muirford House, the butler would set a stable-boy to watch the main road, ensuring the entire staff was neatly assembled on the steps to greet him.

But here . . . there was no one.

Andrew climbed the front steps and sounded the door rapper.

Seconds passed. Then minutes.

Kieran grinned next to him. "Are ye sure yer in the right place, yer lordship?" he quipped.

Andrew simply stared at him, face impassive.

Naturally, this only encouraged Kieran. "Mayhap they dinnae know yer the new earl?"

"Haud yer wheesht."

Andrew rapped again.

Kieran chuckled. And then leaned back, stepping outside the archway, scanning the impressive facade. "I could get us in one of these windaes, if ye decide tae storm the place."

Andrew shook his head and rapped again.

"English lords are rather good at it . . . storming castles and the like." Kieran said this nonchalantly, as if he was merely talking about the weather.

"Remind me again why we're friends?"

"It's ma fair looks. You cannae help yerself."

Andrew was shaking his head when the door *finally* creaked open.

A harried, decidedly top-lofty butler faced them. Though English butlers likely only came in the 'top-lofty' variety, this one was a fine specimen of the breed. The man's gaze flicked up and down, not missing one inch of Andrew's flamboyant Highland kit.

"I trust you are with Lord Hadley's retinue," the man said, his tone two-parts bored and three-parts condescension. "The servant entrance is around back." He pointed to the right.

And shut the door.

Andrew paused, braced his hands on his hips, looked at Kieran . . . and then sighed, shaking his head at the butler's effrontery. Even a *servant* should be treated more kindly than this. The butler's behavior was utterly insupportable.

Gritting his teeth, Andrew knocked again, this time more forcefully. The same man answered the door.

"I am Lord Hadley," Andrew said without preamble, stepping inside, "and you must be ma new butler."

Andrew loomed over the man, giving him the steely gaze he reserved for insubordinate managers and, if needed, top-lofty butlers.

The man blanched, undoubtedly quickly calculating the likelihood of retaining his current position.

Kieran chuckled.

As the butler stammered his apologies, Andrew listened with amusement. He was quite sure it was wrong to be enjoying himself.

He couldn't muster the energy to care.

BY SOME DIVINE miracle, Jane managed to drive herself back to Hadley Park along a side-lane and sneak up to her bedroom without encountering her mother. She might have been muddy, soaked, and frustrated, but thank goodness, she avoided a scolding for now.

Jane rang for her maid, pondering the ridiculousness of being twenty-four years old and fearing having to answer to her mother.

Of course, as she stripped off her wet gloves and waited for Mary to arrive, she repeated her encounter with the Scotsmen over and over in her head. Red Scot and his booming laugh, the shocking strength of his grip, the sheer power in his upper body to heft her, sodden skirts and all, so easily. Her arms still burned from the press of his hands.

Would the Scots inform Lord Hadley of their encounter?

Granted, Lord Hadley knowing wasn't necessarily her concern. It was Lord Hadley mentioning it to her mother that was the true problem. But hopefully, she wouldn't cross paths Red Scot once Hadley arrived. She would likely blush scarlet and reveal herself.

Case in point . . . just the thought of it sent heat flooding her face. Jane pressed her chilled hands to her cheeks.

Her wild, base inner-self had broken completely free for the first time in years. How could she have allowed that to happen? She had worked too hard— molding herself into a model of elegant woman-hood—to regress now.

Become a lady . . . no one will want you otherwise.

She swallowed, pulling her trembling hands from her face and clenching them into tight fists, nails pressing inward.

Jane must make a brilliant marriage. *That* had been Montacute's—and, therefore, her mother's—lodestar for years. Montacute saw Jane as political leverage; her tendency toward 'hoydenish' behavior was an impediment to this.

In his will, her father had bestowed a generous dowry of thirty thousand pounds on Jane. The enormity of the sum, naturally, gave rise to fortune hunters.

To combat that inevitability, her father had wrapped the funds in tight legal bands. Most importantly, Montacute must approve of her choice of spouse. Only then, would her dowry be released to her new husband. Given the stringent requirements and her own struggles to rein in her baser self, Jane supposed it was no wonder she had endured *five* London Seasons without marrying.

Though Jane was often called handsome—not beautiful, not breath-taking—she knew she lacked the vivacity that made other women so appealing. Calling a woman handsome was a polite way of saying she was elegant and well-bred but missing the spark of true beauty.

Grimacing, she unbuttoned her spencer and then sat to peel her sodden stockings off her pruned feet.

When Jane made her debut, Montacute and her mother had even held out hope that one of King George's younger sons—Prince Edward or Prince Adolphus—might take a fancy to her. Royal dukes almost always married other royals (usually cousins), but a royal duke who had six older brothers *might* be permitted to marry a rose of the upper English aristocracy. Montacute longed for a seat on the King's privy council once George III finally passed on; her brother sought to use Jane as a foothold.

However, a marriage into the royal family had not been brokered, to Jane's absolute relief. The royal dukes were a dissolute lot, and a life surrounded by the rigors of court etiquette distressed her.

From there, she had been expected to marry a non-royal duke or marquess. But, again, she had proved a disappointment, unable to keep her baser self completely subdued. She had remained too long in Hyde Park one May and freckled her cheeks so terribly she had to retire to the country in shame. Another year, she had referred to a middle-aged suitor, Lord Birchall, as 'bloody repulsive' in the man's hearing. Montacute's subsequent tongue-lashing had been particularly scathing.

By her fourth Season, Jane was nearly despairing. But that year, she had been taken with Lord Eastman, the young heir to a marquisate. He had been charming and, more surprisingly, Montacute had approved Lord Eastman's courtship of her.

Lord Eastman had been attentive, taking Jane driving in Hyde Park and attending at-home hours. Unfortunately, Jane found herself enjoying his company too much, becoming a little too comfortable. As a result, during an outing to view the Royal Menagerie in the Tower of London, Jane had waved her arms and laughed loudly at the antics of a rambunctious monkey bouncing around its cage.

Eastman had withdrawn his suit the next day.

Montacute reported that Eastman had found her distasteful—*overly-loud* and *vulgar* being his precise words.

Jane had retired to her room for three days.

She had not loved Lord Eastman, but his withdrawal bleakly illustrated her own inadequacy. Her wild self had always threatened to strip away everything she held dear. First, Peter. And now, any chance at a suitable marriage.

Become a lady . . . no one will want you otherwise.

How was she ever to find a place for herself in this world? Marriage was the only option open to her and even *that* was hampered by Montacute's lofty personal ambitions and her own inability to corral her baser impulses.

For her part, Jane would be content to marry a mere baron or even a knight, provided the man was solvent, reasonably young, and most importantly, kind. Actually *loving* her husband was a concept she had given up long ago. At this point, she would happily accept courtesy and respect.

Thankfully, her maid arrived and assisted Jane out of the rest of her wet clothing and into a dressing gown. The girl then left to order a warm bath drawn.

Jane towel-dried her hair, trying not to fret.

If incidents like today persisted—Jane being found wet, tumbled, and swearing in a stream—even her modest aims would not be possible.

She had managed to keep herself and Peter together all these years. She would not permit anything—not Hadley's coming, not Montacute's personal ambitions, not Peter's anxiety over his future, and certainly not her own hoydenish behavior—to separate them now.

She was still pondering her resolve when her maid darted back into the room.

"We must hurry, my lady," the girl said.

"Pardon?" Jane turned around.

"Your mother has requested your presence in the drawing room immediately. His lordship has arrived."

"What did you say?" Jane asked, blinking. "His lordship?"

"Lord Hadley has arrived," the girl repeated.

"But . . ." Jane's mind blanked. "But . . . he isn't expected until tomorrow."

Though she supposed it explained his men in the woods. Hadley, himself, must have arrived via the principal road while his men rambled through the park on country lanes.

How typical of a Scot to flout all rules and arrive before they were prepared for him.

"Yes," her maid replied. "I overheard that there must have been some confusion as to the date of his arrival. Regardless, he is here. We must make haste. Lord Hadley and her ladyship are waiting."

6

Andrew prowled the boundaries of the silent drawing room. Kieran reclined in an over-stuffed chair, resting his heels on a convenient footstool.

The top-lofty butler, Barnsley by name, had stammered further apologies and shown both men into the drawing room with polite murmurs before hastily retreating.

That had been nearly an *hour* ago.

Andrew wasn't sure how a new earl should be greeted, but he was quite positive this was not it.

The drawing room itself was much like the house, a hodge-podge of chairs, sofas, and decorative tables, all elegant but showing their age. A pair of enormous mullioned windows provided ample natural light, at least.

Andrew lifted the lid on a Chinese jar, peering inside. Empty. He then moved on to inspecting the various figurines lining the mantelpiece. They were French, delicately fussy, and not to his taste.

Mostly he avoided staring at the ancestral portraits crowding the walls, men and women in ruffs and powdered wigs with the occasional dog or cat thrown in. So many eyes looking down in judgment.

Andrew didn't feel any particular attachment to them. He simply disliked the personal pain they represented—the group of people who had collectively decided that Andrew and his parents were not worth knowing because of their Scottishness.

He paused in front of a portrait of his great-grandfather. A small gold plaque attached to the bottom of the frame encapsulated it all:

John Henry Langston, 1st Earl of Hadley
Hero of Culloden

Andrew snorted, soft and low.

Hero of Culloden? More like cruel butcher.

One country's champion was usually another's merciless scourge.

Just looking at the first earl set Andrew's skin to crawling. The man had been instrumental in the deaths of so many Scots.

Was it any wonder that hostility still simmered between Scotland and England?

Andrew vividly remembered trying to explain it to an American acquaintance once. They were seated in an inn in New York, and the man made some ignorant comment about how the Scots and English were essentially one unified whole.

Bloody hell had Andrew set the man straight in a hurry.

Andrew had started with the medieval Wars of Independence from England, summarizing the history of William Wallace and Robert the Bruce. He moved on to the Scottish Stuart kings who eventually succeeded to the English throne upon the death of Elizabeth I. *That* should have been Scotland's shining hour, but England disliked being ruled by Scots just as much as Scots disliked being ruled by English. Eventually, the entire country erupted into civil war.

This led to generations of endless conflict.

Ultimately, England executed and exiled her Scottish kings but kept Scotland as a vassal state. Outraged, Scotland wanted her independence returned.

The issue came to a head at Culloden in 1746 when an amassed Scottish army suffered catastrophic defeat at the hands of the English.

In Culloden's wake, the conquering English crushed Scotland's spirit and culture. The Scottish nobility were systematically stripped of their titles and lands. Scots Gaelic was banned, along with the kilt, the bagpipes, and every other emblem of Scottish civilization.

And even now, England pillaged Scotland just as thoroughly as it had in the Middle Ages. English landlords were currently clearing the land of unwanted tenant farmers, sometimes lighting a house on fire with people still inside. These ousted Highland crofters flooded into Glasgow and Edinburgh every month, refugees desperate for work to feed their families. Even more ironically, these unemployed Scots were conscripted into the English army in large numbers, forming the backbone of British Imperial forces around the world, fighting for a country that had brutalized their own.

By the end of Andrew's tirade, his American friend had held up his hands in surrender.

And now Andrew *was* one of these damned English lords. Would his portrait someday sit beside that of the 'Hero' of Culloden?

He turned away from the portrait with a grimace.

Kieran yawned. "Ye suppose they'll feed us eventually?"

Neither of them had eaten anything since breakfast. Kieran's stomach grumbled loudly to underscore the point.

"Aye." Unless his relatives intended to starve them out. It was a tried-and-true English tactic, after all.

"Maybe the new master of the house could ring up his butler and request some victuals?"

Andrew shot his friend a sharp look.

Kieran merely grinned in reply, enjoying himself far too much.

It wasn't a bad idea, actually.

He took a step toward the bell pull but stopped at the sound of murmured voices outside the door.

A woman glided in, dressed in dark lavender satin edged with expensive lace. Her age was difficult to determine, as the lady had that sort of immutable look the wealthy often achieved. More importantly, a matching lace cap covered blond curls, declaring the woman's marital status.

The woman had to be Lady Hadley, his late grandfather's widow.

Andrew tamped down his surprise. Regardless of her actual age, Lady Hadley was clearly significantly younger than the old earl.

She spared him a wan smile. It did not touch her eyes.

"Lord Hadley." She curtsied.

Andrew bowed. It was a reflexive gesture, quite at odds, he was sure, with the roughness of his dress.

"Lady Hadley, I presume," he said.

She nodded, generations of aristocratic breeding in the motion. Her eyes flicked up-and-down his clothing before repeating the motion with Kieran. Her lips pressed into a stern slash.

"May I present ma friend, Master Kieran MacTavish?" Andrew gestured to Kieran who also executed a satisfactory bow.

Lady Hadley simply nodded in Kieran's direction, every line of her rigid spine indicating her disdain for the connection, but unable to risk offending the new earl who effectively held her purse strings. She gestured for them to be seated before elegantly sinking into a sofa herself.

"I must apologize, my lord, as your arrival was somewhat unexpected." Her words were innocuous but implied a world of criticism. After all, she had left them to cool their heels for over an hour. Even if they hadn't been expected, it did not take sixty minutes to walk to the drawing room.

Kieran had the right of it; Andrew should have simply rung the butler and requested a repast.

"Nae bother." Andrew shot her a polite, but assuredly annoying, grin. "I'm sure ye'll be better prepared next time."

Lady Hadley's eyes widened, her nostrils flaring.

"Thank you," she replied, the words seemingly ripped from her throat, nearly choking her. "My children will be down shortly to greet you."

The door cracked open again, admitting a footman carrying a tea tray. Finally.

Lady Hadley motioned for the footman to place the tray on the table in front of her. "May I offer you some refreshment, my lord?"

At least the hour delay hadn't been entirely wasted.

"Thank ye, my lady. That would be verra appreciated." Andrew took in the tray with its sparse biscuits and bite-size sandwiches. "Ye've a good cook here at Hadley Park?"

"Yes, Mrs. Morris is most competent."

Andrew reached for one of the small sandwiches, dispatching it in one gulp. It was, indeed, delicious.

He surveyed the rest with pursed lips. It was a snack, at best.

"Would it be possible tae have something a little more substantial brought up?" he asked.

Lady Hadley's expression froze further, if possible.

Andrew supposed the request was somewhat rude of him, had this been *her* house and he merely a guest.

But the fact of the matter was simple—this was now *his* home, and she was *his* guest, so him politely asking for a repast was most certainly not beyond the pale.

He refused to be relegated to the fringes of his own house—begin as he intended to carry forward.

"Of course," Lady Hadley said, voice tight. "Allow me to step out and have the housekeeper set up a light luncheon in the breakfast room."

Andrew nodded. "Thank you, my lady—"

She rose quickly, the motion cutting off Andrew's words and forcing him and Kieran to scramble to their feet. Even Andrew's manners couldn't slip so far that he wouldn't stand for a lady. The glint in her eye said she had risen so abruptly on purpose. It was petty and vindictive and exactly the kind of behavior Andrew had expected to encounter at Hadley Park.

She swept out of the room, eddying expensive French perfume and annoyed contempt.

Kieran chuckled as he sat back down, popping one of the sandwiches into his mouth, chewing appreciatively. "I ken her ladyship is off tae have a good haiver with the housekeeper. Leave us tae cool our heels for a wee while longer afore returning."

"Aye. I dinnae doubt it." Andrew had no hope that Lady Hadley's son, Peter, would be any better than his mother.

Against his better judgment, Andrew felt his temperature rise again. First, the haughty lady in the stream and now Lady Hadley. *This* was why his father had never spoken of his English family, why he had shrugged off their refusal to associate with Andrew and his Scottish mother.

Andrew dearly loved his mother. She lived with his dey at Muirford House, running the estate and overseeing the house for them both. His father had died from a lung ailment nearly ten years ago now, but his mother said she would never remarry.

Lady Hadley was as different a person from his gentle mother as could possibly be.

Fifteen minutes later, he and Kieran had devoured the meager contents of the tea tray. Ten minutes after that, the door cracked open, sending Andrew and Kieran to their feet.

Lady Hadley returned. A younger, blonde man accompanied her, his expression tense. The expensive cut of his superfine coat and the glossy shine on his Hessian boots—not to mention his identical look of disdain—loudly proclaimed him to be Lady Hadley's son, Peter Langston.

Andrew's half-uncle and heir.

Mr. Langston was considerably younger than Andrew had supposed. The man couldn't be much over twenty.

Lady Hadley made introductions.

Mr. Langston bowed with exquisite precision. "It's a pleasure to finally meet you, my lord." His clipped tone and clenched jaw indicated it was anything *but* a pleasure.

Clearly, Langston resented him. The lad likely saw Andrew's arrival as the end of his wastrel existence. The younger man had no funds, after all, and was now beholden to Andrew for every pence.

Langston raked Andrew up and down, taking in his trews and sash, nostrils flaring. "You are . . . *fond* of tartan, it seems?"

"Aye, I'm verra fond of ma tartan." Andrew raised his eyebrow. "However, I'm no' so fond of puppies who disparage it."

Langston, at least, had the decency to flush and squirm under Andrew's steady gaze. The younger man looked away, swallowing hard.

The door snicked a third time. Everyone turned.

Andrew expected to see a footman or the butler.

Instead, the high-and-mighty lady from the stream walked into the room.

Andrew's aggravation melted into surprise and then devolved further into mischievous delight.

Hah. This should prove interesting.

She was just as pretty when clean, primped, and neat-as-a-pin. Not a speck of mud in sight. The combination of her auburn hair, pale skin, and wide gray eyes momentarily snagged his breath.

Had she been so tall earlier? She was nearly the height of the footman opening the door. So tall that Andrew could look her in the eye himself without having to bend his head more than an inch. The height suited her.

Unlike the version of herself in the stream, this lady held her head with aloof precision, expression remote, every last ounce of her outraged fire tucked away.

More's the pity. Andrew had preferred her spirit.

Their eyes met.

Andrew grinned. It was a slow grin, spreading like honey.

The unknown lady blanched.

Oh, aye. This was going to be fun.

7

S hock jolted Jane in place.

 Breathe. Just breathe.

 Red Scot was here.

 Jane was quite sure every last ounce of color had fled her face.

 Now she simply needed to hold back the vivid blush that threatened. Flushing crimson would do nothing to stem the tide of her mother's curiosity.

 Red Scot surveyed her, standing loose-limbed.

 No, that wasn't quite right. Red Scot did more than merely *stand*.

 He loomed. He hulked.

 He menaced.

 His very presence somehow reduced the air in the room, leaving her lungs gasping.

 Her mother vibrated with aristocratic outrage.

Jane was torn between hysterical laughter and joining her mother's horror.

Oh, who was she fooling? Hysteria was utterly out of the question; horror was her only option.

Unconsciously, Jane pressed a fingernail into her palm, pushing until she felt the bite of pain.

Lady Hadley motioned toward her. Her mother's pressed lips and stern eyes promised a scold later for being so late to the drawing room. Of course.

Her mother half turned toward Red Scot. "Lord Hadley, may I present my daughter, Lady Jane Everard."

Oh.

Oh, no.

No, no, no.

Red Scot was Lord Hadley.

Lord Hadley was Red Scot.

Jane's surprise over seeing Red Scot had slowed her wits. All the evidence was there; she had simply neglected to make the connection.

Jane blinked, trying to rally her sluggish thoughts.

Lord Hadley was the same Red Scot who, less than three hours ago, had commented on her unladylike language and then lifted her from the river . . . muddy, disheveled, and utterly disgraced.

Now what was she to do?

Hadley *knew.*

More to the point, would it be too much to hope that he would say nothing to her mother of her mishap? And which was worse? Her mother knowing or Lord Hadley's impertinence?

Despite the gossip surrounding him, she had assumed that Hadley would be less . . . garishly Scottish. Or, at the very least, have a modicum of shame.

Red Scot exhibited neither.

And *this* was the man who held Peter's future in his hands?

Dimly, she registered her mother's continued explanation. "Lady Jane is the daughter of my first husband, His Grace, The Duke of Montacute."

Reflexive muscle memory jarred Jane to life. She dipped into a polite curtsy, her limbs strangely disconnected from her body, as if they belonged to an intricate automaton from a toy shop in Mayfair.

"Lady Jane." Hadley bowed, hand over the red tartan sash which crossed his shoulder and chest. His bow, at least, was proper and polite; she would give him that.

He raised his head and met her gaze, eyes smirking. Her words from earlier rose between them.

I have not sought, nor do I wish to have, your acquaintance.

Hadley's grin widened. She could practically see him weighing whether or not to accept an acquaintanceship with her. Would he dare to be so rude?

He shot a side glance at her mother.

Oh!

The wretch!

He must sense that she didn't want her mother to know what had occurred. And now he was teasing her in a most abominable fashion.

The Scot was clearly no gentleman. But then that had been well-known before this moment.

What to do? *This* was what came of her inner-self slipping her tether. *This* was why she had to be ever-diligent in keeping her baser instincts silent.

She pressed her fingernail into her hand again. Twice. Three times. Her palms would be fish scales before the hour was through.

Hadley's eyes came back to hers.

Finally, after a lengthy pause, he said, "Pleased tae make yer acquaintance, Lady Jane."

His delay had not gone unnoticed. Peter raised his eyebrows. Even her mother's brow dented in a faint frown.

Heaven help her.

And then, simply to bring home the discomfort of her situation, Hadley motioned to Green Scot.

"May I present ma companion, Master Kieran MacTavish?"

Master MacTavish bowed. Jane curtsied.

Her mother motioned to the footmen to refresh the tea service with hot water and replenish the biscuits.

They all sat down again, Jane wisely choosing a seat beside Peter. She exchanged a weighted glance with her brother, communicating her horror. Peter faintly rolled his eyes before turning his head back to Hadley.

A horrible tense silence descended, as the footmen busied themselves.

Her brother lounged in his chair, waves of aristocratic indifference floating off of him. But Jane knew frustration and anger seethed just below the surface.

Peter wore the uncertainty well. He was immaculately turned out in a dark-red, clawhammer coat, a finely-embroidered silk waistcoat underneath. His valet spent no less than fifteen minutes every day ensuring that Peter's blond hair had just the right amount of devil-may-care swagger.

Her brother's refined appearance stood in contrast to that of Lord Hadley and Master MacTavish. Their colorful tartan trousers and matching sashes clashed garishly with the English elegance of the drawing room, a sharp discordant note in an otherwise harmonious melody.

Hadley met Jane's gaze again, likely enjoying watching her squirm, wondering if and when he would say something.

The silence stretched from tense to faintly hostile as the footmen exited the room.

Lady Hadley rallied, determined to behave with impeccable breeding, regardless of how vexing she found Lord Hadley's behavior.

"How do you take your tea, my lord?" she asked Hadley.

He murmured his response, his rough Scottish brogue rolling over Jane. Something about the deep rumble of his voice . . . the timbre of it . . . called to mind the library at Rosehearth, cuddled into a soft blanket, the fire roaring in the hearth, snow falling outside—

Jane nearly shook her head.

What an utterly . . . *bizarre* thought. Perhaps she had taken a knock to the head earlier after all.

There was *nothing* comforting about Hadley.

If anything, the Scot should remind her of a pagan Viking, raising a hammered goblet in his Great Hall like Odin in Valhalla.

After all, like the Vikings of old, he was a harbinger of doom.

Jane was quite sure Hadley's Scottish ancestors had wielded swords and conquered castles and generally harried her own English forebears at every turn. That was why her pulse sped up, rendering her breathless in his presence.

Ancestral fear. Nothing more.

The lumbering Scottish Viking accepted her mother's teacup and saucer with passable manners—the dainty cup absurdly small in his large hands—but he then ruined the effect by sipping loudly.

Her mother barely avoided flinching.

"That's verra nice tea, Lady Hadley," the new earl proclaimed, setting down his teacup with a harsh clink.

Jane dug her fingernail into her palm again.

Half-moons. Focus on half-moons.

How could this vulgar lummox of a man be the new earl?

Jane could not envision him taking up his seat in Parliament or attending a ball with the *haut ton*. She could barely imagine him wearing less flamboyantly Scottish clothing.

Peter snorted softly. "Rag-mannered idiot," he whispered in her ear.

Jane stilled, refusing to react.

"Pardon?" Hadley turned to look at her brother. "What did ye say?"

Please don't antagonize him, Peter, she mentally pleaded. *Don't give him a reason to expose me. Don't give him an excuse to cut you off.*

"Ah, 'twas nothing," Peter spluttered. "I was merely remarking to my sister—"

"He called ye a 'rag-mannered idiot,'" Master MacTavish cheerfully supplied, taking a long, gusty sip of his own tea.

A pause.

Peter blanched, meeting Hadley's raised eyebrow.

Jane's mother looked faint.

Please stop, Peter, Jane prayed. *I know you are angry over this man's existence, but please say nothing further.*

Only Master MacTavish appeared unaffected. He helped himself to a biscuit.

"And I couldnae agree more, yer lordship," MacTavish continued nodding to his friend before biting into the biscuit and sending crumbs flying. "Yer a right glaikit oaf. Mayhap yer English relatives here could knock some fine manners into ye."

MacTavish grinned at his friend, brazenly unrepentant.

Hadley met his friend's gaze, eyes unreadable.

MacTavish dunked his biscuit into his tea.

The men's behavior managed to break through even Lady Hadley's stalwart reserve. Jane's mother closed her eyes, likely praying to some long-forgotten saint for forbearance.

Hadley set his teacup down and fixed Peter with what could only charitably be called a flinty gaze. "Ye've a lot of cheek for a man who's relying on ma pocketbook."

Peter swallowed, but a sharp look from Jane silenced him. He focused his gaze on a point above Hadley's head, nostrils flaring.

One did not discuss money matters so openly and *never* in front of a lady. A lady may have years of experience in managing household accounts, but such matters were kept private.

The entire exchange was unbearably gauche.

Lady Hadley pressed a distressed hand to her bosom.

Jane punched a few more half-moons into her palm. When would Hadley turn that look on her and expose her exploits? She was an aristo sent to the guillotine, waiting for the blade to drop.

His gaze flicked over her again. And yet, he said nothing.

Mmmm.

What was his game? Perhaps he did not fully understand the power he held over her at this moment? His life, poor and unknown in rural Scotland, had likely not prepared him for interacting in society such as this.

Regardless, this was why young, respectable maidens were always admonished to behave properly. That way ruffians would have no say over them.

Jane needed to keep that thought firm.

She feared she would need it.

ANDREW ADJUSTED HIS sporran and straightened the brooch holding his great kilt together over his shoulder, studying himself in the mirror.

He met Kieran's eyes behind him. "I'm just saying, we drop the act tomorrow morning, that's all. Playing the rough Highlander has been entertaining, but enough is enough, aye?"

"Your relatives are verra high and mighty. I'm no' sure that they would even ken a difference. So why try?" Kieran shrugged, motioning Andrew out of the way so he could tie his own neckcloth before wrapping the ends of his great kilt around his shoulder, securing it with a brooch.

Andrew grimaced, suspecting that Kieran had the right of it. But Andrew would have to interact with Lady Hadley and her children on a regular basis. Did he truly want to keep playing the unruly Scot?

"I'll think upon it," he replied.

The men were in the master's bedchamber dressing for dinner. After their welcome in the blue drawing room, Lady Hadley had not-so-discreetly ushered the men into the breakfast room, leaving them to their small repast. From there, Andrew and Kieran had been shown to their rooms.

Andrew's bedchamber had windows on two sides with sweeping views across the gardens and countryside. A large tester bed dominated the space with fussy furniture against the walls. On one side, an open door led to a dressing room. A small sitting room was reached through another door.

Kieran had joined him, acting as valet, not that Andrew necessarily needed the help, but he didn't mind the camaraderie. In keeping with their Highland theme, both men were wearing great kilts. The bottom half of the great kilt wrapped around the waist and was secured with a belt, while the top half crossed over the left shoulder and was secured with a brooch. Andrew wore the traditional blue tartan shot with the red stripes that hailed from the county of Angus where his estate, Muirford House, was located.

Kieran had opted for the green-and-blue tartan of Argyll, just north of Dumbarton where he was born. Tartans tended to be regional in Scotland, their colors based on the dyes locally available in each area. Or so Andrew's dey was fond of telling him.

Aside from his kilt with its sporran—a fur pouch which hung from his belt in front—Andrew had donned a more English neckcloth, waistcoat, and tailored superfine jacket, though the back of the coat lacked tails in order to accommodate the fabric from his great kilt crisscrossing his upper body.

Andrew shook his head. "I'll likely send a note tae the inn and fetch the coach and the rest of my men in the morning."

Kieran shrugged. "If you'd like tae, yer lordship."

Andrew turned from the mirror and took up the stack of letters sitting on the bedside table. He had arranged to have his correspondence sent ahead to Hadley Park, so it was no surprise that items were waiting for him.

He had already read the correspondence, but he rummaged through it again, sorting the letters into quick piles—two from managers about business matters, four letters from friends, three from various solicitors inquiring after investment opportunities—

Hah! He finally found the one he had been looking for—a missive from the Bow Street Runner Andrew had hired to find his duplicitous business partner. He scanned its contents again. The Runner had found Madsen's trail and was now trying to track down his present whereabouts.

"Regardless—" Andrew tossed the letter back on the table. "—if my Runner finds more information, I might be off to London sooner rather than later." Kieran, as ever, stiffened at the news. Andrew knew the man still grieved Jamie's death; they all did. None of them would ever lose the guilt of it.

But Kieran, in particular, had felt a keen sense of responsibility toward Jamie.

Andrew distinctly remembered the first time he had seen Kieran. The man had been standing on the deck of *The Minerva*, talking intently with one of the ship's officers. Kieran had a relentless energy about him, as if the entire earth were a wind-tossed boat, and he was constantly braced to take on a heavy swell.

His friend had been practically raised at sea. As a child, Kieran had found a mentor in Charles Fyffe, who had taken the lad under his wing. But an accident had ended Charles' seafaring career early, and unable to work, the Fyffe family had fallen on hard times. Kieran had lost touch with them.

Then one day, Jamie had shown up with a letter from Charles, asking Kieran to help his child. Kieran had hired Jamie on the spot to be the carpenter's mate. Jamie had become his responsibility, his charge, more family than friend.

Kieran's guilt over the youth's death ran as deep as his sorrow, a vast, never-ending crevasse of regret. Andrew wondered if any balm could ever heal those depths.

As if to prove Andrew's point, Kieran's eyes flashed. "Good. I hope yer Runner finds Madsen alive and well. Extracting ma pound of flesh will be much more satisfying that way." He nodded toward the business inquiries. "Ye still refusing other investors?"

"Aye," Andrew bit out. "After Madsen, I have no taste for trusting others with my affairs."

"I would say yer a fool, but it's turned out well for ye."

Andrew shrugged in reply.

Madsen's betrayal had cut deep. More importantly, Andrew had been helpless to control the circumstances surrounding it. If he hadn't had a consortium of investors to appease, the situation in the South Pacific could have been resolved without bloodshed. People had died because Andrew had business partners and investors he had to answer to.

Never again.

He had returned home and bought out or sold out of every joint holding. His actions should have nearly bankrupted him, but luck had smiled on him instead. Moving everything into his exclusive control had resulted in enormous financial gains, earning him the title of the Scottish

Vulcan. Naturally, Andrew received endless requests from other men to invest with him, as today's post alone had proved. Most were from English noblemen, eager to profit (yet again) from Scottish industriousness.

No matter the prospective investor's nationality, Andrew's answer would always be, *No*. He would never again find himself so helpless and beholden to others.

Ironically, the *only* business partner Andrew still retained was Madsen himself. As the man hadn't surfaced, Andrew couldn't buy him out. He had to settle for freezing their joint assets.

"We'll find Madsen and finish this matter, once and for all." Andrew straightened his sporran. "Now, let's go horrify some English, shall we?"

The men stepped out for dinner and were met by a footman who had been sent to show them to a different drawing room.

They followed the footman down stairs and across the expansive, beamed Tudor entrance hall. The footman bowed and motioned for them to continue through an archway and up a grand staircase leading to another wing. Nodding to the footman, Andrew and Kieran started up the stairs. But they only made it halfway before voices rang down the stairwell.

Lady Hadley and her children.

Andrew put a hand on Kieran's arm, stopping him.

". . . must admit it is a disaster beyond anything you could have imagined, Mother." That voice had to be Peter. "His manners are revolting. It's appalling that Scots have survived this long—"

"There is naught we can do, Peter," Lady Hadley replied. "That vulgar Scot is Lord Hadley now, and we must all suffer the consequences."

"He's nothing short of ridiculous," Peter grumbled. "My father must be rolling over in his grave."

"That is a certainty."

Frustration lashed at Andrew. These bloody conceited English.

And *Peter*, no less.

"What a useless *get* that lad is, aye?" Kieran muttered.

Andrew huffed. The spoiled lad needed a solid dose of Scottish pragmatism to reacquaint him with reality—

"Perhaps Lord Hadley would be open to some assistance in polishing his manners?" Lady Jane asked. "Given the certain poverty of his parents, he was not genteelly raised, and as a consequence does not understand how to behave—"

Peter snorted. "A sow's ear will never be a silk purse, sister."

Andrew growled.

"Perhaps," Jane said, "but Lord Hadley might be willing to try to soften his accent a little and learn a few rudimentary—"

"Do not be a simpleton, Jane. No amount of tutelage would take the stench out of his upbringing." Revulsion laced Lady Hadley's voice. Andrew could practically see her shudder. "Given your own . . . *struggles*, you clearly do not comprehend the horror of this situation."

Andrew met Kieran's gaze, seeing his own irritation reflected there.

His friend was correct, of course. These English would never see him as an equal. His Scottish mother and grandfather would always be a stain on his character, regardless of how polished and perfect his manners.

Kieran rolled his eyes.

Lady Hadley wasn't done, however. "I cannot imagine how repugnant his mother must be."

Andrew hissed, the barb shooting home.

"Surely he will not inflict that woman upon us?" Peter said, voice alarmed.

"I cannot see how we could refuse to greet her, if he *did* see fit to invite her to Hadley Park," Lady Jane said. "The acquaintance cannot be avoided, I'm afraid."

Andrew's mouth drew into a firm line.

Enough!

He was fine with these Sassenach haivering at him. But once they brought his saintly mother into it all—

Their disparaging words caused a memory to surface—a rare trip to London as a child. He and his mother had gone shopping along Bond Street. He had been maybe nine at the time.

Andrew stared at the bonnet trimmings on the counter.

"What about this one, Ma?" He held out a pretty blue strip with a scalloped edge.

"Oh, I like that one, Drew. But it isnae quite wide enough." His mother smiled at him, running her fingers along the ribbon. *"Do ye have one that is a wee bit wider, sir?"* She asked the fussing haberdasher.

As they turned to look through a box, words floated across the room.

"Such ghastly accents," a decidedly English voice said, speaking in a penetrating whisper. *"Could they not have stayed in Scotland?"*

"Encroaching mushrooms," snorted another. *"As if a fine ribbon could ever perk up a sow's ear."*

An ugly flush washed Andrew's cheeks. He darted a glance at the women standing before a cabinet, heads bobbing in their finery. He moved his eyes to his mother.

She kept a polite expression firmly in place. Only the tightness around her mouth indicated that she had heard the women.

"Pay them no mind, ye ken," she murmured. *"I have you and yer pa and yer dey. I dinnae want for anything else. That lot can keep their scorn. I dinnae want it."* She smiled. *"I will no' allow them power tae change me even a wee bit."*

That had always been his mother's motto: Never allow others to choose how you feel, particularly if someone wished you to feel ashamed.

Dinnae give them the power, Drew. Dinnae do it, she would say.

Andrew took in a deeply fortifying breath. Her advice was unerring.

"Och," Andrew muttered to Kieran. "How dare they bring my ma into this."

"She's a fine, gracious lady, yer ma."

"Aye, that she is. And Scottish to her core." Andrew gave a low growl. He would not bend to these English. He would continue to embrace his mother's Scottish heritage. "I've heard enough of their pathetic whinging. I'll no' be summoning ma retinue tomorrow morning."

Kieran chuckled.

"We'll be right braw Scots." Andrew tugged on his coat, adjusting his kilt. "No bleeding Sassenach will dare fash with us."

8

"This is what you expect of me?" Peter's voice rose in outrage. "To manage your estate for you?"

Andrew mentally sighed and sat back in his chair. This conversation was not going well. Not that he had anticipated it would.

Peter folded his arms, expression a thundercloud.

Lady Hadley sniffed.

The three of them were seated in Andrew's study—Andrew behind the large desk, Peter and Lady Hadley in chairs facing him.

The window at Andrew's back bathed Peter and his mother in dim, blue-tinted light, rain pattering against the panes.

Andrew had spent his first morning at Hadley Park meeting with his steward and setting out a plan for assessing the estate over the next few weeks. This afternoon he had the task of settling affairs with his heir and Lady Hadley.

"You cannot expect Peter to *work*." Lady Hadley spat *work* as if it were any other four-lettered curse.

"I most certainly do, milady," Andrew replied. "I work, my friends work. I'm no' asking Peter tae do anything I'm no' willing tae do myself. Looking after the estate and helping my steward isnae to be frowned upon—"

"*Gentlemen* do not work. They do not exchange their labors for a wage." Lady Hadley huffed. "Even a man of your . . . *breeding* . . . must understand that much."

Lady Hadley primly adjusted the lace edging her long sleeves, blond curls bobbing, her face a mask of icy reserve.

The woman was abominable.

Andrew swallowed his angry retort. Despite her disparaging opinion about his *breeding*, he was brought up to never raise his voice, particularly not to a lady. No matter how provoking.

He had solidified his decision regarding Peter the night before.

Peter needed an occupation. Andrew certainly couldn't be expected to simply sustain the lad for the rest of his life. A real man needed to earn his way.

Earn his way . . . there he went showing his bourgeois roots.

Andrew knew he wasn't asking too much.

Naturally, Peter had violently flinched and paled when Andrew had first approached him about the matter. That said, Peter's surprise had quickly devolved into outrage, particularly once Lady Hadley joined the conversation.

"I dinnae ken it unusual for an heir tae assist in the running of an estate," he said. "It gives the heir experience and prepares him for the possibility of having tae assume the mantle of *paterfamilias*. And in this particular situation, when the current steward retires in a few years, Peter will be well-trained tae take over the management of Hadley Park. Which, in turn, will provide Peter with a long-term income."

And, most significantly, release Andrew from the duties of caring for the earldom from afar.

It was a perfect solution.

Lady Hadley and Peter were simply being recalcitrant, arguing with him because they felt superior.

Andrew met their hostile gazes with one of his own, pressing his point. "The former earl made no provision for Peter in his will. I have no legal obligation tae provide for him. But I'm a fair man. I dinnae want Peter tae be penniless—"

"That is precisely the point, Hadley!" Lady Hadley's eyes flared. "As any other aristocratic gentleman, Peter should receive an allowance from the family coffers. Helping with the estate should not be forced upon him—"

"Och, I dinnae see why I should pay Peter an allowance and get nothing in return."

Peter snorted.

Andrew met the younger man's gaze, giving Peter his steely eyes. The man squirmed in his seat before looking away.

Andrew understood Peter's mindset, even if he didn't agree with it. At only twenty-one, his heir had never had expectations placed upon him, and so he had never tested his own competency. It was evident in this situation, as he allowed his mother to speak for him.

Andrew thought of himself at that same age. He had already graduated with his degree from St. Andrews and had spent years managing his own businesses.

Even Jamie, who had been years younger than Peter, had known the importance of taking pride in one's work, of giving selflessly to others. It had been one of the youth's many endearing qualities.

Jamie turned to Andrew, smile stretching from ear-to-ear.

"Do ye like it?" Jamie handed Andrew the dolphin carved from a piece of rosewood. Andrew knew the youth had spent weeks carefully shaving and sanding the figure until it shone like glass. He ran a hand over the curved, sinuous shape.

"Aye, Jamie, it's bonnie." Andrew smiled in reply, moving to give the carving back.

Jamie laughed, eyes dancing, pushing the dolphin firmly into Andrew's hands. "Nae, I made it for ye."

"For me?"

"Aye."

Andrew stared at the beautiful figurine. "I cannae accept it, Jamie. Ye worked so hard on it. Ye should sell it—"

"Nae." Jamie's eyes turned serious. "I want ye to have it, ye ken? Ye've been a true friend to me. A person couldnae ask for more than that—"

The soul-gutting guilt over Jamie's death surged into his chest, shorting his breath.

Enough. Not now.

Andrew shook the memory off.

Lady Hadley clenched her jaw. "It is painfully obvious you do not understand how affairs work within our class, Hadley. A gentleman is a gentleman *because* he does not have to work, not in spite of it. Peter, as a gentleman, will never have a profession."

"Hear, hear." Peter sank further into his chair, staring in sullen silence.

"Fine," Andrew ground out. "Let's no' call it *work*, then. Would *honorarium* be preferable? *Donation? Stipend?*"

"This is not a matter of *vocabulary*, Hadley. It is a question of honor—"

"Honor?! What does *honor* have to do with Peter providing for hisself—"

The door snicked open.

All three of them turned toward the sound.

Lady Jane entered the room, closing the door carefully behind her. Andrew and Peter scrambled to their feet. She curtsied politely, face expressionless, posture rigid.

"Your raised voices were starting to upset the servants," she said, folding her hands in front of her. "I thought I would investigate."

Andrew nearly rolled his eyes. By 'upsetting the servants,' she meant 'feeding the local gossip mill.' And by 'investigate,' she meant 'I want in on the gossip.'

He gestured for Lady Jane to be seated beside her mother before sitting himself.

Lady Jane was as prim and contained today as she had been the evening before, her auburn curls meticulously styled, her fair skin gleaming against the soft green of her day gown. She sat stiffly, posture regal, her spine held rigidly away from the back of the chair.

She was achingly lovely. But beautiful in the way of a marble statue—captivating to look at but likely chilled to the touch. In fact, if Andrew hadn't seen her spitting angry and raging in that stream, he would think her cold through to her core.

But her freckles outed her, those rebellious wee bits of spirit on her cheeks. His eyes traced them, lingering on her pert nose. He knew there was fire just underneath her surface, perhaps a secret version of Lady Jane she hid from others. Given her expansive vocabulary when upset, Lady Jane could not be the chilly lady she would like others to believe. Not entirely.

And somehow, knowing that, nearly put a smile on his face.

Andrew angled toward her. "We were merely discussing an employment opportunity for yer brother—"

"Peter? *Employment?*" Lady Jane's eyes widened with dismay, nostrils flaring.

Her mother shot her a quelling look, obviously disliking the volume of Lady Jane's outburst. Swallowing, Lady Jane pulled even that brief emotion back behind her mask and sat straighter in her chair, a feat Andrew would not have thought possible.

"Peter most certainly will *not* engage in trade," Lady Jane said, voice measured and calm.

"Employment is hardly the same thing as *trade*, Lady Jane," Andrew said.

"Peter does not *seek* employment," Lady Hadley snipped.

"Precisely. He is the son of an earl, my lord." The leashed outrage in Lady Jane's voice was nearly comical.

"Peter is a grown man who can make his own decisions." Andrew flicked a look toward Peter who remained slumped in his chair.

The lad jerked his gaze away from Andrew's. But his angry, helpless expression said it all—the younger man had never been allowed to choose his own path.

Unbidden, Andrew felt a flicker of sympathy. Peter had likely been smothered and pampered at every turn, never seeing or testing his own inner strength. By assigning Peter to assist his steward in managing the estate, Andrew was helping the younger man build his self-confidence, allowing Peter to eventually take on greater responsibilities and, essentially, grow up.

Not that anyone in the room besides himself seemed to understand that.

"Ye seem tae be unclear as tae what I'm asking Peter to do." Andrew clasped his hands on the desk in front of him. "Allow me to explain it again."

Once more, he outlined his terms.

Peter would assist the current steward with running the vast estate of Hadley Park. In return, Peter would receive a generous allowance.

Lady Hadley and her two children glared at him in sullen silence throughout his speech.

Andrew finished, saying, "I ken that yous dinnae like me much. I'm Scottish. I'm a *rag-mannered idiot*." He flicked his eyes over Peter, who at least had the decency to flush. "I'm no' like yerselves. But that doesnae mean we cannae rub along with one another. All yous are welcome tae live here at Hadley Park, as I have no intention of residing here on a permanent basis, though I will visit at least once a year."

"What about Jane?" Peter asked, darting a glance at his sister. Lady Jane shot him a grateful look in return.

Andrew motioned toward her. "Lady Jane is welcome tae live here with ye, Peter, even though her financial care falls tae Montacute."

Lady Jane sagged slightly. Clearly, there had been some tension on that point. The thread of empathy in Andrew's chest expanded a smidgen.

"I willnae cast any of you adrift," he continued. "You, Lady Hadley, are legally entitled to yer widow's jointure from the estate, and I will ensure it is paid quarterly." He nodded at Lady Hadley. "And, as I said, I'm happy tae further assist Peter by offering him a generous salary."

If Andrew thought his words would be soothing, he was sorely mistaken. Apparently, his largess was already a given, not a gift for him to bestow.

At the word *salary*, Lady Hadley erupted again.

"*Work* is not the answer here." She practically hissed the words.

"Again, we can call it a stipend—"

"My son will not labor like a common farmhand—"

"I'm no' asking him to work in the fields." Andrew felt his temper rising. "I'm offering him money tae make hisself useful, tae learn the craft of caring for an estate."

"That simply isn't done—"

Lady Jane huffed. "Precisely, Peter will not—"

"Leave it be! Both of you," Peter said to his mother and sister, shifting in his chair. "Let me think upon it myself."

That's it, lad. Speak up.

The women fell silent.

"Allow me tae be completely clear." Andrew paused until they met his gaze. "This all stops now." He motioned a hand, indicating the four of them.

Lady Hadley sniffed, plucking at her lace again. "I cannot fathom to what you are referring—"

"Yer endless wee abuses and insults. Ye think me too stupid to understand what yer about." He waited until all three of them met his gaze. "But I ken. Dinnae push me. Dinnae think that I dinnae hear yous talking about my mother or my father—"

Peter harrumphed, his knee bouncing restlessly. "Perhaps you should leave off eavesdropping then—"

"Enough." Andrew fixed his heir with a steely look. "Yer life will be a lot easier, Peter, if ye learn tae cooperate with me. We could be friends, no' enemies."

Peter ground his teeth and averted his eyes, jaw tense.

"As for you, Lady Hadley, may I suggest doing what my mother always told me, 'If ye cannae say something polite, dinnae say anything at all.'"

"My lord, I cannot—"

"Ye need tae just walk away, Lady Hadley. If ye cannae stand me, simply get up and leave the room. I willnae think ill of yous for it. But I will *not* tolerate being abused by you, either in private or tae my face. Have I made myself clear?"

Silence.

Andrew continued, "I anticipate staying for several weeks, sorting through affairs of the estate. Let's all try tae bump along with each other while I'm here. Once I leave, yous can all go back tae pretending I dinnae exist."Lady Jane exchanged a glance with her brother, something passing between them.

"Of course, my lord," Lady Hadley replied, voice stiff and unyielding.

Andrew nodded, acknowledging her grudging acquiescence.

Peter stood up, hands clasped behind his back. He looked at Lady Jane before taking his eyes back to Andrew.

Andrew motioned toward his heir. "Peter, I'll give you a week tae think over my offer. Ye are my heir, and ye ought to learn how this estate functions if, heaven forbid, ye should be called upon to manage it. If ye decide not tae help, I willnae cut ye off entirely, but if ye wish a substantial enough income to someday marry, ye'll need tae assist me in running the affairs of the earldom."

Peter set his jaw, eyes snapping before jerking his gaze away. He made no reply.

Andrew responded with a curt dip of his head before looking down to the papers on his desk. But as his head moved, he snagged Lady Jane's gaze.

A glimmer of that fire simmered there, banked and tamped down, but not entirely snuffed out.

She met his eyes fearlessly, pressing her lips into a straight line, challenging him to take her to task, too.

He nearly smiled.

He had far too much on his plate to deal with a spoiled English lass, no matter how pretty.

He was quite sure Lady Jane would sort herself out.

9

Jane woke to the sound of damned souls screeching in agony.

The searing noise blasted through her slumber, post-slumber malaise, bed lying about, and sent her straight to rising in a gasping burst.

And as Jane was a woman who greatly valued her sleep, *that* was the greatest horror of all.

She swayed on her feet, grasping the frame of her poster bed to steady herself, shaking sleep from her foggy head.

Another moment passed. The ungodly noise continued, wafting in through the bedroom shutters.

It was ghastly—loud and shrill.

Jane decided then and there that whoever was making that noise would *wish* they were a damned soul by the time she was done with them.

Stomping across the room, she rang for her maid before crawling back into bed, pulling the counterpane over her head in an attempt to muffle the sound.

The noise outside was only the last in a string of indignities.

The horror of Lord Hadley's arrival—both her official and *unofficial* introductions to him. The Scot hadn't said anything yet about finding her rumpled and muddy in the stream, but she feared he was only biding his time.

Lord Hadley, after all, displayed a shocking lack of propriety and truly atrocious manners.

Dinner the previous evening had been nothing short of a disaster. Lord Hadley had chomped and snorted his way through the meal, making one vulgar comment after another.

As a woman who had spent the entirety of her adult life stifling her baser self, Jane knew well how difficult it could be to navigate the labyrinth of aristocratic etiquette.

Lord Hadley, however, blithely did not care to exert himself. He sniffed and behaved abominably without a moment's self-consciousness.

Jane witnessed it with half-admiring outrage. It took a certain amount of verve to so thoroughly disregard decorum. It was as if she were viewing her own baser self without any restraint.

Of course, the entire experience underscored precisely *why* English manners were born in the first place.

That Jane found Hadley attractive even in the midst of it all had only heightened her irritation.

Jane, Peter, and their mother had all retired after dessert, leaving Hadley and Master MacTavish to their port.

Honestly, Jane would almost believe his behavior a farce, if she could think of a reason why he would be behaving so. How could anyone truly be so unabashedly Scottish? The man was a caricature of his race.

Her sense of fairness had to allow that Hadley was attempting, at least, to assume the mantle of earl. He had met with his steward and seemed to take an interest in the estate himself. Jane was relieved he had agreed to allow her to stay at Hadley Park.

As for her brother, Jane had slept restlessly, her mind occupied with Peter.

Naturally, Peter fumed over the thought of assisting to manage the estate. He had raged about it in the library the afternoon before, pacing back and forth in front of Jane for nearly an hour, going on and on about Hadley's presumption. Jane had rarely seen Peter so overset. A fact that had probably contributed to her restless sleep.

Though Jane understood her brother's point—he shouldn't be forced to work for his allowance—there was a secret, tiny sliver of her mind which recognized that having a purpose and focus could be helpful for Peter. He had always been somewhat aimless and drifting.

The old earl hadn't wanted his son to seek employment in the few respectable fields open to him—military officer or man of the cloth— and so Peter had floundered for years, lazing about with no direction. Jane knew Peter had attempted to help with affairs once the old earl's health had declined. But even that had ceased once their mother got wind of it; her biting commentary on work and Peter's station had eroded her brother's confidence.

Perhaps with Hadley here, Peter would try anew. Jane desperately wished for her brother to find lasting happiness, but before happiness, he needed to acquire a purpose in life—

Another blast of noise intruded nearly rattling the windowpanes.

Jane groaned and pulled the counterpane higher.

Her bedroom door snicked open.

Jane rolled over in bed, pushing back the covers. Her maid, Mary, stepped inside, bobbing a curtsy.

"Who is making that infernal racket outside?" Jane demanded.

Mary paused, eyes widening. "Erhm . . . it's his lordship, my lady."

"His lordship?"

"Lord Hadley, my lady. He's playing the pipes."

Dead silence.

Lord Hadley's piping gleefully filled the empty space with screeching sound.

"The pipes?" Jane repeated, voice flat.

"Bagpipes, my lady." Mary flinched at a particularly loud wail.

Jane had not needed the point clarified.

More importantly, none of the staff could tell their master to cease the racket. Her mother certainly wouldn't deign to do it.

That left Jane.

Her mother would not approve of Jane interfering.

But . . .

Grating noise sailed through the window.

"I see." Jane's tone was clipped. "Fetch some water, Mary. I must dress."

This ridiculousness ended right now.

"YER NO' DOING it right, yer lordship," Kieran said, wincing as Andrew blew a particular harsh noise through the bagpipes.

"Och, I've been trying to learn the pipes for years." Andrew wrenched another horrific wail from the instrument. "I dinnae ken why I cannae make the sound run true."

The Scottish gardener, Tam MacDonald, to whom the pipes belonged, grimaced.

They were standing on the lawn to the south of the house, enjoying the noon-time sun. Sheep baaed and bleated across the grass, voicing their own opinions of Andrew's playing.

"Aye, milord. It does a body proud tae feel proper Scottish—" Tam's tone was strained. "—but mayhap I could help ye with it?"

"I dinnae know if I can be helped, tae be honest. The pipes escape me." Sighing, Andrew handed the beleaguered bagpipes over to the older man. "I'm pleased tae see a fellow Scot among ma staff here."

"Aye, there be a few of us, milord. Do ye mind if I play a wee song or two?"

"I dinnae mind at all."

Tam began tuning the pipes, adjusting the sound until it all came into harmony. Andrew shook his head. Tam made it appear so simple.

Tam began playing "Johnnie Cope," an old Jacobite tune.

The April sun peeked out from high overhead, bathing the lawn in warm light. Andrew and Kieran were wearing their great kilts again today. Andrew figured he would be wearing a kilt for the foreseeable future.

He didn't object.

He sat down on the grass, legs stretched out in front of him. Kieran laid down, hands crossed behind his head, eyes closed.

Tam finished playing "Johnnie Cope," the final notes drifting across the lawn.

"Can ye play 'Highland Laddie'?" Kieran asked, squinting up at Tam.

"'Heilan' Laddie'?" Tam repeated. "Aye."

"It soothes ma sailor's soul." Kieran closed his eyes. Scottish sailors sang the tune as a call-and-answer while hoisting sails or raising anchor.

Tam launched into the first bars.

"Speaking of ships on the horizon," Andrew muttered.

It seemed the enemy was incoming. A ship-of-the-line, if he wasn't mistaken. Lady Jane sailed across the lawn toward them, expression thunderous under her wide-brimmed bonnet, skirts fluttering in her wake. She appeared ready to deliver a solid broadside of cannon fire, determined to shred them with her sharp tongue and scathing condescension.

Hah!

Though he hadn't intended to draw her out with the bagpipes, he also couldn't feel sorry that he had. Anticipation coiled inside Andrew, sending quicksilver through his veins.

Part of him delighted in seeing the animated version of Lady Jane again. She had been nearly an automaton of a person over the last two days—expressionless and tightly coiled. Prim Jane, no trace of Fiery Jane.

Andrew slowly rose to his feet. The gentleman in him could not remain lounging on the ground in front of a lady, no matter the situation. Kieran joined him.

Lady Jane stopped in front of them, fixing Tam with a baleful look.

Andrew motioned for the gardener to cease his piping. The bagpipe sang one last mournful note and then went silent.

"I assume you have work to do, Mr. MacDonald?" Lady Jane addressed Tam, haughty anger in her tone.

Tam shot a furtive look at Andrew.

As Lord Hadley, Andrew was Tam's employer, not Lady Jane. She had no right to dismiss the gardener, particularly in front of Andrew.

It was a shocking breach of etiquette.

Clearly, Lady Jane wished to have a word with Andrew and did not want a servant to witness it. But she had no right to dismiss the man. She should have simply asked to speak with Andrew in private.

He let the silence linger, becoming more and more damning with each second.

A slow flush burned up Lady Jane's neck. Whether from mortification at her lack of proper protocol or virulent frustration with Andrew's continued presence in her life, he couldn't say.

Finally, Andrew nodded at Tam. "Thank ye for the use of your pipes, Tam."

"Milord." Tam sketched a bow. "Ma lady." He touched his forelock and then strode off across the grass, pipes cradled in his arm.

Andrew faced Lady Jane, keeping a pleasant expression on his face. Mostly because he intuitively knew that remaining cheerful would annoy her. *Why* he enjoyed needling her so much, he chose not to examine too closely.

Her blush deepened, eyes narrowing and flashing fire.

There you are, he thought. *I knew you were not as proper as you seemed.*

"Lady Jane." Andrew bowed.

"Lord Hadley. Master MacTavish." To her credit, Lady Jane greeted them both with exquisite propriety.

"Now that ye've run off ma gardener, how may I assist ye?" Andrew smiled, making sure to show lots of teeth. "Are ye looking fer more people tae command about? Order away from streams and fields and the like?"

It was his first oblique reference to their initial meeting by the river.

Given the flare of her nostrils, she did not miss his meaning.

Lady Jane, however, was made of stern stuff. She swatted away his implied criticism with practiced ease.

"I am sure you are well aware that the racket you call music—" She motioned toward the retreating Tam MacDonald with his bagpipes. "—has roused the entire estate."

"Roused the entire estate?" Andrew glanced upward, lifting a palm to shade his eyes from the sun shining high in the sky. "The servants and ma staff were up hours and hours ago. The sound didnae do anything more than provide accompaniment for their chores." He clasped his hands behind him, rocking back on his heels.

Lady Jane nearly huffed in frustration.

Andrew kept a ridiculous grin on his face.

"You know perfectly well that I was not referring to the *servants*." She said 'servants' with a hefty dose of contempt. "Even one such as yourself cannot be quite such a simpleton."

Unbidden, Andrew felt his own temper rising.

"One such as myself? Ma staff work hard day-and-night, like yon Tam MacDonald—" He nodded in the direction of Tam's retreating figure. "I wouldnae dream of interrupting their rest. But if anyone *were* still asleep at this hour, the pipes would simply encourage them to no' be a laze-a-bed."

Lady Jane said nothing in reply. But she did glare at him, bosom heaving.

Andrew kept his expression cheeky, despite the roil of emotion in his own chest. "Ye know I'm a 'rag-mannered idiot'." He leaned toward her. "I wouldnae ken anything of it were a 'bloody hell' or 'deuce take ye' to escape yer mouth."

It was a second, not-so-vague reference to their initial meeting.

"Oh!" Jane huffed.

Andrew was quite sure she stamped a foot, but the motion was so small, it was hard to be certain.

He pretended to survey her, eyes dragging up and down. He tapped his chin, as if thinking.

"Does she look familiar to ye, Kieran?" he asked his friend.

Kieran, ever quick, scratched his head. "I cannae say. If she does, she's cleaner than I remember."

Andrew folded his arms across his chest, mouth perplexed. "Aye. The lack of mud does make a difference."

"An' polite language."

"Verra true." Andrew nodded his head. "Mayhap she only curses when there's no other gentry aboot."

JANE WAS QUITE sure if she were a teakettle, steam would be pouring from her ears.

Lord Hadley was unbearably obnoxious.

First his implication that she was indolent because she enjoyed sleeping late occasionally . . .

. . . ehr, often . . .

. . . perhaps, frequently . . .

Oh, bother—she mentally threw up her hands in frustration—so she disliked rising before the sun was high in the sky? What did it signify? She was the daughter of a duke, for heaven's sake. She had every right to sleep as long and late as she wished.

His lordship roused the entire county with his caterwauling racket. *He* was the problem here. Not her.

Furthermore, she greatly resented that she had to tilt her head upwards and shield her gaze from the sun in order to look him in the eye. She could practically *feel* the freckles surfacing from the brief exposure to sunlight.

If Hadley had to be insufferable, did he have to be so loomingly *large* about it?

She was a tall woman in her own right. She *never* had to look up to a man, and yet Hadley made her feel positively dainty in comparison.

Hadley was swaddled in that enormous kilt again. He had worn it the previous day, but he had either been seated behind his desk or a dinner table, and so she had not quite appreciated the full effect of it.

The kilt *should* have made him appear feminine or ridiculous.

It was neither of those things.

The fabric wrapped across his broad chest, emphasizing the width of his shoulders. Worse, his folded arms bunched the muscles in his upper arms, making him appear that much larger. A sheathed knife sticking out of the top of his gartered stockings completed the ruthless image.

His face was all angles and planes, a jaw like cut granite. An errant breeze unhelpfully ruffled his light brown hair, lending his stern manliness a tousled, boyish edge that threatened to weaken Jane's knees.

Though she may have simply had knees on her mind.

As she had approached, Jane had noticed a distressingly bare strip of skin between the bottom of Hadley's kilt and the top of his stockings.

She could see his knees.

His *bare* knees.

His bare, *hairy* knees.

It was simultaneously shockingly indecent and unnervingly virile and sent that same heat rocketing through her body—

No!

Again, she brutally squelched that skittering physical awareness, grinding it under her mental foot.

You. Do. Not. Find. Him. (Or his knees.) Attractive!

A woman was in dire straits indeed if she found a man's *kneecaps* fetching.

Jane ground her teeth. Curling her fingers into tight balls, she punched her fingernails into her palms, pressing hard.

And as for his reference to the "River Incident" . . .

"I understand the general direction of your conversation, Lord Hadley—" she began.

"I ken ye do."

"—and I have appreciated that you have not, until now, brought up our unconventional first meeting—"

"It was verra memorable."

"—but I would be grateful if you would never refer to the incident again."

A moment of silence.

Master MacTavish, thank goodness, had stepped aside to chat with one of the undergardeners about the sheep near the ha-ha across the lawn.

Hadley, for his part, scrunched his brow, as if her words simply didn't compute.

"I cannae think why I would wish tae forget such a scene. Ye were a wee drowned kitten—"

"Lord Hadley—"

"—spittin' fire and ragin'. It was verra comical."

"My lord, you must cease—"

"Have ye considered the stage? Ye have a flare for it . . . the comedy. Yer quite a natural."

Jane, quite literally, *spluttered*. Jaw flapping open, breath gasping for words. Her nostrils flared. She closed her eyes and methodically counted to ten, continuing to press half-moons into her palms.

She was quite sure even a duke's daughter would not be excused for murdering an earl of the peerage.

No matter how provoked.

Jane waited until she had wrested her temper and clamoring inner-self into submission.

She opened her eyes. Hadley was still smirking at her.

The beast.

She took a deep breath. "A *gentleman*—" Jane paused, allowing the word to sink in. "—such as all would assume the Earl of Hadley to be—would pretend the incident had never occurred."

Hadley seemed to consider her words.

More silence.

"Are ye wanting me to act the gentleman, then?" he finally asked, tone full of scorn.

Oh!

"You could at least *aspire* to the title," she managed to say, voice so very strained.

He pondered that for a moment.

"If being a gentleman means I can no' have a sense of humor, I dinnae ken I'm interested."

"My lord—"

"I'm the Earl of Hadley, Lady Jane." He said the words with wry humor, but a bite simmered underneath. "An' I'll still be earl no matter how I behave."

"Be that as it may, my lord, but Polite Society and the *ton*—"

"—can go hang itself, for naught I care. The *ton* is no' ma concern. I will not contort myself into a popinjay so's tae blend in with other popinjays. I prefer the life of a lone hawk." He snapped his teeth at her.

Snapped. His. Teeth.

Oh, good heavens.

A host of emotions swept through Jane's midriff. Horror. Outrage. Shock. Anger.

She *should* have ignored them all, but her inner-self was lunging at its tether.

So Jane compromised and sorted through them, landing on *anger* as the one she wished to court.

"Somewhere between behaving as a proper gentleman and devolving into an uncouth *savage*"—she leaned on the word with a nice, sibilant hiss—"I would think you could, at the very least, temper your manners into something more hospitable."

"Why should I?"

Jane clenched her hands so tightly she popped a knuckle.

Hadley looked down at her balled fists and lifted his gaze back to hers, eyebrow raising.

"Need I remind you, my lord, that you are now a Peer of the Realm, not some barbarous Highlander prowling for English cattle to raid—"

"Och! Cattle-raiding is ma favorite hobby." Hadley threw up his arms. "I cannae be fussed with this conversation. Kieran!" He called to Master MacTavish. "Let's go see what other Scottish finds Tam Mac-Donald has for us. Perhaps we can dredge up some whisky and drink a dram tae the Bard."

Jane snorted.

Unladylike and undignified, but ten minutes in Lord Hadley's company and pieces of that wild girl were set loose.

It was as if his feral nature called to hers, forcing it out of hiding. Like wild animals seeking their own kind.

It was not a pleasant image.

But she had spent years waging war on her own inner animalistic nature. She was a battle-hardened general, not a squeamish green recruit.

And so Jane rallied, stiffening her spine as he turned back to her.

"The Bard?" she asked, voice cold and cutting. "I find it hard to believe you know a single line of Shakespeare."

A pause.

Hadley blinked at her. "Who?" he said, face confused.

Oh, for the love of—!

"William Shakespeare. Famous *English* playwright. Perhaps you've heard of him?" Her voice rivaled the Sahara for dryness. "He wrote a play about a wretched Scottish earl who murdered his king—"

"Och! Ye mean Macbeth?" Master MacTavish said, joining Hadley. "The play with the blood-thirsty lady?"

"Aye," Hadley turned to his friend. "I ken so."

"'*Out, damned spot*,'" Master MacTavish quoted. "That lady?"

"The verra one." Hadley's expression turned thoughtful. "She curses, too . . . Lady Macbeth."

They both looked at Jane.

A pause.

They turned back to each other.

"Must be a ladyish thing," Master MacTavish said, shrugging.

"Aye. For the blood-thirsty ones, at least," Hadley replied, tone far too cheerful.

Jane almost pitied Lady Macbeth in that moment. The poor woman had to deal with unruly Scots at every turn. No wonder she had gone mad in the end.

"Yes. Macbeth." Jane closed her eyes, struggling, yet again, to rein in her temper. "Shakespeare—the Bard—wrote it."

"Ah. I ken." Hadley nodded. "Shakespeare may be the *English* Bard, but there is only one Bard to a Scot—Robert Burns."

"Robert Burns?" Now it was Jane's turn to blink.

"Aye," Master MacTavish said, hand over his heart. "Rabbie Burns. The Bard of Scotland."

"Ye've got the right of it, Kieran." Hadley slapped his friend on the back. "Can ye still recite 'Address to a Haggis'?"

"I ken I can." Master MacTavish began to declaim, "'*Fair fa' your honest, sonsie face. Great chieftain o' the puddin'-race!* . . .'"

"I leave ye to yer haivering, Lady Jane. We're off to find Tam."

Hadley sketched a bow in her direction and then took a step closer, leaning down to murmur more softly.

"And I willnae say anything about yer wee tumble into the burn." His warm breath tickled her ear, sending gooseflesh scattering down her arms. "No' because ye ken me a gentleman but because I'm a decent human being. Mayhap someday ye'll care tae see that."

Hadley winked at her before turning around.

Jane watched him walk away, kilt swishing with each step—left, right, left, right.

She pressed her nails into her palms again.

I'm a decent human being.

Jane nearly snorted.

This from a man who had just called her a *blood-thirsty lady*.

Hadley had no idea of what she was capable.

10

L ady Jane, fiery or not, was a force to be reckoned with.

Andrew came to this conclusion fairly quickly the next morning.

Other than the bagpipe interlude and his resulting teasing of Lady Jane, he had spent most of the day closeted with his land steward going over estate records. As Andrew's grandfather had been ill for several years before his death, the steward had been overseeing the extensive property with only the occasional helping hand from Peter. Fortunately, his grandfather had hired an intelligent, competent man. Andrew had no complaints with the steward's method; he had been doing the best he could with the resources at hand.

But the state of affairs was grim. Hadley Park would require a shocking influx of cash to both modernize farming methods and address much-needed repairs. His grandfather's poor investments—the

Caribbean Affair being only one of several—had depleted resources. The estate had been limping along for years.

Andrew arrived at breakfast—great kilt and all—ready for another day with his steward. He had risen early and had already spent several hours going over expenditures and, after a late breakfast, he hoped to ride out and inspect some of the tenants' farms directly. Kieran had taken off earlier in order to deliver business letters and procure a few of their items from Andrew's valet and other staff in the neighboring town.

Andrew helped himself to some eggs and several rashers of bacon from the warming dishes on the sideboard before sitting down at the table. A hovering footman poured him a cup of coffee. Andrew murmured his thanks.

He was halfway through his eggs when Lady Jane arrived. She stopped abruptly in the doorway, skirts swinging, clearly not expecting him.

Andrew rose slowly to his feet.

To her credit, she didn't pause long.

"Lord Hadley." She nodded, expression distant and emotionless.

Ah. He wasn't to see Fiery Jane today. Just polite, chilly Prim Jane.

He refused to feel perplexed about the prospect. But it seemed some small part of him, tickling right beneath his sternum, *did* care—

"Lady Jane." He gave her a partial bow.

He stood patiently, as a gentleman *should*—he was a gentleman to his core, despite Lady Jane's withering comments—while she daintily dished plum cake and eggs onto her plate.

Lady Jane, he noted, was excessively particular about how her breakfast was to be arranged. She carefully ensured that not one particle of food touched another.

Andrew had a feeling that Lady Jane insisted every aspect of her life—emotions, clothing, unruly Scotsmen—should be similarly controlled and wrested into orderly submission. Though *why* she behaved like this was a puzzle. The spirited woman he had caught glimpses of was nothing like this cold, reserved facade.

Perhaps sensing his eyes drilling between her shoulder blades, Lady Jane slowed her already meticulous movements, taking an absurd amount of time to finish plating her breakfast, forcing Andrew to stand on his feet while his coffee cooled.

Was she making him wait on purpose?

He noted that her high-waisted morning dress was of the finest white muslin with small white flowers embroidered at regular intervals, creating a pristine, white-in-white look. Her long sleeves banded around her upper arm before stretching to her wrist. A lace fichu was carefully tucked into the low neckline of her gown. Both sleeves and fichu effectively hid much of her freckled skin.

All that white should have rendered her pale and colorless, but somehow it had the opposite effect and instead highlighted the staggering glory of Lady Jane's auburn hair. Her curls were tied back with a loose bandeau, tendrils escaping here and there to glow like embers in the sunlight.

Finally, she turned around, her face a polite mask. In outward appearance, Lady Jane was every inch the wealthy, purebred aristocrat she professed to be.

But her glorious hair outed her.

She nodded in his direction, and in that glance, he saw the inner spirit her hair represented—fire in her icy gray eyes.

Despite her placid appearance, Lady Jane was fair to crackling with leashed energy.

More to the point . . .

That fire was a declaration of war. She wished to pester and harass him.

Of course, the Scot in him wanted to shake her awake, to convince her to show her vitality even more openly. If she wanted a war, he preferred she rage directly at him. But he was quite sure her English self could never be so gauche.

No, Lady Jane was an utter paradox.

Fire and ice.

Keeping an amused smile on his face, he solicitously held out a chair for her to sit down, knowing that the motion would irk her—that he *could* have good manners; he just chose not to exercise them.

He retook his seat, sipping at his rapidly cooling coffee.

Lady Jane took a small bite of her eggs.

"It appears that we'll have bonnie weather again today," Andrew said, forcing Lady Jane to chew and swallow before answering him.

Naturally, she took her time.

"Yes," she finally replied, voice cool and cultured, eyes still snapping. She said nothing more.

Instead, she rose from the table, forcing Andrew to scramble to his feet.

Again, a gentleman *always* rises for a lady.

She retrieved a freshly-ironed copy of a lady's circular the butler had laid out on a side table.

She sat.

Andrew sat.

She continued to eat her eggs, now looking at the newspaper.

Andrew munched on a rasher of bacon, staring at her the whole time, catching the occasional flash of temper when she moved her head.

Lady Jane rose again.

Andrew lurched to his feet.

She poured herself a cup of tea from the insulated teapot on the sideboard.

Andrew's eyes narrowed. The waiting footman should have done that for her.

She carried her tea back to the table, nodding at Andrew before sitting down again.

He sat.

His coffee was now cold.

He motioned for the footman to remove it and pour him a new, hot cup. Like Lady Jane *should have done.*

She continued to read her circular, as if completely unaware of his presence. Unfortunately, the tense set of her shoulders betrayed her.

He had not forgotten her sniffing disdain from the previous afternoon. He might prefer her fire, but she definitely found his behavior abhorrent. And now she was instigating a battle of her own.

He knew his own intentions, but what was *her* motivation for escalating this wee war? What did she hope to gain? Harass him? Prove that he was a barbarian?

If *that* were the case, he could happily oblige her.

With a dramatic flourish, he pulled his *sgian-dubh* from its sheath tucked into his right stocking garter. The abrupt appearance of the wicked knife immediately shattered the illusion that Lady Jane was not paying attention to him.

Her head snapped upright, eyes wide. She sat back in alarm, gaze fixated on the knife.

"Good heavens!" She pressed a hand to her chest. "Do you often bring medieval weaponry to breakfast?"

Smiling at her—an expression Andrew was quite sure appeared more maniacal than friendly—he stabbed a rasher of bacon. He motioned toward her with the *sgian-dubh*, the bacon flopping on its tip.

"No proper Scot would be without his *sgian-dubh*," was his reply.

"Skee-uhn doo?" she repeated, wrinkling her nose, as if the mere act of saying the Gaelic words pained her.

"Aye. Ye never know when ye might need a knife."

He took an obscenely large bite of the bacon dangling from the knife tip, holding her gaze while he chewed.

She stared at him, light from the window washing her from right to left and catching the flecks of soft gold in her fine gray eyes. With her swanlike neck, porcelain skin, and lush auburn hair, she was abruptly stunningly beautiful.

A white-and-gold goddess, gleaming bright.

Awareness flooded him, scouring his blood and setting his heart to racing. She was so impossibly lovely, fire and ice—

Bloody hell!

Enough!

He did not wish to find Lady Jane attractive. He did not want to be contemplating cupping her cheek and running a thumb over those adorable freckles. He disliked pondering if her lips would be as pillowy as they looked.

The entire experience was monumentally annoying.

But Andrew was male and, like most men, capable of being attracted to a woman he had no intention of pursuing.

It was ironic, to say the least.

In Edinburgh, Andrew regularly received invitations and was often deliberately thrown into the path of eligible young ladies. He was wealthy and genteelly-born and consequently in demand. Many a matchmaking mother had sought to capture his fortune for her daughter.

But even without his exaggerated Scottishness, he was sure Lady Jane would consider herself too highly-born to associate with him. She would hand him his head on a platter should he even dare contemplate courting her.

He took another large bite of bacon.

Jaw tensing, Lady Jane stood.

Andrew set down his *sgian-dubh* with its dangling rasher and reluctantly rose to his feet.

Lady Jane's fine, gray eyes danced with gloating glee. He could almost see the beginnings of a smile at the corner of her mouth. A decidedly triumphant, smug sort of smile, to be sure.

At least she was enjoying herself.

She took her plate and strode to the sideboard, adding a muffin.

She returned and sat.

Andrew sat.

He ate the last bit of bacon off his knife.

Lady Jane stood up.

Rolling his eyes, Andrew slowly rose to his feet.

She replaced her circular on the side table.

She sat back down.

Andrew slumped into his chair.

Lady Jane took another nibble of her eggs.

Oh yes, she was decidedly pleased with herself.

Bloody English.

Sighing, Andrew reached into his sporran, the pouch dangling from his belt. Pulling out a flask, he proceeded to pour whisky into his coffee.

Lady Jane paused, fork raised, watching him with those wide, gray eyes.

"Spirits?" she asked. "At this hour?"

"Oh aye, my lady. I have a feeling it will be verra much needed." Shaking his head, he downed the cup in one gulp.

"SO VERY KIND of you, your ladyship." Mrs. Jones curtsied, as she took the parcel of embroidery threads Jane had prepared for her.

"It was my pleasure," Jane murmured. "I know how you adore the smoothness of floss silk."

"I've been telling my Daniel that you are the best of mistresses."

After dealing with Lord Hadley over the past couple days, visiting the estate's tenants was a gentle balm.

"Has the steward sent a man out to check on your roof yet?" Jane asked. She knew that the roof had leaked terribly with the last rainstorm.

Mrs. Jones lit up, her eyes brightening. "Oh, yes, his lordship came himself, he did. Clambered up on the roof and sussed out the problem in no time."

"His lordship?" Was Mrs. Jones truthfully referring to *that* man? "You mean Lord Hadley?"

"Of course. He was such a gentleman, too." Mrs. Jones blushed like a debutante.

"He was a gentleman?" Jane repeated, head tilting bird-like.

"A perfect gentleman," Mrs. Jones effused. "Polite and kind, asking after my John and saying he would send a man to help mend the south fence. And that's after he fixed up the roof. We're so fortunate to have Lord Hadley here now."

Jane managed a wan smile, before bidding a polite goodbye and making her way home.

She was sure anyone viewing her walking across the south lawn would assume she was placid and calm.

They would be utterly wrong. Inside, she shook an enraged fist at the sky. These were *her* people. Villagers and tenants that she had known her entire life.

And then ridiculous Lord Hadley arrived and turned his Highland charm on them with his 'ochs' and 'ayes' and swinging kilt, earning their loyalty with a few well-placed smiles and boyish charm.

Bloody man with his stupidly handsome face and looming body and complete disregard for the proper order of things.

Was Mrs. Jones simply blind to Hadley's ghastly behavior?

Another thought occurred, this one perhaps more puzzling—

Or . . . did Hadley behave more properly with tenants and exaggerate his Scottishness for Jane's benefit alone?

She was still muttering over the situation a day later. Lord Hadley was everywhere, intent on destroying her peace of mind. Worse, Hadley's presence had turned her mother's mood particularly waspish.

"If only you could marry, Jane," her mother had said just that morning, "perhaps we could all escape Hadley's grasp. But even in that, you have been such a disappointment to myself and Montacute."

Jane had nearly bitten her tongue in an effort not to reply. The half-moons on her palm had come dangerously close to breaking the skin.

Finally, Jane retreated to the library and her mineral collection before she did something ill-advised. Like scream in frustration or beat a pillow or, heaven forbid, roll her eyes in her mother's presence.

Hopefully spending the day with her collection of minerals would bring some emotional equilibrium.

A recent essay by a noted German mineralogist had proposed a fascinating idea regarding stone color. She had spent the last several weeks working to reorganize her own collection according to the theory, but there was yet work to be done.

Along with that, she wished to choose a few stones to show the Brady children. The younger ones had been begging to see some of her 'pretty rocks,' and she didn't wish to disappoint them.

The library was her favorite place in Hadley Park. Spacious and filled with light, the room sported book shelves on two walls, stretching from the floor nearly to the ceiling. Deep-seated, leather armchairs sat at regular intervals near the bookcases and a sliding ladder provided access to the upper shelves. The other two walls featured a bank of three tall windows on one side and a cavernous fireplace flanked by wingback chairs and a plump sofa on the other. A large desk stood in front of the windows and her mineral cabinets provided a neat dividing line between the fireplace seating and the bookcases.

Jane dragged a stool across the floor to sit before one of the cabinets, determined to lose herself in the soothing work of re-examining and re-categorizing her minerals. She leafed through Hutton's *Theory of the Earth*, trying to focus as she referenced things.

But, of course, her riotous thoughts were having none of it.

How had her life gone sideways so quickly? It wasn't simply Hadley himself.

Montacute continued sending his letters, each one setting her heart to pounding. Would this be the letter that removed her from Peter?

But, no, Montacute's latest letter had expounded on his disappointment in her spinster state.

Your lack of a husband grows burdensome, sister. When the old earl was yet living, I knew you were assured a place in society. But with his passing, your own future has become less secure. I have allowed you to remain in the country, buoying up your mother and Peter in their mourning. However, the worst of that is now passed, and your future again weighs heavy on my pocketbook.

I am frustrated with your inability to attract and captivate a proper gentleman. The dealings with Lord Eastman two years past trouble me even now, as they show evidence of your base, wayward nature. You must fully remove that shameful stain from your personality. Your behavior must always be that of a lady. Otherwise, the difficult task of finding you a suitable husband becomes a nearly-impossible one.

Remain at the ready as I may summon you to London should I discover a possible suitor.

Jane flushed, the lingering burn of humiliation searing her cheeks. How critical would Montacute be of her behavior over the past week with Hadley's arrival? Over and over, her wild inner-self had tugged and lunged at the chains that bound it, desperate to challenge Hadley's own coarse manners on more equal terms.

Become a lady . . . no one will want you otherwise.

Jane snorted softly, letting the sting of that long-ago rebuke sink deep. Despite the harsh words, the grain of truth remained:

No gentleman would ever love a woman who tumbled into streams and swore like a sailor. Jane needed to imprison her baser instincts if she wished to have a husband and family of her own. And the older she grew, the more she ached for those things.

If only Lord Hadley didn't make it so difficult to control her temper. As for her other brother . . .

Peter continued to rant and fume over Hadley's ultimatum. He was a gentleman, not a hired hand seeking employment, and how dare Hadley demand this of him!

Peter had taken to doing what men excelled at when there was unpleasantness about—making himself scarce. He studiously avoided Hadley, and by extension, the rest of the household and Jane, herself.

It was that last bit, ironically, that stung the most. Peter spent inordinate amounts of time in the billiards room and then took himself off to the Lion Arms in Alsbourne 'til late in the evening, always returning foxed and muttering.

Therefore, Jane was surprised when Peter stumbled into the library, interrupting her mineral cataloging. He grunted, before hooking a wingback chair with his toe, turning it to face Jane, and sitting down. He was clearly somewhat hungover from the evening before, if his tousled hair and the green cast of his skin were any indication.

"Drinking again, Peter?" Jane saw no reason to begin with polite pleasantries.

Peter moaned, settling further, resting his head on the back of the chair, closing his eyes.

"Sorting *rocks* again, Jane?" he countered, head unmoving.

She hated it when he called her minerals 'rocks.' Which, of course, meant that Peter only ever referred to them as *rocks*.

"Must you spend so much time at the Lion Arms?" she asked.

Peter grunted again, still not moving his head.

She knew Peter was adrift and lost, but she could no longer bite her tongue. Words tumbled free. "I wish you were here more often. I feel as if I've been left to deal with Hadley alone." Didn't Peter see that his was not the *only* future at stake here? Did he not see that his refusal to assist Hadley endangered her own options? Why was he being so recalcitrant on this point?

Peter did not immediately respond to her criticism, which in and of itself, was telling.

He appeared so young in that moment, Jane realized. At one-and-twenty, he was barely three years her junior, but sometimes she felt a lifetime older. Or maybe, it was simply that she took her duties as a lady more seriously.

"I know you think that by avoiding the situation, Hadley will simply disappear. But he is here to stay, Peter," she said into the silence. "Avoidance is a poor strategy."

As much as she disliked some of Hadley's methods, Jane had come to believe that her brother *should* take up Hadley's offer. Helping run the estate would give Peter some much needed direction. Why couldn't Peter see this, too?

Finally, her brother sighed.

"I can't make this better, Jane," he whispered, pinching the bridge of his nose.

Jane scrunched her nose. "Make this better? Your hangover?"

He snorted. "No." He cracked an eyelid, peering at her. "This mess with Hadley."

Oh.

Her brother sat further upright, eyes bloodshot and weary. "Hadley is so much worse than I expected. And my expectations were never high—"

"Peter—"

"Let me say my piece, Jane. I'm sorry I haven't been a particularly good brother to you, as of late."

Jane's heart melted into a puddle at his words.

Peter does see! she wanted to shout.

He continued, "This whole business with Hadley has me flummoxed. Do I accept his offer and spend my days dealing with angry tenants? Do I fight against him until he gives me a more generous allowance?"

She paused. "What do you want to do?"

"Truthfully?" He met her gaze, his blue eyes open and guileless.

"Yes."

"I want this to all go away." He waved a hand and sat back with a huff. "Maybe we could convince Hadley to give me a settlement. If you and I pool our resources—"

"Me?"

"Yes, of course, you. If I had a settlement from Hadley and you had your allowance from Montacute, we could likely cobble together enough to let a house somewhere, escape from Hadley's presence—"

"Peter, you know that is simply not possible. Besides Hadley isn't so bad—"

"You *cannot* mean that, Jane." Peter snorted.

Very well, maybe she didn't mean it, but she wasn't going to back down.

Peter continued, "Hadley is an absolute menace. I cannot abide him. I would leave here tomorrow if I could manage it—"

"Hadley is at least attending to the estate, Peter." *That* much Jane could admit to. "But he doesn't have the funds to settle on us. More to the point, Montacute would never agree to such a scheme."

"Why not? Cheaper than paying your dowry."

Jane knew Peter didn't mean his words to sting, but they did nonetheless. Even Peter dismissed her if she were a commodity that needed sorting.

"Nonsense. My marriage is Montacute's favorite topic," she countered. "I'm endlessly scolded about it, remember?"

"Balderdash," Peter said. "I doubt it will happen."

"Pardon?"

"I've been thinking about it lately. I don't believe Montacute has any intention of letting you marry. He is content to keep the interest from your dowry for himself. He makes noise about marriage, but he isn't truly engaged in finding you a husband. Why do you think no man is ever perfect enough for him?"

"You are incredibly wrong, Peter. I had a letter from him just this morning on the topic." Jane barely suppressed an ill-bred snort. "Many gentlemen have been acceptable to Montacute. It's my own poor manners that have been problematic—"

"You? Are you referring to that dashed business with Lord Eastman?"

Jane flinched at his words. Naturally, Peter knew every last detail of how the situation with Lord Eastman had played out. She bit her lip, helpless to stop a fiery blush of shame.

Peter noted it, a frown denting his brows. "Eastman's actions were not about you, Jane."

She laughed in surprise. "Are you dotty, Peter? I am obviously at fault. Do you not remember the freckle incident, as well? Lord Birchall overhearing me call him 'bloody repulsive'? The problem lies within me. Eastman's actions were *entirely* in response to my own unruly behavior—"

"Says who?"

Jane spluttered. "Uh . . . *Eastman*, of course."

"Did he tell you to your face?"

"Well, no—"

"Of course, not. *Montacute* informed you."

Silence.

"What is your point, Peter?" she asked after a moment.

"Just this—Montacute has every reason to lie to you. I know that Eastman was hard pressed for funds at the time—"

"He wanted my dowry?"

"Naturally Eastman wanted your dowry."

Jane winced.

Peter continued on, "You are a lovely woman, Jane, with sparkling depths and a quick mind. But men are, by and large, simple creatures. We want money, power, and a warm body in our beds. Marriage to you provides all three." His blunt words reignited her blush, but her brother carried on, oblivious as usual. "Eastman would have been a fool not to pursue you. You giving an overly-loud laugh—if it *had* occurred as you say—would not have sent him packing, I can assure you. You are too great a prize to be given up so readily."

"But?" Jane prompted, as surely there was a point to reliving her humiliation.

"Montacute doesn't want to part with your dowry. I'm guessing Eastman was not put off by your behavior at the menagerie. He might have even been charmed—"

"*Charmed?!*"

"—and he applied to Montacute, officially asking for your hand. Montacute, realizing that he would lose your dowry in earnest, sent Eastman packing. And then to cover up his base motives, Montacute concocted a story that it was your behavior that caused the rupture. The other incidences seemed similar. *Montacute* told you Lord Birchall overheard you calling him 'bloody repulsive,' but it could have just as easily been a servant who heard, not his lordship. *Montacute* decided your face was too freckled to remain in London."

Jane bit her lip, struggling to mentally realign the events. The pieces simply refused to slot into place. Peter's ideas went against everything Montacute had said over the years.

And yet . . .

She frowned. "Why haven't you told me this before now?"

Peter shrugged. "I only sussed it out myself yesterday. You have to admit—it makes sense."

That was the problem; it *did* make a sort of sense. Jane could imagine Montacute behaving like that. Her ducal half-brother was manipulative and cruel, seeing others as puppets to bend to his will.

But . . .

"I think you are wrong, Peter." She shook her head. "I *will* marry at some point. I want a family of my own. Montacute knows this. If he truly wished to keep my money for himself, he would be better off encouraging me to make an unsuitable marriage, which would release him from having to bestow my dowry at all."

"And how would Montacute accomplish that?"

"I don't know. Hire a handsome dancing instructor? Or a dashing Italian artist—"

"Nurtured a few fantasies, have you?"

"Enough." Jane rolled her eyes.

"You're wrong, of course," Peter said. "Montacute doesn't do that because such a marriage would sully the family name. He wishes to avoid scandal. It's better for him to keep you in this marital limbo—"

"Hah! You're practically making my argument for me. Montacute wants me to marry well because he sees my marriage as a way to advance his own political ambitions. My inability to control my baser impulses is an impediment to this—"

"That's what Montacute wants *you* to believe."

Jane ground her teeth. Peter was wrong about Montacute; the duke was wealthy and didn't need her dowry. He wanted something that money could not entirely purchase—political influence.

And Jane was merely another card he could play in his bid for power.

She and Peter could argue this all day.

"Enough of me. What of you?" Jane tossed the conversation back at him. "Are you going to accept Hadley's offer?"

"To manage his earldom?" Peter groaned.

"You *are* his heir—"

"Until Hadley marries and has a son of his own," he snorted.

Unbidden, an image flashed through Jane's mind—a child version of Hadley racing down the main staircase of Hadley Park, tartan streaming behind him, a wooden sword in his hand. The lad laughed, streaking toward her, arms outstretched—

Too quickly, the vision morphed into memory. Peter running to her across the central courtyard of Rosehearth, leaping into her outstretched arms, tackling her to the ground, both of them tangled in her skirt, shrieking and laughing—

Jane swallowed, shaking the thoughts away. "That may happen, but regardless, you need to build a life for yourself. Despite your distaste of Hadley, he will only be here occasionally. You will not have to see him often—"

Peter squirmed at her words.

Did he truly dislike Hadley as much as he said? Or was it just one more excuse?

Jane shook the thought off, continuing, "A man can look after an estate and be a gentleman. The two facts are not mutually exclusive—"

"Enough, Jane." Her brother shrugged, gaze moving off. "I'll continue to think on it."

"You know I only want your happiness, Peter." Jane leaned forward and placed her hand over his. "I believe in you. I think you would be splendid watching over Hadley Park. And I would be here with you, to help when you need it."

His red-rimmed eyes met hers.

"Thank you, sister," he nodded. "I'll give it more serious consideration. But I think I have officially hit my limit for maudlin conversation—"

"Whose conversation is maudlin?" Lady Hadley's voice rang from the doorway.

Jane and Peter both looked toward their mother. The stern slash of Lady Hadley's lips spoke tellingly of her mood.

Peter stood, smile strained. "Nothing, Mother. Jane and I were merely talking—"

"Really, Jane? Minerals again?" Her mother advanced into the room, her mouth pulling into a full frown.

"Yes, Mother," Jane all but sighed. "I am attempting to re-categorize—"

"Bah!" Her mother flapped a hand. "I don't wish to hear it. It's no wonder you are nearly five and twenty and unmarried. Just one more example of your wayward tendencies—"

"Mother," Peter said, taking a step toward Lady Hadley, "Jane's minerals are hardly a slight on her character. Simply an innocuous hobby. Come." He placed a hand under her elbow. "Allow me to accompany you on a stroll around the parterre garden."

Lady Hadley shot Jane another displeased look, but allowed Peter to lead her from the room.

For his part, Peter winked at Jane over their mother's head as he walked out the doorway.

Bless Peter.

Jane stared after him, concern banding her chest.

Oh, Peter. What is to become of us?

11

In an effort to reign in her own wayward tendencies, Jane tried to avoid Hadley over the next several days. His ungoverned nature called too strongly to her own; better to remove the temptation altogether. Heaven knew what her mother was saying to Montacute about it.

Unfortunately, avoiding Hadley proved difficult. The man was a veritable menace to sensible ladies everywhere.

For example, she happened upon Hadley as he directed the spring sheep shearing near the river. He stood knee deep in the water, dressed only in his kilt and shirt-sleeves, assisting the men in dunking the sheep to wash the wool before shearing. Hadley was oblivious to the way his wet shirt clung to his shoulders, rendering the linen nearly transparent, his wool kilt swirling in the current.

Jane stared far longer than was proper. So perhaps Peter *was* right— she maybe nurtured a horrifically-improper fantasy or two . . .

As if feeling her eyes on him, Hadley turned and raised a hand in greeting, giving her an impressive view of his linen-soaked chest, muscles bunching, water dripping down his arm.

The sight knocked the air out of her.

Worse, before Jane could manage a response beyond stunned admiration, he had wiped his hands on his kilt and turned back around with that exaggerated swagger.

Dratted man.

Everywhere she went, Hadley had been there first.

He helped Lucas Fletcher mend his south fence, fixed the flue of Widow Iverson's chimney, and even visited the vicar for tea.

How could the man be so vulgar and free-mannered and yet so annoyingly capable at the same time? The sheer audacity of it infuriated her.

The bloody Scotsman should be monolithic in his defects. Vulgar and *in*competent. Coarse and *un*fit.

His mixing of good and bad qualities—kind but unmannered, skilled but boisterous—addled her thinking and sense of order.

This was particularly evident during a visit to the rambunctious Brady clan. She had come to show them her minerals, as promised. The children cooed over the stones but then immediately moved on to talking about the new earl.

Her minerals were utterly forgotten.

The rest of her visit was filled with nothing but 'Lord Hadley is such a kind gentleman,' and 'Lord Hadley helped birth a lamb,' and 'Lord Hadley looks so comely in his kilt with his bare legs showing—'

Fine. So maybe she had made up the last one . . .

Regardless, by the time she bid the Brady family farewell, Jane was fair simmering.

These were *her* people. *Hers!* How dare Hadley sway their allegiance like this!

She quietly contemplated methods of revenge as she guided Thunder toward Hadley Park. It was only after imagining a particularly vivid scene which ended with Hadley groveling at her feet, begging forgiveness, that Jane finally asked herself the obvious question—

Why *did* Lord Hadley annoy her so thoroughly?

Was it simply the spark of attraction that flared between them—the horror that her baser self found Hadley physically appealing?

Or was it more?

Wind filtered through the trees, rustling the leaves. The chimneys of Rosehearth rose before her. A single trail of smoke drifted upward, signaling the presence of the elderly couple, Mr. and Mrs. Carlton, who cared for the house now. Nanny Smith, the woman who had essentially raised Jane and Peter, had passed on nearly a decade ago. Their nanny had been a woman of deep wisdom; Jane still felt the pang of her loss.

She clucked Thunder onward.

Unbidden, words from Nanny Smith surfaced:

Often, when we take a dislike to someone, it is because we see our own failings in them. We hate these faults in ourselves, and so we abhor them in others.

We detest seeing our own flaws reflected back at us.

Jane ground her teeth but faced the truth of the words—

Her own wild, base self had only ever brought her shame and pain. Her inability to completely control her thoughts and actions made her undesirable on the Marriage Mart.

Become a lady . . . no one will want you otherwise.

Hadley, however, readily embraced his baser self, never bothering to restrain his bawdier impulses.

Of course, Hadley was a man and an earl. As such, he might endure the scorn of some of his peers, but he would never know true despair because of his behavior.

Ah.

And therein lay her disgust.

How unfair that Hadley could gad about, acting a complete scapegrace and everyone loved him.

But if Jane were to do such a thing, even in the most trivial way—like make a face or, heaven forbid, *laugh* at a monkey playing in its cage—she suffered the consequences for years.

Despite being an English noblewoman, she had significantly less freedom than a lowly Scottish oaf.

Bitterly, Jane acknowledged the emotion for what it was—*jealousy.*

By the time she turned Thunder down the long lane leading to the front of the house, her blood was at a low simmer.

Shouting reached her from the lawn to her left. Turning in her seat, she saw Lord Hadley brace his hands under a log and lift it, end first.

Wait—

She pulled Thunder to a full stop.

She blinked. And then blinked again to make sure she wasn't seeing a mirage.

No. She had not been mistaken.

Hadley was balancing a log on end.

His kilt swished as he staggered, bracing the enormous log against his shoulder. It rose into the sky at least twenty feet, teetering precariously.

A group of men stood well-back from him, cheering and laughing— the gardeners and gamekeepers, grooms and stable master, even a footman or two.

Truthfully, the sight should not have surprised her.

Of course, Hadley would balance trees on end and parade them around the estate. It seemed as logical as everything else he did.

Was this what her life had come to then? A man hefting trees was now reckoned a normal, Wednesday-morning activity?

And yet . . .

Hadley struggled to keep control over the log. It circled, threatening to topple, but finally, he wrested it into submission.

And then he took off at a run.

Running . . .

. . . with the log . . .

. . . directly toward her . . .

Jane surged to her feet, a scream in her throat.

The Earl of Hadley sprinted across the lawn, still balancing the enormous log on end, kilt flying.

And headed her direction.

Jane tightened her hand on the reins, preparing to move.

However, Hadley abruptly stopped well before reaching her and hurled the log upward. The continued forward momentum sent the thing flying end over end, tipping it with a crash to the ground. The log landed nearly straight in front of the earl, the top of it pointing toward Jane's phaeton.

A cheer went up from the gathered men.

Chest heaving from exertion, Hadley placed his hands on his hips, neck bowed.

Jane pressed a hand to her own chest.

Heavens!

Why—

What—

Hadley remained stationary for another moment before finally lifting his head.

His gaze found hers immediately.

Their eyes clashed.

A devilish grin split his face.

He touched a forelock in salute before stomping in her direction.

Oh, bother.

She couldn't very well cluck Thunder into a walk now. It would be tantamount to fleeing the enemy on the battlefield. It didn't help that his grin grew cockier with each step in her direction.

"My lord," she said coolly as he drew abreast of her.

"Lady Jane." He said her name in a deeply sardonic tone.

She looked pointedly toward the log lying on the ground behind him. "Did you give up on dogs and decide to walk trees instead? Will I see you attempting to corral stones next?"

Naturally, he laughed at her acerbic comment, white teeth flashing.

Jane ground her teeth. "At the very least, you have managed to distract the staff from their duties."

"Och, every man needs tae try his luck at the caber." He wrapped his left hand around the edge of her carriage.

Jane stared down at it. He wore no gloves (of course) and his hand was hardly that of a gentleman. Rangy knuckles and long fingers, bulging veins and a smattering of hair, a long white scar standing out in his tanned skin.

A hand that knew manual labor and work.

Beautiful—

No.

Jane instantly snuffed out the thought. Her unhelpful wild self would *not* be allowed a voice here.

Unsettling. Indecent. Coarse.

Those were the correct words.

Unfortunately, her thoughts meant that it took Jane a moment to filter what he had just said.

"Pardon? The what?"

"The caber." Hadley turned halfway and waved a hand at the enormous log that Master MacTavish and Tam MacDonald were carrying back to the other waiting men.

Jane opened her mouth to speak, shut it, and then lapsed into silence.

She could find nothing to say.

"Tossin' the caber is a Scottish tradition. I ken yer no' a man until ye've tried it," he continued.

Jane stared.

There was so much to unpack there. Scottish traditions involved hurling lumber? Throwing logs was a prerequisite to manhood?

Besides his hand was still holding on to her carriage and she found it *fascinating*—

No. Repulsive. She found his hand *repulsive*.

She did.

Jane pressed two gloved fingers against her brow ridge before retrieving the equilibrium to continue the conversation. "Do Scots habitually throw large things?"

"Oh, aye." Hadley's grin was ridiculous.

"B-but why?" Jane deeply resented that his absurd behavior had reduced her to stuttering.

"Why?" He smiled wider, teeth flashing in his tanned face. "Why tae make the lasses stop and stare, o' course."

"What lass would ever find such a thing as that"—she flapped a hand toward the caber, now being hefted by one of the under-gardeners—"attractive?" Even Jane marveled at her baffled tone. Hadley glanced behind at the men and then turned back to her.

"Well, you stopped, did ye not?"

He clucked Thunder to walk on.

And then had the sheer audacity to wink at her and wave that absurdly *un*attractive left hand in farewell.

Jane did not surrender to watching him walk off, that bloody kilt of his surely swinging back and forth like a bell.

Unfortunately, the image of it stayed in her mind just the same.

AFTER DAYS OF kilt wearing, manual labor, Highland games, and endless deliberate social gaffs, Andrew was unsure if his uncouth behavior was having the effect he intended.

Well . . . that wasn't quite true.

Lady Hadley had begun to avoid him, as he had suggested she do. When his presence became too much, she simply rose and left the room. His only interaction with Lady Hadley was hearing her voice from a distance admonishing Lady Jane to not forget her parasol or to sit up straighter.

Part of him thought it was perhaps time to give up the charade of his excessive Scottishness. As Kieran had said in the beginning, his relatives likely wouldn't notice a difference anyway.

But then Lady Jane would heave a long sigh over his behavior. Or let an acerbic comment slip. Or, when she assumed no one was looking, roll her eyes. He took endless delight in trying to crack her elegant reserve.

And so, Andrew couldn't bring himself to give up the act quite yet. He desperately wanted to see the woman from the stream again—cursing, dripping wet, and spitting fire. The image of an angry, mussed Jane appealed tremendously—a point he chose not to examine too closely.

Andrew simply needed to figure out how to permanently break her formidable composure.

That opportunity came nearly ten days after arriving at Hadley Park.

Andrew tracked down Peter and asked him for his answer. Would he accept Andrew's offer of employment?

The younger man had hummed and hawed until Andrew suggested Peter accompany the steward, Kieran, and himself around the estate for an afternoon.

Peter had been stoic and quiet for the first hour. But then the steward had mentioned repairing the old mill, and they had all tromped over to take a look at it.

The building was in decent repair, but some of the mill mechanisms were damaged. Peter had spent a solid hour listening as Kieran explained to him how the gears turned the millstone, the mechanism being similar to that of a ship's anchor hoist. By the end of the afternoon, the younger man had been brimming with ideas and asking endless questions, laughing easily with Kieran and the steward.

Andrew merely stood back and watched. It had proved his suspicions. Peter had a nimble mind and good intentions. He merely needed someone to have confidence in him.

At the end of it, Peter grudgingly agreed to help manage the estate. Andrew wasn't naive enough to think that Peter would magically come to be a friend, but at least the younger man was no longer fighting him.

Returning to the house in the late afternoon, Andrew and Kieran coaxed Peter into sharing a drink in the billiards room, ostensibly to celebrate Peter's decision.

Andrew hadn't set out to get Peter soused. It was hardly his fault the lad couldn't hold his drink.

But after a single finger of whisky, it was obvious that Peter was an absolute featherweight.

After two fingers, Kieran had convinced Peter to shed his claw-hammer coat and regale them with a song from his Eton days.

After three fingers, Peter had shucked his boots and neckcloth as well and was eager to learn a raucous Scottish drinking song, thanking Kieran over and over for his assistance.

They were two verses into "The Bonnie Lass of Fyvie" when Lady Jane found them. Granted, the door had been left wide open, causing the noise of their merriment to travel. Andrew was quite sure there was nary a corner of Hadley Park that didn't ring with their laughter.

Andrew was honest enough to admit he was slightly foxed himself.

But nothing like Peter who was three sheets to the wind—*roarin' fou*, as a Scot would describe it—sitting on the billiards table and singing, "*O, come down the stairs, Pretty Peggy, my dear*," at the top of his voice. Thank goodness, he was a happy drunk.

Lady Jane froze in the doorway—her gaze swinging between Andrew and Kieran in their kilts and shirt sleeves and Peter in his waistcoat and stocking feet—her face firmly set to Prim Jane.

Bemused, Andrew noted her immaculately-cut day dress, white Indian muslin dotted with small green flowers and bordered with spooling filigree. A green silk ribbon wound through her auburn hair, small curls escaping to frame her face. She looked every inch the reserved, aristocratic lady.

"Hullo, Janie." Peter fixed his sister with an endearing, open grin—his blond hair askew and tumbled across his forehead. "Yer a dear to come hear my shing- . . . my shing-"—*hiccup*— "-ing."

"It's verra accomplished." Kieran raised his glass, taking a small sip.

Lady Jane's brows drew down ever so slightly. A sign, Andrew had learned over the past few days, that she was upset. Her eyebrows were the only expression she permitted. And even then, they were hardly thunderously-angry eyebrows.

More vaguely-perturbed.

Lady Jane didn't do grand displays of emotion when she had an audience. More's the pity.

He liked Fiery Jane—chest-heaving, gaze raging, tongue lashing. Fiery Jane was a magnificent sight. Though at the moment, with color high in her cheeks and her eyes snapping with suppressed emotion, Prim Jane was staggeringly lovely.

She stoically took them all in, head swinging. And for a moment, Andrew thought she might leave without saying a word.

But he caught her eye and smirked, his expression deliberately gloating and triumphant. *I've won this round.*

Her gaze narrowed.

"It smells like a taproom." Lady Jane waved a hand in front of her face. "Have you quite finished corrupting my brother, Lord Hadley?"

Before Andrew could say a word, Peter howled at the implied insult.

"I'm decidedly good at corrupting myself, I'll have you know, Janie dearesht." He jabbed a finger in her general direction, nearly toppling himself off the billiards table. Andrew lunged and snatched him by the shoulder, pulling him back. "I don't need a bloody Shcotshman to help me."

"Aye, lad." Andrew slapped his back and then grabbed him when the momentum pushed Peter too far forward again. "Dinnae let yer woman-folk slander yer manhood."

"He's drunk as a wheelbarrow," Jane observed, wrinkling her nose.

"It's no' ma fault he cannae handle a wee dram or two." Andrew pressed a hand to his chest, weaving slightly.

Hmmm, perhaps he was more drunk than he thought—more proper fou than merely fou-ish.

Was that why Lady Jane looked particularly fetching in that gown?

No. Not *fetching*. Andrew searched for the word he wanted.

. . .

. . .

Mussable.

Hah!

That was it. Lady Jane looked like she needed to be rumpled and tousled and thoroughly kissed—

Whoa.

Andrew swayed again on his feet, blinking to clear his thoughts. They had gone sideways far too quickly.

Yes, he found Lady Jane attractive.

Yes, he had wondered more than once how it would feel to hold her tall, lithe body in his arms, to run his fingers through the silk of her auburn hair.

Yes, she was spirited and fiercely intelligent and he admired those things.

But that was all he would ever do—*admire.*

Admire from a distance. A goodly distance.

A very, *very* far, distant, goodly . . . distance.

Andrew still had no intention of pursuing her.

"Ye've caught us celebrating, I'm afraid." Grinning far too broadly, he winked at Lady Jane.

Her eyebrows inched farther down.

He considered it a glorious victory.

Kieran lifted his glass toward Peter. "Peter is going tae assist on the estate."

"Yesh, I am." Peter nodded emphatically, leaning precariously again. Andrew kept a firm hand on his shoulder.

"How lovely," she replied, tone dry. "However, if you must celebrate, why ply my brother with your . . . your . . ."

"Whisky?" Kieran supplied before belching loudly.

Peter's eyes widened and then he giggled.

"Whisky? I thought only the Irish called it whisky." Jane's frown deepened even further. "Isn't it scotch?"

"Scotch?!" Andrew said the word as if it were particularly repugnant. "Nae. Only a Sassenach would call it *scotch*."

"Aye," Kieran nodded emphatically. "Any proper Scotsman knows its *uisge-beatha*—"

"*Uisge-beatha!*" Andrew repeated.

"*Ushkah-bayah*," Peter hiccupped, trying to copy the Gaelic enunciation.

"The verra breath of life," Kieran said the words in the hushed, reverent tone one might reserve for the archbishop or a particularly beautiful woman. Of course, his loud hiccupping-burp at the end spoiled the effect.

Jane gritted her teeth. "Why must you drink *whisky* at all?"

"Well . . . the whisky willnae drink itself," Andrew said.

"Aye." Kieran belched again. "It's no' self-drinking whisky."

That caused Peter to lean forward, trying to get a better look at Andrew's glass. "Is anything shelf-drinking?"

"I dinnae think so." Andrew shrugged. "Personally, I'd love a self-driving carriage."

He beat back the thought that wondered if whisky—self-drinking or not—would perhaps assist in mussing Lady Jane a wee bit.

"A self-driving boat. That's a thing." Kieran pointed a finger at him. "I took the steamboat service up the River Clyde last June. Ran from Greenock right into the center of Glasgow."

Andrew perked up. "I didnae know that. Mr. Bell's service, aye? *The Comet*, was it?"

"Aye. The verra same."

"How was that?"

"Bonnie, I must say."

Andrew picked up his glass and swirled the tumbler, the amber liquid glinting in the sun washing the room. His mind unhelpfully noted that the whisky was the same color as Lady Jane's magnificent hair—

A man was in a sad state when his thoughts ran to poetry.

For her part, Lady Jane appeared to be chewing on the inside of her cheek. Perhaps to keep from screaming at them?

"Shall I shing for my shishter?" Peter asked Kieran, swaying precariously before pulling himself upright.

"Aye, by all means." Kieran saluted him with his tumbler. "Yer proving a proper drinking companion, ye are, Peter."

"Aye," Andrew said, "I'm sure Lady Jane cannae wait to hear what befalls poor Peggy." He winked.

Andrew wasn't quite sure what he had expected Lady Jane to do, but he was definitely disappointed when she ground her teeth, turned around, and left the room without another word.

Though he took comfort in the fact that she likely stomped her foot.

She definitely slammed the door.

Andrew grinned.

12

J ane shuffled into the library.

No. She did *not* shuffle. A lady never shuffled.

She merely walked with a somewhat tired slide in her step.

Oh, bother.

Even if she *did* shuffle, no one would blame her.

Hadley's whisky-laden revelry had lasted well into the evening. Lord Hadley and Master MacTavish had managed to drag themselves off to bed, leaning heavily on each other and singing loudly. Peter had been found snoring under the billiards table. It took two footmen to haul him to his chambers, Peter slung between them like a sack of grain.

Jane had spent the better part of the morning dealing with the aftermath of their merrymaking.

Worse, she had tried to reign in her *jealousy* over it. She regretted having ever voiced that thought. But once out of its cage, the idea would not be silenced.

How unfair that the men were allowed to drink and make merry? When she must deny herself every ounce of enjoyment?

If she could not drink, then they should not either, right?

Her impulsive self had whole-heartedly agreed, suggesting ways Jane could help temper the men's drinking in the future.

It was for everyone's good, after all.

Once she had tamped her jealousy down to a low simmer, Jane had finally admitted to herself that she was pleased Peter had accepted Hadley's offer.

That did not mean, however, that her brother needed to adopt *all* of Hadley's unsavory ways. She would definitely be having a word with Peter once he emerged from his bedroom. Though given what was surely a monumental hangover, she did not anticipate seeing him anytime soon.

In the meantime, she would take solace in the library and her minerals. She had nearly completed her most recent method of organization, but there were a few questions that needed answering.

To that end, she paused before the bookshelf which held all her books on mineralogy. Hutton's *Theory of the Earth* had been helpful, but she needed even more theoretical background. She had read nearly every work published on geology and mineralogy, and yet it never seemed enough. She pulled Robert Jameson's *A System of Mineralogy* from the shelf before turning to the row of cabinets standing in the middle of the room.

The results of her re-categorization had been utterly fascinating. In her proudest moments, she even considered writing a treatise on it. Not that anyone would read it. She was a woman, after all.

But the thought remained.

Jane set her book down on top of the cabinet and opened the first drawer with a loud *snick*.

"*Ughhhh*," a low moan sounded from the fireplace.

Jumping around, Jane barely stifled a startled squeak.

Good heavens!

"*Ughhhh*," the fireplace moaned again. Or, more specifically, the sofa before the fireplace.

Puzzled, Jane walked slowly over to the sofa and peered over its back.

Lord Hadley was stretched out on its length, an arm over his eyes, the rest of him unmoving.

Surprisingly, he was not wearing a kilt, nor tartan of any sort. Instead, he had on snug-fitting pantaloons in worn, fawn kerseymere, the foot-straps unbuttoned and dangling, his stockinged feet hanging over the end of the sofa, a pair of black shoes sitting on the floor where he had kicked them off.

Of course, he wore no coat. Why would he? He was only an earl, after all. Jane mentally rolled her eyes.

But his shirt was of the finest linen and well-cut. His pantaloons were definitely of the latest fashion. And though his waistcoat was unadorned, it was made of beautiful ivory silk with silver buttons.

Where did a poor Scotsman acquire such a waistcoat? Had he raided some Corinthian's wardrobe? Or had he *finally* visited a tailor and rid himself of his ridiculous Scottish garments?

That would be too much to hope.

Regardless, Jane pursed her lips.

"Are you quite all right, my lord?" she asked.

He answered with a moan, tried to shake his head, stopped, and then moaned again.

"Please do not shout, Lady Jane." His voice was the barest whisper.

Silence.

"I am hardly shouting, my lord," Jane said in a perfectly normal tone.

Fine. Perhaps she was speaking a *tad* loudly. However . . .

"A lady never needs to shout," she added.

Hadley replied with another moan.

Jane took perverse pleasure in his obvious discomfort. Perhaps she wasn't so jealous, after all.

"Have you had a nice morning, my lord?" Her voice was sugary sweet.

"My morning"—Hadley shifted his arm, further blocking the light—"would be decidedly improved if ye could manage tae speak in softer tones, my lady."

Jane blinked. And then frowned.

Hadley's horrendous accent seemed to have miraculously softened overnight. Scotland was still present in his rolled 'r's and expansive vowels, but his usual mangling of the English language was remarkably absent.

It was as if his missing Scottish clothing had walked off with his thick brogue, too.

Jane would have thought that too much strong drink and the subsequent hangover would have had the *opposite* effect—exacerbating his Scottishness, rather than minimizing it.

It was . . . odd.

The scientist in her felt obliged to study this phenomenon further. To that end, she walked around and sat in a chair facing the sofa.

"Is this tone better?" she asked, lowering her voice the smallest degree.

Hadley managed a nod and then promptly groaned.

Jane contemplated torturing him further, perhaps with a cheery regaling of current lace trends, but she decided to be a decent human being first.

Assuage her conscience. *Then* torture the unruly Scot.

"Shall I have Cook send up something to ease your headache?" she asked. "Perhaps some willow bark tea?"

He grunted.

Jane took that as an affirmative answer.

She stood and pulled on the bell rope next to the fireplace.

Hadley's voice rose from behind her. "I should also tell ye that I've had a letter from a friend. He will be joining us in three days' time."

It was eerie how much Hadley's accent had shifted. He sounded almost . . . aristocratic.

How was he suddenly less Scottish today? She *had* often thought his Scottishness a caricature. Was that truly the case then?

Or . . . perhaps the time he had spent with Peter had not been *entirely* without benefit?

Jane sat back down. "Thank you for letting me know. I will ensure that the housekeeper is informed."

Hadley gave no response.

Of course not.

Replying would have been far too gentlemanly a thing to do.

Jane's modicum of goodwill rapidly evaporated.

Hadley remained motionless, his enormous form stretched out and loose.

Must he be such a finely proportioned man? His large body filled a room to such a degree that he seemed positively elemental. As much a force of nature as those that had formed the rocks and stones in her mineral cabinets.

Of a surety, his broad shoulders and long legs dwarfed the sofa. A sudden move would likely send him tumbling off the thing altogether. She was half tempted to clap her hands and see if that were truly the result.

A polite scratching at the open door caught her attention.

"Come," Jane said.

Hadley grunted at the noise.

A maid entered and Jane gave instructions for willow bark tea and a light repast to be brought up for his lordship.

Jane delighted in the loud cheerfulness of the girl's voice.

Hadley simply groaned again.

Jane was feeling positively ebullient as the girl left, shutting the door with a harsh *clack*.

"The sunshine is quite lovely outside today, do you not think?" she asked Hadley. "Perhaps I should see if Tam would be willing to play the bagpipes for us?"

No response.

"After all," she continued, "someone told me recently that only a *laze-a-bed* would be bothered by such noise at this time of day."

That got to him. "You are a cruel, cruel woman."

She pinched her lips, barely stopping a giggle.

"Come now." Jane rose, walking forward. "At least let me open the window. Fresh air will do you good. The birds are chirping away, and the new lambs are bleating—"

"No." Hadley managed to croak, his hand reaching out to snare her skirts as she passed.

Jane froze, partly from shock that he would dare to touch her in any way, and partly out of surprise at the searing heat of his hand so close to her knee.

"Leave the windows." He shifted the arm over his face slightly, revealing one bleary, blood-shot eyeball looking up at her. It was a handsome shade of blue, that eyeball. The soft gray-blue of the ocean on a cloudy day. A dusky sort of blue.

"But the weather is so lovely." Jane arched an eyebrow down at him. "Why don't you wish to enjoy it?"

Hadley's eye narrowed at her daft question. "I'm enjoying the closed window just fine from this sofa."

"I do not believe that you are."

"I am."

"No, you are not. You are lying down and not even facing toward the window."

He groaned, licking his lips. "Please don't shout," he whispered, tugging on her skirts.

Jane's lips twitched. She desperately wanted to smile in triumph. After days of watching him charm the tenants and flout the rules of propriety, it was glorious to have the upper hand.

"Perhaps you shouldn't drink so much," she countered.

"Perhaps ye should simply cease talking." His plaintive tone removed any sting from his words.

He released her skirts with a huff. And then promptly moaned at the pain the movement must have caused him.

Jane smiled in truth.

"Allow me to keep you company then. I shall tell you all about the latest bonnet I am contemplating."

That got a reaction.

Finally.

Hadley removed his arm entirely from his face and stared at her. "Ye cannot be in earnest," he whispered. "I am absolutely in earnest, my lord."

Hadley blinked. "I am sure ye feel I deserve this torture."

Jane intended to simply sniff and look away, but she couldn't help the enormous grin that stretched across her face.

He shook his head ever so slightly, eyes locked with hers.

"Fiery Jane," he whispered. "I do not think I can tolerate Fiery Jane at the moment."

Which, as a response, made no sense.

With a grunt, Hadley pushed himself upright, stockinged feet hitting the floor. He sank his head into his hands.

Jane wanted to dance a jig. At last! She had brought the mighty Scot to his knees—

Well.

The whisky had probably helped, too.

With another groan, Hadley heaved himself to his feet, flinching as the bright sunlight hit his face. His enormous body loomed over Jane. She took a step back, but before she could feel alarmed, he shuffled toward a cabinet sitting beside the fireplace.

"The maid should be back shortly with your tea," she informed his back.

"I need more than tea at this point," he replied.

Opening the cabinet, he uncorked a decanter and poured two fingers of amber liquid into a tumbler.

"Whisky? For your whisky hangover?" Jane asked. "That *cannot* be wise." For quite a few reasons.

Hadley turned around to her, lifting his glass in a salute, eyes squinting against the light. "Sometimes it's the only answer."

Jane was unsure what *precisely* the question had been to necessitate such an answer, but she held her tongue, eyeing the amber liquid sloshing in his glass.

It truly did look exactly like whisky. She would likely live to regret listening to her impulsive, wild self, but in the moment, she was nearly gleeful. She pinched back a giggle.

The next five minutes would not go well, she was quite sure.

Hadley tossed back the liquid.

Jane was already moving for the door before he finishing swallowing.

His bellow reached her in the hallway, followed by the sound of the window being thrown open and violent retching.

Jane knew she should feel at least a smidgen of guilt. A twinge of remorse.

But instead she ran up the grand staircase with a broad smile on her face.

ANDREW WIPED HIS mouth with a handkerchief, hand shaking violently.

Chamomile.

Lady Jane had emptied the decanter of his fine Glenturret whisky and replaced it with cold, unsweetened, chamomile *tea*.

Bloody chamomile tea.

Just the mere thought of it caused nausea to crawl up the back of his throat, gagging him.

He wiped his mouth again.

The damn woman had smiled at him like a cat in the cream, eyes lit and merry. Fiery Jane at last. It had been the loveliest sight—

And then . . . chamomile tea.

That was it.

No English—man or woman—had the right to meddle with proper Scottish whisky. It was sacrilege. Desecration.

A man had his limits.

This was war and Lady Jane had won yet another skirmish.

The gloves were off now.

He would draw Fiery Jane out of her shell.

Preferably kicking and screaming.

13

Andrew and Lady Jane tiptoed around one another over the following days.

Naturally, Kieran had roared with laughter when Andrew informed him what had happened. Worse, Andrew's evenings had been filled with Kieran asking if he'd like 'a wee dram of chamomile' and offering to serve him 'tea' before bedtime.

Andrew was quite sure that twenty years from now, Kieran would still bring up the Whisky-Chamomile Affair, as he now dubbed it.

It only took an hour for Barnsley to empty all the decanters of chamomile and replenish the whisky, but Andrew struggled to move past the episode. Over and over, he relived Lady Jane's smiling face, gloating and triumphant above him. In that moment, she had been incandescent.

He ached to see Fiery Jane again.

But Lady Jane had retreated back into her shell of Prim Jane, giving him monosyllabic answers and expressionless looks. But that didn't stop him from noticing things.

The way the Brady children prattled on about her, the glowing praise heaped on her from the vicar, the thoughtful touches in every tenant household that Lady Jane had provided. There was so much more to Lady Jane than even he had seen.

Andrew wanted her to set her inner-self free. He had dug up nearly every ounce of his Scottishness over the previous week and had only managed to crack her composure now and again. There was only one thing left to do:

Hold a Burns Supper.

"Why should we hold a Burns Supper?" Kieran asked when Andrew mentioned it. "It's not January."

Andrew raked a hand through his hair. Kieran was right. Traditionally, a Burns Supper was held on the twenty-fifth of January, the anniversary of Robert Burns' birth. On Burns Night, Scots gathered to drink whisky, eat haggis, read Burns' poetry, and generally make merry.

"A Burns Night is verra Scottish," Andrew explained.

"That it is, yer lofty English lordship."

It was the most Scottish of Scottish things Andrew could think of to do. Most importantly, it might be the proverbial last straw for one proper, English lady.

Kieran shot him a smug, knowing grin. "Ye realize ye can just pull Lady Jane's hair. Or put a frog in her bed. It will have the same effect."

Andrew frowned, pretending to not understand.

His friend continued to grin merrily. "Rafe should be arriving soon. We should wait for him."

"I've already ordered the haggis to be made. It cannae wait."

"That settles that, I suppose." Kieran placed his fists on his waist, that smile stretching wider. "Haggis waits for no man."

Andrew glared at his friend. Kieran's expression was far too innocent.

"A Burns Supper is the perfect way to put a bonnie English lass in her place," his friend continued.

Andrew grunted. "I'm merely wishing to continue offending my verra offendable English relatives."

"Keep telling yerself that." Kieran winked at him.

"Devil take ye," Andrew muttered and walked off to find the cook. There would indeed be a Burns Supper.

DINNER THAT EVENING began with Andrew motioning to the footmen to pour a small amount of whisky in the tumbler beside each gentleman's plate; the ladies received Madeira. As usual, it was the five of them for dinner: Andrew, Kieran, Peter, Lady Jane, and Lady Hadley. Candlelight flickered from the candelabra on the table and sconces along the walls. A fire in the large hearth kept the cool May evening at bay. Footmen moved around the table with decanters.

Lady Hadley, at the foot of the table, raised her eyebrows.

Peter eyed his glass, clearly unsure if he wanted to travel that path again.

Lady Jane determinedly avoided Andrew's gaze, Prim Jane being in full-force tonight.

Kieran grinned widely.

Andrew stood, shifting his great kilt firmly on his shoulder.

"Tonight, we celebrate the life and works of Robert Burns, the Bard of Ayrshire."

"Hear, hear," Kieran said.

"I suppose that yous dinnae ken much about Rabbie Burns, so I've asked Master MacTavish to tell yous about him." Andrew gestured toward Kieran.

Kieran nodded and stood as Andrew sat back down.

"Rabbie Burns was the Ploughman Poet, born in Ayrshire south of Glasgow about fifty years ago. He wrote poems about Scotland and what it means tae be a Scot. Every year, Scots gather tae celebrate his life and poetry. A Burns Night begins with the Selkirk Grace, if yous could all join me."

Kieran bowed his head. Smirking, Andrew followed suit. Kieran intoned:

"Some hae meat and canna eat,
And some wad eat that want it,
But we hae meat and we can eat,
Sae let the Lord be thankit."

Kieran finished and sat down.

Before anyone could say anything, Andrew stood again.

"Please stand," he said, words solemn.

Lady Jane and Peter looked at one another before gradually rising to their feet. Lady Hadley was even slower to stand.

Andrew motioned toward the footmen at the door. One opened the door with a flourish.

"Now we salute the haggis," Andrew said.

The low hum of bagpipes sounded in the corridor and then burst into song. Tam MacDonald strode through the doorway, himself in a kilt, the sounds of the pipe ringing through the room. Behind Tam, a footman carried a haggis on a silver platter. The humble meat had been stuffed into a sheep's stomach and then cooked until golden brown. The footman held the haggis aloft, as if it were the king of foods.

Which, to Andrew's Scottish point of view, it was.

Two more footmen followed behind.

The men made a full circuit of the room, Tam playing—a Scottish Pied Piper.

They finished by standing around Andrew's chair, the first footman setting the haggis before Andrew with a flourish.

When Tam had finished playing, Andrew motioned for the guests to be seated.

"Now it is customary to recite 'Address to a Haggis'." Andrew cleared his throat. He had been up half the night properly memorizing the long poem. *"Fair fa' your honest, sonsie face, Great chieftain o the puddin'-race!"*

Andrew went on, the poem describing the haggis' humble origins, its place of pride at the Scottish table. As was customary, he drew his *sgian-dubh* as he recited the words,

"An cut you up wi' ready slight,
Trenching your gushing entrails bright . . ."

Andrew slashed into the haggis, causing the ground meat to spill dramatically onto the platter, spreading outward like, well, gushing entrails.

Kieran cheered.

Peter chuckled.

Lady Jane startled.

For her part, Lady Hadley looked faint, shot him a frozen smile, stood . . .

. . . and left the room.

Andrew glanced at Kieran. Kieran shrugged.

Andrew then met Lady Jane's gaze. She raised her chin, daring him to do his worst.

Hallelujah, she was made of sterner stuff than her mother.

He grinned and continued on reciting the poem, finally finishing with a flourish—

"Auld Scotland wants nae skinking ware . . .
But, if ye wish her grateful prayer,
Gie her a Haggis."

Kieran and Peter clapped enthusiastically.

Lady Jane kept her own hands clasped in her lap.

The meal continued on from there. Footmen served cock-a-leekie soup before heaping mounds of haggis and mashed turnips and potatoes—neeps 'n' tatties—onto everyone's plate.

Lady Jane looked at the haggis before her with dubious eyes. She tasted a small bit, mouth pursed. Her eyebrows raised as she chewed. She went back for a second bite. Andrew took it to mean that she didn't find haggis repugnant. Haggis, Andrew felt, was one of the delights of life. It looked strange but was, for all intents and purposes, lamb sausage.

And sausage, in his opinion, was never a bad thing.

After the main course, Kieran stood and gave the Immortal Memory—a tribute to Rabbie Burns, describing his life of poverty and his love of the lasses, all liberally laced with toasts, forcing the diners to raise a glass over and over.

Both Peter and Lady Jane sipped cautiously. Peter because he clearly did not wish another hangover. Lady Jane because, well, she was a lady after all.

From there, it was on to cheese and dessert.

As the dessert plates were being cleared away, Andrew rose once more.

"Heavens, there is *more* to the evening?" Lady Jane asked. "Is it not time for the ladies to retire and leave you to your port or scotch or whisky or . . . whatever?"

"Nae. Now comes the most important part of the evening for the ladies present. Or, in our case, lady." He motioned toward her.

"Truly?"

"Aye. 'Tis time for the Address to the Lasses."

"Address to the Lasses?" Lady Jane wrinkled her nose. "Why does that sound like something I will regret hearing?"

Andrew laughed. She wasn't far off the mark.

"As Master MacTavish stated earlier, Rabbie Burns had a deep devotion tae women from all walks of life—"

"Isn't that a polite way of stating the man was a philandering rake-hell?" Lady Jane crossed her arms.

Andrew shrugged. "I prefer to think of it as an affectionate respect for a wide variety of womenfolk."

Lady Jane's lips flattened into a straight line, clearly not rethinking her opinion.

"Burns said, '*What signifies the life o' man, An' 'twere nae for the lasses O'.*'" Andrew paused, giving Lady Jane a direct look.

She replied by settling back farther in her chair and drawing her eyebrows down.

Fine.

Andrew cleared his throat and continued, "Rabbie felt life was quite meaningless without the lasses. He was devastated when the father of his beloved Jean wouldnae let his daughter marry a poor poet."

"That does happen. Was she too highly born then?" Lady Jane asked.

"Nae. I ken Jean was a laborer's daughter, like Rabbie himself."

Lady Jane blinked. "Why would her father deny his permission?"

"Och, he should have granted his permission." Andrew sighed. "Jean was in a family way, after all."

"Pardon?" Lady Jane shook her head, face confused.

"Jean was with child," Kieran helpfully clarified.

"Yes, I understood that, but the child was—"

"She had twins."

"Fine. Twins. And Burns was the father of her children?"

"Aye."

"And yet her father refused to allow his daughter to marry Mr. Burns, who was her social equal?"

"Aye."

Lady Jane laughed, an astounded gasp of sound.

"Heavens. Allow me to clearly understand this situation." She leaned forward, tapping a finger against the tabletop. "This poor woman, Jean, found herself with child by Robert Burns. Burns offered to make an honest woman of her—thus avoiding the censure of their neighbors, the village, and the church. However, her father refused, feeling that being known as a woman of loose morals and the mother of illegitimate children was preferable to being the *wife* of Robert Burns?!" She clucked her tongue. "And this is the poet you so admire? A man whose reputation and behavior were so appalling?"

Well.

When she put it that way . . .

Andrew screwed up his mouth.

Kieran scratched his head.

Peter laughed. "Good one, Jane. I hadn't thought of it like that. It doesn't quite recommend this Burns fellow, does it?"

Kieran sighed, "Rabbie couldnae help it that the lassies found him so irresistible."

"Aye." Andrew spread his hands wide. "It's a problem for all us Scottish men, tae be honest. Our cross tae bear."

Lady Jane opened her mouth. Shut it. And then shook her head. "I am sure you are both quite delusional."

"Nae, the lasses cannae help themselves," Andrew said.

"Aye. A man strolls by in a kilt, and the lasses go all shoogly in the legs." Kieran sagged in his chair, mimicking the motion of a lady swooning.

"That is simply ridiculous." Lady Jane shook her head.

"'Tis the Lord's own truth, Lady Jane." Andrew pressed a hand over his heart.

"Aye," Kieran chimed in. "They dinnae call a kilt the *passion pleats* for nothing."

"Passion pleats?!" Peter hooted, slapping his knee.

"Dinnae mock a fine kilt, Peter. The kilt swish is no' tae be underestimated."

"The kilt *swish*?" Lady Jane's tone dripped with scorn.

"It's a well-known fact that the lasses appreciate watching a man's passion pleats swish as he walks."

"Particularly from the backside," Kieran helpfully clarified.

"Aye, allow me to show ye." Andrew stepped away from the table, walked to the door with extra swagger in his step, turned, and strode back to the table. His kilt swinging like a bell back and forth with every step.

He spread his hands wide. *See what I mean.*

She shook her head. *I'm not convinced.*

Andrew motioned to Kieran. He stood with a grin.

"Watch carefully," Andrew said.

Side-by-side, he and Kieran walked to the door, shoulders back, head high. Andrew's kilt bumped his knees as it swung. He could practically feel the intensity of Lady Jane's eyes drilling him between the shoulder blades.

Turning around, Andrew held Lady Jane's gaze as he walked back. She tried to maintain a demur posture, but Andrew knew she had been looking.

Rare was the woman who could resist a braw Scot in a kilt.

Lady Jane pressed her lips together, clearly not wishing to give him the satisfaction of a reaction.

Andrew was having none of it.

He wanted Fiery Jane.

Folding his arms across his chest, he angled forward. "Now, I dinnae want to argue with ye, Lady Jane, but I have noticed ye eyeing the kilt swish a time or two. Not just tonight."

"I have done no such thing, Lord Hadley." Lady Jane's brows drew down, while a hot flush crept up her neck, challenging her denial. "Precisely how much whisky have you imbibed this evening?"

"I willnae allow you tae change the subject, Lady Jane."

"I am hardly changing the subject." Lady Jane surged to her feet. "I am merely pointing out that you are wrong, my lord—"

"I'm no' wrong."

"—and furthermore, calling a kilt the *passion pleats* is the most absurd phrase—"

"Accurate. Ye mean the most *accurate* phrase."

"I most certainly do not!" Lady Jane hurled the words at him.

As they spoke, Andrew found himself leaning toward her, fists pressed against the tabletop, his entire body angled. For her part, Lady Jane motioned widely, all pretense of decorum forgotten—gray eyes flashing, chest heaving, auburn curls framing her fine-boned face.

Fiery Jane, at last! Utterly freed and snapping with life.

She was magnificent.

It had taken nearly ten days of constant harassment, but Andrew had finally broken through her reserve.

He felt like crowing from the rooftops.

Right after he throttled her.

"Yer just a wee bit frustrated because ye like ma kilt swish." He waggled his eyebrows at her, deliberately antagonizing.

"You are clearly either drunk or addled in the head."

"I'm no' wrong. And yer no' denying it either."

"Oh!" Lady Jane stamped her foot, hands fisted at her side. "If I were a man—"

"*Uh-hum.*" Someone loudly cleared their throat.

The sound instantly froze Andrew and Lady Jane.

Turning around, Andrew saw Lord Rafe standing in the doorway, a traveling greatcoat still around his shoulders, hat in his hand.

"The butler announced me," he said, "but I believe your argument was so intense, you did not hear." His dark eyes darted between them all, amused and obviously missing nothing.

Before Andrew could say a word, Lady Jane erupted behind him.

"Lord Rafe!"

Andrew watched as Lady Jane blossomed before his very eyes. Every last ounce of reserve and hauteur vanished, her anger and frustration melting away. A welcoming, warm smile stretched across her face, a nearly incandescent light shining in her gaze.

Something panged in Andrew's chest at the sight. It was shocking how much a person could alter in only a moment's time.

Prim Jane was a handsome woman. Fiery Jane was resplendent. But this open, warm Lady Jane?

She was astonishingly, beautifully lovely.

Abruptly, he was utterly tired of playing the Scottish fool, of pretending to be something he was not. He wanted to be his whole self.

And, worst of all . . . if he was fully honest with himself . . .

. . . he wanted Lady Jane to notice.

JANE COULD HAVE cried with relief.

At last! An ally!

"Lord Rafe, how wonderful to see you!" She instantly moved around the table.

Lord Rafe was a cousin of sorts. Their grandmothers were sisters, and so she and Lord Rafe had a passing acquaintance. But as he had a reputation for being something of a rake, they did not move in the same circles and, therefore, rarely saw each other.

But that didn't mean she wasn't delighted to see him. "I had no idea you would be arriving. Mother said nothing about you visiting."

"Ah, well—" he began.

"It is of no concern, regardless." Jane motioned for a footman to take his greatcoat and hat. "You are just in time to regale us with stories of London while you eat dinner." She nodded at another footman, indicating that a plate was to be brought for Lord Rafe.

Turning back to the room, she squared her shoulders. Heaven knew what Lord Rafe would make of Lord Hadley and Master MacTavish.

She expected Lord Hadley to be scowling at his Burns Supper being interrupted, but instead he stood calmly, a bemused expression upon his face.

Shaking his head, Hadley took three steps forward and caught Lord Rafe in a rough embrace, slapping his back heartily.

"Thought ye were going tae abandon me, ye scapegrace," he said.

"I pondered it but decided someone needed to ensure you and Kieran weren't destroying this corner of Sussex."

"Aye." Master MacTavish joined Hadley in greeting Lord Rafe. "It's been a near thing, I must say. Ye've joined us in time for a Burns Supper.""A Burns Supper?" Lord Rafe looked around the room. "But it's not January?"

As the men talked, Jane noticed several disturbing facts all at once.

One, Lord Rafe, Lord Hadley, and Master MacTavish were clearly friends. How and why? She had no idea. The men should have been eternities apart in social spheres and interests.

Two, Lord Rafe's accent had suddenly lost its crisp, aristocratic sound and had developed a strongly Scottish flavor. Jane abruptly remembered that Lord Rafe's mother was the daughter of a Scottish earl, so was that the connection then?

And three . . . had she gained an ally in Lord Rafe? Or acquired another tormentor?

There was only one way to find out.

"Pardon? You gentlemen know one another?" Jane asked.

"Aye." Hadley nodded. "This is the friend I mentioned would be joining us."

Surprise jolted her. "But . . . but, how could you possibly have formed an acquaintance?"

The men looked at each other.

Hadley spoke first, "Lord Rafe and I studied together at St. Andrews. And Lord Rafe knows Master MacTavish through me."

Jane angled her head, trying desperately to imagine the loud, overbearing Lord Hadley as a serious student. "You studied at the University of St. Andrews?"

"Aye."

Jane had precisely twenty follow-up questions to that. How had he found the money to attend St. Andrews? Was he a King's Scholar like at Cambridge, where poor, intelligent boys could receive a proper education? Did St. Andrews even have King's Scholars? And if Hadley had been a King's Scholar, that meant he was studious and frightfully intelligent, right? And why hadn't attending a university tempered his manners and accent?

Or, was it as she suspected—his excessive Scottishness was an act of some sort?

Why must the man be such a puzzle?

And worse, why did she care so much to solve it?

Before Jane could ask anything, she was interrupted by Master MacTavish.

"Yer just in time, Rafe. Lady Jane was about tae give the lass's reply."

"Pardon?" Jane asked.

"Nae, there's no need tae have the lass's reply, Kieran," Hadley said. "I didnae even give a proper address in the first place."

Hadley motioned for all of them to resume their places at the table. A footman quickly set a place for Lord Rafe beside Master MacTavish.

"Andrew, the lasses have to give their reply," Lord Rafe said with a grin as he sat down. "'Tis only sporting."

All three men turned to her, expectantly. Jane sank into her chair.

"The lass's reply?" she asked.

"Exactly." Lord Rafe nodded, still smiling from across the table. "It's where a bonnie lass—that would be your fair self, Cousin—gives a speech which thoroughly abuses the male species."

Silence.

Her impulsive self perked up.

Oh! Abuse the male species? Let loose her opinions as a man would do?

Yes, please.

Of course, she instantly leaped to ponder the ramifications of giving such a speech—something men rarely had to do.

In that moment, Jane felt so very weary.

Weary of the constant worry over making the tiniest mistake, of allowing her baser impulses even an inch of leash.

She always guarded her speech so. Such a display of emotion might—

Oh, bother!

Enough!

Her mother had taken herself off to bed. And Peter lounged indolently across the table. He would say nothing.

Lord Rafe was discrete. Hadley, for all his brazen manners, would not reveal her to her mother.

Tonight, she would allow her wilder self the freedom it craved.

With a sniff, Jane took a fortifying sip of wine and then stood.

Hadley reflexively went to stand too.

Jane held out a staying hand.

"No, I will stand," she said, pointing at them, "and you lot will sit. For once, I will be taller than all the gentlemen in the room."

Hadley sat back down.

Nodding at him, Jane took a deep breath. "I do not know much about Robert Burns, and the little I have heard tonight has not endeared the man to me. Like many men, he seemed the sort to take his pleasure where he could and leave us womenfolk to carry the consequences."

Peter chuckled.

Jane shot him a quelling look.

She continued, "It can be said that we women are cursed . . ." She paused. ". . . and men are certainly the proof of that."

Kieran chuckled.

Delight shivered down Jane's spine. She could feel that wild girl squirming, spreading her wings, testing the air.

She certainly wasn't to be silenced now.

"Some have asked why I have chosen not to marry. I usually reply with nonsense about waiting for a proper match, but that is only partially true. I tend to hold that marriage involves three rings—" Jane ticked off on her fingers. "—the engagement ring, the wedding ring, and the *suffering*."

Lord Rafe guffawed, his choking laughter filling the room. Hadley grinned.

Jane permitted herself a small smile.

"For example," she continued, "men never want to hear what women think. Instead, men prefer to hear what *they* think parroted back at them in a higher voice."

The men laughed.

Jane smiled wider. "Mind you, this is the same body of men who will bravely face cannon fire and whizzing bullets but run in horror if their mothers insist they must attend a London ball. Or, worse, tea with an elderly aunt."

Peter shuddered. Hadley smiled, blue eyes dancing merrily.

"And correct me if I err, but I am quite sure that men would prefer to take a bullet than escort a bevy of debutantes along Bond Street on a bonnet hunting expedition. And why is that?" She tapped her lips. "Men enjoy hunting. Men enjoy the company of women. And, yet, once we combine the two, men become rats abandoning a sinking ship."

All the men laughed. Not polite, quiet laughs, but great gusting chuckles and bursting guffaws.

It was most gratifying.

"Furthermore," she said, "when women are melancholy or out of sorts, we simply swap the trim on a favorite dress. Men, on the other hand, invade another country.

"In summation. I've heard it said that men marry women in the hope they won't change. Women marry men hoping they will. Unfortunately, in the end, both parties are bitterly disappointed."

Jane sat down.

The men whooped and clapped and laughed heartily.

"Well said, Lady Jane! Well done, indeed." Lord Rafe wiped a tear from his eye. "Ah, that did my heart good, it did. Brilliant! You must do every lass's reply from now on."

"I cannot think that I will ever attend another Burns Supper, Lord Rafe."

"Nonsense." Hadley grinned at her. "With such fire in ye, ye must set it free more often."

Jane flushed at his words. Did Hadley truly think that? And how was having fire a good thing?

"Aye," Lord Rafe agreed. "You wear spirit well, Cousin."

And Lord Rafe, too?

What was she to do with this information—

"Though I must pick one bone with your speech," Lord Rafe continued.

"No, you cannae do that," Hadley protested.

"Nae, I must," Lord Rafe chuckled. "It is simply this. Rabbie Burns certainly had his faults, but he did genuinely care for the women in his life. Here's a single verse to capture it—

'Auld Nature swears, the lovely dears,
Her noblest work she classes, O:
Her prentice han' she try'd on man,
An' then she made the lasses, O.'"

A moment of silence followed his words, and then everyone clapped. Lord Rafe stood, taking a bow.

He sat back down, turning to Jane. "That is all I will say on the matter, Cousin. You are the finest of us all." Lord Rafe lifted his glass of whisky. "A toast to the lasses."

"To the lasses," the others intoned, each taking a drink.

Hadley met Jane's gaze as he took a deep swallow.

He wasn't smiling, but there was something different in his eyes.

An awareness.

A knowing.

As if he truly saw *her*, the hidden wild Jane.

Had he meant what he said? About showing her inner fire more freely?

Jane blinked and looked away.

She could practically hear Montacute's censorious voice in her head—

What does Hadley's opinion signify? The man is an ill-mannered Scot. He has no real understanding of what it means to be a gentleman.

Yet, the more she came to know Hadley, the more she wondered how truly ill-mannered he was. Besides, manners alone were not what made one a gentleman—

She mentally shook the thoughts away.

None of it mattered, in the end.

She might permit that inner wild girl a moment in the sun, but she would never be that free spirit permanently.

Her wanton inclinations were a stain to be avoided and shunned.

Become a lady . . . no one will want you otherwise.

Despite her personal dislike of Montacute and his duchess, those words spoken so long ago were still true. No gentleman wanted a termagant for a wife. Her own life experiences had proved this over and over.

A child must become an adult, and the daughter of a duke must become a proper lady.

Jane had left that wild girl at Rosehearth long ago.

Never to return.

14

How goes the petition for your Writ of Summons?" Rafe asked, settling back in his chair.

Andrew grimaced and stretched his legs out before the fire.

He, Kieran, and Rafe had retreated to Andrew's study after the Burns Supper.

Peter had taken himself off to bed. The small amount of whisky he had drunk during dinner had gone instantly to his head, it seemed. It was a wonder the man survived the London Season given his inability to hold drink of any sort.

Lady Jane, of course, had retired with her brother.

Andrew studiously avoided thinking about the joy on her face—the warm sincerity of her expression—when she allowed her reserve to collapse.

Lady Jane had rapidly entrenched herself in his thoughts, and given everything else he had to worry about at the moment, he wasn't quite sure he had mental space to spare. His brain was already crowded enough as it was.

"My Writ of Summons?" he sighed. "The Committee on Privilege are dragging their feet in reviewing the documents they required to prove my parents' marriage and testaments as to character. Every week my solicitor requests an update and every week they tell him they will see to it—"

"But they haven't?"

"Not yet. I have much tae sort at Hadley Park yet, so I'm in no hurry tae take up my seat in Lords. Once I finish here, I plan on swinging through London and calling on Chancery."

"Has the state of Hadley Park been worse than expected?"

"Nae, but there is much to sort yet. Though once I am finished, it should be in good hands."

"Aye," Kieran jumped into the conversation. "Peter is proving a promising manager."

"That he is." Andrew nodded before turning back to Rafe. "What about yourself? What news have you?"

"I met up with your man from Bow Street," Rafe replied.

"You did?"

"Aye. He's slowly unraveling Madsen's path and hopes to have answers within the next week or two."

"It's taken him long enough," Kieran grumbled, tossing back the remains of whisky in his glass.

"Aye," Rafe nodded. "But it seems our vendetta is just the beginning of Madsen's woes. He has his fingers in many pies. The Runner is simply trying to unravel them all—"

"We aren't going tae take this before a magistrate, are we?" Kieran asked. "Ye both know I want ma pound of flesh."

"We may not have a choice," Rafe said. "Our Runner believes Madsen might actually already be in prison on another offense."

Andrew kept his gaze on Kieran. The ship's master snorted, eyes staring into the fire, expression bleak and haunted. The whisky seemed to have softened his armor, allowing all the anger and grief he normally kept well-buried to rise to the surface.

Of course, guilt ate at them all. It wracked Andrew on sleepless nights, replaying those events over and over, wondering how they could have acted differently. If any other outcome had been possible.

Kieran thrashing in Alex's hold, fire raging behind them, red and gold lashing the dark sky.

"Let me go! Jamie cannae be allowed to sacrifice—"

"Jamie made the decision, Kieran!" Alex bellowed, struggling to hold him. "Ye need to honor it. Let Jamie's sacrifice stand!"

No!

Not Jamie.

Andrew struggled to move, pain blackening his vision—

"We will avenge Jamie, Kieran," Andrew said, voice quiet.

"Aye. Jamie's sacrifice and death will not have been in vain," Rafe added. "Ye will have peace."

When it came to justice for Jamie, Kieran would be the one to make any final decisions regarding vengeance and retribution.

Though the carpenter's mate had been a friend and ally to them all, for Kieran, Jamie had been even more. Jamie had been a responsibility, his mentor's child, practically his family. Kieran would have given his life for Jamie's.

But, in the end, Jamie's life had been sacrificed for *them*. Not the other way around.

"Jamie was too young tae die," Kieran murmured, running a shaking palm over his face. "All of life ahead and then whoosh—" He snapped his fingers. "—gone in an instant."

"And it all began with Madsen's treachery," Rafe said. "*Why* did the man set such things in motion?"

"We'll get answers soon. I'll pen a letter to Alex and Ewan in the morning, apprising them of these events. Hopefully, my Runner will find Madsen—"

"Nae. I'm done sitting about and waiting." Kieran shook his head. "I'm off tae London in the morning. I'll assist yer Runner however I can. Rafe is here now tae tend to yer lofty lordship—"

"I have no need of a nursemaid, Kieran."

"Och, ye know what I meant." Kieran waved a hand. "Rafe will see tae reforming ye convincingly."

"I *am* growing weary of being a Scottish caricature all the time." Andrew raked a hand through his hair. "I have enough tae worry about as it is. My English peers may always view me as Scottish first, and a gentleman, second. But I cannot allow that tae stop me from simply being myself."

"Aye."

"Though being extraordinarily Sottish has been most enjoyable," Andrew sighed. He let his accent slip. "I dinnae get a chance tae be ma most Scottish self verra often."

Kieran grunted and pushed to his feet. "I'll take ma leave now. I'll be off in the morning afore yous are awake. I'll let ye know once I have any word about Madsen."

"'Night, Kieran," Rafe waved him off.

Kieran stumbled out the door.

Rafe took a low swallow of his own drink.

Andrew stared unseeing into the fire.

"You want to talk about Lady Jane," Rafe asked into the quiet.

The question caught Andrew utterly unaware. "I can't imagine there is much to say, tae be honest," he nearly spluttered. "Though ye could have been more forthcoming about her when we discussed this in Edinburgh."

"I probably should have. But I didn't know if she was still in residence at Hadley Park. And even if I had, I didn't anticipate you would be so taken with her."

Andrew grunted. In hindsight, he should have known that Rafe could read him like a book. It was the biologist in the man, always interested in understanding how the different sexes of a species interacted with one another.

"Are you truthfully going to deny you have an interest there?" Rafe asked.

"I don't know that I would use the word *interest. Interest* implies that I see Lady Jane as a potential bride, which I do not—"

"Why not? Why not consider Jane?"

Andrew fixed Rafe with his best '*Are ye daft?*' look. "From listening to Lady Hadley talk, I gather that Lady Jane has set her sights high—"

"You're an earl, your lordship. That's mighty high."

"Och, but I'm an earl with little real power, not to mention my own lower-class, Scottish roots. I sense that Lady Jane expects to marry a proper Sassenach lord, not a rough-and-tumble Scot."

"Perhaps. But I noted the way you studied each other this evening, particularly when you thought no one was watching. The heart doesn't always listen to what the mind thinks best—"

"Enough, Rafe." Andrew rolled his eyes at Rafe's teasing. "Am I physically attracted to Lady Jane? Of course. She's a bonnie lass. But I ken that physical attraction can only get ye so far. I need more than a pretty face and refined manners out of my woman. Besides, Lady Jane strikes me as a lass who is still trying to sort herself out."

Rafe arched an eyebrow. "How do you mean?"

"She has a very refined facade, but underneath it all, she burns bright and fierce. I don't like seeing her spirit broken and tethered."

Silence.

The fire popped into the quiet.

Andrew chewed his cheek, reliving again Lady Jane's vibrant smile, the rosy color in her cheeks as she roasted the men in the room, her auburn curls catching the candlelight, ringing her head in a halo of fire. Once more, her hair an emblem of Lady Jane herself, loosing the spark she kept hidden.

Why, why, why, did Andrew long to kindle that spark into a burning flame?

And, perhaps more importantly, why did Lady Jane hide her spark in the first place? Even an English lady was permitted to smile and glow with vivacity, so why did Lady Jane choose to be a shadow of herself?

He knew full well how taxing it was to cloak one's inner self. Playing the Scottish fool over the past ten days, though generally enjoyable, had been time-consuming and exhausting. He was well and done with it.

How much more tiring must it be for Jane?

Andrew puzzled over it for longer than was wise.

A chuckle from Rafe drew him back to the present.

Andrew lifted an eyebrow at his friend.

"Such brooding," Rafe laughed. "I can't think that I've ever seen you like this over a woman. You are well on your way to being truly smitten."

"Haud yer wheesht," Andrew muttered.

Rafe laughed harder, the eejit. "For what it's worth, I think you and Jane are good for each other."

Andrew snorted. "Keep your matchmaking ways tae yourself, Rafe. Don't ye have your own wife tae find?"

"Och, don't remind me," Rafe groaned. "My own search is abysmal, as ever. My father holds my purse-strings tight. I cannot marry without his blessing if I wish to have an income at all. And his choices and my wishes do not align."

Andrew grunted, knowing full-well Rafe's tumultuous history with his domineering, ducal father.

They sat in companionable silence for a moment.

"Do ye think that Kieran will ever heal?" Rafe asked. "Will he ever release his guilt and grief over Jamie's death?"

More silence.

"Nae," Andrew whispered. "Some cuts slice too deep and no amount of grieving can ever heal them."

"That's what I thought."

THE NEXT MORNING Andrew sent for his retinue: secretaries, valet, groomsmen, and baggage. He hadn't been lying when he said he was tired of pretending.

So his English relatives would think poorly of him regardless? What did it signify? He could do nothing more or less than simply be himself.

Naturally, Lady Hadley was overjoyed to have Lord Rafe in residence.

For the first time in over a week, Lady Hadley had tea sent to the drawing room, encouraging Rafe—and by extension, Andrew—to join her and her children.

Andrew arrived a few minutes late, as his valet had felt the need to meticulously brush his superfine coat.

He strode into the blue drawing room, nodding at the footman who opened the door for him. Lady Hadley and Lady Jane sat before the fire, chatting amiably with Rafe. Peter stood near the mantel.

Every head swung his way.

Dead silence descended.

Lady Jane, in particular, sat taller, eyes widening. Not that Andrew noticed . . . too much.

Lady Hadley surveyed Andrew—turned out as any proper English lord in fawn unmentionables, silk embroidered waistcoat, blue tailcoat, and polished Hessian boots—with an approving nod.

"I must say, Hadley," she said, "Lord Rafe has done you a service in assisting you with your wardrobe. I understand he has seen to providing you with a proper valet, as well." She smiled—a brittle, condescending thing—and then poured tea.

Andrew met Rafe's eye as Lady Hadley spoke, a grin tugging at his lips.

Andrew sat and then listened as Lady Hadley cooed and fawned over Rafe, leaving Andrew torn between bemusement at the difference in her behavior and commiserating with Rafe over the depth of her attention.

Lady Jane sat beside her mother, every last ounce of the fire from the night before gone, doused and utterly stamped out.

Lady Hadley poured some tea, dropped in two lumps of sugar, and motioned for Lady Jane to hand it across to Andrew. Lady Jane obligingly took the cup and saucer, but she clinked the edge on the tea tray in the process, sending a wee bit of tea sloshing over the edge onto the saucer. "Heavens, Jane, have a care." Lady Hadley's nostrils flared, glancing down at the cup. "You are fortunate Lord Hadley is not so much a gentleman that he cares about a little spilled tea."

Lady Jane made no reply. She merely smiled tightly and handed the cup and saucer across to Andrew.

Andrew felt his ire rising. Why did Lady Hadley endlessly scold Jane?

Was Jane's placid demeanor her mother's doing then? And to what end? To help Jane secure a husband?

A thinking man did not want a pale milksop as a bride. Such women appealed to men who preferred subservience.

But Lady Jane struck him as far too intelligent to seek such a marriage. And her mother held no real sway over Jane—not monetarily or physically, at least. Nor did she and her mother appear emotionally close.

So why did Lady Jane work so diligently to hide herself? And why did Andrew, more and more, feel like he needed to do something about it?

He worried that Rafe might have the right of it—perhaps he was well on his way to being truly smitten.

OVER THE NEXT several days, no matter how many times he told himself it was none of his concern, his mind insisted on returning to the puzzle of Lady Jane again and again. It was a conundrum that he couldn't solve.

Worse, this meant Jane had claimed a place firmly in his thoughts, chasing away nearly every other concern.

Curse Rafe for placing the idea in the first place.

It was maddening.

Andrew did not brood over a lady.

And yet . . . he was quite sure he was brooding.

Employing some logical gymnastics, he determined the only way to resolve this problem—and, by extension, achieve some mental peace—was to spend *more* time with Lady Jane.

Perhaps if he got to know her better, he would be able to puzzle out why she hid her spirited self and put this perplexing obsessiveness behind him.

However, every time he sought Lady Jane out, she was busy consulting with the housekeeper or off calling on ailing tenants.

After several days, Andrew feared she was avoiding him.

It *shouldn't* have annoyed him.

He *should* have brushed it off and thought nothing more of it.

And yet . . .

. . . he brooded.

How dare Lady Jane simply decide that he wasn't worth knowing? How dare she decide that *she* wasn't worth knowing? It was as if, in her attempts to negate him, she was negating herself. He wanted to shake her, to force her to act and *live*.

In an effort to tame his wayward thoughts, Andrew took to the library one rainy afternoon. He had spent days with his steward and secretaries, going over the estate and addressing needs. The moody clouds begged him to relax and simply be.

He had made a happy discovery the previous day. The cabinets in the middle of the library held an impressive collection of minerals—rocks and stones from all over the world, all meticulously presented.

However, someone had organized them oddly. As best he could understand, the collection was arranged according to color, the stones extending through the cabinets like a rainbow. For example, red sedimentary sandstone was nestled next to pink crystalline quartz, even though the rocks were utterly opposite in nearly every other way.

It made absolutely no sense.

Shaking his head, Andrew took it upon himself to re-categorize everything into a more logical strata of crystalline stones moving through to granular. It would take forever, as he would have to carefully examine each rock, but at least future mineral enthusiasts would be able to find things more easily.

Pushing back the sofa and chairs, he had two footmen lay down several white sheets. From there, he took all the minerals out of the cabinet and spread them on the floor, hundreds of small rocks dotting the white linen, all begging to be examined and reassigned a place in the collection.

Andrew rubbed his hands together, excited about the prospect. Categorizing minerals was always an enjoyable task.

An hour later, he had a magnifying glass pressed to his eye—examining the smoky quartz crystal in a piece of Cairngorm granite—when a loud gasp sounded.

Andrew lifted his head to see Lady Jane standing in the open doorway, a hand to her mouth, horror in her eyes. As usual, she was immaculately dressed in a sage green morning dress, a white lace fichu tucked demurely into her bodice. The green highlighted the red in her auburn hair, turning the curls into liquid amber.

Once again, his irrational brain unhelpfully noted that she was remarkably lovely.

He scrambled to his feet, setting down the magnifying glass and stone. "Lady Jane," he bowed, acutely remembering the last time they had been together in the library.

Things had not gone well for him.

And by the dismayed set of her mouth and the wideness of her eyes, Andrew had a sinking suspicion that this current encounter would go no better than his last.

Though she was not entirely tucked into Prim Jane, so he supposed the situation wasn't an utter loss. That said, she was not quite Fiery Jane either.

"May I help ye?" he asked, tone mild.

Lady Jane said nothing but instead advanced into the room, her eyes scouring the minerals spread everywhere.

Andrew immediately saw the room through her eyes. Stones and rocks scattered about. Her tidy self was likely appalled at the mess.

"I am simply organizing the stones." He gestured around. "They were a bit of a mess, tae be honest. I will ensure that everything is neat—"

He stopped. This was *his* house, blast it. He could make all the messes he wanted. He was hardly some recalcitrant boy. He would not apologize.

"What are you doing?!" she hissed, advancing more quickly now.

Andrew blinked, her tone catching him like cold water in the face. "Organizing the stones, as I said."

"Organizing them?!" She rotated in a circle, chest heaving, eyes still wide.

"Yes. You see—"

"How dare you?!" She whirled back to him.

It was Andrew's turn to look perplexed.

Could he have an interaction with this woman that wasn't contentious?

"Pardon?" He pressed a hand to his chest, forcing himself to keep his voice low and steady. "I discovered a mineral collection in my library and decided to investigate it."

His words only served to upset her further. She stopped inches from his chest, poking a finger at him.

"Not *your* minerals!" She emphasized each word with a jab to his shoulder. For a lass, she certainly packed a punch. The pressure of her finger was a searing stab of heat.

He didn't know what surprised him more. The idea that the minerals were not his, or the fact that she was voluntarily standing so close and touching him, eyes blazing.

Regardless of the answer . . .

. . . he had drawn out Fiery Jane.

Hallelujah!

Heavens but she was magnificent when fire lit within her. Her gray eyes snapped and pink touched her cheeks.

He couldn't resist a grin.

Given her immediate and dramatic frown, grinning was not an appropriate reaction.

"The minerals are not mine?" he asked.

"No!" *Jab.*

"They do not belong to the estate?"

"No. They do not!" *Jab, jab, jab.*

Andrew grinned wider.

"Cease this!" Lady Jane stamped her foot before giving him one last jab. "How dare you come into this house with your Scottish accent and passion pleats and kilt swish and whisky and your big, bloody lummox of a body and then d-drag *my* m-minerals out of *my* c-cabinet and . . . and . . ."

Lady Jane's eyes had grown glossier and glossier as she spoke, emotion clogging her voice. She turned away from him, but not before Andrew saw her swipe at her cheek with a trembling hand.

He had rarely felt more of an ass.
He had wanted to crack her reserve.
So . . . mission accomplished.
But at what cost?

15

Jane crossed the library to the window overlooking the back lawn, desperately trying to wrangle her emotions into submission.

Her tears were horrifyingly humiliating.

She never cried.

Rationally, she knew that Lord Hadley didn't know the minerals were hers. He had simply found the minerals in his library and assumed they belonged to him. It was not an erroneous assumption. Nearly everything else in Hadley Park belonged to him.

But her minerals did not.

She did not.

She clenched her fists, pushing her nails into her palms, focusing on the pain.

You do not cry over minerals. Even if Hadley did just upend weeks of work.

Why would he have understood how she had them organized?

It didn't help that Hadley had lost his more obnoxiously Scottish ways. Lord Rafe certainly had a civilizing effect on his friend. Or, as Jane suspected, Hadley had never been so uncivilized in the first place.

Several men-of-business had arrived right behind Lord Rafe and were now firmly entrenched with the steward. Her mother assumed the men had accompanied Lord Rafe, but Jane was not quite so sure.

Hadley's accent was now only a trace of brogue. And his clothing . . . Jane swallowed.

He had been potent in a kilt. But somehow seeing him tucked and tamed into a London Corinthian—knowing the rough Scotsman that lurked beneath the surface—was even more appealing.

Maintaining her distance had been easier before Lord Rafe's arrival. Jane had been able to convince herself that Hadley was unfit for polite society, despite his rank.

But Lord Rafe's easy friendship with him belied that idea. Lord Rafe's manners were so impeccable that even the highest stickler in the *ton* could find no fault.

And Rafe considered Hadley a peer.

She felt helpless to stop her attraction to Hadley.

But she needed to remain vigilant. What would happen if Montacute learned of this? Would he remove her from Peter?

All of which, she assumed, explained the tears pricking her eyes.

She felt more than heard him cross to stand behind her. A heavy sigh escaped him.

"I fear I have offended ye, Lady Jane." Scotland slipped more and more into his words as he spoke. "I didnae mean to cause offense. The minerals were sadly needing categorizing."

Jane shook her head. The idiot.

"They *were* categorized," she all but hissed, refusing to turn around, refusing to give him the satisfaction of seeing how his actions had overset her.

"They were?"

"Yes."

"I suppose the minerals were verra pretty in the cabinets . . . with all the colors and such." He shifted behind her. "I can appreciate the appeal."

Jane surveyed the scattered stones. She had kept written records, thank goodness, but this would take days to re-sort.

"The colors are not just *pretty*, my lord." Jane bit her cheek, pressing nails harder into her palm. "They are the most significant finding of my categorization. An unexpected ancillary effect." Giving her cheeks one last swipe, she turned around. "For the last while, I have been reviewing my field notes and meticulously organizing my entire collection according to the location where they were found—"

"Location? Why would you organize minerals by *location*?" he asked, his tone stating his low opinion of her intellectual capabilities.

Grrrr.

"It was not as foolish as it sounds, my lord." Unbidden, Jane felt her own temper rising again. "Surprising as it may be, there is more than fan etiquette and forms of address between my ears."

He blinked, nonplussed.

Jane did not back down. She waved a hand over her scattered work. "I was merely testing a theory. But I quickly realized that color *can* be a function of location."

Hadley studied her with what could only be described as *befuddled confusion*.

"Color is a function of location?"

"Yes. For example, that piece of prehnite there—" She pointed to a pale, translucent green stone near her foot. "—and that chunk of sandstone with the strip of glauconite in it—" She pointed to a larger sedimentary rock sporting a wide, green streak in its layers. "—were found near one another."

He looked at the rocks indicated, brows drawing down. His hands went up on his hips, a finger tapping as if thinking.

"The crystalline prehnite was found near the granular glauconite? And both with the same coloration, despite being entirely different types of rock?" he finally asked. "Was there any moss agate in the area?"

It was Jane's turn to blink.

No one ever asked a follow-up question.

No one ever asked her about her mineral fascination—full stop.

It was an embarrassing peccadillo to be kept secret, not something to be celebrated. Peter occasionally teased her about it, but that was it.

Jane swallowed. How was she to manage this?

It was one thing to consider Hadley an attractive brute.

It was something else altogether to see him as a clever intellectual, a kindred soul.

"Uhmm, I would need to check my field notes," she replied, voice softer. "There were more green crystalline rocks than granular in that particular location, but notably, all the rocks were green, regardless of type. Even the marble had green inclusions."

"That is fascinating." Hadley nodded, still contemplating the rocks, still tapping that finger. "I think I read a paper hinting at that very thing just last month—"

"Mr. Johnson's work on Bavarian mineralogy?"

Hadley lifted his head, meeting her eyes directly. His blue gaze plumbed hers, sparking with intelligence.

Something breathless passed between them. A nearly living thing with fluffing feathers, puffing outward and fluttering with excitement.

Hadley swallowed.

Jane bit her lower lip.

His eyes followed the motion and then immediately rose back to her gaze. But even that small movement sent heat climbing up her neck.

Oh, heavens.

"Aye," he finally replied. Was his voice suddenly hoarse?

"I quite enjoyed the article," she continued. "It's what prompted me to examine my own collection—"

"Your collection?" He spread his hands wide.

"Yes."

A long pause.

His eyes found hers again. They stared and stared, the silence lingering and stretching.

Hadley's chest rose and fell, reminding Jane that why, yes, she needed to breathe, too.

They both took a perfectly synchronized breath.

One. Two. In. Out.

"You like tae study and collect rocks and minerals?" he asked.

"Yes."

"Like an amateur mineralogist?" His voice had definitely gone gruff.

"I'd like to think that I'm a bit more advanced in my understanding than an *amateur*."

"I see."

Silence hung between them.

"Will ye please show me your collection, Lady Jane?" His eyes met hers again. "I would very much like tae understand it better. It seems like it might be full of surprises."

And suddenly he wasn't just talking about a mineral collection.

I want to understand you *better*, his look seemed to say.

Jane nodded, a small bob of her head, that same tightness having returned to clog her throat.

When had anyone ever said that to her?

She was so used to be known as the daughter of one duke and the sister of another . . . the breadth of her life easily encompassed within the identity of her male relatives.

No one looked beyond that. No one felt the need.

Until Hadley.

Why would it be him? she wondered. *Why would* he *be the one to want to see past my facade?*

Was it because he understood facades so thoroughly himself?

"Why have you changed?" she asked, unable to stop the question before it tumbled out her.

She had a habit of tumbling in front of him, it seemed—into streams and words and her innermost self.

He blinked at the non-sequitur. But—and this was perhaps what she found most troubling of all—he instantly understood what she meant.

Why are you not the uncouth Scot you were a week ago?

He glanced down at his superfine coat over an elegant satin waistcoat before clasping his hands behind his back.

"None of us are what we seem, Lady Jane," came his reply, still low and gruff. "I think ye ken that better than most."

Their eyes locked.

That breathless fluttering feeling returned, bringing a flock of friends with it, fluffing and growing until it pressed against her chest in a nearly painful ache.

Jane wasn't prepared for this. Not this sense of kinship. Not with *him*.

Swallowing, she turned away, plucking a cushion from beside the window and placing it in an uncluttered space within the stones.

"What is your interest in minerals, my lord?" she asked as she sank down onto the cushion, arranging her skirts carefully.

For his part, Hadley sat opposite her, lounging casually, an arm draped over his raised knee.

"It was my course of study at St. Andrews," he replied, picking up a small piece of pyrite from a collection of minerals she had purchased from a dealer in Plymouth several years before.

"Your course of study? Truly?"

"Aye. Mineralogy and natural sciences. As I have mentioned, Rafe and I met at St. Andrews. Our specialties are in mineralogy for myself and biology for him, but both areas fall under the natural sciences. We studied together at United College, which houses all scientific and medical studies at St. Andrews—"

"Did you study with Mr. James Hutton?" Jane had to know. Mr. Hutton was a celebrated Scottish geologist and had formulated many of the current theories about rock formation.

"Unfortunately, no." Hadley shook his head. "Mr. Hutton passed away a few years back, so I never had the honor of meeting him. But several of my professors at university were avid supporters of Mr. Hutton's writing."

Jane longed to bounce with excitement. "I would love nothing more than to attend university and examine minerals all day."

He lifted his head, studying her. She appreciated that he didn't flinch or blink at her outlandish statement.

"What about minerals fascinates ye?" he asked.

She shrugged. "They're timeless; they don't change. They can be studied endlessly, as new ideas surface in modern journals. I find myself constantly rethinking how I have categorized them."

He picked up a chunk of sparkling, pink quartz. "I would have thought ye liked rocks because they're sparkly and pretty."

She laughed. "That, too."

Silence hung for a moment. Jane plucked at a lovely piece of red agate.

"The truth is perhaps even simpler. When you can control so very little about your life, you take your victories where you can. Rocks never change. They are always the same. And there is a comfort in knowing that something in this world is ever-constant."

LADY JANE'S WORDS hit Andrew with brutal force.

When you can control so very little about your life . . .

Even the daughter of a duke did not have the power to direct her own destiny.

She flushed and refused to meet his eye, her shoulders tensing for what she was sure would be his teasing reply.

Guilt laced through him. He hated that he had put that unease there.

Even seeing glimpses of Fiery Jane had not prepared him for the revelations of the last hour.

"I don't suppose I have ever thought of minerals as being advocates for constancy, but I suppose that is the case," he said, laying his words carefully, desperate to not upset the tentative truce between them. "So often we define ourselves not as we are, but what we are in relation to something else. So ye are not Lady Jane Everard in her own right. But instead, ye are Lady Jane, sister of His Grace, the Duke of Montacute. Or Lady Jane, step-daughter of the former Earl of Hadley. Everyone wants to define ye in relation tae someone else."

Lady Jane gasped, eyes still downcast. His words had struck true.

Andrew found himself staring at the side of her neck and the fine down hair which curled there, sworls of wispy copper . . . achingly vulnerable.

She abruptly appeared viscerally alone and lonely. A commodity to be purchased or admired or used. But did no one ever see her as a person?

I see you. He longed to say.

Or, perhaps more accurately, *I want to see you. Show me your truest self. Trust me with your inner being.*

But her words from earlier intruded: *Why have you changed?*

How could he expect her to reveal herself when he had kept himself hidden for most of their acquaintanceship?

And yet, he had to ask it: "What is it *you* want, Lady Jane?"

She kept her eyes downcast, his Jane.

And suddenly she was no longer Lady Jane in his eyes. Not Prim Jane nor Fiery Jane.

She was simply Jane.

Plain Jane.

He mentally smiled at the words. There was nothing plain about her. The window light raked her face from left to right, tangling in her hair and highlighting the slash of her aristocratic cheekbones.

She shook her head, the smallest movement. And he hoped that she would give him another truth, another small piece of herself.

But . . .

Noise intruded.

Lady Hadley's voice sounded in the entrance hall, her words drifting through the open library door. Someone answered.

The interruption had nothing to do with them, but Jane reacted nonetheless.

Andrew could practically see her rebuilding mental walls, shutting him out, retreating back inside Prim Jane.

Finally, she lifted her gaze, expression politely restrained.

"I have everything that I want or need," she said. The tightness around her eyes belied her words.

"You know that's not true, Lady Jane. Everyone wants something."

"Not everyone, my lord. My wise nanny once told me that unhappiness can be measured by the distance between reality and our expectations of reality."

Andrew drew in a hissing breath. It was a harsh assessment of life.

Jane's answering wan smile said she understood his reaction for what it was.

"Life is easier when your expectations of others are small," she said. "Particularly when their expectations of you are so very large."

He nearly winced.

Ah, Jane.

It all came together in a blinding flash.

She did not dream because her life was not her own. Her mother and Montacute made decisions for her. They had hopes and prospects for her that were already too ambitious. Suddenly, all the wee comments Lady Hadley had dropped over past weeks came into crystal-clear focus.

Jane mustn't forget her parasol. She freckles far too easily, and no gentleman would wish to marry a freckle-faced lady.

Jane, modulate your tones to be more dulcet. The daughter of a duke should always sound mellifluous. I should hate to bring up that incident with Lord Eastman.

For Jane to add her own desires into the mix . . .

Ah, Jane. Sweet Jane.

You deserve freedom.

Her smile remained strained.

He would get nothing more from her on the topic. Not today.

"Well, tell me about your minerals then, Lady Jane. And do not think ye will pull one over me. I know my agates from my schist. So take that as fair warning."

The tension in Jane's eyes eased and a real grin appeared.

The morning flew by. Jane did not disappoint.

It didn't take more than five minutes for Andrew to realize she had a thorough understanding of mineralogy.

Ten minutes after that, Andrew was learning new things.

Fifteen minutes after that, they were arguing over which was superior—hard rocks (like granite, schist, and gneiss) or soft rocks (like fossils, sandstone, and limestones).

"Soft rocks will always be more interesting," Jane insisted. "They hold endless surprises, like fossils—"

"Och, ye cannot be serious, Lady Jane? A stone's worth doesn't reside in its *interestingness*. It's how a rock can be used that makes it worthwhile. Granite, as a building material, is much hardier than sandstone—"

"Yes, but no one wants to spend hours staring at granite. However, one can study an ammonite fossil for days . . ."

They continued to argue back and forth, moving from stone to stone, Andrew helping to reorder everything.

Hours passed.

Andrew could not remember when he had enjoyed anyone's company quite as much as Lady Jane's. Talking with her was supposed to ease his fascination, not throw whisky on the flames.

The more he spoke with her, the more he understood, the more he wanted to know. He wanted to learn her, bit-by-bit, and be learned and understood in return.

Rafe had been right.

He was utterly smitten.

He was halfway through telling a story of wading a river to collect a lovely piece of gneiss before he realized how much time had passed.

"And there I was, standing in my bare feet, breeches soaking wet, trying tae scramble on my tiptoes to reach the thing," he chuckled.

Jane laughed. A tinkling, fey sound. Her eyes crinkled and her cheeks plumped and Andrew was quite sure he had never seen anything so lovely.

Still smiling, he continued. "I would have been all right, but then a wee sheep startled off the riverbank and plowed into my—"

"Heaven's, Jane. Such a racket you are making," a cool, aristocratic voice cut through the room.

Jane's peal of laughter instantly died.

Andrew turned to see Lady Hadley push through the open door, eyes snapping with displeasure. She surveyed her daughter, lounging on the floor with a Scottish 'rag-mannered idiot,' rocks and stones scattered around them.

Andrew scrambled to his feet and then offered a hand down to Lady Jane, pulling her up beside him.

Lady Hadley observed it all with icy hostility. "I have need of you, Jane," she said, eyes still trained on him.

Jane said nothing. Every last ounce of her vitality drained away, leaving an empty shell of a person behind.

Jane curtsied to him and then brushed past her mother without another word.

Lady Hadley surveyed Andrew from head to foot. Not a word of censure passed her lips, but he felt it all the same.

Bloody English with their bloody aristocratic manners.

He could not let this slide without comment. "I appreciate Lady Jane taking the time tae show me her impressive collection of minerals." He kept his expression mild but something hot roiled in his chest.

Lady Hadley gave the faintest of smiles. "Yes, well, I suppose minerals hold some interest when there is little else to occupy the mind." Her tone dripped censure. "I shall leave you to them, Lord Hadley."

Lady Hadley nodded her head and swept from the room, leaving only a chilling silence behind.

16

Jane knew she was going to get an earful. There was no escaping it.

Being found lounging on the floor (!), laughing loudly (!!), with a man and a low-born Scot at that (!!!). In all honesty, she would be lucky to escape with *only* a scolding.

Would her mother turn her over to Montacute? Had her untamed impulses finally brought about her doom?

How could Jane have forgotten herself so? How could she have behaved so abominably?

Her mother started as soon as Jane reached her bedroom.

"I would have a word, if I may, Jane." Lady Hadley didn't wait for Jane to reply. She simply latched the bedroom door with a loud snick.

Jane turned, throwing her shoulders back, face impassive. Lady Hadley surveyed her, surely noting her wrinkled skirts and slightly untidy hair.

"You are nearly five and twenty, Jane. I cannot believe that we are, yet again, having this conversation. Your behavior with Hadley . . ." Her mother tsked.

Jane knew better than to reply. She clasped her hands in front of her.

She didn't point out that the library door had been open, and she and Hadley had been observing all rules of propriety.

She also didn't reiterate that they were guests in Hadley's house now, not the other way around. So when he invited her to do something, it would be impolite to decline.

Of a surety, Jane didn't say that she found herself thoroughly liking Hadley with his easy-going charm and kind eyes and quick intelligence.

Saying such things would only prolong her chastisement.

Her mother did love her, in her way. Lady Hadley's overarching goal in life was to maintain her social position within society. Staying in Montacute's good graces assured this. Being self-absorbed, Lady Hadley assumed that Jane wished for these things, too, and therefore constantly strove to correct Jane's wayward behavior.

"I do not believe I need to go into the minutiae of why your behavior with Hadley is unseemly," her mother continued. "Yes, Hadley is the *paterfamilias* now, and we must pay him some attention. But to spend time with him in such a state, laughing and carrying on . . ." Her mother shook her head. "Your matrimonial prospects are hardly so dire yet."

Jane's head jolted upward at her mother's words.

Matrimonial prospects? Did her mother honestly put Hadley into that category?

Abruptly, Jane realized she had been striving *not* to see Lord Hadley in such a light.

But as the man was always underfoot and so absurdly attractive . . .

She swallowed.

What *if* she considered him?

A life with Hadley flashed through her mind's eye. Hadley grinning and endlessly teasing, his broad accent loud and unabashed. Hadley laughing with his children, chasing them across the grass. Hadley chucking her under the chin when something went south, telling her to 'not ken' what others might say about her. Hadley leaning down, his blue eyes going unfocused, warm breath brushing her mouth—

Oh!

Was she now truly pondering this?

But . . . why *not* Hadley?

"Why do you discount Hadley as a suitor, Mother?" she had to ask. "If I were to marry him, it would remove us both from Montacute's influence—"

"Oh, Jane." Lady Hadley gave a condescending smile that said Jane, despite her age, knew so little of the world. "Hadley is penniless and so is the estate. He must marry an heiress, which you are, and likely explains his interest in you. He would not be the first lord to assume that your dowry was easy pickings."

Jane flinched at that brisk dowsing of cold reality—

Her mother assumed Hadley was courting her. But only because he needed her dowry. Did that truly explain his behavior then?

Lady Hadley continued to press her point. "It is obvious that Lord Hadley has requested Lord Rafe's assistance to lure you and try to win your dowry. Hadley's change in manners and dress cannot be explained any other way. The man intends to court you in earnest, I suppose."

Did he though? Hadley had all but admitted to Jane earlier that his excessive Scottishness had been an act.

None of us are what we seem, Lady Jane, he had said. *I think ye ken that better than most.*

Where did the truth lie? With Hadley's explanation? Or her mother's?

"Hadley is doomed to fail, of course." Her mother wasn't done speaking. "Montacute will *never* countenance you marrying Hadley. Of that I am sure. Your brother would find Hadley abhorrent and would never accept him as a brother-in-law. And if you marry outside Montacute's wishes, he will not release your dowry, so Hadley's suit is doomed to fail."

Is this truly Hadley's aim? Jane wondered. *Why must I question and challenge every person's motives?*

Her mother folded her hands, eyes serious and pity-laden. "You are young yet, Jane, and understand so little of the world. Hadley might be an earl, but he will never be good *ton*. If and when he is accepted into Lords, you may be sure he will not be well-received by Polite Society. Montacute will likely see to that, if nothing else. You know as well as I that not all aristocrats are created equal. Hadley has little more than his title to recommend him. He is impoverished, ill-mannered, and a Scot, for heaven's sake. He will need to look outside the peerage to find an heiress to repair the family finances. Your task, Jane, is to marry well before Hadley runs out of funds to support us."

Jane pursed her lips. By *us*, her mother meant herself. Jane needed to marry well in order to ensure her mother had supplementary funds to maintain her current lifestyle.

Jane had always known her mother was self-absorbed. But every time she thought that maybe a glimmer of maternal instinct yet survived, her mother disabused her of the notion.

Jane was nothing more than a means to an end.

Her mother was still beautiful, despite her years. Her blond hair curled and tumbled around her face, the bit of gray she did have blending smoothly with the rest, giving her hair an attractive silvery-pale appearance. Would Lady Hadley marry again after she finished her mourning for the old earl, if only to get out from under Hadley's thumb and Montacute's constant demands? And if that were the case, why did Jane need to marry anyway?

"It will be at least another year or two before we must stoop to entertaining men of Hadley's ilk. A sow's ear will never be a silk purse, no matter how much it tries," her mother continued on, repeating her favorite aphorism. "More to the point, Lady Whitcomb has informed me that her cousin, the Marquess of Wanleigh, will be coming for a visit in two weeks' time—"

"The elderly marquess?" Jane scrambled to follow the change in topic. If this were the same marquess she remembered from years ago, the man was sixty-five if he was a day.

Lady Hadley shot her an unamused look. "He is a man of mature age and, I am sure, quite young at heart. His wife of forty years passed away last year, and it is my understanding that Wanleigh is looking to marry again. Moreover, Wanleigh was a good friend to your father, and Montacute has written to inform me that he welcomes Wanleigh's suit."

"Oh, you are considering remarrying then, Mother?"

Lady Hadley's mouth formed into a stern slash, eyes narrowing as she shook her head.

Oh!

Jane's heart plummeted.

Lord Wanleigh?

Courting her?

Oh, good heavens, no!

Her mother continued on, gaze pitiless. "As the Marchioness of Wanleigh, there isn't a drawing room in the British Empire that would be closed to you. It is likely you would be called upon to be a lady-in-waiting to Princess Caroline—"

"Does the princess not currently reside in Italy, Mother?"

"Well, yes, but rumor is flying that she will return this year. King George is not long for this world, and once Prinny takes the crown, England will need her queen. We must ensure that you are in a position to benefit from the transition in monarchs. Marriage to Lord Wanleigh will ensure you a place with the highest ladies in the land."

And give Montacute a stronger toehold into the highest levels of government, her mother didn't need to add.

Jane's stomach hurt.

Wanleigh was old enough to be her grandfather. His letters to Lady Whitcomb—which the lady read aloud with regular zeal—showed the man to be a self-righteous, pompous windbag. Good *ton* or no, all of her shrunk from marrying a man who would simply replace Montacute.

You don't need to do this. You could marry elsewhere at any time, an insidious voice whispered. *You are of age. They cannot dictate your choices.*

Hadley . . .

Hadley was here. And there was definitely an attraction there, at least on her part.

Why *not* Hadley?

Or . . . was she simply grasping at straws at this point?

But . . . Hadley *did* need to marry an heiress. He could not support a wife and family otherwise. And marrying her without Montacute's approval would not only negate her dowry but create a powerful enemy of her brother.

Montacute could be petty when enraged. Jane vividly remembered hearing tale of a baron who had challenged her brother in Lords over a bill. Enraged at the man's temerity, Montacute had ensured that no one in Town would extend the man credit, all but chasing him from London. Time and again, Montacute viciously crushed those who opposed him.

So . . . even if Hadley pursued her in earnest, his suit was doomed from the beginning. And why did that thought make her throat tight and her eyes sting?

"Lady Whitcomb will be holding a ball in a fortnight in honor of her cousin, which of course we will attend. Wanleigh is most eager to meet you," her mother continued. "Until then, I expect that you will maintain propriety with Hadley at all times. We would not wish to give rise to ugly rumors or expectations where he is concerned. I know such behavior has been a struggle for you in the past, but I do not need to remind you of the stakes currently."

Lady Hadley fixed Jane with a stern look. Memories of Lord Eastman swirled between them.

Become a lady . . . no one will want you otherwise.

But what did that thought matter now? Jane *had* become a lady and still no one wanted her. Not without a dowry and political gain attached.

Her mother continued, "We are all counting on you to resist the baser parts of your nature, Jane. I presume you will do the right thing by your family."

Jane managed a polite, murmured response.

Her mother pressed a perfumed hand to Jane's cheek before sweeping from the room, the door snicking shut behind her.

Jane tried to move, but a horrid numbness had taken over her limbs.

She hated this feeling. Of being a shiny guinea that her mother and Montacute were eager to spend for their own gain.

What is it you *want, Lady Jane?* Hadley's words from earlier rose in her mind.

I don't want an arrogant, old man as a husband, was her immediate reply. *I don't want to participate in my family's social-climbing schemes. I want out of this gilded cage.*

Jane remained still, fists tight, nails pressing half-moons, as usual.

But thoughts continued to pound her, unchecked.

What is it you want, Lady Jane?

She clenched her jaw. *I want to rage at the sky. I want to hurl heavy logs and throw myself into wet streams and play pipes loudly on the south lawn.*

English ladies, of course, did not do such things.

Only stupidly-attractive Scottish earls with their swinging kilts and boisterous laughs behaved thus.

How easy for Hadley to ask the question: *What is it you want?*

He didn't have to stifle himself. He hadn't been taught to leash and corral and curse his very nature in order to earn others' love and affection.

Become a lady . . . no one will want you otherwise.

Her chest heaved.

A gasping sob escaped.

None of us are what we seem, Lady Jane. I think ye ken that better than most.

Oh!

Foolish, foolish Jane.

How could she have been so blind?

She saw it. She understood.

What is it you want, Lady Jane?

She knew the answer. It tore loose from the deepest part of her soul, stretching hungrily toward the sky—

I want my wild, free-spirited child to be free.

I want to be the girl I once was at Rosehearth.

17

Jane's personal revelation continued to thrum through her mind over the next several days.

How could she *want* to become that rambunctious girl again? She was half a lifetime older and more mature.

Being that girl had only ever brought her pain.

And yet . . .

The idea would not be quelled.

She thought about it as she stitched embroidery by candlelight after supper.

She pondered it as she took the air in the Italian parterre garden and drove Thunder out to visit tenants.

So . . . what *if* she let more of that girl free?

Jane had always assumed that no one would want her if she didn't maintain strict propriety, that no part of that wild child could remain within her if she wished to be a proper lady.

But as her mother had inadvertently pointed out—no one wanted her anyway.

Not for her true self. Not for Jane.

Of course, all these thoughts led to a difficult question—was it even possible to merge that wild little girl with adult Lady Jane?

She had kept her baser self locked away in a tight prison for so many years. Opening the cell door and flooding the space with light was blinding. All she could do at the moment was shield her eyes and try to accommodate the idea of freedom.

These were the thoughts she determined—

That small girl, the one she had been at Rosehearth, had been happy. She had known true joy.

Most importantly, she had been *loved* . . . by Peter, by her nanny. They had loved her, wild impulses and all. And Jane had openly loved them in return.

Moreover, transforming into excruciatingly proper Lady Jane had not brought her happiness or joy. She had been crushed and contorted into something that felt viscerally unnatural.

And all those gymnastics certainly hadn't opened her heart to love. Nanny Smith had passed away years ago. Peter was still the only person she completely loved and who genuinely loved her.

As for a certain unruly Scotsman . . .

Hadley's presence made it difficult to find clarity, as he was ever present, muddling her thinking with his charm and overly-large personality.

His deep voice carried throughout the house, whether he was laughing with Lord Rafe or simply talking business with the estate steward. The air changed from room-to-room as he walked, as if Nature herself were in his thrall. Jane was quite sure she could chart his course through the house based on the energy field that followed him.

Everyone spoke of him.

The steward enthusiastically described Hadley's plan to modernize the home farm, going on endlessly about the new earl's brilliant understanding of land management. Where the money would come from for such a scheme, Jane did not know, but the enthusiasm was palpable.

The cook kept small canisters of shortbread at the ready, as Hadley had a bit of a sweet tooth.

Even Peter had changed. In a few short days, his tentative friendship with the man had blossomed. Peter followed Hadley around on estate business like an infatuated puppy.

Worse, Jane was worried that she might actually feel a smidgen of jealousy over all the time Peter got to spend with Hadley. The two men forming a friendship felt a little too much like her worlds were colliding and merging into one.

She found herself looking for Hadley. Waiting for him. Missing him when she went half-a-day without seeing him.

It was utterly bizarre. Was this what came of accepting her inner-self more fully? Her baser instincts constantly sought out his?

Two days after her mother's scold, Hadley found her pouring over a book of mineralogy in the library.

Jane's proper conscience instructed her to make a polite excuse and leave the room, to avoid him per her mother's instructions.

Her wild, impulsive inner-child told her to admire the breadth of his shoulders and make a teasing comment about chamomile tea.

Neither suggestion was quite right.

And so, she tried a middle-ground—she asked his opinion on her reading. Which led to questions. Which led to enthusiastically debating with him for several hours.

Jane gave up trying to understand her muddled feelings after that.

Hadley came upon her visiting tenants one afternoon and accompanied her through the rest of her social calls. He was charming to the vicar and laughed at Mrs. Jones' terrible puns. And in between houses, their conversation never flagged. She and Hadley had endless ideas to discuss.

Another day, Hadley insisted she, Lord Rafe, and Peter accompany him to a nearby farm to inspect a pair of horses Hadley was considering purchasing. They dined at an inn, making merry as Rafe and Andrew regaled her and Peter with tales of their university days.

One evening, her mother retired early and the four of them played cards into the morning hours.

So it went, day after day, until Jane was quite sure the Hadley she knew was nothing like the loutish, unmannered Scot her mother and others assumed him to be.

And eventually Jane's emotions settled into a knowing—

She counted Lord Hadley as a friend.

She genuinely liked him. Her feelings were perhaps even more than mere *like*.

He was kind and observant. He listened attentively to her questions and gave an ear to her ideas and explanations. He saw her as an equal intellectually, challenging and meeting her head-on in arguments. He had ceased goading her as he had before—as if challenging her to react—and now met her comments with good-natured teasing and dry wit.

Most importantly, he hadn't balked at her 'vibrant' self. Granted, Jane had only been letting her baser instincts out a little at a time. Of course, Hadley had seen her at her worst in that stream, but what would he think if he knew that raging woman was more genuinely herself than the persona of Lady Jane?

But Lady Whitcomb's approaching ball and confrontation with Lord Wanleigh loomed, weighing heavily on her. As if he could sense Jane's wavering obedience, Montacute's letters came with more regularity. His last had been particularly blunt:

> *Dear sister,*
>
> *I have had a letter from Lord Wanleigh requesting permission to court you. Naturally, knowing Wanleigh to be a gentleman of superior moral character and aristocratic breeding, I strongly commended his suit. I would welcome Wanleigh as my brother. It is my wish that you act with decorum and unselfishly consider your family's needs and reputation. We expect you to make the appropriate decision.*
>
> *Montacute*

The letter was a cold dowsing of reality.

Wanleigh had requested permission to court her before even *meeting* her. Was the man so enthusiastic to have Jane as a bride, he would all but offer for her, sight unseen?

Foreboding skittered down Jane's spine. She struggled to see a way to avoid this situation descending into catastrophe.

No matter how often she found her thoughts winging fancifully to Hadley, the facts still remained unchanged.

She was reliant on Montacute's good graces for her financial support and dowry monies. She needed her brother's approval.

Hadley was bankrupt and required an infusion of cash.

Montacute would never agree to a liaison between herself and Hadley, so if the Scot was courting her for her dowry, he would soon be disappointed.

Dowry aside, even if Hadley was courting her for herself alone, how could he withstand the full force of Montacute's displeasure? Hadley struggled to convince Lords to grant him a simple Writ of Summons. Even if Hadley had ample finances, Montacute would wreak havoc on him politically and socially.

No, anything more than friendship with Hadley was doomed from the outset.

Was this how her life would always be? She would free her inner child only to have Montacute imprison her once more?

Would she ever be able to keep who she had been at Rosehearth?

Or would she become like Lady Macbeth, cursed to madness for trying?

THE MORNING OF Lady Whitcomb's ball dawned with fiery color in the sky. The day promised to be lovely.

Andrew was surprised by how much he anticipated the evening's dancing. He didn't dislike balls, per se, yet he couldn't say he was excessively fond of them, either.

But the thought of dancing with Lady Jane had put a small spring in his step. Spending time with her over the past few weeks had been . . . altering.

Lady Jane had shed her mask of Prim Jane at last. Though Andrew suspected she still kept the more fiery parts of her personality tucked away, Jane had taken to laughing and gently teasing. It was like watching a butterfly emerge from the cocoon, slowly stretching its iridescent wings. Andrew had no doubt that Lady Jane would be incandescent once her wings were fully formed.

Over the past two weeks, he had found himself actively seeking her out, eager to learn her opinion on matters, to listen to the soft lilt of her voice.

Part of him was appalled that he had taken a liking to an aristocratic English lady. He could practically feel all his Scottish ancestors shuddering in horror.

But then he would remember that his emphatically-Scottish mother had fallen in love with his aristocratic, English father.

So Lady Jane happened to be English? He was part English himself. When she allowed her reserve to slip, she was clever and witty and irreverent, and he delighted in talking with her.

That was all that mattered to him.

Andrew's valet was in the middle of tying his neckcloth, dressing for the ball, when Rafe entered the bedchamber. His friend carried a paper-wrapped package in one hand and two letters in the other. Andrew met Rafe's gaze in the reflection of the bedroom mirror. Rafe raised an eyebrow, not needing to say anything to indicate he wished a word in private.

Motioning with his hand, Andrew politely dismissed his valet. The man bowed and left.

Rafe set the parcel and one of the letters on Andrew's bed. He handed the second letter to Andrew and then motioned for Andrew to turn his way, clearly intending to take over the valet's task of knotting Andrew's neckcloth.

Andrew flicked open the wax seal on the letter with his thumb and then obligingly raised his chin, chuckling at the same time.

"You don't have tae help me dress," he said, unfolding the letter and raising it high to read.

"Aye, I do. It's the charitable thing to do."

Andrew finished reading the letter with a grimace. Rafe tugged at his neckcloth.

Andrew sighed. "Och. I'm not that helpless when it comes tae dressing myself. I don't need your charity."

Rafe snorted, his polished accent slipping deeper into his Scottish roots. "I didnae say I was doing it for *yer* sorry self. I was thinking of all those poor saps at the ball tonight, having tae look at your blastit cravat. How the poor, wee things will suffer so needlessly."

"Have off," Andrew shoved him aside and looked at his neckcloth in the bedroom mirror. The thing was tied into a perfect mathematical. "For a lofty, English lord, ye certainly know how tae dress a man."

Rafe shrugged. "I've watched my own valet dress me enough, 'twould be a shame if I hadn't picked up a thing or two." Rafe motioned toward the letter still in Andrew's hand. "Bad news?"

"Just a note from my solicitor in London. The Committee on Privilege have further concerns over the documentation proving my parent's marriage, as my mother's character cannot be fully discerned. They now require a signed affidavit from the local sheriff because, '*Given your family connection to Scottish unpleasantness, we cannot be too careful,*'" he read in a singsong voice. "Bloody English bullies."

"Aye. I would speak with my father about it, but . . ." Rafe's voice drifted off.

His friend didn't have to say more. "I would never ask you to solicit his help on my behalf." Rafe's father would exact stiff payment from his son for such a favor. "The Writ of Summons will sort itself out eventually. I *will* win. Chancery and Lords simply want to make their point first."

Rafe grimaced and then nodded. "Agreed. Besides, there is also this." He plucked the second letter off the counterpane and handed it to Andrew. Andrew glanced at the brief address, instantly noting the familiar handwriting.

Rafe began, "It arrived special delivery less than fifteen minutes ago—"

"—from Kieran," Andrew finished.

"Aye."

Andrew ripped into the letter. Words jumped out at him.

. . . found Madsen . . .

. . . arrested for robbery and theft and sentenced to gaol . . .

. . . hard labor on the prison hulk, Bellerophon, *in the harbor at Sheerness . . .*

. . . in haste to meet there tomorrow afternoon . . .

Andrew let out a long gust of air and then tilted the letter so Rafe could read it.

"We found him," Rafe breathed. "Hallelujah."

"Amen," Andrew agreed, heart racing at the news.

At long last! Justice for Jamie and all the others whose lives were lost due to Madsen's treachery.

And, perhaps, a measure of comfort, an easing of the guilt that plagued them.

Andrew continued, "I don't know if it's good or bad that Madsen has already been tried on separate charges."

"Aye. He's in custody now. Always surrounded by guards."

Andrew nodded. Their grievance with Madsen would likely never be brought before a magistrate, for a number of reasons. And Madsen being in prison meant they couldn't administer their own form of justice.

The searing pain of a cudgel to his jaw, endless floating in a fevered haze.

Hands frantically pulling him into a boat, waves lapping, agony rattling his bones.

Kieran's voice. "Stay with me, Andrew. I willnae let them have ye."

"Aye," Jamie's voice piping in. "I'll butcher the lot of them first—"

Andrew shook off the memory.

Madsen deserved whatever horrors awaited him. Andrew took savage comfort in the fact that prison hulks were miserable places to be incarcerated.

The prison ships were a way for the Crown to alleviate overcrowding in its land-based prisons, like Newgate. Many of the older ships-of-the-line—the enormous flagships of the British Navy—were re-purposed during the final years of their lives and outfitted for use as floating prisons. The ships were then anchored in a harbor, the prisoners being rowed to shore every day to labor repairing dockyards and sea walls.

"We are tae meet Kieran at the harbor in Sheerness tomorrow afternoon," Andrew said. "He's going tae need our help to convince the wardens tae let us speak with Madsen aboard the *Bellerophon*."

Unspoken was the knowledge that a Peer of the Realm and the son of a powerful duke should be able to brazen their way onto the ship.

"That's that, then. We'll depart tomorrow before noon."

"I'll leave letters tae be dispatched to Alex and Ewan at first light, keeping them apprised of the situation. They will want to have their say."

"Aye. But first—" Rafe stepped forward, lifting the parcel off the bed. "—one last item for the ball this evening."

Rafe unwrapped the package, revealing two lengths of Jamie's tartan. Andrew's manager had finished having the fabric woven.

Emotion pricked the back of Andrew's throat. How appropriate for it to arrive on today, of all days. Now that they were closer to reaching answers and (perhaps, maybe) justice for Jamie.

Andrew took hold of the fabric, the lambswool butter-soft in his fingers.

Black for their grief and guilt.

Vibrant red for blood spilled and their anger over being betrayed.

Mossy green and gold yellow emphasizing hope and a wish for growth.

White for the purity of their hearts and intentions.

Jamie would have approved.

Rafe helped Andrew into his superfine clawhammer coat, and then each of them wrapped a length of Jamie's tartan across their bodies, a baldric sash secured with a large brooch.

Andrew studied them side-by-side in his bedroom mirror, their formal aristocratic attire and the traditional, Scottish plaid.

"We'll do, aye?" he said.

Rafe slapped his back. "Aye. That we will."

18

Andrew and Rafe took a separate carriage to Chestlehurst, Lord and Lady Whitcomb's estate. Peter, Lady Hadley, and Lady Jane rode in the family barouche.

Andrew had caught a glimpse of Jane's finery as he helped the ladies into their carriage. Her dress was ice-blue satin with an over-skirt of silver netting which caused the fabric to glimmer and shine with every step. But it was the wan, hesitant smile she gave him as their hands touched that had his eyebrows drawing into a frown.

She had donned the mask of Prim Jane for the evening, every last emotion withdrawn and snuffed out. Why?

He would have expected Jane to be sunnier over the prospect of attending a ball. Even her mother could hardly find fault with Jane having a sparkle in her eye and a spring in her step.

Instead, Jane had the air of one heading toward the guillotine rather than a country party. Even Rafe commented on her low spirits.

Had something gone amiss?

Andrew was pondering this same question an hour later, as they waited in line to greet their hosts. Lady Hadley had insisted Jane take Lord Rafe's arm, before taking Peter's herself, leaving Andrew alone.

Andrew knew it was a cutting breach of etiquette, even if Rafe's surprised eyebrows hadn't communicated as much. As the higher-ranking peer, Andrew should have been escorting Lady Hadley. By refusing his escort, she was loudly proclaiming to her neighbors that she considered Andrew unfit for his station.

Worse, Lady Hadley likely assumed that he was too unaware of the rules of precedence to understand what she had done. Over the past few weeks, she had been circumspect in her criticism of Andrew. Apparently tonight she wished to take a bolder stance.

Andrew drew his lips into a straight line, trying to decide if he cared enough to take her to task over it.

Lord and Lady Whitcomb smiled politely when they finally reached the front of the line.

"Lord Hadley." Lady Whitcomb bobbed an elegant curtsy, her eyes straying to take in the length of tartan wrapped around his chest. "'Tis a pleasure to see you this evening."

Andrew bowed in return. Lady Whitcomb turned to the older gentleman standing at her side.

"Lord Wanleigh, may I present Lord Hadley?" she asked the man.

"Lord Wanleigh," Andrew bowed.

Ah, all the small social rules of the English. He wanted to shake his head.

Lady Whitcomb's manner of introduction meant that Lord Wanleigh must be a marquess, as she had presented Hadley to him, not the other way around. This meant that Wanleigh outranked his own title of earl, and as he hadn't been introduced as a duke . . .

Andrew smiled politely at the man. Wanleigh dripped arrogance and condescension, a visual embodiment of the scorn Andrew had already felt at the hands of the peerage and Parliament. Privilege and wealth clung to him, from the haughty inclination of his head to the glittering rings on his fingers to the gold thread of his waistcoat straining across his rounded belly. Andrew took petty comfort in his balding, gray hair, and obviously powdered head.

But it was Wanleigh's reaction to being introduced to Lady Jane that truly set Andrew's teeth on edge.

"Lady Jane." Wanleigh bowed low over Jane's hand, his eyes lighting with almost lurid interest. "It is a pleasure to make your acquaintance." He pressed a kiss to her hand, a decidedly old-fashioned gesture.

Jane's expression didn't change during the exchange. Her face remained passive; her eyes remote.

Lady Hadley was looking back and forth between her daughter and Wanleigh, as if she had *expectations* in that direction.

Were there expectations there?

The very thought made Andrew's stomach churn.

"May I solicit your hand for the supper waltz, Lady Jane?" Wanleigh asked.

Andrew bristled. The supper waltz was the most prized dance of the evening, as the gentleman then got to accompany the lady into supper and spend even more time at her side.

He had thought to ask Jane to bestow the dance on him.

But if Jane had any similar thoughts, she didn't show them. She briefly met Andrew's gaze with a cool one of her own before turning her head back to Wanleigh.

"It would be an honor, my lord," she said.

Wanleigh smiled wider, his eyes skimming Jane as if assessing a prize filly. Lady Hadley positively beamed with approval.

Andrew walked with Rafe into the main ballroom, his eyes following Jane, who had moved off to greet some friends.

"Surely I misunderstood what just happened in the entrance hall?" Andrew murmured to his friend, voice low.

Rafe took one last look at Jane before shaking his head. "I fear not. Is Wanleigh courting her?"

"I have no idea. I suppose Wanleigh courting her isn't a surprise. Jane is a bonnie lass—"

Rafe raised his eyebrow, a smirk hovering.

Andrew rolled his eyes.

"Regardless of Wanleigh's intentions," he continued, "why would Jane act as if she must entertain his suit?"

Rafe shrugged. "Her family has always made it clear that they expect her to marry well."

"But forcing her tae marry a man old enough tae be her grandfather? And a supercilious windbag, tae boot?"

"You're not wrong about Wanleigh," Rafe snorted. "But he is powerful and well-connected, not to mention wealthy. He's one of the few peers to escape the disastrous Caribbean Affair. If Lady Jane's family brings pressure for her to marry Wanleigh, I'm not sure she will be able to extricate herself."

Rafe's words caused the knot in Andrew's stomach to cinch tighter.

Unfortunately, their fears proved founded as the evening wore on. Wanleigh attached himself to Jane's side, talking at her—not *with* her, that would have required Jane to respond beyond a word or two—and monopolizing her entirely.

Andrew tried to lose himself in dancing with several young women local to the area, but the harder he avoided staring at Jane, the more difficult it became.

Why would Jane not look at him? Why did he feel like she was avoiding him? He had thought they were friends, at the very least, given their interactions over the past two weeks. But Jane's cool distance belied even that.

The supper waltz was particularly troublesome.

Jane twirled with Wanleigh, her face studiously averted. Andrew felt forgotten and abandoned.

For his part, Andrew was partnered with a chatty young miss whose father had earned a knighthood during the Napoleonic conflict. He learned that wee bit between her questions about Scotland and outrageous flirting.

He had never been one to discourage the attentions of a pretty lass.

He might have flirted back.

He also may have laughed heartily.

And, he very possibly may have said, "A man cannae help but appreciate a fresh-faced lass," a little too loudly.

Even Wanleigh turned his head in Andrew's direction at that.

But Jane looked steadfastly away, not acknowledging his existence.

Finally, he could take it no longer.

He approached Jane after supper. She stood primly with her mother on one side, talking with Lord Wanleigh on the other. Or rather still being talked *at* by Wanleigh. Jane's lips weren't moving. Wanleigh scowled as Andrew stopped before them.

Andrew bowed. "Lady Jane, may I solicit the honor of your hand for this next set?"

Wanleigh harrumphed from his position at Jane's elbow.

Jane gave the man a quick glance. Wanleigh pursed his mouth and then gave a subtle nod of his head.

Wait—had the man honestly just given Jane permission to dance?

Jane smiled faintly, not misunderstanding Andrew's abruptly thunderous expression. "I would be honored, Lord Hadley."

HADLEY'S ARM WAS tense under Jane's gloved hand. Despite the multiple layers of fabric between them, Jane could feel the muscles stiff and unyielding underneath.

He was an intelligent man, Jane would give him that. He clearly understood that Lord Wanleigh was a feted suitor for her hand.

His opinion of that fact was also blatantly obvious.

What Jane hadn't expected was the rise of her own temper.

How dare Hadley stomp around as if he had a say in her life! Her decisions were her own. If she wished to marry an elderly lord, well, that was her choice to make.

He wasn't her brother or uncle or guardian.

He had not declared himself to be her suitor.

He was a friend and little more.

They took their places for the next set, arm-in-arm, waiting for their turn to *chassé* down the line.

"Ye seem tae be enjoying yourself tonight, my lady," he began, bite in his tone.

"I am," Jane replied in an equally tense voice.

"Are ye?" Hadley glanced tellingly at Wanleigh staring at them from across the ballroom. "I didnae know ye fancied a man in his dotage."

A shiver of surprise slid down Jane's spine. She suspected that Lord Hadley's accent slipped when he felt strong emotions. Was he truly so upset over Wanleigh? Why did he believe her decisions were any of his concern?

How had they reached this point again? Her . . . the icy princess. Him . . . the oafish buffoon.

"I have not sought your opinion on this matter, my lord," she replied, keeping her tone low and even.

"I'm trying tae be a friend, Lady Jane—"

"A friend would be significantly kinder."

"—and merely pointing out that ye have more options. Yer too spirited a lass tae be hobbled like this—"

"Too spirited?!" Jane managed to hiss the words without breaking the mask of her expression.

The bloody man had no idea precisely *how* spirited she could be.

"Aye," Hadley muttered, "Ye deserve tae be free—"

"Enough. I will not discuss this," Jane replied and then turned away from him, allowing the forms of the reel to move her to another partner.

Hadley did not understand her situation. He claimed friendship, but he didn't know her. Not entirely.

And whose fault is that? A soft voice whispered in her mind.

She ground her teeth.

The remainder of the dance passed in silence, as no other opportunity for private conversation presented itself.

Hadley continued to send pointed glances her way throughout the rest of the evening. Jane hated how attuned her body was to his, that she could feel the weight of his gaze drilling her between the shoulder blades from thirty paces away.

His judgment only underscored her own frustration. She detested feeling helpless. She disliked Wanleigh's possessive glances.

But most of all, she hated that Hadley was right.

She *was* too spirited a lass to be hobbled like this.

But she struggled to see another solution. Throwing her problem at Hadley's feet would do nothing to solve it. He couldn't take on Montacute, and he hadn't the finances to marry her without her dowry.

By the time the carriages rolled to the front of Hadley Park, her nerves were a frayed mess.

It didn't help that Peter had emerged from the gaming room three sheets to the wind. He had sung every verse to 'What Shall We Do with the Drunken Sailor?' at least four times on the drive home.

Jane was quite sure, "*Weigh ho and up she rises*," would linger in her ears for the next week.

Her brother stumbled out of the carriage first, leaning on a footman, regaling him with tales of his evening.

Her mother followed with pursed lips.

Lord Rafe and Hadley greeted them in the entrance hall. Hadley shot her mother a thunderous look, clearly holding Lady Hadley somewhat responsible for the evening's machinations. Her mother, not misreading Hadley's expression, kissed Jane's cheek in the hallway.

"I am utterly shattered," she said, voice prim. "I'm for bed. Goodnight, all." And she made her escape upstairs.

Lord Rafe shook his head and waved goodnight as well, taking the stairs two at a time.

This left Jane with Hadley and a happily humming Peter in the entrance hall.

Jane turned to follow her mother up the stairs, but a firm hand on her elbow held her back.

"Yes, Lord Hadley?" Jane asked, turning back around.

"A word, if I may, Lady Jane." His tone was *not* a question.

His expression all-too-clearly stated what his *word* would be.

Peter relaxed against the wall behind Hadley, singing softly, "*What shall we do with a drunken sailor eeeeearly in the mornin'.*"

Lovely.

She did not want to have this conversation at the moment.

Or, really . . . ever.

"I have nothing to say to you," she said, tugging her arm free and turning again for the stairs.

"Ye need to discuss this," he hissed. "You're more than this reserved person. Ye have fire in you, Jane. It's your future you're throwing away."

That got her attention.

Reserved person?

Fire?

Hadley wanted fire?

Oh, she was ready to give him that. Would that send him running for the hills? Would he abandon her like others had? Finally scorn her for simply being her truest self?

Turning around, Jane stomped back to Hadley.

She did what she had longed to do for hours now: planted her hands on her hips, tapped her foot, and prepared to give him the set-down of the century.

"*Chuck him in the long-boat 'til he's shhhhhober . . .*" Peter sang.

"How dare you question me! My future." She tapped her breastbone. "*Mine.* You"—she jabbed a finger into his irritatingly attractive chest— "do not get any say in that."

He folded his arms, causing his biceps to bulge in his tight-fitting coat. Highlighting the perfection of said attractive chest.

Grrrrr. Annoying man to use his absurd handsomeness against her.

"*Heigh hoooo and up shhhe rises.*"

Hadley growled, leaning toward her. "You're my friend, Jane—"

"Lady Jane to you!"

"—and I worry that you keep yourself too tightly wound. You're a wee bit English sometimes."

"I *am* English," she ground out between clenched teeth. "And it's better to be English than a free-mannered Scot with all your 'dinnaes' and *passion pleats* and boisterous laughter."

Naturally, Hadley proved her point by laughing. If she intended to insult him, she should have known better.

Peter instantly joined in, braying like a donkey.

Hadley glanced at Peter and then turned back to Jane. "I think ye could do with some boisterous laughter yourself."

"Oh!"

"When was the last time ye lived a little?"

"Are you truly *daring* me?!"

"Aye! I am! Commandeer your life! What do you wish tae do right now? If ye could do anything?"

Well, what she wished was for Montacute and Wanleigh to simply disappear. Leave her to find her own way—maybe with Hadley, maybe without—but since *none* of those things were a possibility . . .

Peter devolved into giggling. Jane looked at her blissfully swaying brother.

She brought her gaze back to Hadley.

Hah!

Foolish man.

He wanted to see her wild inner child? Truly?

Well . . . she had no problem calling his bluff—

"I want some whisky."

19

Are ye sure this is a good idea?" Hadley asked, expression hesitant. He had stalled in the drawing room doorway.

Jane shrugged, continuing to remove her evening gloves. She set them on the sideboard before moving to pour a finger of whisky into a tumbler.

Something had irrevocably broken loose inside her—that wild girl escaping her cage. To find sunlight, to revel in the fresh air on her face, to breath in deep gulps of *life*.

Anything to banish the chilly numbness she felt in Wanleigh's presence.

"Afraid?" she asked over her shoulder, hefty contempt in her voice. "You literally just ordered me to, 'Commandeer my life.' It was practically a battle cry of *carpe diem* . . . seize the day! Were you lying?"

Peter hummed to one side, slumping onto the sofa. He had happily followed them into the drawing room. Jane hadn't discouraged his presence, as someone needed to act as chaperone at this late hour.

A drunken brother was better than nothing.

Hadley continued to eye her uneasily.

Hah! Had she known it would be so easy to best him, she would have done this ages ago.

Scots were funny creatures, Jane decided.

Mock them and they laughed back at you.

But should a lady *join* them in their riotous behavior, they suddenly became squeamish.

Part of her gloated in triumph.

The other part depressingly observed that even Hadley found her wild self repulsive when loosed completely.

Well, she *had* intended to call his bluff. Better to learn his true feelings now.

Raising her eyebrow in challenge, she pulled out a second glass and poured another finger of scotch. She picked up both glasses, holding one out toward Hadley.

A blatant dare.

Meeting her gaze full on, Hadley stepped entirely into the room and crossed to her.

"I cannot think this wise, Lady Jane." He took the glass from her.

"Because I'm a lady?"

He snorted. "I have no problem with ye wishing a wee dram." He sipped his whisky.

"Then why?" Jane pushed him. She would force him to say the words, to criticize her behavior.

He pursed his mouth before replying, "Ye always think of others and their expectations before yourself."

Jane stilled, thoughts freezing. *Not* the response she had been expecting.

Moreover, she did not follow his logic.

He leaned down, bringing his face closer to hers. "I'm just wanting tae make sure this is what ye truly want, that's all." Concern laced his voice.

Tears pricked Jane's eyes. Why could she handle scorn and indifference, but a kind tone and caring consideration undid her?

More to the point, he did not find her behavior repulsive, after all.

"This is what I want," she replied softly. "I know I haven't mentioned this but . . . I quite like scotch."

Hadley blinked . . . and then nodded very slowly, taking a step back. He swallowed. "I wasnae expecting that answer."

Jane shrugged. "Peter and I found the old earl's stash of scotch—"

"Whisky," he said on a sigh. "How many times must I tell ye, it's *whisky*."

"*Scotch*." Jane leaned on the word a little. "The old earl had forgotten several crates of the stuff in the cellars of Rosehearth. Peter and I would sneak a bottle occasionally."

"That's a right terrible thing for a wee bairn tae do."

He wasn't wrong.

But her past was her past.

Jane shrugged and then took a sip of her whisky before motioning for them to sit in a pair of chairs before the fire. A cheery blaze had been set in the hearth and crackled merrily.

Before he sat, Hadley loosened his cravat and removed his tailcoat and then re-wrapped that same length of tartan back around his chest. The bright red bands stood out in the dark fabric, looking nearly like bloodied slashes in the dim light. Why had he bothered to put it back on? Could he not set aside his blatant Scottishness for even one evening?

Worse, the fabric only heightened the broad strength of his chest and biceps. In his shirtsleeves and waistcoat, Hadley fairly thrummed with vitality.

She clenched her fist, pressing her nails into her palm. The move so instinctive she hardly registered doing it anymore.

With a resigned sigh, he settled into his chair, a foot propped across the opposite knee.

"What shall we drink tae, then?" he asked, tilting his glass slightly in her direction.

Jane raised her eyebrows as the clock in the corner chimed midnight.

"What about until two in the morning?" she replied, giving him an arch grin before taking a healthy swallow of her drink. The fiery liquid burned going down, spreading a lovely warmth through her bones. Jane kicked off her slippers and tucked her feet underneath her.

He shook his head. "I won't be responsible when ye find yourself sloshed."

Jane snorted.

"I'm right serious. Whisky is not tae be trifled with, Jane."

"Well, Andrewwww—" Jane drew out his Christian name, landing hard on the 'd' and stretching the rest. "—I cannot imagine why you think I should be your responsibility."

She tossed back the rest of her tumbler, raising her eyebrows at Hadley. A direct, taunting dare.

He had dragged her wild self out of the prison; he could deal with the consequences.

Shaking his head, Hadley downed the rest of his glass.

Smirking, Jane reached for the decanter and poured herself two fingers.

"Whoa there." Hadley reached for her glass. "We don't want you to end up like Peter." He nodded his head toward Peter, already snoring on the sofa across the room.

"Bah! I'm no lightweight," she scoffed, holding her tumbler away from him. "Peter never could hold his liquor. It drove the old earl quite mad and embarrasses our mother. I, on the other hand, am made of sterner stuff. I promise I will drink your bloody arse under the table."

Hadley huffed, a smile lurking, before he shook his head, clearly skeptical.

But he did pour himself two fingers of whisky.

Jane stared at his hand as it moved, the tendons flexing and rippling just below the skin.

It was just like him. So much mystery hiding underneath a thin veneer.

"You were supposed to be an uncouth Highlander, but you are not."

If he found her *non sequitur* bewildering, he didn't show it. As usual, he effortlessly pivoted with her change in thought.

"Sorry tae disappoint." He sat back.

"You're every bit the proper gentleman, despite the tartan and accent."

"My ma would be right glad tae hear it, but—"

"No . . . don't you dare say,"—Jane adopted her best Scottish brogue—"Och, I thought ye were supposed tae be a lady, and yet . . . "

Hadley smirked and raised his glass to her.

Jane stuck out her tongue.

Hmmm, the whisky *was* strong.

Hadley wisely chose not to respond to her comment about being a lady. She couldn't fault his intelligence.

"I'm nae actually a Highlander at all," he offered.

"You're not?" Jane felt her outrage rising.

"I'm a Fifer."

"A *Fifer?*"

"It means I was born in the county of the Kingdom of Fife."

Jane's brows drew down in confusion. It was far too late in the evening—or was it too early in the morning?—to be contemplating geography.

"Fife is right above Edinburgh." He raised his hand above his head, as if that small visual would help. "Just across the Firth of Forth."

Again, not particularly helpful.

Jane shook her head. *Focus.*

"If you are not a proper Highlander, then what has been the point of all the kilt swishing and haggis stabbing?"

"Hah!" He wagged a finger at her, accent sliding. "I kent ye were looking at ma kilt swish. The lassies cannae help themselves."

"Andrew!"

"Jane!"

"Why do you wear the tartan?" She waved a hand at the fabric still wrapped around his torso.

He followed the motion, head bending down to study the fabric.

"This tartan?" He plucked at it with his free hand. "This tartan is for Jamie."

Jane blinked. Jamie?

"Who is Jamie?"

"*Was*," Hadley corrected her. "Who *was* Jamie."

A beat of silence.

"Who was Jamie?" she repeated, voice quiet.

Hadley sighed, slouching further into his chair. He sipped his whisky, gaze far away.

"'Tis a long tale," he began.

"Pfft." Jane waved a hand, enjoying the warmth now singing through her blood. "We literally have all night. Carry on. I wish to hear the tale of Jamie's tartan."

Hadley smiled at her words. The smile did not, however, touch his eyes. Those remained bleak.

He set down his tumbler and scrubbed his hands through his hair, turning it from fashionably tousled to early-morning scarecrow.

"Who was Jamie then? A brother?" she prompted. Of a surety, this Jamie was someone he had cared about.

Hadley shrugged and then nodded. "Of a sort. Much of the story isnae mine to tell, but I'll give ye the main gist. It all began four years ago." He stared into the fire. "Rafe and I decided that we would like to fund a scientific exploration to the South Pacific."

Shock jolted Jane. "A scientific expedition? Like the one of the HMS *Discovery*?"

"Yes, though obviously on a smaller scale. Ours would be a privately funded endeavor, not one sponsored by the crown, as the *Discovery* was."

Jane shook her head. "What an incredible ambition. What stopped you from completing the journey?"

"Who said we didn't?" Hadley shot her a grim look.

"But . . ." Jane blinked, shaking her head again. "Surely I would have heard about such an expedition. One doesn't conduct an ambitious survey of plants and minerals without publishing something about the journey. It's implausible."

Though, the more she thought about it, the more she remembered someone telling her that Lord Rafe had been away collecting botany samples. She had assumed that meant he was traveling through the

Highlands of Scotland or perhaps the Alps, not scouring tropical islands in the Pacific.

"We completed the journey, but nothing has ever been published about it. Allow me tae finish the story."

"Please." Jane breathlessly wanted to hear more.

"Rafe and I set out tae organize our expedition. I had, at the time, a business partner, Thomas Madsen." Hadley nearly spat the man's name. "We joined together with a consortium of investors tae purchase a ship called *The Minerva*. Madsen, in particular, had deep pockets and agreed tae help us fund the expedition. Madsen, with the approval of all the investors, hired a man, Captain Martin Cuthie and crew. The investors and myself all agreed that tae offset the cost of the trip, we would transport supplies tae Australia and then take on cargo in Sydney. I signed a contract agreeing to these terms.

"Everything seemed heaven-sent at that point. Kieran was hired tae be our ship's master and navigator. Dr. Alexander Whitaker was taken on as our ship's physician and botanist. Ewan Campbell was hired as a ship's artist tae sketch animals and plants. We set out from Greenock, outside Glasgow, laden with provisions and stoked on excitement. All went well for the first nine months of our journey. Captain Cuthie was an odd man, prickly and quick tae anger. But his men served him with unswerving loyalty, and he was competent as a captain.

"We came into port in Portugal, in west Africa, in south Africa. Along the way, we made better acquaintance with the ship's crew. Jamie Fyffe was the carpenter's mate and hailed from a family Kieran knew. In fact, Jamie's father, Charles Fyffe, had been Kieran's mentor for a number of years. Kieran had hired the youth as a favor tae the family. That said, Jamie had a passionate zest for life. Always quick with a smile and a laugh, not tae mention unfailingly kind. Kieran, in particular, felt an enormous sense of responsibility for Jamie. I think Kieran considered himself an older brother of sorts."

Hadley seemed to get lost in memory, his voice fading off.

The fire popped and a log slumped in the grate. Reaching for the fire poker, Hadley leaned forward in his seat, moving the coals around, prompting them to catch flame again.

He sat back and took another sip of whisky before shaking his head. "Where was I?"

"Jamie. The trip to Sydney." Jane supplied.

"Yes. Jamie. As I said, all was well until after Sydney. Based on Madsen's words before we left, I had assumed we would be taking on cargo in Sydney. We had carried down supplies for the colony, so it made sense that we would pick up some other export tae take home.

"But Captain Cuthie said his orders were to take on timber in the New Hebrides, northeast of Australia. Sandalwood had recently been discovered on the islands, he said, and Madsen had requested he fill the hold with the wood." Hadley's words dripped bitterness. "So off we sailed from Sydney, northeast tae the New Hebrides. That's when we learned the true nature of Captain Cuthie and his crew.

"We set anchor in the harbor of one of the islands. A small village ringed the beach there, and the natives greeted us kindly but warily. Rafe and I spent a week surveying the island, gathering plants and minerals. Several of the village lads joined in until it seemed the entire population was helping, bringing us interesting insects and plants. It was absolute paradise. "I had thought that the captain and his crew were negotiating the sale of sandalwood from the villagers, but I was in for a rude shock. The night before we were tae set sail, Captain Cuthie informed me that his men would be bringing some of the villagers aboard the ship the following morning. His orders from Madsen were to—" Hadley choked, as if the words were difficult to get out. "—his orders were to take seventy-five of the healthiest villagers as slaves."

Horror shattered Jane's calm.

"Pardon?!" She sat higher in her chair.

Hadley downed the last of his whisky in one gulp. "I cannae believe it still. Slaves. Those poor villagers."

"But . . . but slavery is illegal. The international transportation of slaves, in particular, is illegal."

"Aye. But the practice continues, as we well know. British law applies to the Atlantic slave trade from Africa, but it says nothing about slaves from other parts of the world, as Madsen and Captain Cuthie well knew.

And slavery may be illegal in Britain itself, but it is still legal in many parts of the British Empire. So, Madsen had instructed Cuthie tae capture the natives from some island in the Pacific and sell them into slavery on our way back to Britain."

Jane pressed a hand to her chest. Her heart *hurt* at the thought.

"That is so terrible. I can scarcely imagine the horror."

"Neither could I. Neither could Rafe. None of us could."

"What did you do?"

"The only thing a truly Christian person could do—we refused tae go along with the plan. Cuthie raged at me, stating I had signed the agreement with Madsen and the other investors, and I needed tae hold to my end of the bargain. Naturally, I countered that slavery was illegal, and I most certainly would not keep a contract that had been presented tae me in false terms. But Cuthie insisted that the New Hebrides was outside English law and slavery most certainly wasn't illegal in the Pacific. As if *legality* were the only problem with the entire idea." Hadley swiped a shaking hand over his face. "It renders me nauseous even now."

"As it would for any decent soul."

"Exactly. We argued and argued and eventually, Cuthie had Rafe and myself taken up in chains and beaten."

"Oh!" Jane gasped. She saw Rafe's white scar in her mind's eye. Was that how he got it?

"I am not sure of the rest of the details, tae be entirely honest. I think Cuthie thought he had killed me, I was so near tae death. But as I understand it, my friends put up a fight and rescued Rafe and myself. I remember someone pulling me into a boat and the lapping waves. I remember Jamie's voice calling encouragement and being pushed up a hill, stumbling in the dark. But much of the night I alternated between delirium and unconsciousness. My most lucid memory is a single scene. Me, lying on the headland overlooking the harbor. The village, in flames. *The Minerva,* under full sail, cruising out of the harbor, leaving Rafe, Kieran, Alex, Ewan, and me behind."

He paused, eyes going unfocused, thoughts far away. Lost in the horror of memory.

Finally, he stirred.

"I only learned later everything that had happened that night. Despite the fire, the villagers were safe, more or less. Kieran and Jamie had warned them in time," he murmured. "But in the process, Captain Cuthie captured Kieran and Jamie and had them chained in the hold of the ship. I believe Cuthie's intention was tae force Kieran to navigate the ship out of the treacherous waters of the South Pacific, using Jamie's safety as motivation. Cuthie didn't know enough himself tae steer the ship through all the hazards.

"But Jamie picked the lock on Kieran's chains, and Kieran was then able to free them both. The problem was getting off the ship. They fought their way tae the top deck. Their plan was tae jump overboard and swim for shore. But at the last second, Kieran was apprehended by the first mate while protecting Jamie. Jamie stabbed the first mate and pushed Kieran overboard, out of harm's way."

Silence descended.

The fire popped into the quiet.

"What happened to Jamie?" She had to ask it.

"I don't kno—" Hadley's voice broke at the end. He swallowed once . . . twice . . . and then continued. "I don't know. Jamie . . . remained on the ship. Without our protection. Without us. Worse, Jamie was guilty of stabbing a crew member and disobeying the captain, both hangable offenses.

"Kieran knew all this, but he was injured and couldn't overpower the entire crew himself. So he swam for shore, rushing to recruit Alex, Ewan, and some villagers tae help rescue Jamie. But the ship sailed before they could return, marooning us five on the island."

He ran a shaking hand over his face. "I was near death for weeks, a fever having set in after my beating. Just as I was slowly mending, a Portuguese whaling ship anchored in the village harbor. They told tale of sailing through the remains of a merchant ship, dashed tae pieces on a hidden reef in the open ocean, bodies floating in the wreckage. The launch skiffs were bobbing and empty. They found no survivors, but they did find a piece of wood with the letters 'ERVA' on it."

"*The Minerva?*"

"Aye."

"And Jamie?"

Hadley shook his head. "There was no way Jamie could have survived it. So many innocent lives lost. But Jamie . . . to die such a death, after sacrificing—" Hadley swallowed again, sucking in a deep breath. "The guilt and grief of it shook us all. But Kieran . . . Kieran was almost incapacitated by it. The pain—"

"Master MacTavish shouldn't blame himself. None of you should," Jane interrupted. "The situation was intolerable. You all did the best you could, given the circumstances."

"Aye, but Jamie's death still hurts. It's an open wound that never heals. I feel as if I have blood on my own hands. The guilt haunts me. And so, we have this tartan." He tugged at the sash. "Black for grief, red for our guilt and the innocent blood spilled, green for hope—"

"—white for the purity of your hearts," she finished.

"Perhaps," he snorted. "Or maybe it's the hope of forgiveness."

"What did you do when you returned home? Surely Madsen must have been brought to justice for what he had done? Ordering Captain Cuthie to take on slaves must have consequences, right?"

"Mayhap, but we need tae find Madsen afore any justice can be meted out."

"*Find* Madsen?"

"Aye. Word must have reached him that his plans had gone awry. He had disappeared by the time we arrived back in Edinburgh. He had an enormous head start, of that I am sure—"

"Running is the surest sign of a guilty conscience, I think."

"I could not agree more. But I had a letter from Kieran today. He believes he finally found Madsen."

"Truly?"

"Aye. Rafe and I are headed for Sheerness tomorrow. We hope tae find Madsen there."

"I pray you find him." Jane spoke with dramatic fervor, her words ringing with outrage. "I hope you make him pay for his actions."

"Bloodthirsty," Hadley winked. "I like that in a lass."

Jane froze, momentarily taken aback. And then she grinned.

He smiled in return, reaching for the decanter. He poured himself another finger of whisky. Jane held out her empty glass. Raising his eyebrows, Hadley obliged and poured her a shot.

His story had been illuminating, in many ways. Perhaps more than he intended.

"So . . . you never answered my question from earlier," she said, "about your haggis-stabbing, kilt swishing behavior."

"I didn't?"

"No, you did not—why do you sometimes play the unmannered Scot when you are clearly a gentleman?"

His eyebrows shot up. She had struck true.

She replied to his unasked question. "I've long sensed that it was an act."

"You have?"

"Ayyyyye." She drew out the word, giving it a strongly Scottish flare.

He sipped his whisky, gaze pensive. Would he answer her?

Firelight skimmed his face, catching the golden highlights in his sandy hair and dancing along the hard planes of his face. Evening whiskers stubbled his chin. He was askew and rumpled, and she found him nearly unbearably handsome.

Finally, he grimaced. "I ken that being Scottish comes with a whole host of preconceptions, and I even admit that I fit those notions in many ways. But I am still a person, unique and individual. However, sometimes others don't want the individual." He leaned forward, elbows on his knees, the tumbler held between his hands. "Often, it is easier tae meet someone's low expectations than tae change their prejudiced assumptions."

His voice hovered in the dark night, silken and knowing.

It is easier tae meet someone's low expectations than tae change their prejudiced assumptions.

Jane's throat tightened. His words . . . it was like hearing her soul made physical.

For the thousandth time, she pondered on the irony of *this* man being the one to inspire such kinship. They should be utterly opposite in every way. And yet . . .

He saw.

He understood.

He *knew*.

"An individual is a mess of contradictions that requires subtlety and observation to understand," she nearly whispered. "A caricature is easier to mentally assimilate."

"Aye."

He lifted his head. Their eyes tangled, entwining. That feeling rose again, fluttery and fluffing outward, choking in its force.

Jane bit her lip and blinked back the swelling emotion, swallowing hard.

His gaze softened, as if he too recognized her.

"I propose a toast." Hadley held his glass aloft. "Tae life. And, more importantly, tae choosing our own path through it."

Trust Hadley to go straight to the heart of the matter.

Could she turn away from her Fate and choose her own path?

Jane said nothing, but she did lift her glass and sip.

I am still a person, unique and individual.

She pressed her fingernails into her palm, marveling at the half-moon shape.

She could feel Hadley's eyes studying her.

Still seeing too much, blast him.

Seeing more than an aristocratic lady in an expensive dress—a pretty bauble to be purchased . . . both the dress and the woman.

He was so unlike Wanleigh, who had stared at her as if she were his property for the taking. As if he already owned her.

"I am not a possession," she said aloud, whisky readily knocking thoughts loose.

She pressed her nails again. Always a half-moon they made, never a full one. And even at that, it was only an imprint. She could only imitate a tiny sliver of heaven, forever relegated to imagining the moon but never able to hold it. Most certainly never achieving the entire thing.

Hadley grunted, settling further into his chair, mumbling something.

Jane paused. Surely he hadn't just said, *I wouldnae mind being your possession.*

She met his gaze, his eyes dark and heated.

Oh my.

Perhaps he had.

20

Andrew didn't mean to tell Jane quite so much about his trip to the South Pacific. But as he took another sip of whisky, he understood why. The quiet of the evening, the popping fire, the smoky alcohol warming his blood, the intensity of her gray eyes, even now, seated across from him . . .

It all simply slipped out.

Fire scorching the ground.

The searing pain of a cudgel to his jaw.

Kieran screaming into the night, fist shaking at the moonlit sails on the ocean. "Ye'll not get away with this. I'll hunt ye tae the ends of the earth, Cuthie!"

They hadn't needed to wait long for the Captain to be brought to justice.

As for the other men involved in financing the journey . . .

Madsen had set it all in motion.

The other investors hadn't known of the arrangement with Cuthie and were, to a man, appalled.

Andrew had bought them all out just the same.

Just Madsen remained.

For the thousandth time, Andrew wondered why Madsen had done it. He had considered Madsen a friend. The man knew Andrew's feelings on slavery. He knew that Andrew and the others would fight tooth-and-nail to prevent innocent villagers from being taken against their will.

Why give Captain Cuthie a task that would surely end in bloodshed?

Madsen had nothing to gain from it. The money involved with transporting slaves was not enough to justify the risk.

It made no sense.

Andrew shook his head.

They would have answers soon enough.

But for the here and now . . .

I am not a possession, she had said.

He may have muttered something about her possessing him.

He surveyed his tumbler. Whisky was dangerous. It had a frustrating tendency to jostle things loose, like top hats or hairpins or truths.

"I dislike feeling like a possession." She didn't raise her head to meet his eyes. "But everyone perceives me to be a commodity. A thing to be bought and sold."

Jane was digging her fingernails into her palm. He had noticed the habit before. Anytime a conversation became tense or difficult, she clenched her fists too tight.

She was doing it now.

"I dinnae think of ye as a commodity," he said, his voice taking on a husky edge. As usual, his Scottishness became more apparent the more he drank.

She downed a healthy swallow of whisky in one hand and methodically pressed her nails into her palm with the other.

The lass could hold her drink, he would give her that. Better than her brother snoring in the corner.

Andrew paused, wondering if he should take her thought further.

He threw caution to the wind.

She had called him on his pretenses; now, he returned the favor.

"You're a brave lass who hides her fire behind a shield of decorum."

Jane's head snapped upright, a low hiss escaping her.

He had struck dead true.

"Why do ye do it?" He pressed further.

Silence.

If she weren't so ladylike, she would be squirming, he was sure of it.

And yet, she did not reply.

Andrew tried a different question. "Why let your mother dictate who your suitors are? Ye be old enough tae no' need their approval."

She pressed her fingers again. Andrew longed to snatch her hand back, to sooth the agitation that caused her to clench her fists so hard.

Finally, she said, "I know I don't need her approval. It is Montacute who controls my movements."

"Montacute? Yer half-brother?" Andrew frowned, his whisky-addled wits trying to catch up. "But ye are well of age. Montacute cannae control where ye marry."

"No, he cannot. I am my own woman, in that regard. But Montacute holds my purse strings. If I disobey him, I lose my allowance. If I marry outside of his wishes, I do not receive my dowry. I would find myself cut off, both financially and socially." She paused briefly, as if this information were important somehow. "My mother had no marriage settlement with my father—as he married her for her beauty, not her money and connections—and my father tied my dowry and allowance to my brother's approval."

Again, she seemed to think this knowledge would be of significance to him, beyond simply answering his question.

"Of course," he replied, trying to puzzle out her tone. "It's a wise way tae prevent fortune-hunters."

"Precisely. If I marry without Montacute's blessing, I receive nothing from my late father's estate. He keeps me on a short tether. Without his support, I have no real options. Few men have the ready cash to marry a woman who brings no money and the censure of a powerful duke to their union."

Her tone still confused him. "And why should ye care about that?

Not every man needs tae marry an heiress."

Jane lifted a skeptical eyebrow, as if she found him adorable in his confusion. "You do realize that is somewhat hypocritical, correct? Everyone says *you* need to marry an heiress."

Andrew paused. Was that the cause of her tone then?

He supposed he understood why people would think that. Very few knew that Andrew Langston, Earl of Hadley, and Andrew Mackenzie, wealthy Scottish Vulcan, were the same man.

A gentleman shouldn't boast about his wealth—and Andrew had no intention of doing so—but Jane needed to know that a gentleman *could* pursue her for herself alone.

I wouldnae mind being your possession.

He settled for saying, "I don't need tae marry an heiress. The gossips have it wrong."

She frowned, clearly not believing him. "So all those men who arrived with Lord Rafe—the clerks and valet and such—those are your men? Not his?"

"Aye. Those are my own people. That's the absolute truth, Jane," he continued in the face of her skepticism. "There are many gentlemen who dinnae need a wealthy wife. So ye marry without Montacute's consent and a few sticklers give ye the cold shoulder at a ball—"

"It's more than that." Jane squirmed in her chair. "Montacute is one of the most powerful lords in Parliament. If my half-brother chose, he could ensure that my husband was thoroughly black-balled. No one would extend us credit. If my husband had a seat in the House of Lords, no one would support his bills. My children would be denied entrance to Eton and Cambridge. The list goes on and on. Montacute is just spiteful enough to ensure that I become a pariah. If I cannot be a jewel in his crown, then I must be cast out altogether. There is no in-between."

"And ye truly believe that Montacute would be so dastardly? He's your brother. Why disgrace his own sister? It seems like a mountain of effort, tae be honest."

Jane laughed. It was *not* an amused sound. "You clearly do not know Montacute. He would control heaven and earth itself, if he could. If I misstep in any way, he will cut me off. And we all know that a lady without funds and connections, no matter how highly-born, has very few options."

"I know yer mother's finances are tight, but surely there would be a relative who would take ye in—"

"And incur Montacute's wrath? Never." She gave that same bitter laugh again. "Despite the apparent privilege of my life, I am caught in a cage I cannot escape."

Andrew allowed her words to sink deep.

I am caught in a cage I cannot escape.

How could she be the daughter of a duke and still have so few choices over her life?

And yet . . .

The evidence was copious.

Andrew was slow to anger. Anyone who knew him would describe him as level-headed and fair-minded.

But . . .

How could Jane's brother be so callous of her feelings? How could he consider his reputation more important than his sister's lifelong happiness?

The cruel selfishness of it boggled his mind.

"Your life is worth more than bowing to Montacute's wishes," he finally said. "You shouldn't have tae marry a man like Wanleigh unless you wish it."

He couldn't see her eyes, but the slight flinch of her shoulders told him his words had struck true. Her hand clenched again.

"I know," she whispered, "and, yet, there are few options available to me."

"You've never longed for a man who did not suit then?"

"No. I've been an obedient daughter, for all the good it has done me." She gave a bitter laugh. "Here I am. Nearly twenty-five years of age, sipping whisky into the night, and complaining of my bitter loneliness."

He smiled. "I can drink to that. I'm quite sure it was what whisky was made for."

He saluted her with his glass. She managed a wan smile back.

Andrew's heart gave a lurching thump.

How could Montacute and her mother squelch Jane's light like this? She should be blazing through the sky, illuminating them all with her vivacity.

Abruptly, he desperately wanted that for her.

No. That wasn't quite right.

The weeks of watching her, trading barbs and witticisms, learning and knowing, the endless pull of her beauty . . .

Ah.

He was such an eejit.

I wouldnae mind being your possession.

He had meant every word of that.

Jane.

His Jane.

She wrapped her arms around her waist, staring into the fire. How had he ever thought her arrogant? She was kindness and light. The goodness in her only matched by the steel of her resolve. Here was a woman who would take on the world for a cause she believed in.

How *dare* Montacute render her helpless.

He wanted to trounce something or chop wood to exhaustion or knock some sense into a specific haughty English duke.

Maybe this was why his Scottish forebears chose to toss heavy stones and logs around. With no English around to pummel, they resorted to whatever they had on hand.

He would take on Hell itself for her, he realized. An arrogant, English duke would be child's play.

She fascinates you as no other woman ever has. You should marry her. The thought drifted through his head before he consciously thought it. He *did* crave her warm eyes and fiery spirit and sparkling intelligence.

Yet . . . admiring a woman was not the same thing as deep love. He wasn't quite sure he was ready to commit his life to hers.

But . . .

The thought would not be silenced either. The potential was there. He could no longer deny it. He could feel the emotion lurking in his soul, waiting to sweep his heart utterly away.

She clenched that fist again.

Abruptly, the distance between them felt intolerable.

"Here now." He set his tumbler down and moved across to her, the motion as natural as breathing.

Her eyes met his, gaze confused.

He hooked a footstool with his foot and dragged it in front of her chair, sitting himself down. Tugging the glass out of her hand, he set it on the small table beside them. His knees brushed against her skirts and legs tucked on the chair. Leaning forward, he took her clenched fist in both his hands.

The silky warmth of her skin burned his fingers, shooting darts up his arm.

She gasped at his touch, her body going impossibly still, as if those same darts had extended to her, too.

Gently, he coaxed her fingers to relax, rubbing his thumbs along the base of her palms.

Her fingers unfurled to reveal the arching imprint of her nails in her skin, just as he suspected.

"Och, ye shouldnae do this," he whispered, leaning forward. "Ye hurt yer fine skin."

He brushed a thumb across her palm.

She shivered in response.

Again, the motion sent a cascade of silvery chills chasing up his own arm. As if they were now bound by a single energy, arcing and sparking between them.

His heart raced.

"I can't help it," she murmured, her head bending down to his, her lips practically in his ear. The brush of her breath and subtle smell of violets swirled around him, a dizzying punch to his senses. "The pain distracts me from saying things I shouldn't."

"But ye dinnae need tae do it with me. What cannae ye tell me?"

She shook her head, ignoring his question. Instead, she lowered her head further, staring at her hand with him.

"I can never get a full moon, do you see?" She pointed to her skin. "Only half-moons. Tiny slices of heaven."

"Slices of heaven?"

"Yes. Just pieces of acceptance, bits of happiness. But ofttimes I feel greedy. I want all of heaven, not just a slice of it. I want to hold the moon, treasure it, not just create a partial, poor imitation."

"Ah." A breath of sound. "What would be heaven to you?"

He asked the question in the barest whisper. She lifted her head.

Their bodies were so close now, he could count the eyelashes fanning across her cheeks. Her skin looked impossibly dewy and soft.

Her eyes skimmed his mouth, staring intently.

"I've never been kissed." Her voice had a plaintive quality, as if the change in topic were perfectly logical.

"Never?"

She shook her head. "No."

"That's a shame. Ye should do something about it."

"I tried. I kissed the back of my hand." She lifted her other hand and pressed a kiss to the back of it. She pulled her hand away, studying it. "I don't think it's quite the same, do you?"

"Nae. I dinnae think it's the same thing at all."

"No," she pouted. The motion forced her plump lower lip to jut out further. Andrew found himself unable to look away.

"You were made for kissing, Jane."

"I know." She tilted her chin upward, nearly aligning their mouths. "I *was* made for kissing."

Andrew chuckled. That answer was so . . . *her*.

Smiling, he cupped her head in his hand, fingers sliding into her thick, auburn hair. Her cheek fit into his hand like a glove, as if his palm had been formed simply as a cradle for her head.

Bending down, his lips found hers.

The first touch was the barest of whispers, a brushing hint of sensation.

The second pass was firmer, a deeper press.

Heaven help him. Had he ever kissed lips so soft?

Andrew intended to pull back, to stop himself right there.

But Jane had other ideas.

Her hand wrapped around the back of his neck, tugging his mouth back to hers.

Of course, Jane would be as high-handed in her kissing as everything else.

She took what she saw as hers, thoroughly, utterly.

He hadn't been wrong. She possessed him.

He vowed, then and there.

Even if she bitterly regretted this kiss. Even if she decided to toss him aside, an unwanted toy.

He would find a way to free her from Montacute's machinations.

His Jane warranted more than a mere slice of heaven.

She merited having the entire universe at her feet.

JANE KNEW SHE liked whisky for a reason. It softened the edges of reality, giving her the courage to grab what she wanted.

Right now, she never wanted to stop kissing Andrew.

He tasted of smoky liquor and stubborn man.

Their lips warred for dominance, each giving and taking. He tried to pull back and she chased him with her mouth, taking more and more.

"I wasn't done," she said, tone dangerously close to begging.

"Ye've had a lot of whisky, Jane. I've already taken more advantage than I should."

"Pffft. You've had just as much liquid courage as I have," she countered. "And I don't think I'm taking advantage of you."

"Jane—"

"You are an adult and if you dislike my kisses, you can say something." She arched an eyebrow. "Do you dislike my kisses?"

Hadley growled. "Ye know I dinnae. Yer deliberately making this difficult for me."

Her smile grew wider. "I'm quite sure that's part of my reason for existing, *Andrew*. To make life difficult for you."

"*That* . . . I dinnae doubt."

Hadley stood, pulling her with him, clasping her tightly against his chest, their bodies pressed together.

His head bowed again to find her lips. Jane reveled in how their bodies aligned. Hadley was the perfect height. So tall she had to tip her head upward to meet his mouth. She felt dainty and protected in his embrace, his strong arms swallowing her.

Heavens, why had she never kissed a man before this? The sensation was sublime. It rendered her loose-limbed and so utterly free.

She realized it then . . .

She wanted a man who tasted of whisky. Who was as bold and fierce and strong as the drink.

She wanted a man who *saw* her, who didn't shrink from her wild self.

A man who would weep over a lad dying half a world away.

A man with a heart so large, it enveloped whole villages.

His words from the ball earlier drift upward.

Ye deserve tae be free—

Oh!

Emotion hit her with blinding force, stinging her eyes.

She had dared Andrew into the drawing room, convinced he would be repulsed by her wilder self.

How wrong she had been.

Andrew didn't like her *despite* her fire.

He liked her *because* of her fire.

The thought trembled the foundations of her world.

Andrew *reveled* in her wild self. He wanted to see *more* of the inner her, not less.

What is it you want, Lady Jane?

The answer rose from deep within.

You.

I want you, Andrew.

She hurled the words back at him in her mind.

I wouldn't mind being your possession.

Perilously close to weeping, she pressed even closer, demanding even more.

Finally, it was Hadley who stopped them. He pressed a kiss to her mouth and then stood back, hands grasping her upper arms, holding her away from him.

Their loud breathing filled the room.

Peter snorted and mumbled from his corner.

Hadley darted one last tormented look at her mouth, bowed, and snatching his coat, practically ran from the room . . .

. . . leaving Jane standing, reeling, trying to accommodate the enormity of it all.

Heaven help her.

Now what was she to do?

21

The prisoners worked in a long line, passing stones between each other to stack them into a wall which bordered the harbor. Three overseers watched the men work, long whips held loosely in their hands.

"We'll start by asking them." Rafe gestured with his chin toward the uniformed overseers.

"Aye," Kieran murmured.

Andrew nodded, stopping himself before nausea could crawl up his throat. The pounding of his head didn't help matters either.

He had definitely had too much to drink last night and not nearly enough sleep. He and Rafe had ridden at a brutal pace in order to meet Kieran at the appointed time.

Memories of the night before with Jane kept darting through his mind.

Jane open and teasing him, face illuminated in the firelight.

Jane fully reveling in her fiery self, unguarded and utterly charming.

Jane's soft lips on his, the warmth of her breath.

The plush give of her body wrapped in his arms.

He had done it.

He had gone and fallen hard for an English lass.

The irony.

You could marry her.

The thought drifted through again.

The more he pondered it, the more real it became.

Jane as his . . . wife.

His breath snagged at the thought.

But . . .

Without the influence of whisky, how would Jane feel about him in the harsh light of day? Would she still welcome his affection—most importantly, his kisses?

He didn't need or want her dowry; just her sweet self was sufficient. Though her warning about Montacute had not been unheeded—*Montacute is just spiteful enough to ensure that I become a pariah.*

Would her brother truly do something so cruel if Jane chose to marry for love instead of power and social position? Andrew's mind boggled at the thought. How could any man be so uncaring about his sister? Surely Jane had to be mistaken.

And yet, he had felt firsthand the petty machinations of the peerage, so it was not entirely beyond the pale.

Little that Andrew cared. Montacute would not stop him from marrying Jane. Let the arrogant duke do what he will. Andrew and Jane would fight him together.

No, the more important question . . . would Jane accept Andrew as a suitor?

Just because she didn't want to marry Wanleigh, it did not follow that she would marry *him*. Lady Jane had remained unmarried for years.

But that *kiss* . . .

A woman didn't kiss a man like that if she were indifferent, right? Even with whisky involved?

Regardless, Andrew vowed anew, even if she rebuffed his suit, he would help her escape Montacute's stratagems. Her brother threatened Jane with penury and abandonment if she disobeyed him.

But Jane deserved more. She merited every happiness, every gift—

Enough.

Focus on the present.

Andrew followed Rafe and Kieran on horseback as they rode down into the harbor. Houses clustered around the bay, edging the coastline like sheep huddled against a shelter. Wash hung on lines, sagging in the overcast light. Add in the line of prisoners, haggard in their issued uniforms, and the scene became one of poverty and desperation. Not even the stray ray of sunlight could alleviate the gloom.

The overseers pointed them in the direction of two officers. The officers watched them approach with guarded expressions.

"How may I help you gentlemen?" the taller of the two asked, his eyes quickly surveying their fine mounts and expensive dress. Only Kieran sported Jamie's tartan wrapped across his chest. Andrew and Rafe had left off the tartan, knowing they were going to need to be their most English, lordly selves today.

Rafe smiled, easy-going and polite. "We seek Thomas Madsen. We believe he is a prisoner aboard the *Bellerophon.*"

The officers looked at each other.

"Madsen is still abed, I believe," one said.

"Aye. Been ill this past week. Gaol fever," the second man explained.

Andrew's stomach sank. Gaol fever ran rampant through British prisons, rendering even a short stay in gaol a near death sentence at times.

"We would like to speak with him," Rafe replied.

"Of course, we would be happy to compensate ye for your effort," Andrew said. "Rowing us out tae the Bellerophon would be no easy task." He nodded toward the ship, bobbing at anchor only a hundred yards from shore. Rowing them out would be simple. The payment was merely a polite way of offering a bribe.

The officers were not fools.

"Madsen's not likely to recover," the first said, "so I expect there's no harm in letting these men speak with him."

"Nay, no harm at all. Come then," the second beckoned.

Tossing a coin to a lad to watch their horses, Andrew, Kieran, and Rafe scrambled into a rowboat. The officer pulled at the oars.

The *Bellerophon* bobbed up and down with the low harbor waves. The ship had clearly seen better days. No sails clung to her rigging and much of her top deck was covered in tarpaulin, the canvas pulled tight with rope. Paint curled and peeled from her side, and even at a distance, Andrew could hear the timbers creaking.

Pulling alongside, Kieran hauled himself out first, scrambling up the ladder to the top deck. Once aboard, the smell of unwashed bodies nearly sent Andrew running for the ship's railing. His stomach was not up to the challenge of this. Swallowing, he breathed through his mouth, and when that still set him to gagging, he pulled out his handkerchief, burying his nose in the lavender and cedar scent of it.

The officer led them down a series of stairways, through the mess deck, and down to the prisoner deck. Hammocks slung from poles, stacked three high. The ceiling was so low, Andrew had to duck his head, even when standing between the roof beams.

The officer directed them to a curtained off area where several men moaned and writhed in hammocks. He motioned toward a hammock in the corner, weak light from a lamp overhead illuminating the space.

"Madsen should be there, if he still lives. I'll be here waiting for ye." The man pointed to where he stood, well back from the area of contagion.

Nodding, Andrew walked forward. The scent of sick and death was stronger here, penetrating hiss handkerchief. The figure in the hammock didn't look large enough to be Madsen. His former business partner had been a booming Highlander.

But peering over the edge, Madsen's face came into view. Haggard, gaunt, and a ghastly shade of gray.

"Does he live?" Rafe murmured.

"I can poke him until he squeals, if ye like," Kieran offered.

"Madsen," Andrew said loudly, imbuing his tone with authority. "Thomas!"

Kieran rocked the hammock.

Madsen moaned, blearily opening his eyes, tongue licking out to cracked lips. He appeared disoriented, gaze unfocused.

"Water," he whispered.

Unbidden, compassion stirred in Andrew's chest even as he tightened his hold on the handkerchief over his mouth.

Why would he *now* develop a conscience? This man had shown no such compassion for the scores of villagers who would have been sold into slavery, journeying aboard a ship in conditions worse than this.

And yet . . .

Sighing, Andrew stepped over to a water bucket in the corner and lifted the dipper out of it. Returning, he tilted a dribble into Madsen's mouth. The man drank a wee bit before choking, ending in a coughing fit.

Opening his eyes again, Madsen finally focused on Andrew's face. His pupils widened.

"Andrew Mackenzie," he whispered, pulling back. He blinked.

"Madsen," Andrew replied, passing the dipper to Rafe.

Madsen moaned. "Come tae send me off to Hell then?"

Kieran snorted.

"I'm quite sure ye will make it there all on your own, Madsen," Andrew replied. "Ye have no need of my help."

Silence. The boat rocked. Timbers creaked. The lamp sputtered overhead.

Madsen's gaze moved between Rafe and Kieran, coming back to Andrew. Andrew didn't expect Madsen to recognize his friends. Despite how thoroughly Madsen's actions had changed their lives, Rafe and Kieran had only met Madsen once before embarking on their voyage.

It felt nearly unreal, to finally be in this moment. So many years he had imagined confronting Madsen, but never like this. Never in these conditions, with Madsen clearly near to death.

It was anticlimactic, to say the least.

"Ye know why I'm here, Madsen," Andrew said. "Why did ye sell out an entire village of people? How could ye be so callous?"

Madsen swallowed, glancing at the ladle Rafe held. Obligingly, Rafe tipped a little more water into Madsen's mouth.

"I hadnae choice," Madsen rasped, voice breathy.

"A man always has choice," Andrew growled. "We could have recovered the cost. There was no need tae enslave innocent people. What could ye have been thinking? We didn't need the return on our investment that badly. Ye had tae know I would never have allowed the villagers tae be taken as slaves."

Madsen focused on him and then laughed, a weak, hollow sound.

"Investment? Ye still think it all was about appeasing investors?" he gasped.

Andrew stilled.

Madsen's breathing was labored; his eyes glazed with fever.

"This was never about that," Madsen continued. "I was well paid fer ma efforts."

A chill chased Andrew's spine. "What do ye mean?"

"I never had any money. It was never mine."

"Pardon?"

"Yer being a bit daft, Mackenzie. I was *hired* tae be yer partner. Some other man wanted a piece of yer business but didnae want ye tae know. So, he set it all up with solicitors and the like, made it appear as if I was yer business partner, but I was never acting as my own man."

Andrew blinked, trying desperately to make sense of Madsen's words.

"How is that possible? We were business partners for two years before the voyage."

"Aye."

"And you were . . . paid? Where did the money for all our investments come from?"

Madsen shook his head before closing his eyes. "I dinnae know. I was told tae no' ask questions."

"Who? Who told you?"

"I'm smart, aye. I dinnae ask questions like that." Madsen snorted softly, voice sinking. "I dinnae know who gave me orders. The solicitors kept it secret."

"Who? Who were these solicitors?"

"Fancy firm in London. Smith something . . . I cannae remember now."

"How about you try harder tae remember?" Kieran growled.

Madsen flinched and shut his eyes, chest sinking. His labored breaths filled the small space.

"Don't suppose ye have a solicitor of the last name Smith?" Rafe asked Andrew.

"Nae. That would have been far too convenient."

"I fear he's unconscious now." Kieran waved a hand over Madsen's hammock.

"Thomas!" Andrew barked. How could the eejit not remember the solicitor's name? That information was vital. He wanted to shake Madsen until every last snippet of information tumbled free.

He got silence instead.

Kieran shook the hammock, rocking it. Finally, Madsen stirred, thoughts clearly meandering. "From the start of the voyage, ye were a marked man, Andrew Mackenzie." He drew a rasping breath. "But then ye didnae die like ye were supposed tae. Always a bloody, stubborn arse."

"Wait—What?!" Shock chased every thought from Andrew's muddled brain. "I was supposed tae *die?*"

"Of course. Cuthie must have known ye wouldnae agree to the villagers being sold. It was his job tae make sure ye didnae return to Scotland. He was tae come up with a scenario that resulted in yer death."

Rafe gasped. Kieran swore.

Andrew's blood turned to ice.

"The villagers were a clever solution." Madsen licked his lips, eyes still closed, voice whispering. "Ye were to die, Mackenzie. That was ma sole job. Make sure ye never returned from the South Pacific. It just needed tae look like an accident. Or something ye had brought upon yerself."

"That was the plan?" Rafe asked.

"Aye. And then ma benefactor cut me off when we heard that *The Minerva* was lost, but ye had lived. Took all the money back, left me with nothin'. Had tae resort to thieving tae pay my way."

"Who did this?" Andrew demanded again, voice raising.

Madsen shook his head again, a soft moan escaping him.

"Who ordered my death?"

"I dinnae know," Madsen whispered, voice drifting in a mumble. "Never asked. Never told me." His shoulders slumped.

"Hell, no." Andrew shook Madsen. "Ye cannae say something like that and then pass out, Madsen."

Madsen whimpered but offered nothing more.

They stared at him for another ten minutes, Andrew willing Madsen to open his eyes again. But it appeared their conversation had exhausted him. Madsen's breaths grew shallower and shallower as they waited, all color bleaching from his skin.

"He's not long for this world," Rafe murmured. "Who knows if he'll ever regain consciousness."

A horrible numbness had taken over Andrew's limbs. Shock, he was quite sure.

How could it all come to this?

For so long, they had assumed that Madsen was the man responsible. But to learn that someone else had been behind his actions. That Madsen had merely been another's puppet. Another man had held Madsen's strings the entirety of their acquaintance.

And, even more horrifying, that Andrew's *death* had been the end goal. And given Andrew's state after that brutal beating aboard *The Minerva*, Cuthie probably thought he had completed the job . . .

Worse, the puppeteer was still at large.

Andrew stumbled back, making his way up to the top deck. Finally, the stench, the whisky from the night before, and his queasiness got the better of him. He stepped to the railing, ducking from under the tarpaulin and was sick over the side of the boat. His stomach heaved over and over.

Someone wanted him dead.

That same person had gone to elaborate lengths to install Madsen as his fake business partner. Madsen had never owned those outstanding business shares; this mysterious man did.

Who?

And, more to the point, why?

22

J ane rose later than normal, her head throbbing and eyes wincing at the bright light. She took a leisurely breakfast in bed.

Andrew was gone, her maid had informed her. Off for London.

Which was . . . good, she supposed. Jane needed some time to mentally sort through everything that had happened the previous evening.

First, the horror of Wanleigh and Montacute's expectations.

Then, Andrew pushing her and daring her to let her inner self free.

And then all the revelations about his voyage and Jamie . . .

The one thing she refused to dwell on was their kiss.

Well, perhaps she did a little . . .

Or maybe a bit—

Oh, bother!

So it was all she could think about, but could anyone blame her?

That bloody kiss.

Her *first* kiss.

How did one arrive at twenty-four years of age without ever having been kissed?

Jane could easily answer that.

Take a careful woman who desperately wished to avoid scandal—such as herself.

Add in a vigilant mother who carefully monitored her every move.

Combine it with an older brother with strict expectations and a tight leash on her.

And, well, it was no surprise.

Though, truth be told, Jane had never really met anyone she found worth the risk of kissing.

Until Andrew.

And even then, without a liberal application of liquid courage, she probably would never have kissed him.

But, oh, that kiss.

Even sober in the light of day, just thinking of it pinked her cheeks and sent heat flooding her body.

Over and over, her mind returned to the gentleness of his hands. The way he held her against him, the leashed strength of his body wrapped around hers.

Jane knew she should feel embarrassed and ashamed. She *should*.

But she mostly just wanted to kiss Andrew again.

And again. And again.

Her heart lurched at the thought.

But did his attachment run as deeply as hers? And, even if it did, what did it alter?

A single kiss was hardly a declaration of love or a marriage proposal. In fact, from hearing acquaintances talk over the years, a kiss often signaled nothing more than a passing fancy. Was that how Andrew saw her?

Despite his words, Jane doubted Andrew had the financial and social clout to marry her without Montacute's support. She equally doubted her ducal brother would ever agree to the match. The duke had his sights set on Wanleigh.

Continued association with Andrew risked Montacute's displeasure, resulting in her being forced to leave Hadley Park and Peter. Though how Jane was to extricate herself from the situation with Lord Wanleigh, she did not know.

Jane was still abed musing when her mother entered her bedchamber. Given her mother's bleary eyes and strained expression, Jane wasn't the only one feeling the effects of the previous evening.

"I've had a letter from Montacute," her mother said without preamble. "He enclosed a message for you."

Jane's stomach plummeted.

Letters from Montacute were never good things. And to receive yet another letter so soon did not portend good things.

Her mother handed Jane a piece of foolscap before sitting at the foot of Jane's bed, the bedcovers dipping to her weight.

Jane snapped the piece of paper in her hand and read her brother's brief words.

I expect you to do your duty as befits the daughter of a duke. Wanleigh will call upon you, and you will show yourself amiable and eager to please him. Do not disappoint me in this. You will not enjoy the consequences if you fail.

Well.

That left little doubt as to Montacute's intentions.

Jane lifted her head, her stricken gaze meeting her mother's. Lady Hadley did not flinch at the pleading she saw in her daughter's eyes.

"We have been most indulgent with you, Jane," her mother said. "But the time has come for you to marry. Wanleigh is an excellent choice. The best marital option on the market at the moment."

"But Mother—"

"No, there will be no argument." Her mother fixed her with a knowing, but terribly firm look.

"Wanleigh is nearly thrice my age, Mother," Jane all but hissed. "I cannot countenance marriage to a man in his dotage."

"It is apparent that the close interactions you have had with Hadley over the past few weeks have somewhat endeared him to your affections. I am not blind to the way you watch him. But need I remind you that Hadley is not suitable as a husband? The man is not good *ton*."

Ugh!

"Mother, this isn't about Hadley, per se." Though, really, it was. "This is about my not wanting to marry Wanleigh." Also true. "One does not necessarily lead to the other."

"Do not split hairs with me, young lady." Lady Hadley's eyes narrowed. "You like Hadley a little too much—"

"Of course, I like Hadley!" Jane ground her teeth. "He's not so far beyond the pale. Besides, he still has all his teeth and doesn't wear a corset!"

"Do not make a poor marriage simply to spite me or Montacute. Yes, Hadley might be a more attractive choice—on the surface, at least—than Wanleigh. But do not look to Hadley to be your savior, Jane. Desperation is not the same thing as love."

Oh!

Jane flinched.

Her mother was not the most intellectual of women, but occasionally, she delivered a barb that shot true.

Desperation is not the same thing as love.

Was that true? Were her feelings for Andrew born of desperation?

How could she separate her desire to avoid a marriage with Wanleigh from her affection for Andrew?

Her mother continued, "How many times must I say this? Birth may have made Hadley an earl, but he will never be accepted by Polite Society. His upbringing was too poor. He sees you as an easy target with your generous dowry and connections to the upper echelons of the *ton*. But you both must give up this fantasy."

Influence. Power. Money. I don't care about such things, Jane longed to rage.

But as ever, she bit her lip and dug her nails into her palm, her eyes surely snapping with suppressed emotion.

"I know you, Jane." Her mother's expression turned pitying. "I know that you think you don't care about money and political influence and being accepted into the highest ranks of the *ton*. But you *will* care. You will care when your children have no financial prospects, and your creditors hound you day and night for payment. You will care when your daughters must marry lesser men, or cannot marry at all, because of your lack of consequence. You will care."

Jane pressed her nails harder.

She wouldn't care.

She was sure of it.

But Lady Hadley had one final blow to deal:

"Do not trade one cage for another, Jane. Do not tether yourself to a man who can offer you little beyond youth. Youth fades. You will live to bitterly regret it."

Jane hissed, breath coming in greater gulps.

"Marriage to Wanleigh is not a trap," her mother continued. "It is a ticket to freedom. He is wealthy, powerful, and best of all, *elderly*. You will likely find yourself a rich widow within a decade. See Wanleigh for the gift he is. Montacute sees this. I see this. Do not be foolish, child."

Marry an elderly peer, raise your social standing, collect your plump widow's jointure when the time comes. Her mother had made the same choice, twice over.

Jane could not reply. The scream stuck in her throat.

How could she find a way out of this?

Jane had always known she lived in a gilded prison. She just hated that every time she rattled the lock and tried to step into the light, her gaolers reminded her exactly how strong the bars were.

"WE START BY making a list of who would wish you dead," Rafe said, sitting back in his chair.

Andrew, Rafe, and Kieran were lounging before the fire in a private dining room in an inn just outside London.

Andrew had some business items to attend to in London, as did Kieran. Rafe was required, yet again, to dance attendance on his father. But for the evening, they were staying in a tidy inn south of Town.

"That's a good question," Andrew sighed. Fortunately, his stomach had settled down. His mind, however, still reeled from the revelations of the afternoon. "I've been pondering it myself."

"The old earl, I'd ken," Kieran said.

"Aye," Andrew said. "My dearly departed grandad certainly had a score tae settle with my father. It could be that he wanted me out of way so Peter could inherit. Keep everything within his English family."

"That is possible," Rafe said. "Are the estates entailed?"

Andrew shook his head. "No. An entail usually has tae be renewed every third generation, and my father never signed an entail. It's actually why I doubt that the old earl wished me ill. If anything, it's the exact opposite. He left me the estates and money in his will, something he did not have tae do, as there was no entail. Peter received nothing. Why do that if he wanted Peter to inherit?"

"It doesn't make sense, I agree," Rafe replied. "Maybe we need to ask a different question: when we left on our trip to the South Pacific, who would have benefited the most from your death?"

Andrew pursed his lips, thinking. "The most obvious answer is Peter. If I had died, he would have inherited instead of me—

"But only the earldom, not your Scottish wealth," Rafe pointed out.

"Aye, but I don't know why someone would have gone after my Scottish holdings before our trip. I was wealthy then, but nothing tae the degree that I am currently."

"Mmmm, so back to the earldom. Are there any other heirs, aside from Peter?" Rafe asked.

"Nae. Peter is the sole remaining heir; he and I are the only living male descendants of the first earl. If neither of us sire a son, the earldom becomes extinct." Andrew drummed his fingers, looking into the fire.

Rafe pursed his lip. "So if you had died *before* the old earl—meaning you had died in the South Pacific, as this unknown person intended—Peter would have inherited all the lands and the estates of the earldom after his father's death?"

"Aye—"

"Och, Peter is no' yer man, I ken." Kieran took a deep drink of his pale ale. "You've been partners with Madsen for how many years?"

"Just over six years."

"And Peter is how old currently?"

"One and twenty."

"So he would have been fifteen when this began? That's a wee bit young to be financing an investment portfolio. He would no' have had the money, if nothing else. Despite having a proper motivation, it's extremely unlikely that Peter is yer man."

"Aye," Rafe nodded, "Kieran has the right of it. Peter wouldn't have had the resources or experience to set it all in motion."

Andrew agreed with them wholeheartedly.

Rafe continued, "Your English title and lands aside, who stood to inherit all your Scottish estates, investments, et cetera?"

Andrew sat back in his chair. "My mother, but I think we can safely remove her from a list of suspects."

"Aye," Rafe said, "she loves you too much, despite your mangy looks and atrocious manners."

Andrew chuckled before tapping his fingers, thinking. "The problem is larger than I think we understand. Madsen had been my partner for several years afore the voyage. If he had an employer who wanted me dead, the man had ample opportunity tae see the task done. Why wait until the voyage? I don't understand."

"Have ye noticed anything off as of late? Anything that makes ye afraid for yer life?" Kieran asked.

"No," Andrew shook his head. "Nothing tae give me pause. Aside from Madsen himself, I can't think of an acquaintance or former investor that wished me ill."

All three men stared at their cups.

Andrew sat back, nearly smacking his palm to his forehead.

"Och! We're a pack of eejits." He shook his head. "We've missed the most obvious question of all—"

"What's that?" Kieran asked.

"Who knows that Andrew Mackenzie and Andrew Langston are one and the same person? When all this began, who knew that Andrew Mackenzie, investor in Scotland, was the heir to the Earl of Hadley?"

Silence.

"We're assuming that whoever wants me out of the way knows that I am the Scottish Vulcan, as well as the Earl of Hadley. That I'm wealthy *and* a Peer of the Realm. But the reality is *very* few people are privy to that information. The question may be irrelevant, but . . ."

"You're right." Rafe sat back. "Did Madsen know you were the heir to an English earldom?"

"No. None of my investors would have known. There was no reason to ever connect Andrew Mackenzie with the Earldom of Hadley."

"Who *did* know?"

"Before our trip? My parents and Scottish grandparents, obviously. A few of the older retainers at Muirford House . . ." Andrew trailed off, thinking. "I can't think of anyone else for sure. Maybe my father's solicitor? Possibly the old earl knew, but I have no definitive proof of that. Peter certainly didn't know." He drummed his fingers on the tabletop.

"You have been listed in *Debrett's* as the heir to the earldom," Rafe said quietly. "So that was common knowledge among those who took the time to look."

"Aye, but listed as Andrew Langston, not Andrew Mackenzie. My middle name isn't in *Debrett's*. More to the point, who had such a grudge against me that they would wait years and spend a small fortune to ensure my demise?" Andrew countered.

Kieran chuckled. "Sounds like an English aristocrat, if ye ask me. Sneaky, conniving bastards."

Rafe snorted. "Kieran isn't far off the mark. It does sound like something a man of power would put in motion. But to what end?"

More silence.

"Whoever they are, they are still my business partner." Andrew gritted his teeth. "I can't buy out shares from a person who remains in hiding."

"Can they harm you through that?"

Andrew shrugged. "Not without stepping into the light. I have frozen all monies attached to the shares." He let out a long breath. "Our best hope at this point is the solicitor Madsen mentioned, a Smith with offices in London—"

"Bah! Do you know how many solicitors there are in London with the surname of Smith?"

"True. But this solicitor would surely know the name of his client—"

"If he is willing to tell us."

"That's why we'll hire another Runner to ferret it out. Find this Smith fellow and see what he knows."

"Good idea," Kieran nodded. "I'll let Ewan and Alex know what has happened. Mayhap they have some ideas, too."

"Thank you," Andrew said.

THE NEXT MORNING, Andrew rode into London proper, turning the facts over and over in his mind.

Aside from Peter, and possibly the old earl, who would benefit from his death?

Lady Hadley and other English step-relatives had no financial incentive. His Scottish mother and grandfather certainly wished him no ill.

It was a puzzle.

First, he stopped by the offices in Bow Street and spoke with his Runner. The man would immediately begin a systematic search of all the solicitors in London with the surname Smith.

Next, Andrew visited his own solicitor. The man had much to report.

The Committee of Privilege was still stalling on recommending him for a Writ of Summons. The solicitor had begun making quiet inquiries to discover which lords were blocking Andrew's summons.

The man also confirmed the current state of the Earldom of Hadley.

"What happens to the earldom if both Peter and I die without heirs?" Andrew asked his solicitor.

The man shrugged. "The earldom and its attendant properties revert to the Crown."

"And then what?"

"The Crown usually bestows them on another Peer. Someone close to the Sovereign or someone who has helped the Crown in some way."

It was plausible that someone wanted their hands on the earldom. But why? To what end?

More to the point, aside from Rafe, Andrew knew no one in the peerage. Looking for his enemy within the English aristocracy seemed futile.

But . . .

Did someone within the peerage know that Andrew Mackenzie and Andrew Langston were the same person? Andrew had never actively hidden the connection; he simply never spoke of it. A determined man *could* sleuth it out. Had someone wanted him dead, and Peter too, in order to take over the earldom?

The idea seemed far-fetched, but given the difficulties he was having with the Chancery and the Committee of Privilege, it was hard to dismiss the possibility entirely. Someone within the peerage clearly wished him ill. He had assumed until now that it was merely a bigoted reaction to his parentage and Scottish heritage. But was there more to it than that?

Too many questions and not nearly enough answers.

Andrew left his solicitor and made his way to The Strand.

He had one more stop to make, this one having nothing to do with Madsen. He smiled when Mrs. Mawe's mineralogy shop came into view.

23

I cannot marry Wanleigh, Peter. It is insupportable." Jane set down her embroidery, pressing a hand to her forehead, before raising her eyes to her brother.

Peter lounged in the chair opposite, legs loose-limbed, hair tousled. The afternoon sun streamed through the mullioned oriel window to one side of the drawing room. Lady Hadley had taken to her room with a headache, leaving Jane to stew over Montacute's missive and her mother's harsh words.

Desperation is not the same thing as love.

Was that truly why she found herself falling for Andrew? Because she saw him as a lifeline out of her current situation with Wanleigh?

Worse, she couldn't say for sure that the idea did *not* influence her emotions. Jane had pondered it over and over until she had induced a headache to go along with her heartache.

Peter sighed at her words. "Jane, I cannot see how you can avoid it, to be honest."

"I had hoped you would be supportive." Jane stabbed her needle through the fabric. She was feeling decidedly *stabby* today.

"Jane, you know this isn't how the world works. I haven't liked the fact that I must work alongside Hadley to earn my keep—"

"Please. Working on the estate is hardly the same thing as being forced to marry a man old enough to be your grandfather. Besides, you seem to have settled into it. To be very honest, I think you enjoy it."

Jane struggled not to dwell on the unfairness of it.

Stab, stab.

Peter shrugged. "I grant you that Hadley isn't as horrid as we both supposed."

Ugh.

More than *not* horrid.

She *did* like him for himself. She did. She was quite sure of it.

Kind, funny, generous, clever, with lips that—

Grrrr.

Stab, stab.

She was not driven by desperation. She was not.

"*You* will be permitted to marry where you will," she said through gritted teeth.

Her brother groaned in frustration. "Jane, you have to marry well. That is hardly a surprise."

She pulled her thread through with more force than necessary. She couldn't open her mouth to reply without screaming.

Stab, stab, stab.

"Is Wanleigh really so bad?" Peter continued. "He isn't long for this world, and if the marriage settlement were generous—"

"Honestly, Peter?!"

Jane didn't anticipate him supporting her in everything. But when something was truly this important, she *did* expect Peter to take a stand with her.

His caving was demoralizing in the extreme. It pointed to how dire her situation truly was.

"I have options," Jane replied.

One always had options. No one was without a choice.

Even if that choice was simply to live or die.

"Do you? Hadley himself, perhaps?" he asked. "None of us are blind to the looks you two exchange—"*Peter.*" Her tone a stern warning.

"—all doe-eyed and longing. It's obvious the man courts you. Do you intend to encourage him further when he returns?"

Jane said nothing, stabbing again with unnecessary force.

Andrew had been gone for three days, but they expected him shortly. She hoped that, for his sake, he had been able to locate Madsen and receive the answers he sought.

And then returned to her as soon as possible.

Jane bent over her embroidery. "Hadley is not a poor choice—"

"This is all quite sudden, Jane," Peter continued. "You couldn't tolerate the man just a month ago, and now you are suddenly contemplating encouraging his attentions. It is quite appalling, to be honest. Are you sure you like Hadley for all the right reasons?" Her brother shook his head. "It smacks of desperation to me, grasping at straws."

Bloody hell.

Et tu, Peter?

Jane clenched her jaw.

"If I ask you to support me against Montacute, will you?" She had to know.

"Jane, why are you harping on thi—"

A knock sounded at the door before it opened.

"Lord Wanleigh, to see you madam," the butler intoned.

Oh, no.

Please, no.

Jane shot Peter a look. *Don't you dare leave me.*

"Please show him up, Barnsley," she said.

Peter snorted but he didn't leave her alone.

Thank goodness.

Lord Wanleigh was no better in daylight than he had been three nights ago at the ball. His girth strained the buttons of his waistcoat, and he clearly wore a corset which creaked as he bowed over Jane's hand.

"To what do I owe this visit, Lord Wanleigh?" Jane asked, lips pressed, gesturing for Wanleigh to be seated.

"Why the pleasure of your company, of course." He smiled, easing himself down onto the sofa, his knees cracking. "Or more precisely, I wished to enjoy the refreshing elegance of your refined manners, Lady Jane, without the unruly stench of a certain Scot clouding the air."

Oh, heavens!

Jane froze, Wanleigh's words having utterly stolen her breath.

Peter, noting her wide eyes, rescued her.

"You are too kind, my lord," he said.

Silence descended.

She knew she should fawn over Wanleigh. She should be polite and simpering. But she just couldn't do it. She couldn't make her tongue form the words.

Despite her mother's jaded opinions and Peter's assumptions, Jane could not stomach such a man as a husband.

She shot a look at Peter, practically pleading with him to continue to help her.

Her brother offered a comment on the weather.

Five minutes later they had covered the spring weather, earlier winter weather, and had now moved on to the upcoming summer weather.

Jane was floundering for another topic that would not lead to Wanleigh declaring himself when the door cracked open again.

"Lord Hadley," the butler announced.

Jane lurched to her feet, relief rushing through her so quickly, it made her knees weak.

He has returned.

Hallelujah!

Andrew walked into the room, his broad shoulders filling the doorway, the scent of the outdoors and fresh, living things eddying behind him.

The sheer magnetism of his person stole Jane's breath.

This fluttery, happy, anxious feeling could not be desperation. It had to be much more than that. She was quite sure Andrew had ruined her for any other man.

His eyes snagged hers, and it took every ounce of Jane's self-control to halt the deep blush threatening to scour her cheeks.

Andrew was still in his riding breeches, a leather crop and gloves in his hands. He passed them off to the butler before coming forward.

"Lord Wanleigh, tae what do I owe the pleasure?" He bowed politely to Wanleigh before smiling and repeating the action to Jane. "Lady Jane. Peter."

"Hadley," Wanleigh nodded. He had not, Jane noticed, risen to greet Andrew. It was a small snub and could be overlooked because of Wanleigh's obvious age.

But Jane knew better. Wanleigh had stayed seated to make a point—Andrew was not one of them; he did not deserve any sort of deference.

If Andrew understood the slight, he did not allow it to show.

Jane sat back down, arranging her skirts carefully. If she looked too long at Andrew, would her heart shine in her eyes? Would everyone know?

Andrew sat beside Peter. His eyes darted between Jane and Wanleigh, clearly not misunderstanding the intent of the situation.

Silence descended again. Jane rallied, as any proper hostess should.

"I trust your journey was well, my lord?" she asked Andrew.

"Yes, my business was concluded satisfactorily."

Jane longed to ask him what that meant. Had he found Madsen then?

As he spoke, Andrew kept his eyes on Wanleigh. Was he silently warning the man off? *Could* she ask him to warn off Wanleigh?

"I understand you are struggling to settle into the role of earl," Wanleigh said after a small pause. "It must be difficult to manage for a man of your understanding."

"Ah," was Andrew's terse reply.

He stared at the older man, the taut line of his shoulders stating that he would not dignify Wanleigh's comment with a further response.

A silent battle of wills ensued.

"I understand you are struggling to receive your Writ of Summons?" Wanleigh said at last. He met Andrew's gaze, unaffected, completely sure of his position of power and wealth.

"Aye," Andrew met the man's stare with unflinching ease. Steel resided beneath his blue eyes. "Someone has been wanting tae cause a wee bit of trouble."

Chills chased Jane's spine. Here was the true Andrew. This strong, unmoving behemoth. Wanleigh appeared a round slug in comparison.

Wanleigh smiled, his thin lips stretching in condescension. "A word of advice, Hadley. It can be tempting to want to indulge in the finer things, once you have had a taste of them." He flicked his eyes to Jane. "But a man must be wary of the danger of reaching too high for something. The tumble from such a height can be . . . unpleasant."

Andrew's eyes narrowed.

Jane opened her mouth to interrupt before hostilities proceeded, but Peter beat her to it.

"I say, Hadley—" Peter gave an awkward laugh. "—have you had a look at how we're coming on in the south field? I had some ideas for improvements."

Affection rushed through Jane. *Bless Peter.*

His words forced Andrew to break eye contact with Wanleigh.

"I have. I rode by on my way tae the house. Ye have been busy down there."

The men moved on to talking about agriculture, Peter gently nudging the conversation to stay on civilized paths.

Jane was buoyed. Peter perhaps couldn't say so in as many words, but he loved her. He supported her.

Peter wouldn't leave her to go at this alone.

ANDREW PULLED OUT another drawer, setting it on his desk. Notebooks sat helter-skelter on top of each other. Correspondence was tied into loose bundles along one side.

The estate's bookkeeping might be neat and tidy, thanks to his steward.

The late earl's personal correspondence and records . . . not so much.

He sighed, running a hand over his face. A clock chimed the hour on the mantelpiece of his study.

This was the fifth drawer like this.

And so far, nothing—

A polite knock on the door interrupted his thoughts.

"Come," he said.

Lady Jane pushed the door open, peeking her head into his study.

"Lady Jane," he smiled, rising to his feet. "Come tae assist me in my woes?"

He hadn't seen much of her since returning yesterday afternoon. After their *tête-à-tête* with Wanleigh in the drawing room, her mother had summoned Jane away, both of them taking supper in her bedchamber. Likely attempting to keep Jane from spending too much time in Andrew's company.

So today, Jane was a welcome sight.

Matching his smile, she entered the room, but left the door open for propriety's sake. As usual, she was dressed to perfection in a blue muslin day dress dotted with small orange flowers. A matching blue silk ribbon threaded through her auburn hair, the color bringing out the amber highlights of her curls.

The soft grin on her face lit her gray eyes, chasing away the stern shadows that often haunted her.

Ah, there she was. There was his Jane.

Achingly beautiful and tenderly brave. Life dancing in her eyes.

His heart thundered at the sight, emotion banding his chest.

Andrew swallowed.

Despite having hours upon hours of travel time to ponder this moment, he honestly hadn't contemplated how he would proceed.

The uncertainty of it hit him like a cricket bat to the skull. He was abruptly nervous and oddly . . . bashful.

It was not pleasant. In fact, the entire experience was bizarrely revolutionary.

Was this love, then?

If so, no wonder poets bemoaned and described this feeling as a curse.

It was decidedly uncomfortable.

The uncertainty of it nearly unmanned him.

He had never courted anyone before. He had never found anyone who captivated him so thoroughly. He certainly had never pursued a lady as loftily-born as Lady Jane.

But . . .

This was Jane, and he liked her far too well to allow a few jittery nerves to stand between them.

"I hope I am not interrupting," she said, noting the scattered drawers and piles of correspondence strewn about.

"Not at all. Please, join me." He motioned for her to come in and be seated.

Still smiling, Jane glanced at the doorway before venturing farther into his study. They both knew that Lady Hadley would ring a peal over Jane's head for spending time with him like this.

Vividly, their last private encounter rose to his memory. The shattering revelation of her kiss.

He knew, as a gentleman, he should say nothing about it. But as he greatly wished a repeat of said kiss, it was difficult to keep quiet. She approached his desk and the ledgers he was currently examining.

"I wish to thank you for your interference yesterday." She moved a bundle of letters off a chair beside his desk and sat down, her body elegantly perched on the edge of the chair, hands clasped in her lap. "Wanleigh's presence was unexpected."

"I gathered as much," he said, sitting back down.

More to the point, Andrew was more than happy to interrupt any intentions that the Marquess of Wanleigh had upon Jane.

"How fared your trip to London? Did you discover what you needed to know?"

"Aye," he said. "We found Madsen aboard the prison hulk in Sheerness."

"That's good."

"Aye, but he only muddied the waters, not clarified them."

"How is that possible?"

Andrew sighed, leaning forward on his forearms. "Because it would appear that Madsen had been hired tae see to my demise."

"Pardon?" Her eyes widened in alarm.

Andrew found it most gratifying.

In a low voice—mindful of the open door—he repeated what they had discovered from Madsen, though he omitted discussing his deeper business ventures as Andrew Mackenzie.

Jane made suitable noises, flinching and gasping in all the correct places.

He adored her for it.

"Worse," he concluded, "I received word late yesterday that Madsen had passed on shortly after our visit. So there is no hope in thinking he had any more information tae divulge."

"What will you do?"

He sat back in his chair. "Well, I've had a pair of days tae ponder the problem. And it is this simple—who might wish me dead?"

She shook her head, bewildered. "Have you angered a rival Scottish clan?"

Andrew gave a bark of laughter. "Nae, that's not likely. First, I'm not a Highlander, and the strict clan structure faded long ago in Fife. We've already traversed this conversation. Second, Scots tend tae make their grievances in the open. If we have a problem with a man, we'll go a round or two of fisticuffs until we work out the frustration and then hare off to the nearest pub for a libation together. This slow nurturing of a murderous grudge worked in secret is more of an English trait, I must say."

Jane attempted to look surprised but gave up and instead shrugged. "You Scots never seem to see us coming, you know."

Andrew laughed again. "Ye have the right of it."

"Have you an explanation?"

"Perhaps. I took a step backwards in my questioning and asked— who knew that I was the heir to the Earldom of Hadley? When I ask *that* question, I always come back to the old earl. He knew of my existence. It's also obvious that my dearly departed grandfather had a grudge and, perhaps, a vested interest in my demise."

"The old earl? Truly?"

"Peter, with his impeccable English pedigree, would have been a preferable heir than my Scottish self." Andrew shrugged. "It's a place tae start."

She frowned, brows slanting down.

"Ye dinnae agree with me?"

"No, it's not that."

"Ye knew the old earl—"

"I agree that the old earl most certainly was the sort to have planned something like this. He had the means and, perhaps, the motivation. But it makes no sense. Why leave you everything if he planned to have you killed?"

"That thought has occurred more than once. It could have been an alibi of sorts, I realized. If he had me as the main beneficiary of his will, then it would be harder to accuse him of wishing me ill if I *did* pass away under mysterious circumstances."

"Ah, I think I see . . ." She thought for a moment. "If you were to die anyway, then naming you as the primary heir would not matter. Once you were dead, Peter would inherit regardless."

Thank heaven for her intelligence. Was it any wonder he liked her so well?

"Exactly." Andrew spread his arms wide. "So, I decided there was no harm in digging through my late grandfather's correspondence."

"I'm assuming you haven't found anything."

"Nothing yet. But there is more tae go through."

"May I help?"

"I was hoping you'd ask." Andrew shot her a grateful look. "I assume ye can read and understand an account book?"

"Of course. I have been managing the household accounts for years."

"I ken ye have a quick head for numbers."

"Perhaps that, too."

Smiling, he handed her a pile of letters to sift through. His grandfather had at least attempted to bundle letters together. But none of it was particularly orderly. Personal correspondence was stacked next to business inquiries.

The problem, of course, was that nothing pointed to Andrew and his businesses. There most certainly wasn't any correspondence with Madsen. In all his weeks sorting through the old earl's affairs, he had yet to see anything unusual. Granted, he hadn't been looking for anything that connected his grandfather's affairs with his own, either.

Unfortunately, working side-by-side with Jane proved a further distraction, a delicious sort of torture. The light scent of her perfume eddied through the room whenever she walked to pick up another item to examine. The rustle of papers as she flipped through pages. The soft sigh of her breathing mingling with the ticking clock.

He waited, but she didn't bring up their kiss. Andrew was adrift, unsure how to act. He knew he shouldn't mention it. A gentleman wouldn't say a word. But it was hard to stay silent, particularly as the clock on the mantel ticked on and on.

Each tick into the silence heightened his awareness of her.

Jane did nothing in a large way. But wee signs betrayed her inner world.

A puff of air indicated frustration.

A faint grunt meant she found something interesting.

A soft *snick* of her lips suggested boredom.

Andrew forced himself not to simply stare at her in fascination.

When had he ever been so besotted?

The silence stretched until it became a living thing, his body vibrating to the slightest movement from her, aching to take her into his arms again. He could practically see the tension in the room, dripping down the walls, hanging from the sconces.

Fortunately, Jane broke the silence before he did something rash.

"I suppose—" She stopped abruptly, tapping her lips.

Andrew forced himself not to stare at her mouth. "Yes?"

"I've just thought of something."

"You have?"

"Oftentimes, the old earl would conduct business at Rosehearth when he wished more privacy."

"Rosehearth? The old dower house at the edge of the woods?"

"Yes. He didn't visit Rosehearth much in the final years of his life, but there might be something there. The caretakers can let us in."

It was a brilliant suggestion. He had visited Mr. and Mrs. Carlton earlier in the month, munching shortbread and taking tea with them.

"Will you accompany me?" he asked. "You seem tae know more about it."

It was a shameless ploy to spend more time in her company.

"Of course."

24

Jane couldn't help the smile on her face, despite the nature of their excursion.

Her mother had given them both disapproving frowns as they drove out, but a stern glance from Andrew had prevented Lady Hadley from saying anything.

Thank goodness.

Simply being with Andrew was stepping out of a prison and into the light.

The sunny May day had turned unseasonably warm, as English spring days did on occasion. The sun decided that it should be summer and sent temperatures soaring.

The day was nearly uncomfortably hot; Jane fanned herself incessantly. Crossing the river brought a breeze of blessedly cool air, but by the time they reached the old quarry, Jane was sweltering again. As they skirted around it, she resorted to removing her gloves, as it was too stiflingly hot with them on. Hadley had chosen not to wear any tartan at all—the day was too warm for extra wool layers—and instead sported a swallowtail coat and top hat, looking every inch the London gentleman.

Jane struggled to decide which she liked more—charmingly Scottish Andrew or urbane Lord Hadley.

They both had their merits. But in her mind, he had become simply Andrew, even though she lacked the courage to call him by his Christian name with regularity. She needed a finger or two of scotch before she did that.

Andrew drove them across the small drawbridge and through the arched entrance into the central courtyard of Rosehearth. Ancient stone flanked age-darkened oak doors and wavy, mullioned windows. Wisteria climbed over one wall of the courtyard, putting on a flashy show of purple blooms.

Mrs. Carlton came out of the house to greet them, her weathered face ringed with cheer.

"Lady Jane! It does a body good to see ye," she said, dipping a curtsy.

"Mrs. Carlton, it's always a pleasure." Jane smiled, nodding her head in return. "We intend to tour the house and see if the old earl left some correspondence here."

"Of course. Ye'll be wanting to see the library then. His lordship always liked to conduct a spot of business there."

Jane led Andrew into the house, the cool interior a relief. She removed her bonnet, and he handed off his hat and driving gloves to Mrs. Carlton. The caretaker bobbed another curtsy and said she would prepare some tea and a small luncheon for them.

The entrance hallway was the same as always—rough-cut stone, a worn rug on the floor, dark doors and a beamed staircase leading upwards. As the house was four hundred years old if it was a day, nothing was plumb. Floors dipped and sagged. Windows were askew. Not a single timber remained straight.

Jane adored every nook and cranny of the place.

She led him through the entrance hallway and into the great hall with its imposing stone fireplace and glittering stained glass window. Andrew walked over to inspect the fireplace.

"Ye seem quite fond of Rosehearth," he noted, running a hand along the fleur-de-lis carvings etched in the stone mantel.

"Yes," she replied truthfully. "I grew up here."

That stopped him.

Andrew froze and turned slowly around, staring at her.

"You grew up here? At Rosehearth?"

"Yes. Peter and I," she all but whispered. "My mother and the old earl were always off in London, entertaining and being seen. I think that they both preferred to forget about us here in the country. When they came down from Town, they always brought guests with them. It was easier for Peter and me to remain here with Nanny Smith, as we were out of the way and never seen. I can't say that I minded."

Andrew surveyed the room again, as if seeing it anew. "It appears tae be a lovely, homey sort of place tae grow up."

"Sometimes I think Nanny Smith was more a mother to me than my own."

A pause.

"I'm verra glad you had someone like Nanny Smith." He met her gaze. "Ye need light and love in yer life, Jane. It seems tae be sadly lacking at Hadley Park, if I can be honest." Something tight and aching lodged in Jane's throat. She blinked, once, twice.

"Did you grow up with light and love?" she finally asked.

"Aye, I did. That's why I know its value. Show me yer Rosehearth, Jane."

He extended his hand to her. The motion should have been rote, but something in his expression told her otherwise.

This . . .

This was why she cared for this man.

Because he not only saw her. He not only accepted her.

But he also wanted to know more and more of her.

She realized, in that moment, that there was nothing in her so ugly or unwelcome that Andrew wouldn't extend his hand, asking to listen and understand.

He would accept her without judgment.

Oh.

Could anyone ever ask for more than that from a fellow human being? To understand and be understood in return?

It was a gift without price.

Tentatively, Jane reached out, her bare palm sliding across his. Logically, one simple touch shouldn't have the ability to spark a fire atop every nerve in her body, and yet here was scientific proof of it. His skin was shockingly warm and smooth, enveloping her hand with quiet strength.

He threaded his fingers through hers, holding tightly.

A small smile tugging at her lips, Jane led the way through the rest of the ground floor—the small receiving room, the dining room, the breakfast room. Their hands clasped the entire time.

All the while, Jane talked about growing up here with Peter. Their endless games of tag, keeping a menagerie of pets including a fox, hunting for a suspected priest hole left over from the Reformation era, and pinching cheese and bread from the larder in midnight raids. Peter had been the first bring her interesting rocks from the old quarry. Jane had been the one to sit at his bedside for days when a particularly virulent fever swept the neighborhood.

Upstairs, she led him through the long gallery, which ran the entire length of the south wing, windows regularly lighting the space, a large oriel window at one end.

"Peter and I would race here." She pointed to the worn jute mats. "Sometimes just foot races, but once we sneaked our ponies up from the stables."

Andrew laughed. Not a polite chuckle, but a head-back, eyes-shut, white-teeth-flashing, belly-rumbling sort of laugh.

"I would have paid a wee fortune tae see such a sight. Something tells me Nanny Smith didn't appreciate having horses in her house, ponies or no."

"She did not. I think Peter and I had to eat bread and milk for a week."

"Ye were a rare pair, the two of ye."

"We were." Jane was quite sure her eyes shone with fondness. She cleared her throat. "I've been meaning to thank you for helping Peter, for forcing him to shoulder some responsibility. It's been lovely to watch him grow over the past several weeks."

"Och, the lad was fair brimming with stifled energy. I simply nudged him in the right direction—"

"Nudged? Don't you mean 'dragged kicking and screaming'?"

"Perhaps," he chuckled, "but regardless, Peter will fill his role well, I ken."

"Not everyone would have taken the time to help him find a place, so thank you."

Andrew looked at her, something fond and gentle shining in his gaze "Think nothing of it."

Jane bit her lip before turning her head away. The tenderness in Andrew's eyes was causing feathery feelings to build in her chest again.

She waved them on to the library. It was a magnificent space, dominated by a fireplace on one side and a bank of mullioned windows on the other. From everything Jane understood about the house, the library was actually a medieval lord's Great Chamber—the place where he would listen to tenants' complaints and mete out local justice. White plasterwork dotted the ceiling with carved wood paneling on the walls. A cozy sofa and chairs crowded around the fireplace while a desk stood in front of the windows. Bookcases lined one of the walls.

Jane breathed in the space, the singular smell of woodsmoke, books, and lavender which would forever say 'home' to her heart.

She told him of reading *Robinson Crusoe* to Peter late into the evening, tucked together on the window seat. She pointed to the small scorch marks in the carpet before the fire, relating a comical incident involving toasted cheese that went awry.

And then Jane found herself telling him about Montacute, about the tumble into the river, and her subsequent humiliation. The end of her idyllic life here at Rosehearth.

"Do you miss that carefree wee lass?" he asked when she was done.

"More than I can say," she whispered, blinking as the room turned blurry. She bit her lip for long seconds before raising her head.

Andrew stared at her, his eyes still holding that gentle fondness.

"I like ye at Rosehearth, Jane," he said at last. "Ye appear tae be yerself here. Less Lady Jane and more simply . . ."

"Jane?" she supplied.

"Aye."

That tight feeling returned to her throat.

How did Andrew do this? How did he see through her barriers so easily? Once again, she felt that tug, that sense of homecoming—soul-to-soul.

It was finding the other half of her and finally being able to breath freely.

Of finally, at last, being whole.

ANDREW ACHED FOR Jane, for the spirited girl who had been so thoroughly tamed and bridled.

Her revelations over the morning had been . . . revelatory.

Not misreading his expression, Jane sucked in a deep breath. "Well, I do believe I have reached my allotment for maudlin conversation today. Shall we begin our search?"

Andrew nodded, turning away from Jane before he did something impulsive himself, like kiss her again. He longed to comfort her, to pull her close, and soak his soul in her sorrow, allow her to release her anguish into his shoulder.

Would that he had that right.

Images rushed through him.

Jane laughing with him, feet tucked underneath her, chin resting on her hand. Jane cuddled into his arms, arguing mineralogy in her crisp, aristocratic voice. Jane handing him a wee babe with her eyes and shock of red hair—

Heaven help him.

He was sinking fast.

He ached for that future.

His Jane would be free. Somehow, Andrew would see to it. And if she chose to marry him at the end of it, so much the better.

He pushed the thoughts aside. He would plot his strategy later this evening. For now, he would enjoy the luxury of being in Jane's company.

She fetched a key from an Italian vase on the mantelpiece and unlocked the drawers of the desk.

"You certainly know your way around this room," he said.

"I was an inquisitive child, and the old earl was a creature of habit."

Andrew lifted bundles of papers, letters, and several jotters onto the desk surface.

"Shall we?" he motioned toward the stack. Jane nodded and sank into the desk chair. Andrew pulled another chair over to sit beside hers, a little closer than propriety dictated, but much farther apart than he wanted.

Elbow to elbow, they began to sort through the papers, making the occasional comment.

Unlike the financial records at Hadley Park—which had benefited somewhat from the organizational efforts of the earl's steward—the documents here were in absolute chaos. Letters from stewards about farming investments were mingled with solicitor's requests for funds and creditor's demands for payment.

The documents in Hadley Park painted a picture of an earl who was not prosperous but neither on the brink of despair.

The records here told a different story. It was obvious fairly quickly that the Caribbean Affair was simply the tail end of a lengthy series of poor investment choices. The earldom had been in trouble for many years. The Caribbean Affair of 1814 had simply been a last bid effort to recoup finances.

"So many bad decisions," Andrew finally said, sorting another report of a failed canal scheme.

"How did the earldom have any money at all in the end, I wonder?"

"Hadley Park is just prosperous enough. It's the only thing that kept him afloat."

Jane pursed her lips. "Still nothing about Thomas Madsen or investments in Scotland."

"Nae. I haven't seen anything either. But we have drawers tae go through yet."

Another hour passed; they continued to sort through items. Andrew pulled another drawer out.

"I've been thinking quite a bit about this, and there is one point that I'm struggling to understand," Jane finally said.

Andrew lifted his head, his eyes a question mark.

"All of these papers refer to business issues before 1815," she continued.

He paused, glancing quickly back through the dates of the letters before him. Jane was right. He had yet to see anything after 1815.

"What are you thinking?" he asked.

"I don't know how much you know about the old earl's death—"

"I thought he died of an apoplectic seizure."

"He did. But it wasn't the first seizure he had. He had his first stroke in 1815. Mother thinks it was due to all the stress from that Caribbean Affair."

"Ah. I take it the first stroke affected him?"

"It did. His capacity was greatly diminished from that point onward. In fact, I can't think that he came to Rosehearth again after that. But he continued to have strokes. By 1817, he was no longer speaking. The old earl was insensible."

Andrew sat back in his chair. "I first went into business with Madsen in 1813, so the old earl would have been in charge of his faculties still. We left on our journey in autumn of 1815. When did he have his first stroke?"

"The previous winter, in February of 1815, I think."

"So before we left."

Mmmmm.

Andrew drummed his fingers on the desktop. "Madsen and I had been exploring the possibility of a voyage before winter of 1815, but nothing had been decided. We hadn't hired Captain Cuthie and *The Minerva*. That happened over the summer of 1815. This is all conjecture, of course. If the old earl were involved with Madsen, he could have set things in motion before his stroke. I forgot to ask Madsen when the order to have me killed was sent."

"Or, more likely, the old earl isn't responsible in any way."

Glumly, Andrew nodded. "Aye, that is the more logical assumption, given the facts currently. But sorting through these papers is providing me with a broader understanding of the earl's finances and risk-taking."

He pulled a folder of loose letters toward himself, while Jane opened a wooden box that appeared to contain letters.

He was riffling through tailor's bills when Jane harrumphed.

He lifted his head.

"This is different." She flapped the foolscap she held and then waved it over the open box. "This entire box is full of letters from a man named Wilson reporting to the earl about a boy he keeps referring to as Mackenzie. Why would the old earl care that Mackenzie can ride a pony better than any other eight-year-old he's seen?"

Andrew's heart hiccupped for a moment and then abruptly started again, racing at full tilt. He stared at the paper in her hand, fluttering harmlessly.

Something in his face must have communicated his astonishment. Wordlessly, she handed the letter to him.

Dear Lord Hadley,

I hope this missive finds you in good health. I have received your requests and will get to them shortly.

First, allow me assure you that young Master Mackenzie has completely recovered from his fall last month. The bruise has faded from his forehead. In fact, I saw him riding with his father just five days ago. The lad has a fine seat and can handle the reins of a horse better than any eight-year-old I've ever seen . . .

The letter went on and on, detailing Mackenzie's riding with his father, his attendance at church on Sunday—*he squirmed only a little, wedged between his parents*—and his superior performance in a footrace against the other village lads.

Andrew set down the letter, staring at the box before Jane. There were scores and scores of letters, likely *years* of reports.

This could only mean one thing.

"Andrew?" Jane's concerned voice intruded. A gentle hand on his arm. "Are you quite well? You appear overset."

Dazed, he shook his head. "This is me." He tapped the letter. "These reports are about me."

"Mackenzie?"

"Aye."

"Are you positive?"

"Aye. My father took tae being called by my dey's last name of Mackenzie. He didn't want tae be known as a Langston. So, I adopted it, too. I've always been Andrew Mackenzie, not Andrew Langston or any other title associated with the earldom. Growing up, no one knew we were related tae the Earls of Hadley. Not even Madsen."

Jane looked back at the box. "The earl had you watched?"

"'Twould appear so."

More to the point, the old earl *knew*. He knew that Andrew Langston and Andrew Mackenzie were the same person. Here was proof positive.

Andrew took the box from Jane and riffled through it. So many letters, some of which had clearly been read over and over, the folds creased and worn. Wilson, whoever he was, wrote every month or two.

At the very bottom of the drawer, Andrew found what appeared to be the first letter.

Dear Lord Hadley,

I have news at last. Mrs. Mackenzie was delivered Sunday last of a healthy baby boy. It is said that the child and mother are doing well. The baby is the toast of the village, healthy and braw . . .

Emotion pricked his throat. He read the next letter. And then the next.

Why had his grandfather done this? The reports glowed with pride, from Andrew's first tooth to concern over a persistent fever. There were no letters from his grandfather, obviously, so the conversation was entirely one-sided. Pity there was no return address on the letters. Was this Wilson fellow still alive?

Regardless . . .

"The old earl certainly seems to have been taken with you," Jane said, setting down another letter, this one detailing his success at St. Andrews, including firsts in Latin and mineralogy.

"Aye."

"This doesn't seem like a man who wished you ill," she continued.

That was precisely Andrew's thought. Why would the old earl spend *years* following his every move, and *then* decide to have him murdered?

It made no sense.

"We also haven't found any proof that my grandfather was the investor behind Madsen," he countered.

"True."

Andrew continued to read about his teenage fascination with a village lass named Mhairi. The old earl seemed concerned that Andrew would marry beneath his station.

In Andrew's defense, Mhairi had been beautiful, if a bit flighty. Last he heard, she had married a ship's captain and was happily raising her family in Aberdeen. But that was neither here nor there.

Jane stirred at his elbow.

"So what, precisely, was your Scottish grandfather's profession?" she asked.

"He began as the owner of some iron works outside Perth."

"Hmmm."

That got his attention.

He lifted his head, fixing Jane with a bemused smile. "Ye have a question. I can feel it longing tae break free."

Jane gave a puff of laughter. "It's just . . . the way this Wilson fellow goes on, it sounds as if your grandfather was quite prosperous." She met his eyes, brow raised in question.

He shrugged, not particularly comfortable with discussing the immensity of his fortune with her. It felt a little too much like bragging.

He settled with saying, "As I've said before, I can well meet my financial needs, both my own and those of the earldom."

Jane paused, head tilting before nodding slowly.

I can take on Montacute for you, he willed her to understand. *I am not powerless.*

Finally, she broke his gaze, turning back to the box.

They read through letters for the better part of an hour, description after description of Andrew's life growing up, each one filled with pride and, even more surprising, affection.

Which explained why the last letter in the box caught Andrew utterly unaware.

> *Lord Hadley,*
>
> *Forgive the brevity of this letter, but I didn't want to let this opportunity slip me by. I have heard news that young Mackenzie is seeking a business partner. The investment appears to be sound. I know you wish to remain anonymous, but I am acquainted with a man, Thomas Madsen, who could act as an agent for yourself . . .*

25

Andrew hadn't spoken a word in nearly thirty minutes.

Jane was quite sure she had never witnessed him go so long without uttering a sound.

The letters from Wilson to the old earl were at times charming and hilarious. Andrew had certainly been a handful, but it was obvious that Wilson admired and respected the boy he had been.

With each letter, Andrew had grown quieter and quieter, as if lost in memory, perhaps wondering why his grandfather had spent so much energy understanding him, but never reaching out to him.

Then came the letter mentioning Madsen.

Andrew had read it aloud, Jane listening. He shook his head. A further look through the remaining papers in the drawer revealed solicitor's documents from a Mr. George Smith, Esq., transferring the shares of Andrew's business from Thomas Madsen to the old earl.

Andrew had stared at the documents and then pocketed them, declaring they needed to return to Hadley Park as the afternoon was wearing on.

Andrew drove the phaeton competently, but clearly lost in thought.

Jane understood that sometimes when one had experienced a shock, a lengthy quiet stillness was needed. That didn't stop her from pressing her nails into her palm, the familiar sting nearly unconsciously done.

Jane disliked seeing his cheery countenance so dark and troubled. Andrew was light and sunshine, forever ready with a smile and happy quip.

There was something decidedly wrong with the universe when his mood dipped. She felt helpless against it, the urge to cheer him up any way she could almost overpowering.

Was this love then? This aching tenderness? This maddening desire to set his happiness above her own?

Oh!

Jane quite feared it was.

She loved him.

She loved Andrew.

She truly did.

What was she to do with the information?

He stirred, clucking the horse to continue walking on, circling the quarry's edge. "Thank you."

"Think nothing of it." She swallowed, attempting to quiet her racing heart.

"I didn't ken it would upset me like it has. After all, I went looking for the proof that my grandfather was my missing business partner, that he was the man who ordered my death—"

"Are you certain of that? Those letters don't sound like a man who wished you ill—"

"That Wilson fella? Perhaps not. But Madsen said that he received orders from the true business partner to set the entire catastrophe in order, so it must have been the old earl in the end."

"Again, we don't have proof of that—"

"Och, it's simply a matter of time. I'm sure the evidence is buried in Rosehearth's library. I just have yet tae uncover it. The writing is on the wall, as the Bible says—"

A rider burst through the trees ahead—a groom from the stables.

Andrew pulled the phaeton to a stop, as the lad reined in his horse beside them.

"I'm bade to give you this, my lord. Lady Hadley says 'tis urgent." He handed a folded piece of foolscap to Andrew.

"Thank you."

The lad saluted and wheeled his horse back toward Hadley Park.

Frowning, Andrew read the note, grimaced, and then passed the paper to Jane.

> *Hadley,*
>
> *I just received word that Montacute comes tomorrow. Please return to Hadley Park with haste, as there is much to prepare.*
>
> *Lady Hadley*

Jane's heart performed an acrobatic leap, lodging instantly in her throat.

There could only be one reason why Montacute would be coming.

He would either force Jane to accept Wanleigh.

Or remove her from Hadley Park.

Or, most likely, both.

Too many shocks stacked on top of each other.

First . . . realizing the old earl had likely ordered Andrew's death.

Then . . . her love for Andrew.

And now . . . Montacute coming . . .

Her lungs heaved, and she pressed a trembling hand to her forehead. Her right hand clenched tight, pressing deep into her palm.

What was to be done? This was too soon. She had not had a moment to—

"Here, now," Andrew's voice broke through her terrified ramblings. While she had been panicking, he had descended the carriage and was now standing on the ground beside her. He snagged her hand and helped her down, his hands tugging her close to him. "Is it really as bad as that? Montacute will not harm ye—""You can't know that," she whispered.

"Ah, but I can."

Jane stepped back, raising an eyebrow.

"Are ye truly going tae argue with a Scot about this?" He winked at her. "Ye'd be a right wee dafty tae do that."

She managed a weak chuckle, but that didn't stop her from wrapping her arms across her chest.

"Why is Montacute coming?" Andrew asked, clasping his hands behind his back, resting his weight on one Hessian boot. "I can make several educated guesses, but I'd like tae hear your insight into this."

Wasn't that so like Andrew? He never tried to take her words from her. Instead, he asked and listened.

Was it any wonder she had fallen so hard and fast for him?

"Montacute wishes to pressure me to marry Wanleigh," she replied tonelessly. "I'm sure my mother has already informed him that you and I—" She motioned between them. "—that you and I have become . . . close."

"He wants tae assert his authority over ye?"

Jane nodded.

A pause.

"I meant what I said the night of ball," Andrew continued. "I want ye to have choices, Jane."

She swallowed. It was his first allusion to that night and their kiss.

Biting her lower lip, she pressed her nails into her palm again. "I want to have choices, too."

"Well, that's settled then. Ye'll tell your lofty brother that ye will not be marrying Wanleigh. I'll support ye in your claims, and Montacute will leave."

Jane almost laughed at the absurd naivety of his explanation.

"Montacute will not be so easily pacified, Andrew."

"So he rants and raves and makes threats—"

"They won't be idle threats. If you defend me, you'll only incur his wrath, too."

"Jane." He took a step toward her.

"Andrew." She replied, matching his aggrieved look.

He took hold of her bonnet and gently loosened the ribbons, tossing it onto the phaeton seat behind them. Grasping her hands, he tugged her to him, wrapping both his hands around her waist, pulling her even closer.

A hug.

Andrew Mackenzie Langston was giving her a hug. He ran a hand up her back, soothing her with soft sounds.

She relaxed against him, sagging her head onto his shoulder, arms twining around his neck.

It was so lovely to be held. To breathe in the scent of sandalwood and woodsmoke of his coat. To feel the soft superfine cloth and flex of his shoulder muscles under her cheek, the roll of his throat as he swallowed, the deep rasp of air in his lungs.

She remembered this. How perfectly they fit together, puzzle pieces neatly aligned, her face tucked into his neck, head resting on his shoulder. How gently he held her, as if she were precious and treasured.

He released a long breath of air, lungs heaving out and in. He slumped further around her, pulling her that much closer.

Jane was quite sure she would be content to remain in his arms for the rest of her life.

Yes, please. Let it be you.

She was truly and utterly lost.

"I dinnae care about Montacute's censure, Jane." Scotland thick in his voice next to her ear. "I wish I could properly communicate that tae ye."

"Andrew, but—"

"Nae, let me say my piece." He pulled her that much closer, breath touching her neck. "I'm sure it hasnae escaped your notice that I've developed a distinct fondness for ye."

Something lodged in Jane's throat.

Oh, you beautiful, wonderful man.

Would he offer to marry her himself? To save her from Montacute? But did he truly wish this?

He continued, answering her question. "I fully intend tae court ye and woo ye proper-like."

Jane pushed away, needing to look him in the eye. "Andrew, I cannot allow you to marry me simply to spite Montacute."

"I know." He regarded her solemnly. "I refuse to marry you to spite Montacute."

Jane blinked.

Not *quite* the answer she had expected.

She took a step backwards. He reluctantly slid his hands off her waist.

"I'm not explaining myself right." He grasped her hand, holding it loosely between both of his. He waited until she met his gaze. "You, Lady Jane Everard, deserve more than a marriage of convenience. If and when ye marry, ye deserve tae know that the man you're marrying loves and adores ye for your beautiful, kind, witty, intelligent, remarkable self. Not for your family name, or your dowry, or your brother's machinations, or even kind desperation."

Tears pricked her eyes, turning Andrew into shimmery shades of gray, cream, and blue.

"Ye deserve tae know that only the purest of love sent your beloved to the altar."

Jane hiccupped, biting her lip in earnest.

"Now, here's the part that gets a wee bit difficult for myself." He cleared his throat. "I want that man tae be me, Jane."

Oh!

Tears splashed down her cheeks. She couldn't stop herself from launching onto his chest. His arms banded around her, pulling her tight against him with gratifying speed. His nose dipped into the space between her earlobe and shoulder, nuzzling at her neck.

Jane shivered.

"This isnae a proposal of marriage, Jane. I want tae make that verra clear." His breath tickled her ear.

"It s-sounds v-very marriage-ish," she whispered.

"Nae. It's yer poor English hearing that's thinking that."

"Andrew!" she laughed helplessly, tightening her grip around his neck until he squeaked.

"I mean it, Jane." His tone turned serious. "I may be a wee bit love-sick for ye, but I willnae allow this situation with Montacute tae hurry things along. We both deserve better than that. If and when we decide tae be together, I want us tae both know that it was only for love."

This dear, sweet impossible man.

How had she ever thought him anything but absolutely perfect for her?

He nuzzled her neck more insistently.

"We havenae spoken about that night after the ball," he murmured, brogue rumbling in her ear.

"No," she whispered. "We haven't. I wasn't sure you even remembered."

He laughed, husky and low. "A man always remembers when he kisses a beautiful lass, particularly one as sweet as you, Jane."

Oh, heavens.

"I thought you literally just said that we were not going to court each other until *after* we resolved Montacute's threats," she chuckled.

"Nae, I said we were no' going to affiance ourselves. As for the courting, *that* I have no intention of ceasing."

He kissed her jawline, likely wishing to prove his point.

Her knees sagged. Andrew easily bore her weight, holding her upright.

He snagged her hand at his neck, his larger one dwarfing hers. The press of his calloused fingers sent chills skittering down her arms.

He looked at her palm, noting the half-moons from her nails.

"Ah, Jane," he tsked. "You've made moons for me."

"It's a terrible habit." She flushed and tried to pull her hand away. But his firm grasp held her fast.

"No, ye cannae go. Not until I've soothed this away."

He flashed an impudent grin and then pressed a slow, bone-melting kiss into the palm of her hand. Jane's fingers curved inward, reflexively cupping his face as he pressed another kiss and then another.

Dropping her hand, he bent down, his nose dragging across her cheek, his destination obvious.

Jane turned her head and met him halfway.

His lips were as soft and delicious as she remembered. The heady give and take of his mouth.

He was utterly addicting.

Prim, proper, ever-restrained Lady Jane Everard had fallen for a scandalous, uncouth Scotsman.

And yet . . .

Scandalous, well . . . she supposed he might be that.

But uncouth? No.

And as for the Scottish bit, she was quite certain she had fallen in love with Scotland, too.

Heaven help her.

She did not expect Montacute to accept Andrew as a suitor, earl or no. Her brother had his sights set on Wanleigh as her husband, and she knew from bitter experience that Montacute would be unmovable once he had decided on a course.

Would Andrew be strong enough to withstand Montacute?

Jane didn't know.

The thought made her want to weep.

She kissed her Scottish earl instead.

JANE WOKE THE next day to her maid opening the bedroom shutters and placing a tray of hot chocolate and warm scones on the bedside table. Sun streamed through the window, promising another golden day. The girl bobbed a curtsy and exited.

Today was the day, then.

Montacute would arrive just after luncheon.

Drawing in a steadying breath, Jane sat up.

Yesterday with Andrew . . .

If and when we decide tae be together, I want us tae both know that it was only for love.

His words would not leave her.

She wanted that for him. She wanted that for her.

How had he become so wise?

Not that she would tell him as much. His confident Scottish head did not need to be inflated further. She smiled at the thought.

Sitting up, she finally noticed the small, velvet pouch resting beside her scone on the tray. Curious, she pulled it open. A note tumbled out, along with a heavy bracelet that gleamed red and black.

I cannot bear to see moon prints marking your fair skin. You merit more than a wee imprint of heaven. I would give you entire universes, but until then, please accept this as a paltry substitute.
—A

Her giggling laughter surprised even herself. Whatever had Andrew done?

She picked up the bracelet, examining it.

Polished black beads shimmered, alternating with ruby garnets set in gleaming silver. The garnets were beautiful, but the black stone beads puzzled her for a moment. The opalescence trapped in the black flickered as she rotated the bracelet in the light.

Oh!

The stones were meteorite, pieces of the moon tumbled to earth.

He had literally given her a 'bit of heaven,' as he said. Tangible, perfectly-round little moons to dot her wrist.

Jane was quite sure her heart would burst.

But, of course, such good bonhomie could not last. Jane descended the grand staircase of Hadley Park, the bracelet upon her wrist, eager to find Andrew.

She was met, instead, by her mother walking quickly away from the housekeeper.

Lady Hadley's eyes had gained a mercenary, flinty edge as she scanned Jane up and down. Such a look never boded well.

"We have much to do today, Jane. Montacute arrives soon. Wanleigh and Lord and Lady Whitcomb have been invited to dinner." Her mother raised her chin. "You should prepare yourself to act as your brother expects the daughter of the Duke of Montacute to behave."

Normally, such an announcement would send panic flooding her limbs, but not today. With Andrew's promises from yesterday yet ringing in her ears and his bit of heaven around her wrist, Jane was able to merely nod at her mother's words.

She and Andrew would face Montacute together.

26

The Duke of Montacute was an unbearable ass.

Andrew did not describe a man thus lightly. But there was no other word that so perfectly encompassed the sheer pompous self-importance that clung to Jane's older half-brother.

The first indication of Montacute's asinine-ness—asinanity? asinancity?—was the brief missive awaiting Andrew when he returned to Hadley Park after visiting Rosehearth.

> *I will be arriving tomorrow afternoon. Please see that all is in order for*
> *my arrival.*
>
> *Montacute*

That was it. No salutation. No question if the duke would be welcomed or inconveniencing Andrew's staff or himself. Worse, no indication of how long he would be staying.

Nothing more.

It was unbearably rude. The haughty decree of a man who had never heard the word, *No*.

Andrew struggled to focus in the hours leading up to Montacute's arrival.

So many concerns crowded his mind.

Not unsurprisingly, Jane loomed largest. Andrew had declared himself, and Jane had been gratifyingly receptive.

But he also meant what he said.

Andrew refused to allow the situation to hasten his own attachment to Jane, and hers to him. They both deserved to know that their affection for each other was genuine and not born of convenience, or worse, desperation. He hoped that his promises gave Jane something to hold to as they faced down Montacute together.

But other thoughts lingered, as well.

His grandfather had been the owner of those outstanding shares. Ironically, that meant Andrew owned them now.

He struggled to reconcile that the man who had watched him grow from infancy, seemingly interested in the minutest details of his life, had also wanted him dead. That his grandfather had set in motion plans to have Andrew killed. Had the old man's stroke addled his thinking?

Andrew's problems with the Committee on Privilege and Chancery were still ongoing. How long before Lords agreed to allow him his seat? And given that Andrew would likely make an enemy of Montacute once this business with Jane concluded, how much more difficult would the process become?

Montacute arrived in splendor, his carriage suitably gilded and polished as befitted a duke.

Their greeting in the entrance hall was tense as Jane introduced Andrew to her half-brother.

"Hadley," Montacute acknowledged Andrew with the barest dip of his head before giving a similarly arctic nod to Lady Hadley and Peter.

He then turned his attention to his sister. He greeted Jane with similar reserve, replying with one-word answers to her polite questions.

Yes, his journey had been uneventful.

Yes, he was in good health.

No, he did not find the country air particularly refreshing.

Jane had not overstated her half-brother's arrogant, petty nature.

But Andrew had not anticipated the familial resemblance between them. Though Montacute was dark-haired, he and Jane shared the same gray eyes and lean height. They were clearly siblings, despite Montacute being nearly twenty years Jane's senior.

After a minute of conversation with Jane, Montacute flicked his gaze over Andrew and stated, "You may go, Hadley. Your presence is not needed here. Jane and I have family matters to discuss."

Andrew felt palpable shock at Montacute's unbearable rudeness. To be so dismissed? And in his own *home*?

Jane maintained a polite expression on her face, but even her eyes widened at the insult.

Andrew bowed—curt and short—and took himself off to the estate office to consult with his steward over a drainage problem in a lower field before he did something rash.

It was the better part of an hour before his blood calmed from boiling to a low simmer.

Of course, all the effort was wasted. When walking back through the house to dress for dinner, he couldn't help but hear Montacute's voice in the library—his cool aristocratic tones already unmistakable.

". . . your mother informs me that you are not showing a proper interest in Lord Wanleigh. I am most disappointed in you, Jane."

"I appreciate your concern, Duke, but I do not find Lord Wanleigh's attentions desirable—"

"I have had great patience with this matter, Jane. But you will be five and twenty soon. You are far too old to still be unwed. I have indulged you long enough."

"If I were to look a little lower than a marquess—"

"Lower? Bah. The blood of the Dukes of Montacute runs thick in your veins. You cannot, for a second, consider that I would allow you to mingle with those of lesser standing?"

"Perhaps, but if I could simply—"

"Enough, Jane. Enough of this selfish thoughtlessness. You are making this situation unpleasant. You will be obedient to my wishes. If and when Wanleigh declares himself, you will accept him. Do not force me to behave in a manner that would be injurious to you. I will say no more on this matter."

Andrew stood outside the library for a solid three minutes, chest heaving, fists clenching and unclenching, listening as their conversation moved on to their grandmother's health.

He knew storming into the room and releasing his anger on Montacute would not help Jane's situation. And, yet, the urge to do so was powerful.

Was Jane all right? Would Montacute only use words to wound?

Jane would not be forced to marry Wanleigh. Andrew would steal her away before watching such a farce.

Their voices retreated into murmurs. And yet it took another couple minutes before Andrew could force his feet to move on.

Tomorrow, he and Jane would sit down together with Montacute and make the situation excruciatingly clear to the duke.

As he dressed for dinner, Andrew briefly considered donning his kilt. When confronted with such jackassery, his knee-jerk reaction was to force others to assume the worst.

But as he stared at the length of plaid folded in the armoire, he realized he truly was no longer that person.

Yes, Montacute was a bully—a cruel tyrant.

Yes, he wished to hurt and offend, using his words as weapons to control others.

Montacute wanted Andrew to react, and by doing so, acknowledge the duke's mastery over him.

His mother's words from that haberdashery so long ago rang in his head: Never allow others to choose how you feel.

He needed to heed her words more thoroughly.

Andrew straightened his shoulders and instructed his valet to dress him with impeccable care.

In the end, he donned only one nod to his Scottish heritage—Jamie's tartan.

"I AM SURE understanding the intricacies of land management and your potential duties in the House of Lords has been overwhelming for you," the duke said over their soup course, fixing Andrew with his gray eyes.

Montacute had a distinctly aristocratic face—sagging cheeks, hairline slightly receding, all suspended over an exceptionally long nose.

The better for looking down upon lesser mortals, Andrew suspected.

Everyone seated at the table turned their heads in Andrew's direction. They were a small group tonight in terms of numbers. Lord and Lady Whitcomb had arrived with Lord Wanleigh in tow. Peter, Jane, and Lady Hadley rounded out the dinner guests.

Andrew dabbed at his mouth with a napkin before answering. "I feel that I have been able tae execute my obligations with relative ease, Duke."

Andrew allowed his gaze to drift to Jane down the table. She shot him a wan smile, a paltry thing that didn't touch her eyes.

Andrew hated that Montacute had stolen her spirit yet again. But she wore Andrew's bracelet. He caught the glimmer of its polished, round stones in the candlelight. He willed Jane to remember what it stood for—that she deserved better than mere half-moon impressions of reality. She merited whole worlds.

Something in his eyes must have buoyed her up.

"Lord Hadley spent the afternoon meeting with his steward, did you not?" Jane offered, taking a slow sip of soup.

"Aye, I did, Lady Jane."

"How is the south field coming?" Peter asked, further turning the conversation and drawing Montacute's attention from belittling Andrew. "Has the drainage improved?"

Andrew smiled, acknowledging Peter's help. The two of them had come a long way in their relationship, forming the beginnings of a true friendship.

Lady Hadley set down her spoon. "Please do not speak of agriculture, Peter. I see quite enough of it out my window at present." She sent Montacute an apologetic frown.

Everyone smiled politely at her comment, allowing the conversation to drift back to the duke.

Peter flashed his mother a dark look before taking a large gulp of his wine. If the conversation continued like this, he would be deep in his cups before dessert.

Andrew noted Jane twisting the bracelet on her wrist, turning the round moons with her thumb, strumming the stones almost like a talisman.

"You are quite confident, Hadley." Montacute turned back to him. "I am sure managing the expectations of the earldom must be difficult for a man of your . . . upbringing."

"Hear, hear," Wanleigh agreed from his seat beside Jane.

Andrew took a sip of wine, mentally debating the pros and cons of antagonizing the Duke of Montacute.

Hah! It was a short-lived debate.

The devil in him couldn't resist baiting the bull.

Besides, it was a quick way to take Montacute's full measure. Would the duke directly threaten? Or use more subtle tactics?

"My upbringing?' Andrew asked, tone mild and genuinely curious. "What, pray tell, do you know about my upbringing?"

Montacute smiled. His expression said he found Andrew's impertinence vaguely amusing, in the way of a rambunctious child. "I do not wish to sully our present conversation with a lengthy list of the objectionable nature of your parentage, Hadley. Suffice it to say, if you must ask the question, you would not understand my explanation." *Ah.* Subtly direct.

Bloody hell.

The man was a menace.

"Are ye so sure?"

Montacute missed the implied sarcasm in the question. Or if he *did* catch it, he didn't care. Andrew guessed it was the latter.

Regardless, Montacute decided to indulge Andrew.

"One's station in life requires a minute understanding of social etiquette and aristocratic obligations. The peerage rule Britain, and as such, have a responsibility to understand that which we govern." The duke leaned back in his chair, fingering his wine glass. "Most peers begin learning this lengthy list of rules while still in leading strings. Some, however ..." The duke paused. "... *some* do not receive this instruction, much to their own detriment."

Andrew longed to roll his eyes.

Wanleigh nodded his head. "You reach to the heart of the matter, Duke. Our responsibilities are not easily assumed and mastered."

"Precisely," Montacute replied with languid ease. "When one is raised among one's own, you make important friendships early. More significantly, one intuitively understands power and how the world works." He sipped his wine. "A true *English* lord would never be at a loss as to how to behave properly. He commands his world with ease."

Andrew chose not to reply. He felt no compunction to defend his skills as a manager and administrator. His business ventures over the years had proved his capabilities there.

Montacute continued talking, waxing on the importance of camaraderie in social position and the power wielded through familial and friendship ties. The gist of his monologue was clear:

Noblemen who stepped outside the rigid bounds of the *ton* risked financial and social ruin.

Of course, Andrew would have to want to be part of the social whirlwind of the *ton* to care. As for finances, he had no need of the *ton* for that.

However, he was curious why Montacute wished to convince Andrew that connections and friendships mattered. What was the man's agenda?

Andrew had thought Montacute was here only to push Jane into a marriage with Wanleigh, but his current conversation was unrelated to that.

Did Montacute simply like to hear the sound of his own voice?

Or was more afoot?

"The upper echelons of *ton* take care of ourselves. We know where and when to offer encouragement," Montacute commented over roast fowl. "For example, I know that your predecessor, the former earl, carried investments with a Scottish man named Mackenzie."

Andrew froze, shock jolting him, a stupefied tingling spreading through his body like wildfire.

What had the duke just said? His comment had come out of seemingly nowhere. Surely the man couldn't be referring to Andrew's own business in Scotland?

Andrew set down his cutlery, staring at the duke. What was Montacute about?

"Mackenzie?" he managed to ask, face numb and stiff.

"I've heard talk of Mackenzie," Wanleigh said around a mouthful of pheasant. "They call him the Scottish Vulcan, don't they? The man owns multiple iron and gas works and is rich as a god."

"The very same," Montacute nodded.

Andrew's brain scrambled to catch up. Why had the conversation taken this turn?

Montacute knew the old earl had invested with Mackenzie.

Did he know that Andrew *was* Mackenzie?

So far the conversation would indicate he did *not*, but . . .

Andrew chanced a glance down the table at Jane. She met his gaze with wide eyes, her fingers freezing their worrying of his bracelet.

Are you truly that wealthy? He could feel the question in her.

He shot her a tight smile and turned back to Montacute, giving her all the confirmation she needed.

Montacute continued, perhaps mistaking Andrew's silence for awe. "Thus far no one has been able to lure Mackenzie from Scotland. I hope to encourage the man to make an appearance in London."

Montacute truly believed this? This was news to Andrew.

What was Montacute up to? Was he playing more cat-and-mouse games?

Did the duke know that Andrew was Mackenzie and was trying to . . . what? Manipulate him to some end?

Or did Montacute have another aim here?

How to tread this conversation?

"I've heard of Mackenzie," Andrew said after a moment's pause, rapidly deciding how much to divulge. "But I did not realize it was commonly known that the Earldom of Hadley had formed a business partnership with the man. I only learned of the connection yesterday. I was unaware that you were in such close confidence with the old earl, Montacute."

Montacute smiled, a chilling expression. "The old earl kept his finances private, as I am sure you are aware." The duke's tone implied that Hadley had few financial options in the first place.

But Montacute, did *not* in fact, answer Andrew's implied question. How had he known about the old earl's investment in Andrew's enterprises?

Was Montacute involved with Madsen? And if so, why?

Andrew's mind spun with possible theories.

He pressed his point. "So the old earl shared with you the details of his relationship with Mackenzie?"

It was a direct question this time. A simple yes-or-no answer.

Wanleigh let out a bark of laughter, jumping into the conversation. "We all know the former earl was a tad senseless the last years of his life. Thankfully Peter stepped up to lend a hand, didn't you, lad? Set investments with Mackenzie aright." Wanleigh winked at Peter, turning towards him. "Though you do tend to talk when you are deep in your cups, Peter."

Andrew raised his eyebrows, turning his eyes to his heir, who had reached for his wine glass again, expression pale.

Peter?

Andrew knew that Peter had helped the steward a wee bit during the last years of his father's life. But Peter had known about the old earl's investments with Mackenzie?

More to the point, had Peter known that Andrew Mackenzie and Andrew Langston were one and the same? Someone with access to the old earl's papers at Rosehearth might have deduced the connection. The more Andrew pondered it, the more likely it seemed that Peter could have known.

And if Peter had known, why not mention it to Andrew? Why hide the information? Unless, of course, Peter *had* something to hide.

And how much had Peter told Montacute?

Given how quickly Jane turned to her brother, her thoughts were similar to Andrew's.

Peter did not meet either of their eyes and chose instead to take another swallow of wine.

"Careful, lad," Wanleigh continued. "You might end up disguised sooner rather than later."

"Indeed." Montacute gave a rigid smile. "We shall discuss this later over our port, as I am sure the ladies have already tired of our business conversation."

Andrew's mind spun through the remainder of the meal.

Peter continued to avoid his gaze, face pale and withdrawn.

Overall, his heir's actions spoke loudly to some lingering guilt.

Jane's words from the previous day resurfaced. *The old earl was insensible.*

The more Andrew pondered it, the more snippets of conversation and pieces of the puzzle slid into place.

Was *Peter* the person who had commanded Madsen to engineer Andrew's accidental death? Not the old earl? If so, Peter would have been young, only sixteen or seventeen at the time.

Or had Peter told Montacute about Andrew's business dealings and the duke had been the one to arrange things with Madsen? And to what end? Why would Montacute wish Andrew's death?

And how odd to be slicing roast beef and wondering which of his dinner companions had ordered his murder?

When Lady Hadley finally motioned for the ladies to retire and leave the men to their port, he was fairly bursting with questions.

And yet, Andrew remained silent.

Montacute struck him as the kind of man who would use every iota of information for his own personal gain.

Jane shot him a concerned look as she followed her mother out of the room. Andrew could only imagine how she longed to stay. It was ridiculous that women were excluded from discussions of business.

And with Montacute bringing Andrew's businesses into the mix, what did that mean for Jane herself?

How had everything suddenly become so utterly intertwined?

After the door clicked behind the ladies and the footmen had left the room, Montacute poured himself a small glass of port before sliding the bottle towards Andrew and sitting back in his chair. "So, you know about the former earl's investments with Mackenzie, then?"

If Montacute knew Andrew *was* Mackenzie, he was remaining mum on that score. What had Peter told him?

"Aye," Andrew replied, keeping a tense eye on Peter. "But now I'm left wondering why ye care tae bring it up, Duke?"

Montacute shrugged. "If you had enough education in these matters, it would be obvious enough, but as you don't, I shall spell it out for you. You are without funds, Hadley. You have little to no ready cash and everything is mortgaged to the hilt. Your lands and properties are in disrepair. You need money."

Andrew drummed his fingers on the tabletop. "So you say," he said.

Obviously, the fact that he had paid off all the earldom's debts had not become common knowledge. And the longer this conversation continued, the more Andrew suspected that Peter had *not* told Montacute the truth of Andrew's finances.

The duke raised his eyebrows at Andrew's tone.

"I come offering you salvation, Hadley." Only a simpleton would miss the steel in Montacute's voice. "Wanleigh and I are ready to give you a handsome offer for Mackenzie's shares. Consider it a gift."

"Ye want me tae sell Mackenzie's shares to ye?"

"Precisely."

Sell the last remaining shares of his business that an outside party owned? And to Montacute no less?

Over my dead body, was Andrew's instant response.

He'd sooner climb into a bed lined with snakes than do business with the likes of Montacute. The duke would take and manipulate and exploit anything he saw as his to his own ends.

Never.

Besides, Andrew needed to help Jane escape this man's clutches, not tether them both to him.

Montacute didn't misunderstand Andrew's silence.

"You are weighing the pros and cons of selling to me, I can see. Possibly contemplating seeing what others will offer you."

Andrew decided to nibble a wee bit on the bait Montacute dangled. "I ken that Mackenzie has supposedly sold out of *all* of his shared business interests. The shares I hold might be the only ones still outstanding." How odd to be talking about himself in the third person. "If so, that would make them even more valuable."

Montacute snorted. "Tell me, Hadley," the duke said, languid hauteur in his tone, "how goes your suit with the Committee on Privilege? Finding it difficult to take your seat in Lords, are you?"

Montacute swirled his port in his glass, eyeing Andrew over the rim. Candlelight flickered in the duke's eyes.

Ah.

Puzzle pieces slotted into place.

"You've been blocking my Writ of Summons, have ye? I'm assuming ye were behind me being black-balled from White's, as well, aye?"

Montacute offered a bland smile in reply. "Friends, Hadley, help friends. I am asking a favor of you. Sell me Mackenzie's shares—"

"At a fraction of their value?"

"At a price I name," the duke replied, as if somehow that were different. "It will be . . . enough. And in return, I will see that the Committee on Privilege and Chancery straighten out this small mess they have made with your Writ of Summons."

Andrew's jaw ticked. "Because you and I are . . . *friends?*"

He desperately wanted to laugh. The duke was an arrogant eejit.

The man had deliberately blocked Andrew's acceptance into the

House of Lords and was now using that fact to blackmail him into selling valuable business shares at a fraction of their value. More money to line Montacute's already wealthy pockets.

It was diabolically cruel and unsporting and exactly the kind of behavior Andrew anticipated from a man like Montacute.

Montacute misunderstood Andrew's hesitation. "Allow me to put this in plainer terms, ones that even an uneducated Highlander can understand: You are outmaneuvered, Hadley. You are a green novice in a field of masters. Withdraw while you still have opportunities. Take my offer—a sum for Mackenzie's business shares and your seat in Lords. Use the money to improve your estates. Marry the daughter of a wealthy cit and line your pockets further. Face the truth now—you will never be good *ton*. But if you make careful choices, you can at least remove the stench of your lowly Scottish beginnings. Your children will reap the benefits of your prudent behavior."

Unbelievable.

Montacute was truly a snake.

Andrew would never agree to such terms, obviously.

But one thing had become clear—Montacute did *not* know Andrew *was* Mackenzie. If so, he would know that Andrew didn't need funds.

In fact, Montacute had nothing Andrew needed.

The Committee on Privilege *had* to approve his Writ of Summons eventually. Montacute could make noise and be difficult, but he couldn't block it forever. Andrew would wait him out.

As for the business shares . . .

He nearly snorted.

The bigger question was how to untangle himself from Montacute without creating a powerful enemy in the process. Montacute had the ear of the Prince Regent. He could make Andrew's life difficult if he chose.

And Andrew was desperate for Jane's freedom. Something Montacute, thankfully, did not know.

Montacute mistook Andrew's silence for acquiescence.

"In time, you will learn the importance of allies and trust within the *ton*," he said. "For example, I know that I will soon welcome Wanleigh as my brother-in-law."

The duke's abrupt change in topic dowsed Andrew in cold water. "Pardon?"

He shot a glance at the aging marquess downing his port in eager gulps. Montacute followed his gaze.

"Lady Jane will be the most fortunate of women. Do you not agree, Wanleigh?"

Wanleigh smiled. It made Andrew's stomach crawl.

"Of course," Wanleigh said. "Naturally, I shall consider it my duty to ensure her happiness. She will make me a decorous, reserved wife."

Andrew met Montacute's eyes. The warning there was unmistakable. *My sister is not for you. Do not think otherwise.*

"We shall all celebrate Lady Jane's happiness, will we not, Hadley?"

Andrew couldn't force an answer past his lips. His heart galloped and bucked, flooding his veins with forceful energy.

A decorous, reserved wife? Jane? Clearly neither man knew the woman at all.

No. He would do whatever he could to prevent *that* fate.

Andrew would be patient. Montacute thought he was the cat to Andrew's mouse. The man was in for a rude awakening.

But for now, Andrew had another problem.

He let his eyes drift down the table to Peter.

Montacute hadn't known about the connection between Andrew Mackenzie and Andrew Langston. Therefore, he likely hadn't ordered Andrew's death.

But Peter, on the other hand . . .

As if confirming his guilt, his heir continued to avoid Andrew's gaze, choosing instead to sink lower and lower into his chair.

As if that would spare him questioning. Andrew's chest heaved, his breathing tight.

Too many revelations. Too many questions.

He counted Peter a friend . . . or, at least, he had.

What did Peter know?

And, more to the point, what had Peter done with that knowledge?

27

J ane sat with her mother and Lady Whitcomb in the drawing room, neatly stitching flowers. The ladies discussed Paris fashions and the latest gossip surrounding a local squire.

Jane wanted to stab herself with her embroidery needle. If she never heard a conversation about bonnet trims again, it would be too soon.

No, she *needed* to know what the men were discussing in the dining room.

Wasn't this a woman's lot in life? Her world could be tumbling down around her, but a proper lady would sit and calmly stitch poppies and butterflies despite the chaos.

Embroidery, in moments like this, was not nearly violent enough for Jane's taste. Clearly, a sadistic man had dreamed up the pastime.

Her emotions were a see-saw.

First, there was frustration.

What did Montacute know? Was there more to his coming than simply forcing Jane's compliance?

Second, there was panic.

And what had Peter done? She knew her brother. He had some finger in the old earl's business dealings.

Third, there was elation.

Andrew was this Scottish Vulcan? Wealthy as a god? Truly?

Jane wanted to feel outraged over his reticence. He had decidedly downplayed his wealth.

But instead, the knowledge simply led to . . . relief. Utter, blessed *relief.*

Andrew truly didn't need her dowry.

It also explained how he was able to instantly address all the needs of the floundering earldom. It showed his diligence as a landlord that he assumed responsibility for his lands and his people.

His bracelet dangled from her wrist, a solid promise.

They would fight Montacute together.

And then they would choose each other. Of *that,* Jane was sure.

The men lingered over their port so long, Jane began to worry she wouldn't see Peter or Andrew at all.

Finally, the men's voices sounded in the entrance hall, crossing from the dining room to the drawing room.

Jane turned her head toward the door.

Peter was the first one through, swaying slightly on his feet, obviously a trifle disguised. Montacute followed and then Whitcomb. Wanleigh entered last and met her gaze with a smug, possessive look that set Jane's skin to crawling.

But no Andrew. Where was he?

"Hadley had some urgent estate business to attend to," Wanleigh explained.

Montacute smiled. It was his self-satisfied smile that always sent chills skittering down Jane's spine. "He can give his properties all the attention in the world, but without ready funds . . ."

Wanleigh laughed.

Peter stared at the door, clearly longing for escape, too. Her brother's reaction spoke loudly to some guilt.

Oh, Peter. What did you do?

Jane gritted her teeth, barely avoiding flinching. If she had to listen to another minute of this, she would resort to violence.

She had an embroidery needle, after all.

"Jane, dear, are you quite all right?" Lady Whitcomb asked, having noted Jane's wince.

Hallelujah. Salvation, at least.

"I am afraid I have developed quite the headache, Lady Whitcomb." Jane pressed a trembling hand to her forehead. "Perhaps it would be best if I withdraw for the evening."

Her mother murmured a few words, voice strained. Peter raised his eyebrow a fraction, expression stating he knew full well that she wasn't ill. Montacute's gaze promised a lengthy scold for daring to escape the drawing room and Wanleigh's attentions.

Jane all but ran from the room.

She intended to retire to her bedchamber, truly she did. But as she walked down the corridor to her chamber, she noted a faint light coming from underneath Peter's door.

Oh!

Who was in Peter's room at this hour?

Another dreadful thought occurred:

Was this the 'estate business' then that had sent Andrew rushing off?

Jane pushed open her brother's door. As a son of the house, Peter had a suite of rooms, including a small sitting room and dressing room which adjoined the main bedchamber.

The light came from Peter's sitting room, a rectangular strip stretching across his bedroom.

Jane crossed to the open door, gripping the frame, skirts flowing around her.

It was exactly as she feared.

Andrew stood over Peter's private desk, riffling through papers. A candelabra on the desk outlined him in golden light, brows drawn down, expression grim. The candles sputtered and flickered, acknowledging Jane's arrival.

Andrew didn't even raise his head to look at her. A quirk of his eyebrows being the only tell that he even knew she was there.

"You cannot invade Peter's privacy like this," she hissed, advancing on him.

"I can and I will," was his reply, continuing to flip through a set of papers.

"Let Peter explain himself. You are invading his inner sanctum here. You're a better man than this, Andrew."

"Nae, I'm a rag-mannered idiot." His tone dripped sarcasm. He pulled out a sheet of foolscap, and then another, setting them aside. "We do things like this all the time, ye ken."

Jane ground her teeth. "Stop trying to pick a fight with me."

"Is it working?"

She shook her head. "Don't do this, Andrew. Talk to Peter." He paused, fixing her with his blue eyes, cold and steely. "People I loved died, Jane. *I* nearly died. I will have justice for them. I will have justice for Jamie. I will have justice for myself."

"And is this how you achieve justice?! Ransacking a young man's rooms?"

"Justice comes in many forms, Jane. Peter knows a wee bit more than he's let on. Enough tae inform Montacute."

"So Peter knew about the old earl's ties to you." Jane threw her hands in the air. "That doesn't follow that he is guilty of attempted murder! You don't know who set events in motion with Madsen."

"You're right." His head snapped upright, eyes boring into her. "I don't ken what happened with Madsen. That's why I'm here—tae see for my own eyes what Peter may have done."

"This is absurd! Peter would have been, what? All of seventeen when you set out on your journey? He was practically a child—"

"Seventeen is old enough tae be a man, Jane. Soldiers kill and die at seventeen. Men marry and become fathers at seventeen. I need tae know the truth before Peter or anyone else has a chance tae destroy it." He waved a hand over the documents.

"This is madness, Andrew. Please. Talk to Peter. If you have any affection for me at all, please stop."

That got his full attention. He snatched the handful of the papers he had set aside off the desk and stomped over to her. His shoulders blocked the light, painting him in backlit shapes of black and white.

Jane stood firm. Though given the heat in his eyes, she may have been wise to beat a retreat.

"If *I* have any affection for *you*?" His nostrils flared. "Ye would tie this tae my love for ye?"

Love?

Oh!

They hadn't spoken of love out loud until now.

Did he love her, then? Truly?

Andrew continued, seemingly heedless of what he had said. "If ye had any affection for *me*, Jane, ye would want tae know the truth. Ye would stand with me in avenging Jamie and all those lives lost. Ye would not ask me tae step aside—"

"I am not asking you to step aside but to give Peter a chance to explain this himself. Will you condemn my brother without proof? Is *that* your idea of justice—"

"Nae. I'm no' that person—"

"—judge and jury before finding evidence—"

"What is going on here?!" A voice came from behind them.

Jane and Andrew whirled.

Peter stood in the door, hand leaning against the frame. His hair askew, eyes bleary from drink. He swayed on his feet.

"Peter!" Jane stepped closer, holding out a staying hand to her brother, tears setting in earnest.

Peter scanned the room, the papers strewn across his desk. Candle-light flickered, illuminating the bookshelves along one wall and a small cabinet next to the desk.

"How dare you invade my personal study?!" he spluttered, eyes staring at the cabinet.

Peter moved to push past Jane angling his body forward, but she stopped him with a hand to his chest.

She couldn't bear to see Andrew and Peter at odds. They were two halves of her soul.

How had events come to this?

Andrew stared at Peter before shaking his head and turning back to the desk and the correspondence there. He moved a few more pieces of paper before rotating around with a sigh.

"This will be easier if ye cooperate, Peter." Andrew tapped the papers on the desk. "What did ye know about the old earl's investments with me and my trip tae the South Pacific?"

Peter stood taller, his jaw tensing, face pale. "I know nothing."

Jane's stomach sank.

Her brother clearly knew *something*. Why not admit it? Why was he hedging?

Worse, why was he wearing his mulish expression, the one he adopted when he wished to be his most intransigent?

Peter took a side-step, as if he were going to inch along the wall.

"Peter, just tell Andrew what you know," Jane said, shooting him a beseeching look.

"I know nothing!"

"Och, ye knew enough tae tell Montacute about it—

"Andrew, please." Jane turned to him. "Peter would have been too young to *do* anything, a mere youth, as I keep saying. This is absurd."

"Is it? Is it, Jane? I was making business investments at his age." Andrew's voice rose. "As I said, good men died. People I loved and fought for. I almost died myself. We. Deserve. Justice."

"I don't understand what you're referring to," Peter growled. He inched forward again, his eyes dropping to the cabinet against the wall. Without thinking, Jane's eyes followed the movement.

Andrew's gaze followed suit. But he was quicker than Jane to pick up on it.

"Why do you appear concerned about that cabinet?" Andrew asked, waving a hand toward the small chest standing thigh-high next to the desk. It was a mahogany chest of drawers inlaid with flowers. Jane knew Peter kept the two narrow drawers at the top continually locked.

Peter glanced at the cabinet.

"I am not concerned about the cabinet," her brother said.

Jane nearly closed her eyes.

Peter was *definitely* concerned about the cabinet.

Andrew was no slow-top.

"Prove it," Andrew replied. "Open it."

Peter bristled, voice rising as he talked. "I do not have to answer to you. These are my private quarters and my private papers and my private things—"

"My house!" Andrew jabbed a finger toward his own chest. "My life that was threatened. My people and friends who died. My right tae seek justice—"

"I have done nothing!"

"Then prove it, Peter. If there is nothing tae hide, then open the cabinet and show me its contents."

"Hadley, this is ridiculous—"

"Open the bloody cabinet, Peter. Or so help me, I'll smash it tae bits. I'm happy tae play the barbarian you English ken that I am."

Growling, Peter stomped away from the cabinet, running his hands through his hair.

He did *not*, however, open it.

Shaking his head, Andrew snagged a letter opener from the desktop. A sharp jab into the keyhole destroyed the locking mechanism.

Peter began pacing as Andrew worked.

"I am appalled that you are destroying my privacy like this, Hadley," Peter raged from across the room. "How can you let him do this, Jane? Have you no care for me now?"

Jane wanted to wring her hands from the tension. How could things have come to this? Trapped between her love for her brother and her love for the man she hoped to marry?

Andrew pulled out the top drawer. It was littered with tailor's bills and other odds and ends.

The second drawer consisted entirely of letters.

Peter snarled, continuing to pace.

Andrew pulled them out, letter after letter, flipping one open after the other, scanning them in the candlelight.

"Well? Have you found anything?" Jane asked at last. "The least you can do is find proof of some wrongdoing after putting on this ghastly charade."

Andrew's face turned weary. He blinked and took a step back.

"Aye." He looked down at the papers in his hand. "Aye. I've found enough."

Jane snatched the top one from his grasp. Words leaped out at her.

. . . you have suggested a brilliant plan . . .

. . . Mackenzie needs to be brought down a peg or two . . .

She swallowed.

Oh, Peter! What have you done?!

She held out her palm for another letter. Andrew handed it to her, his expression wordlessly communicating his anger and agitation.

. . . found the right captain for this venture . . .

. . . Cuthie says he will ensure the deed is done with exquisite discretion . . .

. . . no one will ever suspect us . . .

. . . yours to command, T. Madsen . . .

She pressed a trembling hand to her brow.

No! Her heart screamed. *No, this can't be! Not Peter. Not this.*

But these were clearly letters from Madsen, addressed to Peter, discussing their plans to arrange for Andrew's death.

What was she to do? Panic and anger and terror converged in her throat, clogging her breathing and blurring her eyes.

She simply couldn't assimilate it all. Her mind struggled to rearrange her life to accommodate the horror.

The guilt.

The grief.

Peter was all she had.

If Andrew brought charges against him, Peter could be hanged for attempted murder of a Peer of the Realm.

What was she ever to do?

She looked back and forth between the men. Peter's sullen countenance. Andrew's angry, troubled gaze.

"T-there has to be s-some other explanation," she began, teeth chattering. "Peter had to have been t-too young to arrange this—"

"Not too young, Jane. Foolish, definitely, but not too young." Andrew shot his heir a tight glance before taking the papers from her lifeless fingers, adding them back to the stack. "Peter arranged for my murder. He hired Captain Cuthie. He authorized the illegal kidnapping of those innocent villagers."

"Murder? Villagers?!" Peter reared back in alarm.

Jane and Andrew ignored him.

"Peter is a good m-man!" she nearly shouted, swiping at an errant tear that escaped to tumble down her cheek. "He wouldn't order a sea c-captain to enslave innocent p-people!"

"Enslave people?" Peter was appearing more and more alarmed with every passing moment. "What on earth—"

"These documents would say otherwise." Andrew shook the stack of papers at her.

"I know my brother, Andrew! There must be some m-mistake—"

"There is no mistake, Jane."

She bit her lip. "But—"

"There is no *but* here, Jane! Cannae ye see? Yer brother saw an opportunity and he took it."

"But why—"

"Why? *Why?!* The answer is glaringly obvious! We asked, who benefits from ma death? The answer is simple—Peter does." Andrew jabbed a finger in Peter's direction. "He was the next in line. If I had died *before* the old earl, Peter would have inherited everything—the title, the lands, everything!"

"This is absurd," Peter spluttered. "I never enslaved anyone! I'm sure there is some logical explanation—"

Andrew whirled toward him. "Explanation? For this?" He spread his hands wide, encompassing the disheveled room, brandishing the papers still in his hand. "What excuse can ye give, Peter? What justification merits condemning innocent people tae death? What about the blood staining yer own hands?!"

"Death? People?" Peter flinched. "I don't know to what you refer."

"Hah!" Andrew threw the words at him. He shook the letters. "I'm holding proof right here that ye knew enough. Did ye think tae remove me as the heir and set yourself up as the Earl of Hadley?"

Peter's eyes followed the papers, seeming to gauge if he could rip them from Andrew's hands. "I know nothing about villagers or slavery. I ask you again, Hadley, to leave my private chamber at once—"

"Your private chamber?! Yours?! I'm the bloody earl here, Peter, not ye—"

"Really, this is a most unbecoming scene," a new voice cut through the room.

Jane turned, eyes closing.

Of course, Montacute would follow them here. Granted, their shouting had likely carried all the way to the drawing room.

Both her brothers were here now. Both scapegraces for one reason or another.

"This is none of your affair, Montacute," Andrew barked, all pretense of politeness gone. He finished gathering all the letters together, tucking them under his arm.

"You are closeted with my sister in a private bedchamber, yelling at your heir like a shrieking fishwife," Montacute tsked. "This is what comes when a peer allows his bloodline to become so contaminated."

Deadly silence greeted that particular speech.

Andrew and Peter's loud breathing punctuated the stillness. Jane swiped another tear away.

A vein bulged in Andrew's temple, his blue eyes nothing more than icy chips. Montacute met his gaze with the typical ennui arrogance of a powerful lord.

"May I remind you, Montacute, that this is my house." The deathly quiet of Andrew's voice only heightened the menace of it. "My room." He spread his arm wide. "My heir." He pointed at Peter. "And, the most salient point, none of Your. Damn. Business."

Montacute reared back, eyes flaring. Jane was quite sure no one had ever dared speak to him in such a manner.

"How dare you—"

"How dare I?"

"I'll see you ruined for this!"

Andrew snorted. "I have larger issues than the prickly pride of a spoiled duke. Please leave, the lot of ye."

"Hadley, this farce has dragged on long enough," Peter walked forward, eyes on the papers Andrew had tucked under his arm.

Andrew's returning look would have peeled paint. "You are trying my patience, Peter. I suggest ye leave before I do something rash."

The tension in Andrew's jaw and vibrating tautness of his shoulders must have communicated the seriousness of his intents.

With a low growl, Peter turned on his heel and pushed past Montacute, storming out the door.

"Peter!" Jane turned to rush after him.

A firm hand on her upper arm stopped her.

Jane looked up into Montacute's furious face.

"You will stay, Jane," he commanded. "I will not have you running about like a common shrew."

Hah! If she had to choose between her brothers . . .

"Go to hell," she spat, and yanking her arm from Montacute's grasp, ran after Peter.

28

J ane raced down the main staircase, intent on confronting Peter.

She barely held back the sobs wrenching her chest.

Oh, Peter! What did you do?

Oh, Andrew! How can our love survive this?

She was impossibly trapped, stuck between two immovable forces. How was there ever to be a peaceable resolution?

She found Peter standing in the Italian parterre garden, hands clasped behind his back, chest heaving. The moon peeked out from the clouds, casting the garden into dim shadows. Only Peter's blond hair gleamed, quicksilver bright.

"Peter?" Just the sound of her voice made him flinch. He turned around.

"You don't believe those lies, do you?" The moonlight rimmed his head. "I had nothing to do with villagers or slavery. What was Hadley even referring to?"

Jane stilled.

She needed answers. She needed to understand.

"To be honest, I don't know what to think, Peter." She ordered her racing heart to slow down, to tread carefully. "Why don't you tell me what those letters meant?"

Peter scrubbed a hand through his hair, shaking his head, a loose laugh escaping.

"You don't believe me," his bitter words clanked between them.

"Tell me. I want to believe you. I want to believe *in* you."

Silence.

Peter rocked back on his heels, eyes staring sightlessly into the reflecting pond at the center of the garden. Jane walked to his side, slipping a hand into his.

He swallowed, the noise loud in the quiet night. "What does Hadley accuse me of?"

Jane nearly sighed. This had always been Peter's tactic when he was in trouble.

What do you *think I've done wrong?*

The question gave him time to sort through an appropriate excuse while the accuser outlined his supposed crimes.

Oh, Peter. How could you?

Who knew that one's heart could literally break in two?

She stepped back, releasing his hand and turning toward him.

Jane was no coward. She would face this head-on, as she did everything in life.

And so she told him. "Hadley had a business partner, Thomas Madsen, who betrayed him." She outlined everything she knew—the promise of cargo on their voyage, the enslaved villagers, Andrew beaten and left for dead, the horror of scores of lives lost in the sunken ship, particularly Jamie Fyffe.

Peter's expression grew stonier and stonier the longer she spoke, until Jane had no doubt left.

Peter was guilty.

Suddenly, all of Peter's actions over the past months came into sharp focus. No wonder he had been so angry. No wonder he abused and resisted Andrew so thoroughly at the beginning. What Jane had thought of as resentment had likely been the product of a guilty conscience.

"Why Peter?" she whispered, licking a tear off her lip. "Why did you do it?"

He shrugged. "Are you really interested in hearing a defense?"

"Yes!"

He shook his head and kicked at the ground. The motion at once so familiar and so heartbreakingly sad Jane was not sure she could bear it.

"My father wasn't particularly demonstrative, as you well know. He generally avoided us both."

"That he did." Jane nodded. This topic was a well-worn path between Peter and herself. "But what does the old earl's lack of affection have to do with Andrew?"

Peter scuffed the ground again. "It didn't initially. But then the old earl had his first stroke. I wanted to help out with the estate, so I started reading through the old earl's papers. I discovered his correspondence with a man, Wilson, about Mackenzie. I found it incredibly odd that my father showed such an avid interest in a Scottish stranger, more interest than he had ever shown in me, to be honest.

"So, I dug further. That led to his letters with Thomas Madsen and how my father went about investing with Mackenzie, using Madsen as a go-between. The monies from that investment were the only thing keeping us afloat. I did not, at the time, realize that Mackenzie was Andrew Langston, the earl's grandson and heir."

Peter ran his hands through his hair, before placing them back on his hips.

"Anyway," he continued, "I used the business shares as an excuse to ask my father about Mackenzie. Why not correspond with Mackenzie directly, at the very least? The arrangement with Madsen seemed cumbersome." He swallowed. "But when I asked Father about it, he smiled, proud as Punch. And then proceeded to tell me all about Andrew Mackenzie Langston, his grandson and heir. He explained hiring Madsen to pose as an investor, allowing my father to do business with his grandson anonymously. The old man had thoroughly doted on Andrew from a distance . . .”

Peter's voice trailed off.

A nightingale sang somewhere in the trees. Leaves rustled.

Jane closed her eyes, heart in agony.

“In thirty minutes, my father lavished more praise on Andrew than he had on me in a lifetime of living under his roof.” Peter paused. “And I hated him for it.”

“Andrew? Or your father?”

A beat. And then his answer:

“Both.”

More silence.

Jane absorbed his words, shock rooting her in place.

“And then Father had another stroke, nearly incapacitating him. By that point, I had seen a copy of Father's will. He had cut me out entirely, Jane. Andrew *had* to inherit the title—that I accepted—but the estate wasn't entailed. Father could have left something to me. But he *didn't*. Can you understand how that f-felt?” His voice broke. “I was his *son*. The one who had stayed, who tried to earn his love—”

Jane ran a hand down Peter's back, desperate to soothe him. She had known that Peter harbored pain over the old earl's cold emotional distance, but she had not realized how profoundly deep the wound cut.

How could she have failed Peter like this?

He continued on, “My father cast me aside and, instead, left *every-thing* to Andrew Mackenzie Langston—money, lands. Worse, Father was insensible by that point, so there was no way to convince him to alter the will.” He snorted. “It seemed so bitterly unfair. I had my name. Nothing more. But if something were to happen to Andrew . . .”

“Oh, Peter. How could you wish a man dead?”

“Judge me, if you must, Jane. But many a man in that position has done the same thing—”

“That hardly excuses your behavior, Peter—”

“I was seventeen, Jane, and desperately angry. I knew if something were to happen to Andrew—before my father died—I would inherit everything attached to the Earldom of Hadley—the title, the estates, what money remained. In my seventeen-year-old head, it seemed the perfect solution. And so I wrote to Madsen, offering him more money to ensure that Andrew never returned from this trip he was planning.

"Madsen and I discussed ways to . . . remove . . . Andrew without anyone the wiser. A 'convenient accident' is what Madsen promised me. I never dreamt that others would pay the price, too. I knew the boat went down. But I didn't know why. The entire crew was lost?" Peter asked, strain in his tone.

"That's what Andrew reported."

"And Cuthie wanted to take a whole village as slaves?"

"Yes."

"That—" His voice broke, head shaking. "All of that . . . it was never my intention. I would never have agreed to slavery and the sinking of a ship and her crew. You have to believe me, Jane—"

"I do, Peter. I do believe you." She wrapped her arms around his waist, hugging him tight. He returned her embrace, holding her for a moment.

"What are we to do, Jane?" he asked, pushing out of her arms.

"I don't know," was her honest reply.

That same nightingale sang again.

"I haven't been good at keeping my promises to you," he finally said. "I can't save you from Wanleigh—"

"No, Peter, I should have thought of *you* more. I should have realized how deep the old earl's lack of affection cut. 'Tis I who have failed *you*—"

"Never, Jane."

"Allow me to talk to Andrew. You aren't guilty of the choices Madsen and Cuthie made. Let me fight for you."

"Jane—"

"Please? Just promise me you won't do anything stupid," she said.

"Anything stupid?"

"Yes, like challenge Andrew or run off. Let me see what good I can work first."

"Jane—"

"P-promise me, Peter." Her voice broke. "L-let me see what good I c-can do. I c-can't l-lose you."

He paused.

"I promise you, Jane."

She hiccupped, a sob nearly working its way free.

Launching herself forward, Jane wrapped her arms around him, the familiar feeling of his hug almost overwhelming her.

How could her life have come to this? To lose Peter?

Oh! The pain of it . . .

It was a lash worse than death.

She refused to let this be the end of the story. She would not give up. She would fight for them to be together, as she always had.

Even at the risk of losing Andrew? a small voice in her head asked.

She cried harder.

Heaven help her.

Because she couldn't answer that question.

ANDREW SPENT HOURS riffling through the letters and other papers in Peter's private study before leaving it to Peter in the early morning hours. The evidence Andrew found was thoroughly damning.

Peter may have been hazy on the precise details, but he clearly understood the consequences of his actions. He knew he was signing a death contract with Andrew's name on it.

Peter had intended to murder Andrew just as surely as if he had pulled the trigger on a pistol.

And now, in the early morning light, Andrew was unsure what to do.

Of all the possible scenarios he had outlined in his mind when thinking about bringing Jamie's killer to justice—when he finally contemplated an end to his guilt and a balm for his grief—this had not been it.

He had always imagined a hardened criminal, someone with malicious eyes like Captain Cuthie. A man who cared naught for all the pain and suffering he had caused. Someone like Madsen, whom Andrew would have sent to the hangman's noose without flinching.

But now?

Accusing the beloved brother of the woman he thought to marry? Sending his own heir to the gallows? Condemning a young man he had helped and guided?

How could this be their victorious retribution? Their vengeance?

But Jamie . . .

Jamie's face rose in his mind's eye, green eyes guileless and cheery. And then those same eyes, sightless and empty, drifting into an obscure grave in the South Pacific—

No, he owed Jamie justice.

He owed justice to them all.

For Kieran's endless grief and the white scar tracing Rafe's cheek. For Kieran's screams piercing the inky night. For Andrew's own months of recuperation and agony.

For all their guilt and pain over the past three years.

There was no easy path out of this.

And in the end, the choice would not really be Andrew's to make. Kieran, in particular, had the most say as to what would happen to Peter.

Andrew wrapped Jamie's tartan around his shoulders before seeking his bed, curling into the plaid like a blanket.

Let nothing be forgotten.

He managed to sleep a few fitful hours, but as soon as the sun peeked over the horizon, Andrew rose. He dressed quickly but still took time to wrap Jamie's tartan around his chest.

He penned urgent messages to Kieran and Rafe, who were both yet in London, asking them to join him with all haste. He also wrote to Alex and Ewan, telling them of the change in events. They would not have even received his letter regarding Madsen yet, much less this one about Peter. What would they say?

He then set two footmen to guarding Peter's bedroom door, not wanting to give his heir a chance to flee. He left strict orders to inform him once Peter arose and wished to leave his bedroom.

As he was walking back to his study, his butler handed him a note from Montacute.

Hadley,

I expect an answer from you soon regarding the Mackenzie shares. Do not delay, as I am currently displeased with your obduracy and offensive behavior. I am extending an olive branch of diplomacy, offering you a way forward, both financially and socially.

Do not be a fool.

Montacute

Andrew longed to slowly beat his head against a stone wall. The reality was simple: he would not be selling those shares to Montacute.

Andrew had already mentally reconciled to having the duke as an enemy, as he intended to thwart Montacute's efforts to marry Jane off to Wanleigh—

He winced at the thought of Jane.

Ah, Jane.

His sweet Jane.

Jane whose brother had hired a man to kill him.

There was no harmonious solution to this.

Could their fragile affections survive Peter's betrayal?

His stomach knotted.

As if hearing his thoughts, Jane appeared. She stopped Andrew as he crossed the entrance hall.

She was so lovely, his Jane. The morning light tangled in her auburn hair and the blue of her simple morning gown lent her gray eyes a bluish cast. Andrew's heart burned in his chest, the pleasure and agony of simply staring at her almost more than he could bear.

However, the dark circles under her eyes spoke of her own sleepless night.

"A word, my lord," she said, tone stern.

My lord?

That did not bode well.

He nodded and led her into the library, leaving the door ajar.

The memories of their time together assaulted him. Jane, laughing and pliant in his arms. The soft touch of her lips.

"I trust you found all the proof you needed last night," she began. Her tone was tight, her face expressionless.

Prim Jane.

"Aye, I did," he replied.

Her eyes flicked to Jamie's tartan wrapped across his chest. Jane hugged her arms around her waist, as if trying to hold herself together through sheer will.

A stone settled on his chest.

Ah, Jane.

How was he to resolve this? Had she retreated into Prim Jane because she accepted the impossibility of their situation? Tight bands constricted his lungs at the thought, choking his breathing.

Please, no.

"And what will you do now?" Jane kept her arms across her stomach, refusing to meet his gaze.

"I've sent for Kieran and Rafe from London. We'll decide together what course tae take."

A pause.

"You haven't summoned the magistrate?"

Andrew tapped his fingers on one of her mineral cabinets. "I *am* the local magistrate, as it turns out, but I haven't brought charges as of yet."

"Oh." She lifted her gaze to his, hope abruptly lighting her eyes. "So you are contemplating mercy, then? Peter was so young—"

"Jane—"

"He was only seventeen, Andrew." She rushed toward him, placing a hand on his arm. "That's hardly old enough to understand the ramifications of his actions."

"Jane, please—"

"He was young and stupid. Is he to die for that?"

"Jane, please! Stop!"

She froze, eyes still wide and so bloody hopeful.

"Jane, I am so sorry." Andrew forced the words through stiff lips. He pulled his arm from her grasp. "I cannot remove the consequences of Peter's actions."

"But . . ." Her voice drifted off. She stared at him, clearly noting the resolve in his eyes.

She took a step back.

And then another.

But his Jane was no coward. She was an Amazon, born to fight for those she loved.

And so, she rallied, head shaking.

"No," she said . . . and then more firmly, "*No*. I refuse to accept this." She threw back her shoulders. "I have fought to be with Peter since the day he was born. I will not stop now."

Her courage nearly unmanned him. How could he hurt her so?

But to deny Jamie justice . . .

"Jane, there is nothing tae fight for." He tried to make his tone kind, but nothing could remove the sting of his words. "Peter ordered my *death*. He wanted me dead. That order had devastating consequences—"

"You don't have to do this. You could grant him clemency—"

"Jane, ye know I cannot do that." He laid the words down as gently as he could, his hands shaking from the effort. He ached to comfort her, to save her from this. "Ye must ken this. Jamie and all those others deserve justice. Peter must atone for their deaths—"

"No! He may have agreed to *your* death, but you cannot place the actions of Madsen and the ship's captain on Peter's shoulders. He never agreed to their decisions—to take the villagers as slaves, to kidnap Jamie and sail off into treacherous waters. Peter was guilty of one crime. But Madsen and Cuthie committed many, many crimes—"

"I ken all this, Jane. But ye were no' the one there." Emotion thickened his voice, deepening his accent. "Ye were no' the one beaten and left for dead. Ye didnae see the village in flames, the women crying because they didnae have wherewithal tae feed their bairns. Ye didnae hear the ghastly description of the wreckage of *The Minerva*, the bloated bodies floating in the ocean, being feasted upon by sharks. Jamie . . ." He sucked in a fortifying breath. "Jamie was one of those bodies. And that is one wrong—" His voice broke. "—one wrong that must be brought tae justice. Ye ken what I'm saying, Jane?"

She stifled a sob, palms pressed to her face.

"Peter may not have foreseen or sanctioned everything that happened," he continued, tone emphatic, "but he set it all in motion. None of the horrors would have happened if Peter hadnae instructed Madsen to ensure I met with an accident."

"You cannot know that!"

Andrew clenched his jaw, chest heaving.

She was not entirely wrong . . .

But . . . actions had consequences, even if the outcome had been unintended.

Jane sensed his inner struggle.

"You cannot know that, Andrew," she repeated. "You cannot lay the repercussions of other's actions at Peter's feet."

"Peter meant to kill me. *Me!*" He tapped his chest. "And *that* led to the events that caused Jamie's death—"

"Peter was so young and foolhardy, Andrew! Show mercy!"

"Jane, you dinnae—"

"No!" She took two steps toward him and placed her hands on his chest, peering into his eyes. "Jamie is *dead*, Andrew. You will never get his life back."

Silence. His lungs heaved under the heat of her palms.

"Jamie is lost forever. It's done," she continued, tears tumbling. "Your guilt *c-cannot* save him—"

"But I *can* bring justice—"

"No. You cannot." She shook her head. "All you can do is sacrifice another young life. Destroy another family—"

"Actions have consequences, Jane."

"Yes, but you can choose how far those consequences rage, Andrew."

A pause.

She licked a tear off her lip, gray eyes glistening and pleading.

"Have mercy, Andrew," she whispered.

"Jane, please do not ask it of me—"

"Justice cannot save those who d-died." She hiccupped. "But m-mercy . . . mercy *can* save the living."

His lungs seized. How could he even contemplate granting Peter clemency?

She pressed her advantage. "Nothing can bring Jamie back. Nothing can save his life. But you have a chance here to save another young life, another young man, like Jamie. A boy who led a blameless life up to the point that he made one foolishly rash decision. Have mercy."

Andrew pushed away from her.

Have mercy?

Memories washed him. Jamie's laugh. The screams of the villagers. Kieran's raging grief. So much pain and endless guilt—

No. Justice had to be served. Mercy wasn't possible. Not in this.

And yet . . .

How could he do this? How could he destroy her heart?

And more importantly, perhaps . . . "Mercy isnae my decision alone, Jane." He turned back to her. "There are five of us, four other men and their guilt and grief. I cannae speak for them. Kieran, most of all, has much reason to seek vengeance. And none of this takes into account legal issues. English law must have some say, too."

Something in his tone reached her. A sense of his own turmoil, of the weight of knowing he caused her pain.

Jane chewed on her lip, blinking furiously, head in profile to him. The morning light washed over the contours of her face, rendering her in painted shades of gold, red, cream, and finest gray.

She turned to him, eyes bright. "But will you fight for Peter? Will you be a voice for him?"

He paused, struggling.

His silence was her answer.

"B-but he'll h-hang," she gasped.

She was right.

Peter could hang.

He held her gaze, forced her to read the truth there. He *would* seek justice. Peter's actions had consequences.

Andrew saw it—

The moment *hope* died.

Her eyelids dropped. Her shoulders crumpled, followed by her knees. All of her rolling downward like a marionette doll, tumbling into despair.

Andrew caught her before she hit the floor, pulling her tight into his arms.

Her despair shattered him, shredding his soul with agonizing shards.

Could he truly condemn Peter to death?

But . . . did he have any other choice? Laws existed for a reason. He had a duty to the other members of the Brotherhood. To society as a whole.

Actions had consequences.

Jane's tears wrecked him.

She clung to his arms, shoulders heaving, soundless as she soaked his waistcoat with her weeping. Of course she made no sound. His Jane didn't do grand histrionics or noisy emotional displays.

Her quiet, anguished suffering was all the more devastating for it.

"I c-cannot b-bear this g-g-grief," she hiccupped. "It is t-too m-much."

"*Mo chridhe*, I am so sorry," he murmured into her hair, stroking her back. "I dinnae know what to do. I cannae negate the law. I cannae deny justice for Jamie and all the others. It would no' be right."

She shook harder. "P-Peter is my entire w-world. M-my brother. H-he is the only p-person who loves—"

. . . who loves me . . . Andrew finished the sentence for her.

He is the only person who loves me.

An aching knot clung to his throat, choking him.

That was not true.

"Not the only person, Jane." He stroked her hair, kissing her head. He offered her the only truth he could. "I love you. I love you, too, *mo chridhe*."

She sobbed harder, clinging to him.

How could he do this to her? How could he watch her shed her layers of prim behavior and encourage her to find herself, just to shatter her with Peter's betrayal?

How could Andrew hand her his heart and yet destroy her own?

But . . .

He couldn't rescue Peter from the consequences of his ghastly decisions. He couldn't send Wanleigh packing or swap Montacute for a kinder brother.

But he could be her rock in the eye of the storm. His chest was broad enough for her grief. She clung to him, hands fisted into Jamie's tartan, watering it with her tears.

Her heartbreak was his own.

But the harder she cried, the more she shook her head . . . back and forth, right, left. Finally, she shoved his chest, pulling on Jamie's tartan.

"No." She shook her head again. "No!" She pushed away from him, staggering to her feet. "I will not accept this! I will not allow my brother to hang! I will not give up on Peter!"

"Jane—" He stood.

"No!" She backed away from him, face splotched and red from her crying. "I have f-fought my entire life for Peter. I gave up my childhood. I c-contorted and changed my very soul to keep us t-together." She swiped an angry hand across her eyes. "Again and again, I gave in to every *ridiculous* d-demand Montacute and my m-mother threw my way just to ensure that Peter and I were not s-separated."

She continued to retreat, swiping at her cheeks.

"Please, Jane, let me—"

"No! What don't you understand?!" She hurled the words at him. "Peter has always been my entire world! You *cannot* have him. I will not let you!"

"Jane, this isnae only my decision—"

"You can't steal my whole world, Andrew! No, worse!" She jabbed a finger at him. "You cannot condemn *my* world to hang and then expect that I will have a heart left for you."

She gave one last angry swipe of her cheeks with clenched fists, surely pressing nails into her palms.

"I *reject* your love, Andrew." She nearly spat the words. "I will *not* accept it. My heart is too broken to *ever* accept yours."

"Jane—" He took a step toward her.

She whirled and raced from the room.

The slammed door reverberated behind her.

The sound echoing that of his own soul shattering.

29

Andrew stumbled through the day, mind in a fog, the painful conversation with Jane a haunting refrain in his ears.

It didn't help that Montacute emerged from his room determined to make Andrew's life a living hell. He made ducal demands and kept Andrew dancing in attendance until the dinner gong sounded.

After their discussion in the library, Jane wrapped herself in brittle silence, her face an expressionless mask, her manners excruciatingly polite. Montacute, of course, had complimented Jane on her 'impeccable' behavior.

Surely her inner turmoil was as chaotic as Andrew's own.

I reject your love.

His useless heart thumped and panged every time he replayed her words in his head.

Half of him ached to agree with her. Peter *had* been young. More to the point, Andrew *knew* the young man. Peter might be impetuous and spoiled, but he wasn't mean and cruel. He could grant Peter mercy, reclaim Jane's affection, and bask again in the joy of her glowing eyes.

But the other half remembered the horror of those days in the New Hebrides. The suffering. The catastrophic loss. The vow they had all made, over and over, to bring Jamie's killer to justice.

Andrew honestly didn't know which half to side with. A decision had to be made. He was simply waiting until Rafe and Kieran arrived.

It wasn't until after dinner, when night had truly fallen, that the butler pulled Andrew aside.

"Mr. Langston is nowhere to be found," the man said without preamble. "I sent a footman with a dinner tray, only to find that Mr. Langston's bed had not been slept in. I then made inquiries and realized one of the horses is missing from the home farm."

Damn and blast!

Peter had fled.

Andrew placed his hands on his hips, the sounds of Montacute's languid voice carrying from the drawing room.

Peter had a full day's head start. He would be on a boat to heaven-knew-where before Andrew caught him now.

Had the decision been taken from them?

"This also came for you via the evening express post." The butler handed him a letter. Its contents were brief.

We arrive tomorrow morning.
    —*Rafe*

Andrew stuffed the note into his pocket. His mind screamed at him to saddle his horse and take off after Peter. But there was no moon tonight and travel would be difficult.

He had to wait for his friends to arrive.

"I GET TAE bloody him afore we start asking questions," Kieran said.

"You can't pummel a man without giving him a chance to speak," Rafe replied.

"Watch me."

"I thought you had become fond of Peter?" Rafe asked.

Kieran shrugged, swallowing hard.

Andrew was standing in the stable yard with his friends, waiting for his horse to be saddled and fresh mounts prepared for Rafe and Kieran. Early morning mist rose from the surrounding fields, threading through the trees.

"How is Jane?" Rafe asked Andrew, pulling on his riding gloves.

Andrew grimaced, adjusting his tartan sash. They all wore Jamie's tartan this morning. "Poorly. Her heart is fair broken. She took tae her rooms early last night and hasn't come out."

More to the point, after storming out of the library, she had not uttered another word to Andrew.

Jane's heartbreak would not ebb. Andrew felt it pounding against his own.

"Do ye think she'll ever forgive me for this?" he asked.

A beat of silence.

"I don't know," Rafe replied. "Peter is the only person who genuinely treats her like family."

"Aye."

Andrew knew it to be more than that.

He is the only person who loves me.

"Damn idiot lad to set all this in motion." Rafe settled his hat further on his head.

"Aye. He may not have kent all the consequences of his decision—"

"He put a price on your life, Andrew."

"And *that*, even without the rest, is a hangable offense," Kieran finished.

Andrew huffed. "If it were only me that he offended, I could easily show mercy to the man. But we all know it's much more involved—"

"Bloody stupid lad," Kieran spat. "Did he think we were too dumb tae ever figure it out? How could he have thought tae get away with this?" "She begged me to show Peter mercy," Andrew said. "Justice will not save Jamie's life, she said. But mercy will save Peter."

Rafe scuffed his foot. "That's not an untrue point—"

"Ye cannae be serious?" Kieran turned to him, eyes wide. "We have been seeking justice for *years*—"

"Aye," Rafe nodded, "but sometimes even justice has cruel consequences. I'm merely acknowledging that Jane has a point about mercy—"

"Mercy?" Kieran all but spat the word. "Jamie *died*—" His voice broke. He clenched his jaw. "Where was the *mercy* in that? Where is the *mercy* for ma hurting heart? For Jamie's kin mourning their loss? We deserve justice."

Andrew nodded. He did not expect Kieran to feel any differently.

What were they to do?

Light filtered through the trees. Andrew shifted his feet, eager to be off. At last, a pair of grooms led the horses out of the stable block.

"We all know that this situation is not so simple," Andrew said. "Attempted murder of a Peer is a capital offense. This means the charge would be referred to the assizes where it would be a public spectacle. Every part of our voyage would be examined frontwards and back. I'm not sure we can withstand such scrutiny."

"Aye, we seem to be caught between Scylla and Charybdis," Rafe agreed, pulling himself into the saddle. "At the very least, the undue publicity would destroy everyone's reputation by association—Lady Jane, the Earldom of Hadley, even Montacute himself."

"Hadn't thought of that." Andrew settled into his saddle.

"Mark ma words, there *will* be justice for Jamie. I'll find a way," Kieran growled, heaving upward. "But we have to catch the scabby eejit first."

"Aye," Rafe agreed. "It might be a lost cause at this point."

Andrew kicked his horse into a gallop, the others close behind. They would cut across his lands to the northern road.

Wind rustled through the trees, sending a portent hum through the air. They tore over the wee bridge where Andrew had first met Jane and climbed the hill surrounding the old quarry.

They were nearly past it when Andrew spotted the figure sitting on the ground near the quarry's edge, knees drawn up, calmly throwing rocks over the cliff. A horse was hobbled away from the insecure rim, contentedly munching on grass.

Andrew instantly slowed, recognizing the set of the man's shoulders.

"Well, that's an anticlimax," Kieran muttered.

Peter swiveled his head, noted their approach, and then turned back to the quarry. He tossed another rock over the edge.

They pulled to a stop beside Peter's horse, all swinging down from their saddles.

Peter remained impassive, keeping his back to them.

"Och!" Kieran grumbled, waving a hand toward Peter. "I cannae bloody a man who doesnae present a fighting stance."

Holding out a staying hand to his friends, Andrew approached his heir, stopping well away from the dangerous edge.

"You've found me. What will you do now?" Peter asked, head turned away from them.

It was a fair question: what *was* he going to do now?

"Would it do any good to ask *why* ye did it?" Andrew asked.

"I dinnae care why he did it," Kieran called behind Andrew. "I demand justice for Jamie and all the others."

Peter pitched his head to the side, registering Kieran's words, but still keeping his back to them.

"Why *did* ye do it?" Andrew repeated.

Peter shrugged, shifting to be sitting sideways to the rim, face in profile to Andrew. "Do you truly care for an answer?"

"Aye. I genuinely do."

The young man shook his head. "Shall I tell you of my indifferent father, his distant affection and hazy regard for me? I spent my childhood desperate for his love and felt the pain, over and over, of being unworthy of it. Jane would tell me that the old earl's indifference was just a symptom of his person. That my father valued his station and position in society more than his spare heir. That I received no kindness nor affection because the old man had none to give."

Peter gave a bitter laugh. "And then I found those damnable letters, oozing pride and affection. He adored you, Andrew Mackenzie, his beloved grandson and heir." He jabbed a finger at Andrew. "I was so jealous—"

"Jealous? Of me?"

"Yes, of *you*, Hadley." Peter laughed, a caustic burst of sound. "The worst part? The old earl's affection for you showed me that the man was *capable* of love. He just didn't find me worth any."

Andrew winced.

"And then you show up here, Hadley," Peter continued, "with your rustic ways—which we all now know were an act—and you . . ." His voice drifted for a moment, chest heaving, swallowing back emotion. ". . . and you *saw* me. You believed in me, treated me like a brother. You understood that I needed a purpose, something of my own to feel satisfaction and pride in doing. I tried to hate you for it. I honestly did."

Peter tossed another rock over the cliff, a slightly larger one this time. A thin section of the edge sloughed away.

Peter appeared unconcerned.

Andrew couldn't say he felt the same.

"*Do* you hate me?" Andrew asked.

A long pause.

And then, so softly . . . "No, I tried, but I cannot. You have this wretchedly-annoying habit of being almost unbearably likable."

Rafe snorted. "Aye, it's our trial to bear as his friends," he muttered too low for Peter to hear.

"So I ask you again, Hadley, what will you do with me now? Drag our family name through the filth of a public trial? Take the law into your own hands and execute me yourself here and now?"

Peter punctuated his comments by tossing a much larger stone into the quarry, deliberately clipping the edge, causing more of it to fall away.

Execute me yourself?

The sheer unexpected audacity of his questions stopped Andrew's breathing for a moment.

"Why are you here, Peter?" Andrew asked instead.

Peter snorted, slowing rising to his feet, kicking a few more stones into the quarry. Andrew longed to tug the young man back from the edge, ensuring his safety.

He stayed planted in place.

"I thought you would be on a boat bound for New York by now," Andrew continued.

"I intended to be." Peter turned to face Andrew. "I rode to Dover and was going to board a ship to Calais and, from there, to America. Start a new life."

Silence.

"But . . ." Andrew prompted.

"But . . . I arrived in Dover at an inopportune time. A ship had sunk overnight in the channel. A crowed was gathered in the harbor, awaiting news." He paused. "There were no survivors, in the end. The wailing of the women and children over their lost loved ones, the grief and pain."

Ah. Andrew thought he understood.

His heir's face washed with emotions: horror, misery, heartache.

"I didn't mean to harm so many people." Peter dashed an angry hand across his eyes. "I was stupid and rash and young, but that doesn't excuse my decisions. I *did* intend to harm you." He stabbed a finger at Andrew. "Of that, I am one hundred percent guilty. I can live with that particular guilt. But the deaths of so many others, of the lives ruined because a father never came home . . ." His eyes filled with anguish. "That I cannot forgive myself for."

"Nor should ye!" Kieran spat from behind Andrew.

Andrew shot his friend a silencing look, hoping to stem Kieran's bloodthirsty need for vengeance.

Peter clenched his fists. "I tried to run away, but as I watched the women sobbing on the wharf, I realized I would never be free. The deaths of all those people will haunt me until I die. I'm not the boy I was at seventeen, cocky and arrogant." He waved a hand in Andrew's direction. "I figured throwing myself on your mercy and the mercy of the courts would be easier than living with my conscience for the rest of my days. I deserve to hang for my actions. I truly do. So . . . do with me what you will." Peter glanced back at the quarry's edge, a speaking glance.

Almost a dare.

Take your vengeance, his look said. *Toss me over the edge and no one will ever know I didn't die an accidental death. No one would contest the word of an earl.*

Andrew looked back and forth between the edge and Peter. Such a simple solution. Jamie and the rest would be avenged. Jane would have closure, and Andrew could potentially win her back.

But . . .

Andrew shook his head. Such a solution did not give him even a moment's pause.

Easy answers were a child's way out.

Andrew had become an adult long ago.

There was a better way here.

"Come, Peter," he beckoned.

Notching his chin higher, Peter crossed the few steps separating them.

Andrew grabbed the younger man into a rough hug, slapping him hard on the back. For his part, Peter stood stiff in Andrew's arms, mutely accepting the offered affection.

Andrew pulled back, keeping a hand around Peter's elbow. "I'm proud of ye for doing the right thing."

Peter blinked. "Thank you," he whispered.

"You're a good lad, for all that. I forgive ye for trying tae have me killed."

Peter sighed. "I truly dislike how ridiculously likable you are, you know?"

"I ken that. But don't go offering me praise quite yet. Me forgiving ye doesn't change the result of your actions. I am by no means the only wronged party in all this. There will have to be consequences, but I am willing tae work those out if others agree." Andrew grimaced, taking a step back and motioning behind him. "Kieran? What say ye?"

Kieran clenched his teeth, but Andrew saw the anguished acceptance in his friend's eyes.

Kieran swallowed.

And then swallowed again, Adam's apple bobbing.

"Jamie would want me tae show mercy," Kieran finally said, nearly at a whisper.

"Aye," Rafe agreed.

Andrew nodded. That was true.

There would be compassion for Peter. The lad would not hang, at least.

"But," Kieran continued, voice stronger, "actions do have consequences."

With that, Kieran patted Andrew on the shoulder . . .

. . . took two steps forward . . .

. . . and tumbled Peter to the ground with a savage blow to the jaw.

30

Jane was quite sure her nerves would send her to an early death. Or, at the very least, result in an apoplexy of her own.

Andrew had left with Rafe and Master MacTavish to hunt down Peter and bring him to heel. Jane had been pacing ever since, her eyes dry.

How was she to bear such agonizing grief? To lose the two men who professed to love her?

Andrew's words hummed in her brain.

I love you, too, mo chridhe.

The shock of that moment, of hearing that Andrew Langston, Lord Hadley, loved *her*.

And loved her, not because she was Lady Jane Everard, but in *spite* of her Englishness.

In spite of her condescending mother and ducal brother.

In spite of another brother who had condemned Andrew and his friends to death.

Andrew loved her uncouth, unlovable inner self.

The very thought sent tears pricking her eyes.

Case in point, instead of punching half-moons into her palm, she twisted Andrew's bracelet on her wrist, round and round. Just that small, nearly-insignificant difference painfully highlighted how much Andrew Mackenzie Langston had changed her.

And all for the better.

And what had Jane done? She had hurled Andrew's affections back in his face.

I reject your love.

Just the memory of it banded her chest in a painful ache. She hadn't meant it. The words had boiled out of her in a moment of agony.

But, was she wrong? Even if she didn't outright reject his love, surely any love they shared would not outlast this trial with Peter. She and Andrew would never agree on what was to be done about her brother.

Their love was doomed, even if Andrew forgave her for her harsh words.

How could she be in the position? Having the love of two men, but set to lose them both?

She dashed a tear away. Blasted things. How did she have any left to shed?

She had cried more tears than she thought possible over the past thirty-six hours, stoically enduring Montacute's endless requests.

Lady Hadley remained oblivious to her son's perfidy, entertaining Montacute and unconcerned about Peter's absence. Jane hadn't had the courage to inform her mother of the crimes of her only son. Worse, Wanleigh arrived, closeting himself with Montacute.

Wishing to avoid them all, Jane sneaked down to the library to watch the front drive, desperately waiting for a messenger to arrive. She knew it was far too soon for any news but felt helpless to do otherwise.

What would happen to Peter now? If Andrew caught her brother, would Andrew instantly bind him over for trial? Or would he take a few days to consider other options?

What if Peter were not caught? Would Andrew continue to hunt for him?

The sheer uncertainty of waiting nearly reduced her to a puddle of nerves.

She paced, over and over, nibbling on her lower lip, occasionally pausing to stare out the window.

It was during one of those pauses that she saw four figures emerge from around the edge of the house, clearly coming from the stables.

She pressed against the window, heart in her throat.

Was it?

Could it be—

Snick.

The door opening unexpectedly caused her to yelp in surprise.

Jane whirled to meet Montacute's frosty eyes.

"Wanleigh wishes a word with you in private, Jane," he said without any preamble. "He awaits you in the south drawing room with your mother. I expect you will give careful heed to his, and my own, wishes. Come." He extended a hand to her.

All the air rushed from her lungs.

Truly? *Now?!*

She looked back out the window at the figures climbing the front steps.

Andrew, Rafe, Master MacTavish, and . . . Peter.

Peter!

Peter was returned with them.

Oh—!

"Jane, I am waiting." Montacute's impatient voice cut through the room. "I am willing to overlook your atrocious behavior of the past twenty-four hours provided you obey me *now*."

Jane was too distracted to care. She craned her neck, trying to see more of Peter. Was he unharmed?

There was no sign of chains or shackles. In fact, her brother moved with the other men in easy companionship.

Perhaps . . .

Had Andrew listened to her pleas for clemency? Would Peter be granted mercy? What had transpired? And, more importantly, what would happen now?

Hallelujah!

Wait—was that blood on Peter's cravat? Was his cheek *bleeding*?!

"Jane!" Montacute barked.

She whirled around.

Montacute faced her with barely leashed fury.

"You will come! Now!" he repeated, voice taut. "Do not disappoint me in this. You will not like the consequences—"

The very idea that she would consider Montacute and Wanleigh in a moment like this.

Peter had *returned*—

"No!" She shook her head and dashed past Montacute's outstretched hand, racing for the front entrance hall. She skidded to a stop just as the butler closed the door behind the men.

"Peter!" she shrieked, throwing herself onto his chest.

"Jane," he murmured, enfolding her in his arms. She sagged against him in relief, sobbing yet again.

She had tears in her yet.

He was *here*.

He had not been imprisoned or condemned.

Yet.

"I'm here, Jane." Peter echoed her thoughts, voice low in her ear. "I couldn't run, in the end. I have to face my crimes, such as they are."

She pulled back running her hands over his chest before getting her first solid look of his face.

"What happened?" She touched his split lip and drifted her fingers lightly over cut on his upper cheek and the lump already swelling along his jaw. "Who did this?"

"That would be myself," Master MacTavish replied. His gaze flitted over Peter, eyes murderous. "I had a pound of flesh owed me."

"Master MacTavish! Well—"

"Do not trouble yourself, Jane," Peter interrupted. "It is the least of what I deserve. Hadley has already been merciful."

Oh!

Jane risked a glance at Andrew.

"No one will die, Jane," he confirmed. "We've come to terms with Peter as to what will happen." Warmth glowed in his eyes, that glorious affection she had thought gone forever.

What did that warmth mean?

Hope squirmed its way into her heart.

"Truly?" she asked.

Andrew nodded. "You were right. Peter's life will not bring back Jamie. There are ways for justice to be served." A pause. "But mercy, also—"

"Jane," Montacute's icy voice interrupted, "why are you yet here?"

All heads swiveled toward the sound.

The Duke of Montacute walked into the entrance hall, cold anger on his face. He didn't spare a glance for Andrew or the rest.

"I believe you were told to go to the south drawing room," Montacute continued, eyes drilling her. "Lord Wanleigh awaits you there. Lady Hadley will allow you a word in private with him."

Jane froze.

Andrew stiffened.

Peter's arm tensed under her hand.

No one misunderstood what Wanleigh wished to speak with her about.

Before she could say anything, Montacute fixed Andrew with his haughtiest look. "Your presence, Hadley, is not required at the moment. This is a family matter between myself and my sister. If you will excuse us."

As he spoke, Montacute took a few steps forward and set a hand under Jane's elbow, tugging her out of Peter's loose grasp.

Jane resisted, pulling her arm back. "I have other matters to attend to at the present, Duke—"

"I assure you, Jane," the duke replied, bite in his words, "there is nothing in your life more important, at the moment, than your acquiescence to my request to speak with Wanleigh."

He pulled Jane forward again, this time more roughly.

She stumbled, pressing against his arm to keep herself upright. Behind her, she sensed Andrew surging forward in outrage.

"Enough, Montacute." The command in Andrew's tone was unmistakable.

The duke froze, slowly pivoting to face them all.

Jane yanked her arm free, backing until she felt the heat of Andrew's body behind her, his hand drifting to rest on her waist. Montacute's eyes darted down, noting the physical contact between them.

"How dare you lay a hand upon my sister, Hadley." Montacute's tone vibrated with menace. "You have not been given leave to take such a liberty—"

"I am tired of this farce, Duke. It ends now," Andrew replied. The steadiness of his palm on Jane's hip relayed his calm assurance.

"You appear to have not understood my wishes, Hadley." Montacute took a step forward. "Perhaps I need to make myself exquisitely clear, one final time. I hold all the cards here. You were born into nothing, and you will only become something if I condescend to grant it to you. Therefore, you will retreat from this situation with your tail between your legs. If you do not, I will ruin you, utterly and completely. No one will receive you. No one will extend you credit nor listen to your voice in Lords. You will be friendless and penniless. *Go.*" He pointed.

Jane craned her head around just in time to see Andrew raising one eyebrow, clearly unimpressed.

Jane ached to kiss him.

Wonderful, stupid, lovely man!

Peter gave a bark of laughter.

"He still doesn't know, does he?" he asked Andrew.

Andrew shook his head.

Montacute's gaze narrowed, bristling to deliver another set-down.

Not this time!

Montacute's heavy-handed control of her life was onerous. She couldn't allow Andrew to suffer the same fate.

"Enough!" Jane moved between Montacute and Andrew, facing her brother. "You're making an ass of yourself, Duke."

"Pardon?!" His gray eyes snapped. Eyes so like her own and yet impossibly different.

"Lord Hadley," she said, taking a step sideways to glance at Andrew, "would you be so kind as to inform my brother of the name you went by before being raised to the peerage?"

Andrew chuckled, biting and short. "With pleasure, Lady Jane. Andrew Mackenzie, at your service, Duke." Andrew's sardonic bow was a masterpiece of elegance. "Though I believe you know me better as the Scottish Vulcan."

"Wee bit of a grand title that," Master MacTavish chimed in cheerfully.

Jane had the exquisite pleasure of witnessing Montacute blanch. She was quite sure his shocked face would be a treasured memory for years to come.

"The rumors of my poor parentage, impoverished upbringing, and general uneducated state have been grossly exaggerated," Andrew said.

"Yet another reason why one should never listen to gossip," Master MacTavish said.

"So you see, Duke," Andrew continued. "I am anything but power-less. I have more money than any one person could spend in a score of lifetimes. I may not have friends in the highest echelons of government, but I do have significant economic reach. I do not need your assistance."Montacute blinked, looking between Jane and Andrew, brows drawing down.

"You lie," he spat. "You are nothing—"

"Try me," Andrew bit out. "You said over dinner that you wished to invest in my business ventures. My portfolio of holdings is vast and exceptionally lucrative. Fur trading in the Hudson? I have a company for that. Building steamships along the Clyde? I have a company for that, too. Financing jute sales from India? . . . You get my point, I think."

Montacute was silent, eyes promising murder. He did not like to be thwarted. Andrew was on thin ice, even now.

Jane chewed on her lip.

"Many a man has wished to invest with me, but I grew weary of untrustworthy partners. So I sold or bought out the lot of them."

Andrew's eyes slid over Montacute, silently condemning the duke to that same pile. "As you know, the old earl owned the only business shares held by someone else."

Montacute still said nothing.

Andrew stepped forward, placing a hand on Jane's waist again. She felt his eyes drift to his bracelet on her wrist. "I once promised your sister that I would bring her a piece of heaven. But I will do one even better. I have an offer for you, Montacute."

"An offer?"

"Aye. I *will* sell the old earl's share to you, and for a bargain price at that, but . . ."

Pardon?! Jane froze with surprise. Why would Andrew do such a thing?

Montacute's head reared back, eyes lighting with surprise and avarice. Jane frowned. What game was her brother playing?

"But?" Montacute prompted.

Her heart stilled.

Why was Andrew doing this? Why was Montacute so eager for those business shares?

"But, in return—" Andrew glanced down at Jane. "—you must set Lady Jane free."

She gasped, whirling to face Andrew directly. He didn't meet her gaze, his eyes trained on Montacute behind her.

"Set Jane free?" her brother repeated.

"Aye. Ye must settle her dowry on her, free and clear. Allow her tae choose who she will marry. Or, perhaps, she will choose not tae marry at all—"

"Bah!" Montacute thundered. "That's hardly a choice. I will not surrender Jane's dowry to her care."

"Why not? She is perfectly capable—"

"Jane has a duty to her family, and she will abide by it. It is none of your affair, Hadley."

"If you want the shares, you must agree to my terms," Andrew countered. "Free Jane or there is no deal."

He lowered his gaze, meeting her eyes.

Jane's heart lodged in her throat, tears threatening again, understanding what hadn't been said.

I choose you, his actions stated.

I will show mercy towards Peter despite my own personal vendetta. I will set you free from Montacute's tether and take it on myself.

Moreover, the emotion in his eyes said even more clearly, *I will* always *choose you.*

I love you, too, mo chridhe.

When had anyone ever chosen *her* over something else they valued?

Surely not her mother. Definitely not Montacute.

Not even Peter, really.

And what had she done? She had taken this man's incredible heart and, in a fit of temper, thrown it back at him. She bitterly regretted her words.

And yet . . .

His very actions in this moment showed the enormity of his heart. That he would forgive her, just as he had forgiven Peter.

Jane had never understood love until that very instant. She had never realized how thoroughly it crystallized the important facets of life, blowing away all the unnecessary chaff.

She loved Andrew.

She couldn't let him tie himself to Montacute like this.

She had to choose him, too.

"This is outrageous, Hadley." Montacute was still spluttering behind her. "I will never agree to release Jane in such a fashion. How dare you interfere with a personal family matter!"

Jane's temper spiked. Andrew was making an enormous sacrifice for her, and Montacute was cruelly rejecting it.

Money and power were *everything* to Montacute. Andrew's business shares would give Montacute both of those things. In return, he only had to release Jane.

And yet, Montacute refused. Her brother was so bloody stubborn, always grasping for more and more. He would argue and belittle Andrew into relinquishing so much more than those business shares.

And given the determined set of Andrew's jaw, the idiotic man would likely cave. Because he loved her.

No.

She loved Andrew too much to watch him do this on her behalf.

Montacute was her cross to bear. Moreover, it was high time someone told him, *No.*

She would fight this battle.

"You are very gracious, Lord Hadley, but I kindly decline your offer on behalf of Montacute," Jane said to Andrew.

That sent Montacute to spluttering even more loudly. "Jane! You are unhinged!"

She turned to face him, placing her hands on her hips.

Half a lifetime ago, her half-brother had placed a spirited, courageous little girl into a cage.

Now he would reap his just desserts—the sharp claws and suppressed rage of a chained creature finally set free.

Never to be caged again.

She fixed Montacute with that same steely gaze they shared, courtesy of their father. "Montacute, I will not be marrying Lord Wanleigh or any other man of your choosing."

Montacute reared back, her attack on him unexpected. "I am the head of this family, Jane, and you will be obedient—"

"No! I will not marry to please you. I am of age. You cannot force me into it—"

"Can I not?!"

"—Moreover, when our father bestowed my dowry, I know he did not intend it to be used as a cudgel to beat me into submission. I ask you, a sister entreating her brother, to allow me to choose my own husband in my own time."

"Never!" Montacute raged.

But in his roaring denial, Jane saw something she hadn't expected.

Panicked desperation.

Abruptly, it all clicked together—those snippets of conversation with Peter and her mother, small changes in Montacute's behavior, rumors buzzing through the *ton* about financial concerns. All the pieces of the puzzle slotting into place.

What if Peter were right? What if her dowry were more important to Montacute than she supposed?

His insistence that Jane marry a man of his choosing must have greater bearing than she presumed. And his concern appeared to be hinged on her dowry, as he refused to relinquish it.

And why Wanleigh? The man had heirs from his previous marriage. He was wealthy and didn't need her dowry. Why was he the only suitor Montacute deemed worthy?

Montacute valued money and power above everything else. He would do anything to protect them.

Which logically meant that Jane's dowry and marriage to someone other than Wanleigh threatened his love of power and money . . .

Her jaw nearly dropped, knees sagging in shock.

"*Ah,*" she almost whispered, head falling back. "Oh, Montacute, what did you do?"

Silence.

Jane shook her head, eyes wide and dazed. "You can't give me my dowry because you don't have it, do you, Montacute?"

Montacute flinched. It was subtle and fleeting, but Jane was looking for a reaction.

Got you.

Behind her, Peter gasped.

Rafe swore.

Andrew whistled.

"How dare you—" Montacute seethed, but Jane had seen all she needed.

Blind fury surged in behind her stunned surprise.

"How dare *I*?" She rushed at him, finger pointing. "How dare *you,* brother dearest?!" So many years of heeding his grueling wishes, of listening to his endless chastisements. "How dare *you!*"

She jabbed her finger at his ducal chest.

Montacute took a step back, hands raised. "Jane, you are hysterical—"

"Hysterical?!"

"—and it is most unbecoming."

"Hah! I'm only just beginning, Duke. Allow me to guess how this came to pass." Jane continued to point a finger at him, pressing her advantage. "You were invested in that Nassau bank, too. The former Earl of Hadley was. Rafe's father was." She waved a hand toward Rafe. "Of course, the Duke of Montacute joined his *friends* in the endeavor. That's what aristocratic friends are for, aren't they?"

Her tone took on a heavy mocking edge. She couldn't help it.

Montacute flared his nostrils. Jane could practically see the steam rising off him. But beyond his smoke and mirrors, though, there was true panic.

"But you lost your investment in the Caribbean Affair. You lost too much," she continued. "So, you had to dip into my dowry in order to meet your financial obligations. And skimming your sister's dowry, well, that's not legal. I know our father took great care to ensure that my money was legally protected from *every* kind of fortune hunter, even filial ones."

Gasps of astonishment and several murmured curses echoed through the entrance hall.

"Jane—" Montacute tried to catch her arm. Jane dodged, taking a step sideways. "—you are clearly overset. This hysteria troubles me."

He reached for her again. Andrew shifted placing himself partway between Jane and her brother, offering silent protection.

"I am nothing of the sort, brother," she retorted. If anything, she was seeing and thinking as clearly as she had in years. Like waking from a feverish dream to a brilliantly crystal reality. "Even dukes can be held accountable for their crimes, if my future husband decided to take you to court over the issue. They can't imprison you, naturally, or force you to repay what you took. Being a duke affords you protections no one else enjoys. But you can be tried and hung in the court of public opinion. You and your duchess can become *persona non grata* in the eyes of the *ton* and lose the confidence of the Crown. Hurt your ability to command credit, to direct and govern. After all, only a lowlife cad would steal his own sister's dowry."

"Hear, hear," Andrew murmured.

"I am done with this ridiculous conversation." Montacute turned, intent on the door.

How dare he!

"I have not finished speaking!" She darted forward and grabbed Montacute's elbow, digging in with her heels, using the weight of her entire body to stop him. "You *will* listen to me."

"Jane!" Montacute roared, wresting his elbow from her grasp.

The sound of knuckles cracking shot through the entrance hall, loud and sharp. Rafe? Master MacTavish?

"You will let my sister speak, Duke," Peter said sternly.

"I suggest ye listen to yer womenfolk, Duke," Andrew said behind her.

"Aye," Master MacTavish agreed.

Montacute's gaze flicked over Jane's shoulder. Whatever he saw there stopped him.

"As I was saying, Duke, you took my dowry but how to cover your crimes?" She tapped her chin and then snapped her fingers. "I know. First, repeatedly scare off eligible suitors who need my dowry, like Lord Eastman. Next, find a trusted friend to marry your sister. Someone like Wanleigh who is willing to forgo your sister's dowry. Someone who won't raise a fuss over the missing funds. Silly little Jane will never have to know. It's something her brother and future husband will settle between men. No women allowed."

Andrew huffed behind her. "And then blackmail a foolish sap—that would be myself—tae sell you a profitable business investment for a pittance, thus starting you on the road tae recouping your losses. No one the wiser."

Montacute's expression had grown stonier and stonier as Jane and Andrew spoke.

"What do you think we'll find once we go digging, Montacute?" Rafe asked mildly.

"Indeed," Peter murmured. "No one in the *ton* looks kindly on a gentleman who robs his own womenfolk, duke or no."

"I don't even know if such a man could be called a *gentleman*." Andrew said.

"These are all lies." Montacute stared at Jane. "My sister is clearly under some hysterical delusion, as I know afflicts some women—"

"Lady Jane is as fine and sound a woman as I've ever known. Ye should take care how ye refer tae her." Andrew said, tone menacing. "I think I formally withdraw my offer tae be a business partner after all. I don't do business with known liars and cheats. It's the secret tae my success."

Montacute's nostrils flared. "This entire conversation is absurd. You cannot threaten me—"

"Oh," Andrew's voice rumbled with suppressed promise, "I think by the time we're done here, ye will be begging for us tae leave ye be."

Montacute continued to berate them all, throwing around epithets and threats. Jane recognized it as her brother's typical ducal bluster. But his panic was evident the more he raged.

Andrew bore it all with almost frightening calm.

Finally, Montacute agreed to discuss Jane's dowry with Peter, Rafe, and Andrew—man-to-man, as he put it.

Andrew would have none of it. "This is Jane's future life and Jane's dowry. She, more than anyone, should be allowed tae participate in conversations that pertain so personally tae herself."

And so Jane argued with the men as they hammered out an agreement. Montacute's affairs were, indeed, in shambles. Jane was relentless in forcing her brother to acknowledge his wrongs against her. Andrew said little, but his resolute strength gave Jane the courage to counter Montacute's threats and silence him.

Eventually, Montacute realized he had been bested. He agreed to settle twenty percent of the dowry on Jane—six thousand pounds—for use as she saw fit, the rest having been lost due to his mismanagement. He also agreed to rescind any claims to selecting a husband for her and to support whomever she eventually did decide to marry.

In return, Jane sweetly agreed not to bring a suit before the House of Lords for embezzlement of her personal funds.

Andrew saw the entire thing informally drawn up and signed. Fully legal documents from solicitors would follow.

Her ducal brother wasted no time in packing his bags and departing.

"Do ye think he'll seek revenge?" Andrew asked as they stood on the front stoop, watching Montacute's carriage pull down the drive.

"He may," Jane murmured at his side, "but I do not think so. The threat of his misdeeds will always lurk in the background, waiting to come to light. He will wash his hands of me." She sniffed. "Thank goodness."

Jane turned back to the house just in time to see her mother leading Lord Wanleigh through the entrance hall.

Oh, heavens! She had utterly forgotten about her former suitor.

But given how her mother giggled and batted her eyelashes, placing a hand on Wanleigh's arm, it was obvious that neither Wanleigh nor Lady Hadley had remembered Jane, either. Wanleigh leaned down, whispering something in her mother's ear that set her to blushing.

Jane struggled to decide if she should laugh or feel mildly nauseous. Could she do both simultaneously?

Lady Hadley smiled at them all as Wanleigh took his leave, promising to return to pay his respects to the 'lovely Lady Hadley.'

Clearly, Lady Hadley was on her way to marrying yet another elderly peer, a marquess this time. Which after being the wife of a duke and an earl, seemed only logical. Would her mother eventually round out her husband collection by adding a viscount and a baron?

Jane laughed once the man had driven off.

"Hallelujah," she said.

Andrew grinned at her side.

But her smiles quickly disappeared as she turned to survey Peter.

He met her expression with a grim one of his own.

Andrew rocked back on his heels.

"Come, Peter." He motioned toward his study. "We've already sorted your sister's future today. Now let's contemplate yours."

Jane took a step forward. "I want to be part of the discussion."

The men all looked at each other.

It was Peter who spoke. "I'm sorry, Jane, but this is my affair to sort. You have always been good to defend me, but it's time that I stepped up and took care of matters on my own."

Andrew thumped him on the back, clearly agreeing with Peter's sentiment.

Andrew and Peter disappeared into his study with Rafe and Master MacTavish.

It was late into the night before they emerged. Only then did Jane learn of Peter's fate. After much discussion and letters from their friends—Alex and Ewan—the men had agreed on penance for Peter.

He would return to the New Hebrides and devote five years to caring for the villagers, assisting however he could to rebuild the island and help it prosper.

"Peter will face, first-hand, the consequences of his actions and learn to be responsible for others," Andrew had explained. "It is a fair compromise."

Though Jane choked up at the thought of going years without seeing Peter, she had to agree. Anything was preferable to the gallows.

Peter was given two days to say his goodbyes. Kieran was headed for Dover and his ship. He would take Peter with him.

When she was informed of all that had transpired—Peter's crimes and chosen punishment—Lady Hadley took to her rooms, prostrate with grief, telling one and all to leave her be. But naturally, Lord Wanleigh called upon her the next morning and Lady Hadley rallied enough to receive him. Jane did not doubt that wedding banns were in her mother's near future.

Jane hardly saw Andrew. He was busy with his solicitors and secretaries, likely hammering out official documents for everything.

Nothing had been said between them regarding her cruel words the day Peter left. Andrew's every action showed that he cared deeply for her, but he had not attempted to speak with her.

Did he still love her, as he had said? Or had her words killed his love, turning it into a more friendly affection?

And given the roil of her own emotions, Jane could not think clearly enough to articulate her thoughts. Not when she faced Peter's imminent departure.

She hadn't set out to avoid Andrew, but that was how events happened regardless. Peter consumed her focus. Every moment of the two days before his departure she spent with him, altering between laughing at his quips and sobbing at losing him so soon.

The morning of his departure was particularly brutal.

"I am so sorry to put you through such grief," Peter murmured, pulling her into a tight hug. "But it's only for five years."

Jane clung to him. "It is still a long time to be apart."

"Ah, Jane. This moment would have come eventually anyway. We have to grow up entirely and move on to our separate lives—"

"But I dislike being parted so soon. And you are going so far—"

"My punishment is less than I deserve, Jane. I feel I have been touched by grace itself. Not everyone receives such a reprieve. And Hadley has arranged for me to write to you as often as I can. I am not lost to you."

"I know." Her brain knew all this, but her heart struggled to accept it.

Of course, Peter's parting words did not help her find clarity. "Don't let Hadley slip through your fingers, Jane." Peter kissed her forehead. "He is a good man. Better than either of your brothers."

He kissed her cheek and left to say goodbye to their mother.

An hour later, Peter rode out with Lord Rafe and Master MacTavish, intent on Dover.

Jane stood at the window, tears falling, watching until her brother faded into the distance. It was only as she crumpled into a nearby chair, convulsed with hiccupping sobs, that she realized Andrew had been behind her the entire time, silently standing witness to her grief.

He retreated without a word, locking himself in his study with his steward and solicitor.

Jane took to her room, eventually crying herself to sleep. But chaotic dreams plagued her—Peter calling her name from across the sea; Andrew walking away from her, disappearing into a dense fog. She woke well after noon with puffy eyes and a heavy heart.

But one thing she had resolved.

Peter was right.

Andrew was a good man, better than she deserved. She would find him immediately and beg forgiveness for her words—a groveling apology.

Even as bitterly as she grieved Peter, she *had* to let Andrew know that she appreciated what he had done. He had to know the depth of her love for him.

The house was chillingly silent as she descended the main staircase. She strained to hear the booming sound of Andrew's voice, but only the ticking of the drawing room clock and chirping birds outside the windows greeted her.

Barnsley emerged from the dining room.

"Ah, Lady Jane, I am glad to see you have risen." He walked over and retrieved a thick letter from a small side table. "Lord Hadley bade me give you this when you arose."

He handed the letter to her. Jane took it with numb fingers, a terrible suspicion looming in her mind.

"He has gone?" she asked, though it was hardly a question. "Yes, my lady. First thing this morning."

Oh!

Jane nodded a dismissal to Barnsley before walking into the drawing room, her feet sending her to the window overlooking the long drive. Wind rustled the trees and ravens called.

Andrew had left.

Without saying goodbye. Without uttering a word.

Without hearing her apology or her heartfelt gratitude for saving Peter.

Instead, he departed with her cruel words still ringing in his ears.

The trees went blurry beyond the glass.

She swallowed, turning the letter over in her hands.

She was nearly afraid to open it, as it was heavy and clearly contained several sheets of paper.

What had he written?

But Jane was no coward. If the letter contained recriminations, she would face them head on.

Sitting down, she cracked the seal. A sheet of foolscap, lined with strong, bold handwriting, sat atop other documents:

> *Dearest Jane,*
>
> *I apologize for not speaking to you in person, but perhaps our goodbyes are better this way. I received my Writ of Summons via special courier last night. I am to make my knee before the Prince Regent in just two days' time. I must away to London at first light. I do not know when I shall return to Hadley Park, as I have business to attend to in Scotland afterwards . . .*

Oh.

He was well and truly gone.

He hadn't abandoned her, per se, just moved on to the business of being a peer. Her logical mind knew this.

But her heart saw it as abandonment. It felt like being cut adrift.

She bit her lip, licking back her tears, before continuing reading:

> *I ken that I'm not your favorite person right now. Ye have lost two brothers in the space of as many days because of me, though I suspect ye are content to have lost Montacute. However, it was never my aim to take Peter from ye. I ken ye miss him sorely, and for that, I am most sorry, my Jane. Unfortunately, mercy and forgiveness do not negate all consequences in Peter's case. I did what I could to ease them. I pray you find some peace.*
>
> *These last few days have been a whirlwind of emotions for both of us. As for me, I meant what I said that day at the quarry. My feelings toward ye have not altered. But, as I also said then, I do not want us to come together—if that is what ye wish—out of anything other than*

the deepest love and affection. We both deserve to know that we chose the other, free from any other pressures.

I will always want you, Jane. But the more important question remains—do ye want me? Will your heart ever heal enough to accept mine?

I ken ye need a wee while to sort out what ye would like. So I'm going to give ye that wee bit of time. Let your grieving heart heal. Think about what ye want, Jane. If it's a future with myself, I'll be right happy to oblige ye. If not, then know I wish ye every happiness.

Love,
Andrew

Jane stared at the letter, wiping her damp cheeks.

Of all the infuriating, maddening, stupid—!!!

She was torn between laughing and crying.

The *eejit*, as he would say.

Why couldn't he have simply *told* her all this? Then she could have apologized and kissed his handsome face.

Instead, she confronted the daunting task of waiting for him to return.

How could she do that? How could she wait and wait for him?

Ugh! Men!

She swiped a hand over her cheeks again.

The other papers crinkled in her lap, reminding her that there was more than just his letter.

What else had he included? And why?

She set the letter aside, causing a slip of paper to tumble to the floor. Bending, she picked it up.

Regardless of what happens between us, I never want ye to lose the girl you once were. Ye were born to shine bright.

Andrew

Jane spread out the rest of the papers, blinking when the print went blurry.

Oh.

The dear, impossible, impetuous man.

He had given her Rosehearth.

32

Andrew missed Jane.

He had missed her five minutes after leaving Hadley Park.

He had missed her through his entire two weeks in London, meeting with the Prince Regent and greeting other members of the House of Lords.

He had missed her on the ten-day journey north to Scotland, every mile breaking his heart a wee bit more.

And now, a week later in Scotland, he missed her to distraction.

Every morning he convinced himself to stay in Scotland a little longer. To not go haring off to Sussex again so soon.

Jane needed time.

He had robbed her of both brothers in a matter of hours. Her tears over Peter . . .

It had all nearly unmanned him.

She needed more than a mere month's time to grieve, to heal, to learn her own heart.

He had told her he loved her, and what had she done?

I reject your love . . .

He didn't believe she had meant it. But he knew his own heart could not bear hearing her reject him a second time.

And so, he had taken the coward's way out and simply left her a note.

But since then . . . he had heard nothing. Not that he expected her to write to him. She was a lady after all, and unmarried ladies did not write unmarried gentlemen.

But . . .

He was like to go mad from the silence.

Finally, he had resorted to letting out his aggression in time-honored Scottish fashion—

Throwing absurdly-heavy things.

Which explained why he was currently in breeches and shirt sleeves on his south lawn, hurling a large block affixed to a thick chain.

He had started by tossing stones from the nearby river, heaving them onto his shoulder and launching them like a shot put.

But that had lacked a deeper element of aggression that his soul craved.

So, he had affixed a metal chain to a heavy stone block and had taken to twirling and throwing the thing, over and over. Two footmen assisted, measuring the distance with each toss and dragging the stone back to him.

Muirford House sat behind them, the enormous house dwarfing the horizon. His grandfather had spared no expense when building it nearly thirty years ago, adopting the newly-fashionable neo-Gothic style. Its turrets and arched windows stretched into the sky, looking like a romantic, medieval fortress but hiding more modern comforts within.

Wiping sweat from his face, Andrew took the chain in his right hand, spun in a circle three times, building momentum with each rotation, before releasing the block to soar across the lawn.

One more day.

He could last one more day without racing back to Jane.

Discipline. He had discipline.

He turned and walked back, intent on throwing the stone again.

A figure emerged from the house, moving toward him.

At first, he scarcely glanced up, assuming it to be a maid bringing some refreshment.

But several things grabbed his attention.

First, the woman wasn't carrying anything.

Second, she was wearing an earasaid, the female version of a great kilt, though for women, it was more of a cape. No servant of his would wear an earasaid while on duty.

Third, the earasaid was made of Jamie's plaid.

And fourth, he would know *her* gait anywhere. The loose-limbed grace with which she walked, the long line of her body, the glint of auburn hair in the weak sunlight.

It was like seeing a mirage.

Andrew was running toward her before another thought could cross his mind.

She had *come*.

His Jane had come to him.

He had scarce hoped for this outcome; that she would seek *him* out.

But she was clearly here, wearing Jamie's tartan.

And if he had any doubts as to *why* she had come, the light in her eyes as he drew near told him everything he needed to know.

She extended her hands.

He needed no other encouragement.

Andrew swept her up into his arms, both of them laughing.

"Ye're here." He pressed his face into her hair, breathing her in deeply. "Ah, fair, sweet lass. Ye're here at last."

She hugged him tighter in reply.

Andrew needed no further encouragement. His lips found hers, hungry and eager. Jane returned the kiss with gratifying enthusiasm, before pulling back slightly.

"Ah, Jane. Sweet, sweet Jane," he murmured. "How I've missed ye—"

"About that." She lifted her head. "I have a bone to pick with you," she said, voice stern.

He would have been more worried about it, but as she still had a hand threaded into his hair and was pressed against him, he merely smiled.

"Aye," he nuzzled her cheek.

"I am angry with you." She pulled on his hair, forcing him to lift his head.

But then she kissed him and it was glorious.

"I think I like ye angry," Andrew whispered.

"So angry," she repeated. "Furious, even."

"What should I apologize for?"

"You left me!"

A beat. Andrew froze.

"I told ye why I left. Ye needed time—"

"Just like a man to assume what I need without asking!"

"Ye were greetin' yer wee heart out, weeping away. Ye rejected me because I took Peter from ye—"

Jane may have growled a bit. "Well, yes, I was upset but not at you. Your actions with Peter showed me the true depth of your soul. You found a way to grant him mercy—"

"Och, Peter accepted responsibility for his mistakes. It's much easier to extend clemency tae a repentant man."

"Yes! And I realized, after I calmed down, that you were acting with the utmost honor. You are right. Mercy and forgiveness do not negate consequences. I was upset and angry, but I forgave you quite quickly."

More silence.

"You forgave me? Why didn't ye tell me that?"

"Because you didn't stay around to hear it, you bloody fool. You left!"

Andrew laughed.

"*Now* you laugh, you wretched man." She shook her head, but she kissed him again, taking any sting out of her words.

"I am most sorry then." He pecked her mouth. "Because I could have been kissing ye all these weeks."

"Exactly! *Now* you are understanding."

Nothing was said for another moment as Andrew thoroughly reacquainted himself with the delight of kissing his Jane, pulling her flush against him, hand delving into the silky softness of her hair.

Eventually, she pulled back, holding his head between her hands.

"But, most importantly, I owe *you* an apology, Andrew." Her eyes went shimmery as she spoke.

"An apology?"

"Yes. I said cruel things that I did n-not m-mean—"

"Ah, Jane."

"—and you need to know that I w-will never reject your heart—"

He silenced her with another kiss, helpless to do anything else. His Jane left no doubt as to her affection in her response.

"I forgive ye, *mo chridhe*," he murmured against her mouth. "All is forgiven."

She hiccupped and sighed and cuddled into his chest. Andrew hugged her closer, deeply content to simply hold her.

"And one more thing," she said, pulling back, wiping her damp cheeks. She tossed a thumb over her shoulder. "How many rooms, exactly, is Muirford House? I knew you were wealthy, but the house behind us is a little ridiculous, your lordship. And I say that as the daughter of a duke."

Andrew chuckled. "Ye like my home, do ye?"

Jane leaned into him. "I like it verra much," she said in a decent Scottish accent. "But I think I like it best because you are here."

"Ah, lass, *mo chridhe*—"

"I couldn't stay away." She snuggled into him again. "You left and took everything I wanted with you. And seeing how a good friend encouraged me to embrace the wild Jane of my youth . . ."

"Ye figured a trip to Scotland would be in order?"

"Precisely."

Silence hung for a moment.

"I spent a portion of the journey north reading the poems of Robert Burns," she said.

"Ye did?"

"Aye," she teased. "He had a way with words, Burns did."

"Most Scottish men do—"

She kissed him, laughing against his lips. "I have a favorite Burns poem now."

"Oh aye?"

"Aye."

Andrew pulled back, looking down at her expectantly.

She pressed a kiss to his jaw and then recited.

"She asked why wedding rings are made of gold;
I ventured this to instruct her;
Why, madam, love and lightning are the same . . .
Love is the soul's electric flame,
And gold its best conductor."

He smiled as she finished, the meaning behind the poem coming through loud and clear.

"Are you telling me that you love me, Lady Jane?"

She kissed him in earnest. "I stand here and say, without any doubt—I love you. You. Andrew Henry Mackenzie Langston."

Andrew couldn't contain the burst of joy bubbling through his veins. It bounced through his blood and set his head to spinning.

Naturally, several minutes of kissing followed.

Eventually, Jane murmured against his lips, "So . . . I was also hoping I could convince your very Scottish self to consider a more permanent alliance with England—"

"Are ye proposing marriage tae me, lass? A glorious union of our own?"

Jane laughed. "Aye, I am."

He grinned in return. "I can think of nothing I would like more."

EPILOGUE

EIGHT MONTHS LATER . . .

What do ye make of this, Lady Hadley?" Andrew asked, stretching out his hand, offering a small stone.

Jane smiled at her husband.

Her husband!

She took the stone from his palm, examining it closely. "Is it a small bit of ammonite?"

"I cannot decide. There is opalescence in the stone."

Indeed, there was.

They continued back and forth, debating different theories.

Even though they had been married for over six months now, she could scarce believe it at times. When she thought of herself a year ago—alone and tightly contained, awaiting Andrew's arrival at Hadley Park—she wanted to shake that foolish woman and tell her to wake up. To seize her own future and take the life that she wanted for herself.

She and Andrew had not been separated since the day she arrived in Scotland. They had been married from Muirford House on a sunny morning in August, Andrew looking resplendent in a great kilt made of Jamie's tartan. They had traveled to London for the Little Season and winter Parliament session, allowing Andrew to officially take up his seat in Lords.

While there, they had called upon her mother, who had indeed married Lord Wanleigh, and was now happily enjoying London as the wife of a marquess.

Jane had received several letters from Peter, his latest announcing his safe arrival in Sydney and preparations to leave for the New Hebrides. She desperately missed Peter, but she also saw the good assuming responsibility for his actions had wrought. In time, he would become a remarkable man.

Today Andrew and Jane sat in the library at Rosehearth. She sorted through a stash of minerals Andrew had purchased for her as a surprise, while Andrew caught up on his correspondence. A fire popped in the hearth, cheering up the room despite the incessant February rain drumming against the mullioned windows.

Jane pulled a length of Jamie's tartan tighter around her shoulders. She had left off carrying Paisley shawls and only wore tartan ones, a more obvious nod to her husband's ancestry. In return, Andrew had his factory create tartan shawls for her of the softest Kashmiri wool.

"I've had a letter from Rafe," Andrew said, shifting through the pile of correspondence in the writing slope resting on the small table beside him. "He wants to know if we will be holding our annual meeting of the Brotherhood of the Black Tartan next month."

Jane frowned, looking up from her minerals. "Why would you not hold your reunion?"

"We have met our initial aims." He shrugged. "We have resolved the issue of Madsen, and Jamie would approve of how we handled the situation with Peter. We have honored Jamie's memory in that way."

Her frown deepened. "Surely, the Brotherhood is about more than vengeance—"

"Aye, I suppose that is true. I do enjoy the company of my friends."

"Well, there you are. Why not alter the Brotherhood meetings from a mere reunion to being more of a house party?"

"At Muirford House?"

"Why not?"

Andrew's face turned thoughtful. "That's an excellent idea, Lady Hadley," he said.

"Of course it's an excellent idea. I thought of it, after all."

He grinned.

Jane continued, "Even better, use the meeting this year to discuss and plan future meetings."

Andrew laughed. "Spoken like a true bureaucrat, Lady Hadley."

Jane stuck out her tongue at him before turning back to her minerals. Which, of course, simply made her husband laugh harder, the wretch.

"I shall write Rafe immediately," he said.

Silence descended, a comfortable sort of stillness. Jane sorted through a few more stones. Andrew's quill scritched as he wrote his letter and then sanded the ink. The fire cracked in the hearth, a log collapsing in a flush of cheery sparks.

"Thank you," Jane said.

Andrew lifted his head, eyes a question mark. "Thank you? Why do ye thank me, lass? For existing?"

She laughed. "In fact, you are absolutely correct."

"Och, I am *always* correct. I'm right glad ye're finally admitting tae it—"

He yelped as the pillow she threw hit his head.

Giggling, Jane moved closer to him.

Never slow, Andrew sat back, pulling her onto his lap, cradling her in his arms. Jane sighed, sinking against him, soaking in the sheer delight of being held.

"Thank you for seeing me," she whispered into his neck, tugging Jamie's tartan over them both as a blanket.

Andrew kissed her forehead. "Ah, *mo chridhe*, 'twas selfishly done. Ye were too fair a lass. One look at ye, dripping and raging in that stream, and I was a lost man. I had tae make that fiery lass mine forever."

"But you took the time to draw her out first."

"Aye, I did. I ken it was the kilt swish that did the trick in the end."
Jane smiled. He wasn't wrong.

"The kilt swish is no' to be underestimated," he continued.

"Or maybe it was just your overwhelmingly manly charm?"

"Oh, aye." He nearly preened. "I'm most glad that we have come to such a level of understanding in our marriage. When did ye become so wise, Lady Hadley?"

"The day a handsome *eejit* handed me the moon." She lifted her wrist, his bracelet jingling.

Andrew's booming laughter bounced around the room. "I can kiss tae that."

And so, he did.

AUTHOR'S NOTE

As an author, I find that I bond more with some characters and books than with others. For the record, *Suffering the Scot* was an absolute joy to write. I loved delving deep into Scottish culture and history.

First of all, a note about Scottish language and pronunciation. It's always a struggle to know how to write an accent, particularly in a historical novel. Scotland today recognizes three distinct languages: Scottish Gaelic, Scots, and English. Historically, Scottish Gaelic has been spoken in the Highlands. Most Lowland Scots in the early 1800s (i.e. those from Glasgow and Edinburgh) would have spoken a mix of Scots and English, as we see in the writings of Robert Burns. (Sidenote: If you want to read some Scots, Wikipedia actually has an entire dictionary written in Scots—sco.wikipedia.org.)

Of course, I realized fairly quickly that a modern, primarily American, audience would struggle to understand Scots or the language of Burns' time period.

So, what to do?

After much consideration, I decided to go with a slightly more modern Scottish accent and syntax, simply to aid readability. I write novels, after all, not history texts. I've used modern spellings of Scottish pronunciations and, even then, restricted myself to a few key words to give a Scottish flavor to the text. So at times, the accent as written is not perfectly consistent; this was done to help readability. That said, I have continued to use more common Scots words wherever possible—e.g. *ken/kens/kent* (think, know), *eejit* (idiot), *glaikit* (foolish), *fou* (drunk), etc.

Along those same lines, as editors went through the first couple drafts, I realized that most American readers only have a loose understanding of tensions between Scotland and England. I was endlessly adding more historical background information into each draft, trying to bring my readers up to speed. I acknowledge that, even then, I did not fully capture the nuance of the conflict between Scotland and England, particularly in relation to the Battle of Culloden.

I'll be honest; I didn't fully understand the tension myself until moving to Scotland. Even today, Scotland is very much a place apart from England. Nowadays, Scottish/English historical hostilities are usually framed as good-natured rivalry and ribbing, but the undercurrents remain.

In 1819 when this novel begins, Scotland was finally emerging from generations of English dominion. After being lost for 111 years, the Scottish Crown Jewels—the Honours of Scotland—had been found in 1818 by Sir Walter Scott. (The event resulted in Scott receiving that 'Sir' in front of his name.) In 1822, the newly crowned King George IV, visited Edinburgh. These two events ignited what would become the Victorian fascination with all things Scottish. Much of our modern-day opinions on Scotland are filtered through that Victorian obsession. Victorians romanticized the savage Highlander and took it upon themselves to assign tartan patterns to every clan. The list goes on and on. I've tried to strip away the Victorian lens and give the gist of Scottish/English relations at the beginning of the nineteenth century, which were hardly as amicable.

Of course, Victorian perceptions did not end with Scotland. Rituals surrounding mourning the dead were decidedly more lax during the earlier Regency era. The strong mourning customs we normally think of—years of endless black dresses and heavy veils—only came into existence during Queen Victoria's reign after the death of her husband, Prince Albert. In *Suffering the Scot*, I've tried to capture mourning customs per the time period.

Along those same lines, we often impose later Victorian morality onto earlier times. So, for example, Lady Jane jaunts about everywhere without a chaperone. In the later Victorian era, such behavior would be sternly forbidden. However, a quick survey of earlier literature and visual prints, reveals that such things were considered acceptable before about 1830. A study of Jane Austen shows that genteel women regularly traveled short distances from their homes without any escort. They also drove with unmarried men, as long as the carriage was open top, like a phaeton or curricle.

The one thing that Victorians didn't change is a Burns Supper. Celebrating the birthday of Robert Burns on January 25th began in 1801 and has never stopped. The format of the evening as described in the book has remained unaltered for over 200 years. In fact, I was drafting and researching that section of the book in early January of 2019 and had a long laugh when a Scottish friend asked my husband and me to give the Ode to the Lasses and the Lass's Reply for a Burns Supper. Of course, we said, "Yes," (though how well we did is a matter of debate, haha). If you have never attended a Burns Supper, I strongly suggest checking one out. Most cities around the world will have a band of Scots somewhere eating haggis and singing 'Old Lang Syne' around January 25th.

Prison hulks were very much as described in the book. They were an effective way to relieve over-crowding in land-based prisons and provided a ready-supply of cheap labor to repair harbors. Many of the large ships-of-the-line from the Napoleonic Wars—the flagships of the time—ended their lives anchored on the Thames as prison hulks.

There are many other little snippets of history in the story. Scientific expeditions were a huge thing, most being funded by governments (like that of Darwin and *HMS Beagle*), but there were privately-funded ventures, as well.

Slavery did continue unabated even after being outlawed in the Atlantic. The South Pacific, in particular, became a hotbed for conscripting labor during the 1850s and 1860s.

Scotland, specifically Glasgow and the Firth of Clyde, was the first to launch a commercial passenger steamboat service in 1813. In fact, much of the Industrial Revolution began in Glasgow, Edinburgh, and the surrounding areas.

I have created an extensive pinboard on Pinterest with images of things I talk about in the book. So if you want a visual of anything—including Jamie's tartan or Robert Burns, etc.—pop over there and explore. Just search for NicholeVan.

As with all books, this one couldn't have been written without the help and support from those around me. I know I am going to leave someone out with all these thanks. So to that person, know that I totally love you and am so deeply grateful for your help!

To my beta readers—you know who you are—thank you for your editing suggestions, helpful ideas, and support. And, again, an extra-large thank you to Annette Evans and Norma Melzer for their fantastic editing skills.

Again, I cannot thank Rebecca Spencer and Erin Rodabough enough for their insights. Rebecca, in particular, spent so many hours helping me sort through plot problems, all while pregnant and then sleeplessly dealing with a newborn baby. Thank you. And a shout-out to Julie Frederick for her keen observations.

And, finally, thank you to Andrew, Austenne, Kian, and Dave for your endless patience and support. I particularly appreciate Andrew putting on a great kilt and being my cover model for my hero, Andrew. I love you all.

READING GROUP QUESTIONS

Yes, there are reading group questions. I suggest discussing them over lots of excellent chocolate (solid, liquid, frozen, cake . . . I'm not picky about the precise state of matter of said chocolate. Chocolate in any form is good chocolate.)

Also—fair warning—there are faint spoilers inherent in these questions if you have not finished reading the book as of yet.

1. *Suffering the Scot* begins with an epigraph from Robert Burns:

> *But to see her was to love her,*
> *Love but her, and love forever.*

Jane and Andrew do not fall instantly in love, so why do you think the author still chose to use that particular Robert Burns excerpt as the epigraph? Is Burns talking about physical sight and physical beauty, or is he alluding to something deeper?

2. Continuing on with the epigraph above, what does it mean to love someone? Can anyone truly love someone without 'seeing' them fully? When thinking of the book, what does that mean in a romantic relationship? A familial one?

3. Clearly, this book contains a lot of information about Scotland and Scottish culture. Did you learn something new or unexpected? If so, what was it?

4. Along those same lines, does Scotland and the Scottish language, as portrayed in the book, reflect your own previous understanding or preconceived ideas about the country? Why or why not?

5. The first half of the book strongly addresses issues of stereotyping based on one's culture and heritage. Did you feel that the characterizations were accurate? Why or why not? Have you experienced something similar within your own life? If so, what?

6. Along with that, how can we acknowledge and appreciate differences while still respecting our own heritage? Is it helpful to admit fault and weaknesses in our own culture/heritage/lifestyle and learn from others? Why or why not?

7. How do the characters' assumptions and opinions change throughout the book? Did you feel those changes were believable? Why or why not?

8. Did you agree with how the love story progressed? Did you truly feel like Andrew and Jane had come to genuinely love each other? Why or why not?

9. Throughout the story, Jane creates semi-circular prints in her palm as a coping mechanism. How did the author morph and change this imagery as the story went on? Have you ever used a similar coping mechanism in your own life?

10. Did you suspect the person who was eventually revealed to have been the instigator of Jamie's death? How did you feel about that reveal?

11. The last several chapters of the book explore ideas of justice and mercy. Did you agree or disagree with the opinions the characters shared regarding the situation? Do you feel the situation resolved itself satisfactorily? Should the characters have had more or less mercy toward the villain? Why or why not?

OTHER BOOKS BY NICHOLE VAN

BROTHERHOOD OF THE BLACK TARTAN

Suffering the Scot

Romancing the Rake (Rafe's story, coming Fall 2019)

OTHER REGENCY ROMANCES

Seeing Miss Heartstone

Vingt-et-Un | Twenty-one (a novella included in *Falling for a Duke.*)

BROTHERS *MALEDETTI* SERIES

Lovers and Madmen

Gladly Beyond

Love's Shadow

Lightning Struck

A Madness Most Discreet

THE HOUSE OF OAK SERIES

Intertwine
Divine
Clandestine
Refine
Outshine

If you haven't yet read *Seeing Miss Heartstone*,
please turn the page for a preview.

SEEING MISS HEARTSTONE

. . . My lord, news of your current financial pressures has reached many ears. I know of an interested party who would be honored to discuss a proposed joint venture. They have asked to meet you along the Long Water in Hyde Park tomorrow morning, where they shall endeavor to lay out the particulars of their proposal . . .

—excerpt from an unsigned letter posted to Lord Blake

In retrospect, Miss Arabella Heartstone had three regrets about 'The Incident.'

She should not have worn her green, wool cloak with the fox fur collar, as Hyde Park was warmer than expected that morning.

She should not have instructed her chaperone, Miss Anne Rutger, to remain politely out of earshot.

And she probably should *not* have proposed marriage to the Marquess of Blake.

"P-pardon?" Lord Blake lifted a quizzical eyebrow, standing straight and tall, rimmed in the morning sunlight bouncing off the Long Water behind him. A gentle breeze wound through the surrounding trees, rustling newly-grown, green leaves. "Would . . . would you mind repeating that last phrase? I fear I did not hear you correctly."

Belle straightened her shoulders, clasped her trembling hands together, and sternly ordered her thumping heart to *Cease this racket.*

Swallowing, she restated her request. "After much consideration, my lord, I feel a marriage between you and myself would be prudent."

Lord Blake stared at her, blinking over and over. Belle was unsure if his reaction denoted surprise or was simply the result of the dazzling sunlight off the water behind her.

Silence.

Birds twittered. Branches creaked. Leaves rustled.

Eternities passed. Millennia ended and were reborn.

Belle gritted her teeth, desperate to bolster her flagging confidence. *You are strong and courageous. You can do this.*

In the past, her passivity over the Marriage Matter had nearly ended in disaster. So, Belle had set her sights on a more forthright course—propose marriage herself. Yes, she struggled to talk with people and preferred anonymity to attention, but her current situation was critical.

She needed a husband. Decidedly. Desperately. Immediately. As in . . . yesterday would not have been soon enough.

At the moment, however, her mental encouragement barely managed to convince the swarming butterflies in her stomach to not free her breakfast along with themselves. Casting up her accounts all over his lordship's dusty Hessian boots would hardly nurture his romantic interest.

At last, Lord Blake stirred, pulling a folded letter from his overcoat. He stared at it, eyebrows drawing down, a sharp "V" appearing above his nose.

"You sent me this message, asking to meet me here?" He flapped the letter in her direction.

"Yes." Belle bit down on her lip and darted a glance behind at her companion. Miss Rutger stood a solid thirty yards off, studiously facing the Long Water. "Well . . . uhm . . . in all truthfulness, Miss Rutger wrote the letter."

Lord Blake raised his eyebrows, clearly uncaring of the minutiae involved. "So you are *not* a gentleman interested in my business venture in the East Indies?" He unfolded the letter, reading from it. "'*I know of an interested party who would be honored to discuss a proposed joint venture. They have asked to meet you along the Long Water,*' et cetera. This 'interested party' is yourself?" He returned the letter to his pocket.

"Yes, my lord." Belle commanded her feet to hold still and not bounce up and down—the bouncing being yet another effect of those dratted nervous butterflies.

Lord Blake's brows rose further. "And you are offering . . . marriage?"

"Yes, my lord," Belle repeated, but she had to clarify the point. Apparently, she had no issue with being thought forward and brazen, but heaven forbid Lord Blake imagine her a liar, too. "Though . . . I *am* proposing a joint endeavor."

"Indeed," he paused. "Marriage usually implies as much."

Lord Blake shuffled a Hessian-booted foot and clasped his hands behind his back. A corner of his mouth twitched.

Was the man . . . amused? If so, was that good? Or bad?

And at this point, did it matter?

Belle soldiered on. "There would be significant advantages to both of us with such a match."

More silence. An errant draft of wind tugged at his coat.

"You have me at a disadvantage, Miss . . ." His voice trailed off.

"Heartstone. Miss Arabella Heartstone."

"I see." He removed his hat and slapped it against his thigh. "And why have we not met in more . . . uh . . . typical circumstances? A ball, perhaps? A dinner party where we could be properly introduced and engage in conversation about the weather and the latest bonnet fashions before leaping straight to marriage?"

"Oh." It was Belle's turn to blink, absorbing his words. *Oh dear.* "We *have* met, my lord. We were introduced at Lord Pemberley's musicale last month. We did discuss the weather, but not bonnets or . . . uhm . . . marriage."

She hadn't expected him to recall everything, but to not even *recognize* her? To not remember their brief conversation—

"*How do you do, Miss Heartstone? It's a pleasure to make your acquaintance.*" Lord Blake bowed.

"*The pleasure is all mine, my lord.*" Belle curtsied. "*Lovely weather we're having.*"

"*Indeed, we are.*"

It did not bode well.

The butterflies rushed upward, eager for escape.

"Right." Blake let out a gusting breath and shook his head, sending his hair tumbling across his forehead. The morning sun turned it into molten shades of deep amber, curling softly over his ears.

Lean and several inches taller than her own average height, Lord Blake was not classically handsome, she supposed. His straight nose, square jaw, and high forehead were all too exaggerated for classical handsomeness.

And yet, something about him tugged at her. Perhaps it was the breadth of his shoulders filling out his coat. Or maybe it was the ease of his stance, as if he would face the jaws of Hell itself with a sardonic smile and casual *sang-froid*. Or maybe it was the way he ran a gloved hand through his hair, taking it from fashionably tousled to deliciously rumpled.

Mmmmm.

Belle was going to side with the hair. Though sardonic smiles were a close second.

Regardless, her decision to offer marriage to him had not been based on his physical appearance. She was many things, but *flighty* and *shallow* were two words that had never been attached to her.

Replacing his hat, Lord Blake studied her, blue eyes twinkling.

Yes. Definitely amused.

That was . . . encouraging? Having never proposed marriage to a man before, Belle was unsure.

"Enlighten me, if you would be so kind, as to the particular reasons why you think this . . . joint endeavor . . . would be profitable." He gestured toward her.

Oh! Excellent.

That she had come prepared to do.

With a curt nod, she pulled a paper from her reticule.

"A list?" His lips twitched again.

"I am nothing if not thorough in my planning, my lord." She opened the paper with shaking fingers, her hands clammy inside her gloves.

"Of course. I should have expected as much. You arranged this meeting, after all." He tapped the letter in his pocket.

Belle chose to ignore the wry humor in his tone and merely nodded her head in agreement. "Allow me to proceed with my list. Though please forgive me if my reasons appear forward."

"You have just proposed marriage to a peer of the realm, madam. I cannot imagine anything you say from this point onward will trump that."

"True."

A beat.

Lord Blake pinned her with his gaze—calm and guileless. The forthright look of a man who knew himself and would never be less-than-true to his own values.

His gaze upset her breathing, causing something to catch in her throat.

Belle broke eye-contact, swallowing too loudly.

"Allow me to begin." She snapped the paper in her hand. The words swam in her vision, but she knew them by heart. The paper was more for show than anything else. She had done her calculations most carefully.

Taking a fortifying breath, Belle began, "Firstly, you have newly inherited the Marquisate of Blake from a cousin. Your cousin was somewhat imprudent in his spending habits—"

"I would declare the man to be an utter scapegrace and wastrel, but continue."

"Regardless of the cause, your lands and estates are in dire need of resuscitation." Belle glanced at him over the top of her paper. "You are basically without funds, my lord."

"As my solicitor repeatedly reminds me." He shot her an arch look. "It is why I am trying to fund a business venture in connection with the East India Company, as you are also undoubtedly aware."

"Yes, my lord. That is why I am proposing an enterprise of a slightly different sort. Allow me to continue." Belle cleared her throat, looking down to her paper. "My own family is genteel with connections to the upper aristocracy—my great-great grandfather was the Earl of Stratton—though we have no proper title of our own, leaving my father to make his own way in the world. I, as you might already know, am a considerable heiress. My father was a prominent banker and left the entirety of his estate to me upon his death three years past."

Belle clenched her jaw against the familiar sting in her throat.

Blink, blink, blink.

Now was *not* the time to dwell upon her father.

"Are you indeed?" he asked. "Though I do not wish to sound crass, I feel we left polite discussion in the dust several minutes ago, so I must enquire: How much of an heiress are you, precisely?"

Did she hear keen interest in his tone? Or was Lord Blake simply exceedingly polite?

"I believe the current amount stands somewhere in the region of eighty thousand pounds, my lord," she replied.

Lord Blake froze at that staggering number, just as Belle had predicted he would.

"Eighty thousand pounds, you say? That is a dowry of marquess-saving proportions."

"My thoughts precisely, my lord."

Her father had originally left her a healthy sixty thousand pounds, but she was nothing if not her father's daughter. Numbers and statistics flowed through her brain, a constant rushing river. She had used these skills to grow her fortune.

It was what her father would have wanted. Refusing to see her gender as a barrier, her father had taught his only child everything he knew—financial systems, probabilities, market shares—even soliciting her opinions during that last year before his death.

By the age of sixteen, Belle understood more about supply-and-demand and the mathematics of economics than most noblemen. Knowing this, the conditions in her father's will allowed her to continue to oversee her own interests with the help of his solicitor, Mr. Sloan. At only nineteen years of age, she currently managed a thriving financial empire.

She could hear her father's gruff voice, his hand gently lifting her chin. *I would give you choices, my Little Heart Full. A lady should always have options. I would see you happy.*

Belle swallowed back the painful tightness in her throat.

Now, if she could only land a husband and free herself from the guardianship of her uncle and mother.

Family, it turned out, were not quite as simple to manage as corn shares.

Her mother, hungry for a title for her daughter, was becoming increasingly bold in her attempts to get Belle married. She had all but forced Belle to betroth herself to a cold, aloof viscount the previous Season. Fortunately, the viscount—Lord Linwood—had asked to be released from their betrothal.

But the entire situation had left Belle feeling helpless.

She *detested* feeling helpless, she realized. And so she used that unwelcome sensation to suppress her inherent shyness and overcome her retiring personality.

Belle would solve the husband problem herself. She simply needed to reduce the entire situation to a statistical probability and face it as she would any other business transaction.

"Eighty-thousand pounds," Lord Blake repeated. "Are husbands—particularly the marquess variety—generally so costly?" He clasped his hands behind his back, studying her. "I had not thought to price them before this."

"I cannot say. This is my first venture into, uhmm . . ."

"Purchasing a husband?" he supplied, eyes wide.

Heavens. Was that a hint of displeasure creeping into his voice?

"I am not entirely sure I agree with the word *purchase*, my lord—"

"True. It does smack of trade and all polite society knows we cannot have *that*."

A pause.

"Shall we use the word *negotiate* instead?" she asked.

He cocked his head, considering. "I daresay that would be better. So I receive a sultan's ransom and your lovely self, and you receive . . ." His words drifted off.

"A husband. And in the process, I become Lady Blake, a peeress of the realm."

"Are you truly so hungry to be a marchioness? Surely eighty thousand pounds could purchase—forgive me, *negotiate*—the title of duchess." His words so very, very dry.

"I am sure my mother would agree with you, my lord, but I am more interested in finding a balance between title and the proper gentleman." She cleared her throat. "You come highly recommended."

"Do I?" Again, his tone darkly sardonic.

Oh, dear.

But as she was already in for more than a penny, why not aim for the whole pound?

"I did not arrive at the decision to propose marriage lightly. I had my solicitor hire a Runner to investigate you. I have armed myself with information, my lord."

Belle wisely did not add that, after crunching all the statistical probabilities, Lord Blake had been by far and away her preferred candidate. She was quite sure that, like most people, he would not appreciate being reduced to a number.

"Information? About me?" he asked.

"Yes. For example, I know you recently cashed out of the army, selling the officer's commission you inherited from your father. All those who served with you report you to be an honest and worthy commander—"

"As well they should."

"Additionally, you are a kind son to your mother. You send her and your stepfather funds when you are able. You visit regularly. Your four older sisters dote upon you, and you are godfather to at least one of each of their children. You are a tremendous favorite with all of your nieces and nephews. All of this speaks highly to the kind of husband and father you would be."

After her disastrous betrothal to Lord Linwood last year, Belle was determined to not make the same error twice. She learned from her mistakes. Her mother and uncle would not browbeat her into accepting one of their suitors again.

If nothing else, eighty thousand pounds should purchase—*negotiate*—her a *kindhearted* husband of her own choice.

Lord Blake shuffled his feet. "I-I really am at a loss for words, Miss Heartstone. I am trying to decide if I should be flattered or utterly appalled."

Belle sucked in a deep breath, her mouth as dry as the Sahara.

Stay strong. Argue your case.

She pasted a strained smile on her face. "Might I suggest siding with flattery, my lord?"

Visit www.NicholeVan.com to buy your copy of
Seeing Miss Heartstone today and continue the story.

ABOUT THE AUTHOR

THE SHORT VERSION:

NICHOLE VAN IS a writer, photographer, designer and generally disorganized crazy person. Though originally from Utah, she currently lives on the coast of Scotland with three similarly crazy children and one sane, very patient husband who puts up with all of them. In her free time, she enjoys long walks along the Scottish lochs and braes. She does not, however, enjoy haggis.

THE LONG OVERACHIEVER VERSION:

AN INTERNATIONAL BESTSELLING author, Nichole Van is an artist who feels life is too short to only have one obsession. In former lives, she has been a contemporary dancer, pianist, art historian, choreographer, culinary artist and English professor.

Most notably, however, Nichole is an acclaimed photographer, winning over thirty international accolades for her work, including Portrait of the Year from WPPI in 2007. (Think Oscars for wedding and portrait photographers.) Her unique photography style has been featured in many magazines, including Rangefinder and Professional Photographer. She is also the creative mind behind the popular website Flourish Emporium which provides resources for photographers.

All that said, Nichole has always been a writer at heart. With an MA in English, she taught technical writing at Brigham Young University for ten years and has written more technical manuals than she can quickly count. She decided in late 2013 to start writing fiction and has since become an Amazon #1 bestselling author. Additionally, she has won a RONE award, as well as been a Whitney Award Finalist several years running.

In February 2017, Nichole, her husband and three crazy children moved from the Rocky Mountains in the USA to Scotland. They currently live near the coast of eastern Scotland in an eighteenth century country house. Nichole loves her pastoral country views while writing and enjoys long walks through fields and along beaches. She does not, however, have a fondness for haggis.

She is known as NicholeVan all over the web: Facebook, Instagram, Pinterest, etc. Visit http://www.NicholeVan.com to sign up for her author newsletter and be notified of new book releases. Additionally, you can see her photographic work at http://photography.nicholeV.com and http://www.nicholeV.com

If you enjoyed this book, please leave a short review on Amazon. com. Wonderful reviews are the elixir of life for authors. Even better than dark chocolate.